The Ushers

Edward Lee

THE
USHERS
EDWARD LEE

OBSIDIAN PRESS
SEATTLE • 1999

First Edition:
ISBN: 1-891480-04-9, $45.00 Hardcover
ISBN: 1-891480-03-0, $16.00 Trade Paperback

Epigraph is an excerpt from a poem by Ryan Harding entitled "The Ushers." It is used here with the permission of its author.

This edition Copyright 1999 by Obsidian Books. No part of this book may be copied or quoted, except for brief passages in reviews, without written consent of the publisher. Manufactured in the United States of America. This is a work of fiction. Any similarity to person living or dead is purely coincidental.

The publisher wishes to acknowledge the following for their help and general friendliness: Mike Paduana (I AM smiling), Paul Mausbach, Rich Chizmar, Oly, Kit, Bil, two weirdos at Nightshade, Dick, Erin, and most of the folks the author already thanked.

Obsidian Press
37800 38th Ave S
Auburn, WA 98001
MJobsidian@aol.com
www.horrornet.com/obsidian.htm

Other books from Obsidian Press-

Shifters by Edward Lee and John Pelan (out of print)
The Exit at Toledo Blade Boulevard by Jack Ketchum (out of print)
Dancing With Demons by Lucy Taylor

Coming soon:
Mondo Zombie edited by John Mason Skipp

Flap copy:
Russell Mullen

Book layout & design:
David G. Barnett of Fat Cat Design

For Dallas, to whom I am forever in debt.

Get behind the razor...

Story Afterwords and Foreword, copyright © 1999 by Edward Lee
"Death, She Said," copyright © 1993 by Edward Lee. First appeared in *Bizarre Bazaar 93.*
"The Wrong Guy," copyright © 1993 by Edward Lee. First appeared in *Cyber Psychos A.O.D.,* Summer 1993-issue; appeared again in *Into The Darkness #4.*
"The Decortication Technician," copyright © 1999 by Edward Lee.
"Secret Service," copyright © 1998 by Edward Lee. Shorter version first appeared in *The UFO Files,* ed. by Martin Greenberg (DAW). The version included in this collection is uncut.
"Mr. Torso," copyright © 1994 by Edward Lee. First appeared in *Hot Blood: Deadly After Dark,* ed. by Jeff Gelb and Michael Garrett (POCKET).
"The Hole in the Wall," copyright © 1999 by Edward Lee.
"The Seeker," copyright © 1992 by Edward Lee. First appeared in *Sex, Truth, & Reality,* a chapbook by Tal Publications.
"Almost Never," copyright © 1991 by Edward Lee. First appeared in the Autumn-1991 issue of *Cemetery Dance*; appeared next in the Autumn-1994 issue of *Bloodsongs*; appeared next in the anthology *The Best of Cemetery Dance* (CD PUBLICATIONS).
"The Man Who Loved Clichés," copyright © 1992 by Edward Lee. First appeared in *Bizarre Bazaar 92.* The version included in this collection has been slightly revised.
"Grub Girl in the Prison of Dead Women," copyright © 1997 by Edward Lee. First appeared in *Wetbones #2.*
"Please Let Me Out," copyright © 1994 by Edward Lee. First appeared in *Voices From The Night,* ed. by John Maclay (MACLAY & ASSOCIATES).
"The Horror of Chambers," copyright ©1982 by Edward Lee. First appeared in *Eerie Country Six.*
"Shit-House," copyright © 1995 by Edward Lee. First appeared in *Palace Corbie Six,* ed. by Wayne Edwards (MERRIMACK BOOKS).
"Goddess of the New Dark Age," copyright © 1992. First appeared in *Sex, Truth Reality,* a chapbook from Tal Publications.
"The Salt-Diviner," copyright © 1999 by Edward Lee.
"Scriptures," copyright © 1999 by Edward Lee
"Xipe," copyright © 1993 by Edward Lee. First appeared in *The Barrelhouse: Excursions into the Unknown.*
"Hands," copyright © 1999 by Edward Lee
"The Ushers," copyright © 1999 by Edward Lee

CONTENTS	PAGE
Forward	1
Death, She Said	5
Hands	17
Secret Service	49
The Wrong Guy	67
The Decortication Technician	81
Almost Never	99
The Hole in the Wall	115
The Seeker	121
Grub Girl in the Prison of Dead Women	139
Please Let Me Out	153
The Horror of Chambers	167
Scriptures	177
The Goddess of the New Dark Age	189
The Salt-Diviner	201
The Man Who Loved Clichés	225
ShitHouse	235
Xipe	249
Mr. Torso	259
The Ushers	279
Edward Lee Publishing History	297

You will find no solace
In what you have created.

—Ryan Harding,
from the poem "The Ushers"

Foreword

OTHER WRITERS HAVE frequently related to me that what they like most about selling a collection is the opportunity to write pretentious and/or esoteric forewords—so allow me to indulge in the same with this little preamble.

I've written a bunch of horror—nine mass market paperbacks, small-press novels and collections (collaborations and solo), short stories, comic scripts—close to two million words' worth, and its been a bunch of fun. In the old days, however, just when I was starting out, I'd never hesitate to scoff when I'd overhear other writers remark that it's harder to write a short story than a novel. Yes, I'd frown to crease my face. But one day it occurred to me that perhaps I was being a trifle judgmental—for I'd never really seriously written short stories. Then I embarked, and—

I ain't frowning now.

It is harder, a *lot* harder. It's a different terrain, and a terrain bound by proximity. Not just word-count but something subjective too. Like trying to cut out a tiny piece of yourself just right, where as a novel is more akin to summary amputation where all that's necessary is a crude, simple swoop of the ax.

But it's still fun—*more* fun in many ways—and it's provocative too, and one thing I've always believed is that fiction *must* be provocative, it *must* make us think about things: the world, the people around us, ourselves. Without that mode of provocation, however unseemly, however fantastic, grotesque, or perverse, the fiction isn't honest.

Honesty's the best policy, right?

So I gotta be honest, too, about why I write the stuff that I write. It ain't for everybody, I'll tell you that. To say that horror should be a joyride isn't quite good enough for me. More like a joyride through a whorehouse in hell—the point is what you see while you're along for the ride—or taking a break-neck trip down a waterslide only to land in a wafting, hot corpse-pile. The point is how you feel once you've landed, and who you see. Sometimes we see ourselves.

Edward Lee

Perversity, sadism, sexual aberration, etc. are parts of the nomenclature of the human spirit—just like altruism, fellowship, love, and all that. No, I'm not saying it's cool to be perverse, sadistic, and sexually aberrant, but I think it's honest to be curious about the very worst that humanity has to offer, and the very worst manner in which mankind has presented itself. Not only is it honest, I dare say it's healthy, and the soil of that same curiosity is where I grab my trowel and start to dig.

I'm not trying to be the Proust of horror, nor will I ever presume to scribe the genre's equivalent to *The Sound and the Fury*. The literary analysis of societal design is fine—but I'll take gut-eating any day. Fiction as philosophical symbology and epistemological allegory is terrific, but, Christ, I'd rather look into that corpse-pile or that psycho-killer's fridge or that whorehouse in hell. Sartre, Kierkegaard, Heidegger: cool guys, smart, lotta meat between the ears on those fellas, and certainly trying to define who we are in the world or the universe is a noble undertaking. But isn't it somewhat as legitimate to try to define the reason why people do the horrible things they do? It's a fascinating query for me. It's a *kick*.

Hence, my plight. I write horror. I love it. A number of the stories in this book are technically reprints, but some of them are "un-cut" versions. The original versions were either toned down by me because, at the time, I didn't have the balls to submit them as is, or I cut them because of editorial advice. The new stories are pieces written the way I want them published: gross, unrepentant, profane, perverse, pathological. Down and dirty, ya know? 'Cos *life,* all too frequently, is down and dirty. Aberrant, erotopathic, disgusting, politically incorrect. Yeah. Groovy.

Because, like I said, it's healthy to be curious, and after all, the end of the 90's is a health-conscious age.

Anyway, that's my pretentious and/or esoteric foreword. If you like your horror the way I do—straight up, no beating around the bush, the fresh guts and karyiolitic rot and throbbing, reeking pudenda right in your proboscis—then I hope you like these stories, and I thank you for buying this. Furthermore, I thank all my loyal and very wonderful fans out there whose support has made this collection possible.

There's plenty of fresh, rich, worm-laden soil to till in this book, and as I just got done saying, I *like* to dig.

And, who knows? Maybe I can dig a hole big enough for both of us.

We'll have a hell of a party.

Edward Lee
Seattle, Washington
December 31, 1998

Death, She Said

"LIFE," I SAID.

I'd said it to myself, to my reflection in the rearview as I peeled the cardboard cover off the razor blade. Yeah, life.

I was all set; I was going to kill myself. Oh, I know what you're thinking. Sure, fella. All the time you're hearing about how suicidal tendencies are really just pleas for attention, cries for help. Fuck that. I didn't want help. I wanted to die.

I had one of those Red Devil brand blades, the kind you cut carpet with, or scrape paint off windows. Real sharp. I'd read somewhere that if you do it laterally, you bleed to death before the blood can clot. I sure as shit didn't want to pull a stunt like that and blow it. I could picture myself sitting in some psyche ward with bandaged wrists—a perfect ass. I wanted to do it right.

Why? Long story. I'll give you the abridged version.

I'd spent my whole life trying to make something good for myself, or maybe I should say what I thought was good turned out to be nothing. It was all gone in less time than it takes you to blow your nose. We had two kids. One ran off with some holistic cult, haven't seen him in a decade. The younger one died a couple weeks after her senior prom. "Axial metastatic mass," the neurologist called it. A fuckin' brain tumor is what I called it. Worst part was I never really knew them. It was my wife who brought them up, carried the load. I was too busy putting in 12, 14 hours a day at the firm, like airline trademark infringements were more important than raising my own kids. But I still had my wife, her love, her faith in me. She was behind me every step of the way, a real gem. She quit college to wait tables so I could go to law school, gave away her own future for me. She was always there—you know what I mean? We were going to get the house painted. She went out one day to check out some colors—I was too busy suing some company that made bearings for airplane wheels—but she never made it home. Drunk driver. I still had my job, though, right? Wrong. A Month ago I was a senior partner in the number three firm in the country. A couple of associates decided it might be neat to bribe some jurors on a big air-wreck case I was litigating. They get disbarred, but I get blackballed. Right now I couldn't get a job jacking fries at Roy Fucking Rogers my name stinks so bad. So I guess that wraps it up nice and neat. I'm a 48-year-old attorney with no job, no family, no life.

There.

I didn't want anyone saving me, calling the paramedics or anything like that. I decided I'd do it in my car. The repo people were already after it, so I figured let 'em have it with my blood all over the suede-leather seats. I backed into an alley off the porn block. Rats, oblivious to the cold, were hopping in and out of garbage cans. Lights from an adult bookstore blinked in my face. Up ahead, I could see the hookers traipsing back and forth on L Street. They were like the rats; they didn't feel the cold. You should've seen some of the wild shit they were wearing. Leopard-skin leotards, sheer low-cut evening dresses, shorts that looked like tin foil. It was kind of funny, that my last vision in life would be this prancing tribe of whores. I had the razorblade between my fingers, poised. Each time I got ready to drag it from the inside of my elbow to my wrist, I kept looking up. I wasn't chickening out, I just felt distracted. But distracted by what?

That's when I saw her, in that last half-moment before I was going to actually do it.

She'd probably been standing on the corner the whole time, I just hadn't noticed. It was like she was part of the wall, or even part of the city—darkness blended into brick.

She was staring right at me.

I stared back. She stood tall in a shiny black waistcoat whose hem came up to mid-thigh. Long legs, black stockings, high heels, I sensed she wasn't young—like the streetwalkers—yet she seemed more comely than old: graceful, beautiful in wisdom. Somehow I knew she couldn't be a hooker; looking at her, I thought of vanquished regalities—an exiled queen. She had her hands in her pockets, and she was staring.

Go away, I thought. *Can't you see I'm trying to kill myself?*

I blinked.

Then she was walking toward the car.

I stashed the razor blade under the seat. It didn't make sense. Even

Death, She Said

if she was a prostitute, no prostitute would approach a barely visible car in an alley. Maybe she'd think I was a cop. I could give her the brushoff and get back to business.

Her high heels ticked down the alley. Was she smiling? I couldn't tell. The rats scurried away.

She stopped beside the driver's window.

"I'm not sportin', I'm not datin', and I'm not looking for someone to tickle my stick," I said. "Buzz off."

Her voice was weird, like a wisp of breeze, or two pieces of silk brushing together. So soft it almost wasn't there. "Providence is a mysterious thing," she said. "It can be very nourishing."

I squinted. She was standing right there, but I couldn't see her, not really. Just snatches of her, like my eyes were a movie camera and the cameraman was drunk. All I could say in response was, "What?"

"Think before you act," she said. "There are truths you haven't seen. Wouldn't it be regrettable to die without ever knowing what they are?"

She couldn't possibly have seen what I was trying to do in the car; it was too dark, and she'd been too far away. Besides, the razor blade was under the seat.

"I can show you providence," she said. "I can show you truth."

"Oh, yeah?" I challenged. "What the fuck do you know about truth?"

"More than you think," she said.

I looked at her, still only able to see her in pieces, like slivers. I sensed more than saw. I sensed beauty in her age, not haggardness. I sensed gracility, wisdom...

"Come with me," she bid. "I'll show you."

I got out. *What the hell,* I thought. The razor would still be there when I got back. In my gut, though, it was more than that. In my gut, I felt *destined* to get out of the car.

She walked away.

I had to nearly trot to keep up. I could imagine how I must look to the people on the street: an unshaven, shambling dolt in a crushed $800 suit, hectically pursuing this...woman. Her high heels ticked across the cement like nails. The shiny waistcoat glittered. She took me back through the alley. Ahead, windows were lit.

"Look," she said.

Crack vials and glass crunched beneath my feet. Rotting garbage lay heaped against vomit and urine-streaked brick.

I looked in the window, expecting to see something terrible. What I saw instead was this: A subsidized apartment, sparse but clean. Two black children, a boy and a girl, sat at a table reading schoolbooks, while an aproned woman prepared dinner in the background. Then a black man walked in, a jacket over his shoulder, a lunchpail in hand. Beaming, the children glanced up. The woman smiled. The man kissed his wife, then knelt to hug his children.

But this wasn't terrible, it was wonderful. Jammed in a ghetto, surrounded by crime and despair, here was a family *making* it. Most didn't in this environment. Most fell apart against the odds. I was standing on crack vials and puke, looking straight into the face of something more powerful than any force on earth…

"Love," said the old woman.

Yeah, I thought. Love. I'm a lawyer, which means I'm also a nihilistic prick. You've heard the joke: What happens when a lawyer takes Viagra? He gets taller. But this made me feel good to see, the power of real love, real human ideals.

But why had the woman shown me this?

She was walking away again, and again I was huffing to keep up. Now I was curious—about her. Where did she come from? What was her name? She led me through more grimy alleys, more garbage and havens for rats. A single sodium lamp sidelighted her. My breath condensed in the cold.

I tried to look at her…

All I could see was one side of her face from behind. Fine lines etched her cheek and neck. Her short, straight hair was dusted with gray. Yeah, she was up there— 60ish, I guessed—but elegant. You know how some women keep their looks in spite of age—that was her. Well-postured, a good figure and bosom, nice legs. But I still never really got a look at her face.

In the next alley, muttering rose.

It was getting colder. I was shivering, yet the woman seemed comfortable, she seemed warm in some arcane knowledge. She pointed down.

Aw, shit, I thought. Strewn across the alley were bundles. They were people, the inevitable detritus of any big city. They lay asleep or unconscious: shivering dark forms wrapped in newspapers or rags. Many slept convulsing from the cold. The city was too busy repaving commuter routes to build more shelters. It was astonishing that on a night this cold they didn't just freeze to death. And all this time I thought I had nothing. Jesus.

"I don't want to see this," I said.

"Wait."

I heard footsteps. Then a bent shape was moving down the dark, stepping quietly between the twitching forms. It was a priest, an old guy, 70 at least. Slung across his back were blankets. I don't know how a guy his age

Death, She Said

could manage carrying all of them, especially in cold this bad. The guy huffed and puffed, stooping to cover each prone figure with a blanket. It was the look on his face that got to me most. Not pity, not fanaticism, just some kind of resolute complacency, like he was thinking *Well, tonight I'll get whatever money I can lay my hands on, buy some blankets, and cover up some homeless people. No one else is gonna do it, so I'm gonna do it.* It was simple. Right now your average person was watching the Ally McBeal, or getting laid, or sleeping in a warm bed, but here was this old priest doing what he could for a few people no one else gave a pinch of shit about.

"Compassion," the woman, my companion, said.

I watched as the priest went about his business, shivering himself as he lay a blanket over each figure, one after another after another. Then I touched the woman's shoulder. "What is this?" I asked. "Why are you showing me this stuff? I don't get it."

"Providence," she whispered. "Come on."

Providence, I thought. She led. I followed. Now we were walking down Connecticut Avenue, the power drag. Lots of ritzy schmucks getting out of limos in front of restaurants where dinner for two cost more than the average working person made in two weeks. There were a lot of lawyers too, tisk, tisk. Whatever this tour was she was taking me on—it was making me think.

Next we were walking past Washington Square, where I used to work, and 21 Federal, where I stopped for cocktails every day, or had power lunches with the managing partners. Jesus. A couple of blocks away people were sleeping in the fucking street, and we were too busy to care. Too busy hiding behind Harvard law degrees and clients who paid seven figures per annum just in retainers. This bizarre woman was showing me what I used to be. And she showed me this: I may have been a good attorney, but that sure as shit didn't mean I was a good person. An hour ago I was going to kill myself. Now all I could feel was shame. I felt like a spoiled baby.

"One more stop," she said. "Then you can go."

With the less I understood, the more I wanted to know. But one thing I *did* know: There was a reason for this. This was no ordinary encounter, and she was certainly no ordinary woman.

I half trotted along, always just behind her, never quite keeping up. It reminded me of the Dickens story, the wretched cynic shown his future and past by ghosts. But the woman was no ghost. I'd touched her; she was flesh.

She was real.

Minutes later we were standing in a graveyard.

Yeah, this was like the Dickens story, all right. My breath froze in front of my face. The woman stood straight as a chess piece, pointing down at the stone. But I already knew it wasn't *my* grave.

It was my wife's.

"Truth," the woman said.

Thoughts seemed to tick in my head; my confusion felt like a fever. First love, then compassion, and now…truth?

What truth was there in showing me my wife's grave? She'd been dead for years.

"Does it nourish you?" the woman asked. "The truth?"

Dead for years, yeah, but even in death she was the only real truth in my life.

"I loved her," I muttered.

"Indeed. And did she love you?"

"Yes."

"Yes?"

"Yes."

She paused, gauging me, I guess. "There, then," she told me. "There's truth even in memory. You should remember her love for you—the truth of it. It raises us up, doesn't it? It *nourishes* us." Her gaze seemed to wander. "The truth."

I wanted to cry. Now this final vision made sense. I'd had love. My wife had loved me. Lots of people, most people probably, never had love, not really. Just sad facsimiles and bitter falsehoods. I wanted to fall to my knees at this old woman's feet and blubber like a little kid. Because it wasn't cruelty that made her bring me here. It was the same force behind all the things she'd shown me tonight. Things to make me think and to see. Things to make me realize that life really was a gift, and that even when people died, even when the shittiest, most fucked up things happened, the gift remained…

We followed back the way we came, back through the bowels of the city. It was different now—everything was. The streetlights made the pavement look gritty with ice. It began to snow but all I could feel was the warmth of what she'd shown me.

That's how I felt. I felt warm. I felt nourished.

She took me back to the alley, to the car. We got in. She sat beside me in the passenger seat.

"Time means nothing," she said. Her voice was soft, sweet in its age. "It never has."

"Who are you?" I asked.

She didn't answer. Instead she smiled, or at least she seemed to, because I still really couldn't see her. Just fragments of her, just shards of vision that never quite came together.

Death, She Said

"You're some kind of angel, aren't you?" I finally summoned the nerve to ask. "You were sent to keep me from killing myself."

"Love, compassion, truth," she replied. "They add up to something. What a waste for a person to die alone, unnourished of the truth."

Yeah, she was an angel or something. The first thing she'd said to me was something about providence.

Greed, selfishness, cynicism, and God knows what else, had brought me to the brink of suicide but I'd been saved at the last minute by seeing the good things out there, the things that transcended the bad, the evil.

"The truth," she said.

"Thank you."

Somehow it didn't surprise me. She slipped out of the black waistcoat. She was nude beneath. Her breasts were large, with large full nipples. They sagged but gracefully. The gentle roll of flesh at her waist, the fine white skin of her throat, shoulders, and thighs, her entire body—seemed softly radiant in its age, beautiful in its truth.

That's what this was about—truth. And I knew why she'd taken off the coat. She hadn't brought me all this way just to fuck me in a Porsche 911. All night long she'd given me things to see. That's why she was naked now, to let me, at last, see *her*.

And I wanted to. I wanted to see the body which carried so resplendent a spirit. The light from the streetlamp shined through the windshield. I could see her body now, but still not her face, and I guessed I never would. This seemed appropriate, though, you've got to admit.

The face of an angel shouldn't be something you can ever really see.

"We're all here for a reason," she said, leaning over to look at me. "And this is my reason. To show the truth, to make people see the truth."

I held her hand, ran my fingers up her arm. I slid over close and began to touch her breasts, smoothed my fingers across her abdomen, down her thighs, and over the thick plot of her pubic hair. She seemed to expect this, like it was some kind of calm precognition. It wasn't lust, it wasn't sexual at all. I just wanted to touch her.

I needed to know what an angel felt like.

Her skin, though it had lost some of its elasticity, was soft and smooth as a baby's. Cool. Palely clean. The groove of her pubis sheathed my finger in heat.

Then she asked: "Are you ready to see the rest?"

"There's more?"

She paused. I think she liked this a lot, lazing back in the plush seat, being touched. "I've shown you love, compassion, and truth. I've nourished you, haven't I?"

"Yes," I said, still touching.

Her cool fingers entwined in mine. "But I need nourishment too, through something else."

"What?"

"Death," she said.

I stared at her. My hand went limp.

"The truth is like people. Sometimes the real face is the one underneath. Look now at what you didn't see before—the *rest* of the truth. The *real* truth."

She leaned over and kissed me. I turned rigid. Her cool lips played over mine, her tongue delved. All the while my eyes felt sewn open. I couldn't close them. The kiss reached into me and *pulled*. Yes, the kiss. It forced me to stare whimpering into the wide-open black chasm that was her face.

The *real* truth.

First, the future: The family in the window. The man, unemployed now, and drunk, was steadily beating his wife's face into a bleeding mask. Then, the boy, older, was holding a woman down while four others took turns raping her. He crammed a handful of garbage into her mouth to keep her quiet. "Watch me bust this bitch's coconut," he said when they were finished. He split her head open with a brick while the others divvied up her money. Meanwhile, blocks away, his sister spread her legs for the tenth stranger of the night, her arms, hands, and feet pocked by needlemarks, her blood teeming with herpes, hepatitis, AIDS.

Next, the present: The alley of the homeless. The priest was gone. A gang of faceless youths chuckled as they poured gasoline over the huddled forms, drenching the new blankets. Matches flared. The alley burst into flames, and the gang ran off, laughing. Human flesh sizzled in each cocoon of fire. Screams wheeled up into the frigid night.

And last, the past: First, brakes squealing, a collision of metal, and my wife's neck snapping like a wine stem as her head impacted the windshield. Then the vision reeled back an hour. A hotel room. A bed. Naked on hands and knees, my wife was busily fellating a young man who stood before her. He held her head and remarked, "Yeah, Duff, this is one class-A cock-suck. She's fucking me with her tonsils." "Best deep throat in town, just like I told ya," remarked another man who then promptly inserted his vaselined penis into her rectum. "Bet your hubby would shit if he could see this, huh?" Eventually he ejaculated into her bowel. "Here comes lunch," said the first man, whose semen launched into her mouth. My wife swallowed it, purring like a cat. Then she lay back on the bed. "Can you believe it? I told him I was going to the paint store to check out color schemes for the house." "When you gonna dump that limp shithead?" inquired the second man. She began masturbating them both. "Why should I?" she said. "A deal like this? Come on! He keeps me in jewelry, and you guys keep me in cock." Then the three of them burst into laughter.

The kiss broke. I seemed to fall away from it, a rappeller whose line had just been cut. I sat slack in the seat. The old woman was looking at me, but I could see she wasn't old at all. She looked like a teenager. The meal she'd made of my truth left her robust, vital, glowing in new youth. Her once-gray hair shined raven-black. The pale skin had tightened over young muscle and bone; the large white orbs of her breasts grew firm even as I watched. Their fresh nipples erected, pointing at me like wall studs.

I couldn't speak. I couldn't move.

Greedy new hands caressed me; her eyes shined. She kissed me some more, licked me, reveled in what I was to her. Her breath was hot in my drained face.

"Just a little more," she panted.

She was drooling. She reached under the seat. The Red Devil razor blade glinted in icy light. Then, very gently, she placed it in my hand.

¤   ¤   ¤   ¤   ¤

At least it didn't hurt. It felt good. It felt purging. Know what I mean? Can't see much now. Like lights going down in a theater. All I can see is the little girl. She's watching me. She's grinning, getting younger and growing more alive on the meat of providence, on the sweet, sweet high of truth.

DEATH, SHE SAID
AFTERWORD

Probably the most popular story ever told is Dicken's "A Christmas Carol"; I think I read somewhere that more printings of this story have been published than any fiction in history. I believe it. But I can also say that the first story to have any serious impact on me personally was "Was It A Dream?" by Guy de Maupassant. Here I've mixed both elements of influence. It's probably the most negative story I've ever written. Even though I consider myself a positivist...I'm not quite sure what compelled me to write this one. I've considered the question for years, but I'm fairly sure no answer will ever arise.

HANDS

WHEN THE EMTS brought the guy in, it looked like he must've sat down in a bathtub full of blood. "Damn it!" Paduana shouted, thinking *I'm off duty in five minutes! I ain't got time for a cut-down!* Dr. Paduana was in charge of Emergency Room Cove 4 tonight, and had been for the last twelve hours–or make that eleven hours and fifty-five minutes. He was pulling noon-to-mids for eight days straight, but he had tomorrow off. It would sure be nice to just go home and get some sleep, but this bleeder looked like a two- or three-hour string-job at least.

"Don't forget your Hippocratic Oath," Mullen, his intern, remarked with a mordant grin. Mullen had a short beard and a wise ass. "Looks like you miss Jerry springer tonight, daddy-o."

"Just get the meat on the table," Paduana ordered. He smirked as Mullen and the gurney-jockey hoisted the unmoving patient up onto the crash table. "What's the guy's stats, Ben Casey?" he asked the EMT.

The EMT gave him the finger. "Looks like a single GS high and inside of the right thigh. We slapped a tourniquet on and brought him in."

"Don't EMTs have to go to school anymore?" Paduana said. "How come you didn't ligate the wound in the ambulance?"

"Because we picked him up on Jackson Street, about two minutes away, Dr. Dickhead," the EMT replied.

These fuckin' meat-wagon jocks, Paduana thought. *They got no respect for doctors anymore.*

"All that blood?" Mullen observed. "The bullet might've hit the femoral artery."

"Duh," Paduana said. "At least the Two Stooges out there know how to strap a tourniquet."

"The guy's type is A-pos, Shemp," the EMT added. "Have fun. I'm out of here."

"Thanks for staying to help out," Paduana shot back.

"Hey, that shit's your job, I just drive. You're the guy getting a hundred and fifty k a year. Have fun."

The EMT left. *Eat shit and die,* Paduana thought.

"We need three pints of A-pos in C4, stat," Mullen said into the phone and hung up. Then he leaned over the victim, squinting at the blood-drenched groin. "Looks small, looks like someone popped him with a .25, maybe a .32. Aimed for his cock but missed by an inch."

Close but no cigar. Paduana snapped on Tru-Touch sterile gloves. "They picked him up on Jackson, at this hour? He's probably a john, picked up a hooker, got rough, so she shot him." Paduana got them all the time. "Can't say I blame her."

"Probably right–"

A draft wafted. The cove door swung open, and it was the EMT again. "Oh, and I forgot to tell ya. We checked the guy's wallet when we picked him up–he's a homicide captain with city PD."

"Move it!" Paduana yelled. "Fuck!"

But Mullen was shaking his head. "Come on–the guy's dying."

"I don't want a damn *cop* dying on my table! Get the hemos and the shears! We're doing a cut-down right now!"

Shiny instruments clinked; Mullen rushed the tray over, then raised the pair of Sistrunk-brand German fabric shears.

Paduana put on his monocular, a plastic headset sort of thing with a single lens fitting over the eye; he'd need it to see the broken arterial walls. Once the wound was exposed, he would cut laterally along the femoral artery and with a nearly microscopic needle and thread, perform a pre-op ligature in order to effect a cessation of the arterial blood flow. "Go!" he shouted. "Cut his pants off!"

"Roger that," Mullen said. The shears cut right through the waist of the slacks and the leather belt like onionskin paper.

Paduana turned momentarily, snapped up an Arista 3LA scalpel. Its stainless-steel flash winked at him in the overheads. But before he could turn back around to the patient, he heard Mullen's dismal mutter.

"Oh, shit.–"

"What!" Paduana barked. "Don't tell me he 64'd!"

"Naw, but... You better take a look at this. I think we got the guy they've been writing about in the papers..."

Dr. Paduana finished turning. He closed the eye over which the monocular rested and looked down with his other eye. Mullen had indeed expertly cut the patient's pants off with the shears, and the boxer shorts as well. And when Paduana saw what lay there, he knew immediately what his intern meant.

Hands

The "patient" had been carrying a severed human hand in his undershorts.

¤   ¤   ¤   ¤   ¤

I guess I knew Jameson was the one the moment after the police shrink explained the psychiatric profile. But what tagged it was when Jameson took me to his Belltown condo and showed me those pictures. He introduced me to his wife, then showed me the row of framed snapshots over the mantle. One was a picture of him as a child, his father's arm around him.

But no mother.

The lack of the facilitation of a nurturing touch...

My name's Matt Hauge; I'm a crime reporter for the *Seattle Times*. The other papers were calling the killer the "Handyman," and I guess that's why Captain Jay Jameson had come to me in the first place. A couple weeks ago, he walked right into my office and said, "I need your help."

This was a cop, one of the bigwigs–a captain up for deputy chief. Cops generally hated press people but here's this tall, imposing guy flashing his shield in my face and asking *me* for help.

"This Handyman shit–that's my case," he said. .

"It's my case too," I countered.

"Yeah. That's why I'm here." He sat down, pulled out a cigarette, asked if I minded if he smoked, then lit up before I could answer. Now that I think back, I should've known even then. This guy *looked* like a perv. He had lines down his face like a James Street speed freak. One eye looked a teeny bit higher than the other. And he had this weird dirty blond hair spiked with grey and a tan, roughened complexion like a waterman. He didn't look like a cop. He looked like a killer.

"I know it's your case," he said. "You think I'm here for shits and giggles?"

"Pardon me, Captain?" I said.

"Every newspaper in the goddamn *state* is printing all this tabloid shit about the case. They're making me look like the most incompetent cop in the history of the department. And this 'Handyman' tagline they're pushing? It sounds ridiculous, and it makes *me* look ridiculous." Jameson got up, closed my office door, then returned to his seat. Plumes of cigarette smoke seemed to follow him around like lingering spirits. "What is it with press people anyway?" he said next. Then the son of a bitch tapped an ash on my carpet. "The first thing you do is accuse the police of inefficiency, and then you gotta slap these horror-movie taglines onto any repeat crime you can get your hands on."

"It's a way of increasing the indentifiability of the event to a mass readership, because it helps sell papers. But I might remind you, Captain—before you flick more ashes on my floor—that I'm one journalist who's never used that tagline and has never criticized the police in their efforts to catch the killer."

"Yeah. That's why I like you."

By the way, the so-called "Handyman" Case involved a fairly recent sequence of murders in the downtown area. Three women so far: two known street prostitutes and one homeless woman. All three had been found strangled to death, their bodies carefully hidden along the Jackson Street corridor. And all three had been found with both of their hands missing. Cut off with an ax or a hatchet.

"And don't worry about your floor," he went on. "What? Your big paper can't afford janitors?"

"Captain Jameson, for a man coming in here asking for help, you might need to learn a few lessons in sincerity."

"Oh, fuck that shit. Don't be a creamcake. The only good journalism about this case that I've seen has been written by you. I want to make a deal."

"A deal? For what?"

"There've been more than three girls. That info's gonna get leaked eventually. I want you to break it first. I'll tell you everything about the case the press *hasn't* heard. You'll look good."

"Yes sir, I guess I would," I realized. "But what's the catch?"

"You make me look good along the way. You write for the most respectable paper in the city. All I'm asking is for some slack. I give you the goods, but when you write it, you say my unit's doing its best. And when we catch this fuck-up…you put in a good word for me. Deal?"

"No deal," I said. "You're bribing me. You've got balls coming in here telling me this. I'm a newspaper reporter for God's sake!"

"I wouldn't call it bribery." Jameson showed a big toothy grin, then flicked more ashes on the floor. "That descrambler you got? Sounds smalltime, but did you know it's now an FCC first-degree misdemeanor? A federal crime? Get'cha a year in jail and a five-grand fine for starters. Then let's talk about your Schedule C deductions. Newspaper writers with freelance gigs on the side? You pay Miscellaneous income tax, right? Those pseudonymous articles you wrote for *The Stranger, The Rocket,* and *Mansplat*?"

You son of a bitch, I thought.

"Can we talk?" Jameson asked.

¤   ¤   ¤   ¤   ¤

Seattle's never been a city known for its crime rate. Thirty-six murders last year in the entire Seattle-Metro area. Compare that to L.A., New

York, Washington D.C. and at least a dozen others tipping a thousand. What we're known for instead is the Space Needle, the Monorail, and the largest fish depot in the hemisphere. Microsoft and Boeing. Happy times and happy people. Low unemployment, and no state income tax. No partisan politics and no potholes. And more NEA and college grants per-capita than any major metropolis in the country.

A good place to live.

But then there's the downside that no one sees. Higher temperatures in the winter and wide-open welfare policies wag false promises to the destitute–it's a magnet to the hopeless. They come here looking for the yellow-brick road but all they get is another bridge to sleep under, another dumpster to eat out of. Just take a walk around Third and James, Yesler Street, the trolley bridge on Jackson. You'll see them trudging back and forth on their journey to nowhere. Stick-figures in rags, ghosts not quite incorporeal yet. Their dead eyes sunk into wax faces and bloodless lips asking for change or promising anything you want for twenty dollars. There are so many of them here, so many of these non-people with no names, no backgrounds, no lives.

The perfect grist of a psycho-killer.

"Our total's sixteen so far," Jameson admitted. "But that's not even the worst consideration–"

"God knows how many others are out there you *haven't* found," I said.

"You got it."

Jameson had brought me to his office at the city district headquarters. A large tack-board hung on the wall with sixteen pieces of paper pinned to it. Each piece of paper showed a victim's name, or in several cases just the letters *No ID* and a recovery date.

"How'd you manage to keep it quiet for so long?" I asked.

"Luck, mostly," Jameson grumbled. "Until recently, we'd find one here, one there. Isolated incidents, the victims were all nobodies: hookers, street trash. And we have our ways of keeping stuff away from the press."

"So you knew about this all along," I said, not asked.

"Yeah, for over three years." He was standing by the window, staring out as he talked. "Every single police department in the area is still the laughing stock over the Green River thing. What could we do? Have another one of those?"

"That's not the point, is it?"

He turned, a tight sarcastic smile on his face like a razor slash. "You fuckin' press guys. My job's to protect the residents of this city. It's not gonna do me or them any good if they find out this shit's been going on for years."

"And the victims?"

"So what? I don't give a shit about a bunch of whores and crackheads. I don't work for them—I work for the real people. And it sure as shit doesn't help when you press people bend over backwards to trash the police. If you're not complaining about increased burglary rates you're complaining about kids buying cigarettes. It's all our fault, huh? The police aren't doing enough."

I almost laughed at his insolence.

Jameson winced. "I'm just generalizing so don't be an asshole. Fuck, I'm forty-nine years old, been breaking my ass out there since I was a nineteen-year-old cadet. I'm a shoe-in for deputy chief, then all of a sudden a couple of dead junkies make the papers, and there goes my promotion."

"So this is all about you," I said. "You're just worried that this case will queer your promotion."

"I don't deserve the shit, that's all I'm saying."

That may have been true, at least in a sense. Eventually, I found out that Jameson had the highest conviction rate of any homicide investigator in the state. A lot of promotions, commendations, and even a valor medal. But now, after so many years on the department, his bitterness was draining like an abscess.

"You've covered this up for three years," I pointed out. "How'd the papers get wind of these last three?"

He sputtered smoke in disgust. "One of the construction crews building the new stadium found two in one day, and one of the workmen's wives writes for *Post-Intelligencer*. So we were fucked. Then a couple days later some egghead from UW's botany department finds the third body stuffed into a hole in one of the original drain outlets to the Sound. That fuckin' outlet had been out of service for seventy years, but this guy's in there with hipwaders collecting samples of fuckin' kelp and sea-mold. Then we were really burned. Three bodies with the same m.o., in less than a week? Next thing I know, me and the rest of my squad are getting pig-fucked by the press."

"Your compassion for the victims is heart-rending, captain," I said.

"Let me tell you something about these 'victims,'" Jameson shot back. "They're crack-whores. They're street junkies. They steal, they rip people off, they spread AIDS and other diseases. If it weren't for all this walking garbage that this candyass liberal state welcomes with open arms, then we wouldn't *have* a fuckin' drug epidemic. Shit, Health and Human Services *pays* these fuckin' people with our tax dollars! They sell their goddamn food stamps for a quarter on the dollar to buy crack. The city spends a couple hundred grand a year of our money giving these animals brand-new needles every day, and then millions more in hospital fees when they OD. Sooner or later society's gonna get fed up...but probably not in my fuckin' lifetime."

"That's quite a social thesis, captain. Should I start my next article with that quote?"

"Sure," he said. "But you'll have to have it transcribed."

"Transcribed?" I asked.

"They won't let you have a computer or typewriter in prison. Between the FCC violations and the tax-evasion, they'll probably give you five years, but don't worry. I'm sure they'll parole you after, say, a year and a half."

Okay, so maybe I've cut a few corners on my taxes, and I almost never use that descrambler...but I didn't know if he was kidding about this stuff or not. And Jameson didn't look like the kind of guy to kid about anything.

"Now that we've got that settled–come on. I need a drink."

¤   ¤   ¤   ¤   ¤

Jameson wasn't kidding about that either, about needing a drink. He slammed back three beers–tall boys—in about ten minutes while I sipped a Coke. Of all places, he'd taken me to The Friendly Tavern at James Street and Yesler, what most people would call a "bum" bar. It was on the same block as the city's most notorious subsidized housing complex, a couple of liquor stores and two bail bondsman's. Right across the street was the county courthouse.

"You sure know how to pick the posh spots," I said.

"Aw, fuck all those ritzy socialist asshole pinkie-in-the-air places up town," Jameson replied. "I want to drink, I don't want to listen to some bald lesbian read poetry. I don't want to listen to a bunch of fruitcake men with fingernail polish and black lipstick talk about art. I'll tell ya, one day Russia and the Red Chinese are gonna invade us, and this'll probably be the first city they take. When they get a load of the art-fag freak show we've got going on here, they'll just say fuck it and nuke us. All this fuckin' tattoo homo goth shit, women in combat boots, guys with Kool-Aid-colored mohawks swapping tongues in public and girls sticking their hands down each other's pants while they're walking down fucking Fifth Avenue. Everybody wearing black, of course–'cos it's *chic,* it's *sophisticated.* Everybody with all this ridiculous metal shit in their face, fuckin' rings in their nose and lips, rivets in their tongues. Nobody gives a shit about global terrorism or the trade-deficit–all they care about is getting their dicks pierced and picking up the next Maryland Mansion album."

"I think that's *Marilyn Manson,*" I said, "and, boy, you're packing a whole lot of hatred, Captain."

"I wouldn't call it hatred."

"Oh? You consider the homeless, the drug-addicted, and destitute to be, and I quote 'walking garbage' and you've just railed against alternative lifestyles with more invective than a right-wing militia newsletter. If that's not hatred, what is it?"

"Focused objection."

"Ah, thanks for the clarification," I said, amazed at this guy.

"The world doesn't ask much, you know? Work a job and obey the law–that's all anyone needs to do to be okay in my book." He slugged more beer, then glanced around in loathe. "The art-faggots, the dykes and the pinkos? I guess I can put up with them–most of 'em got jobs and they tend to stay out of the per-capita crime percentages. I'm just sick of seeing it, you know? I'm tired of seeing men swapping spit and holding hands. I'm tired of seeing fat 300-pound bull-dykes lumbering into the Bon Marché with asses wider than a fuckin' Metro bus. Then you've got these swish blue-jean queers at First and Pike selling their no-dick commie newspapers and yelling about how bad America is. Let 'em move to North Korea if they don't like it here, see how long they last pickin' rice for the fuckin' commissar twenty hours a day. Fuckin' pinkos."

"Didn't that term die out in the '70s?" I speculated. "Like when *All In The Family* went off the air?"

Jameson didn't hear me. He took another slug of beer, another loathsome glance around at the bar's patronage. "But this shit here? The rummies, the winos? They're the ones that get my goat. Ever notice how shit-hole bars like this are always full the first week of the month?"

I squinted at him. "I don't know what you're talking about."

"It's 'cos on the first of the month, they all get their three-hundred-dollar SSI checks. Then they come here and sit around like a bunch of waste-products and drink till the money's gone. The rest of the month they pan-handle or mug people for booze money."

I had to protest. "Come on, Captain. I read the crime indexes. Incidences of the homeless mugging citizens are almost non-existent. They pan-handle because there's nothing else they can do. And they drink because they're genetically dependent on alcohol. They can't help it."

"Gimme a break," he said. "I'm not surprised at something like that from lib journalist. Jesus Christ. Everything's a *disease* today. If you're a lazy piece of shit, you've got *affect disorder*. If you're a fat fuck, it's an inherited *glandular imbalance*. If your kid's a wise-ass, smart-ass punk fucking up in school, it's *amotivational syndrome* or *attention-deficit disorder*. What they all really need is a good old fashioned ass-kicking.

Hands

Crack 'em in the head with a two by four enough times and they'll get the message that they gotta pull their own weight in this world. And these fuckin' rummies and crackheads? Oh, boo-hoo, poor them. It's not their fault that they're dope addicts and drunks, it's this *disease* they have. It's this thing in their *genes* that makes them be useless stinking fuck-ups on two legs. Put all that liberal shit in a box and mail it to someone who cares. I'll bet you give money to the fuckin' Civil Liberties Union. If they had it their way, we'd all be paying sixty-percent taxes so these fucking bums could drink all day long and piss and shit in the street whenever they want."

This hypocrisy made me sick. If anyone in this bar were an alcoholic, it was Jameson. "You know something, Captain?" I said. "You're the most hateful, insensitive asshole I've ever met in my life. You're an ignorant bigot and a police-state fascist. You probably call African-Americans niggers."

"Naw, we call 'em boot-lips and porch monkeys. You don't see white people prancing down the street rubbing their fuckin' crotches and playing cop-killer rap out of those ghetto blasters, do you? I'se Amf-nee, I'se Tyrome. Kill duh poe-leece.. Kill duh poe-leece."

"I'm leaving," I said. "This is incredulous. What the hell am I doing even sitting here with you? What the hell has this got to do with your psycho killer?"

"Everything," he said, and ordered his fourth beer. "It doesn't matter what my views are–you're a journalist, you're supposed to report the truth. Even if you hate me...you're supposed to report the truth, right?"

"Yeah, right."

"Well none of the other papers are doing that. None of them have even queried my office to ask anything about the status of our investigation. It's easier just to write these horror-movie articles about the three poor victims who were brutally murdered by this killer, and about how the big bad police aren't doing anything about it because they don't care about street whores or the homeless. They want to make this look like Jack the fucking Ripper so they can sell more papers and have something to talk about at their pinko liberal bisexual cocktail parties."

I finished my Coke, grabbed my jacket off the next stool. "I'm out of here, Captain. You've given me no reason to stay and listen to any more of this bullshit. You want me to write a news article about police diligence regarding this case? That's a laugh. You haven't shown me anything. In fact the *only* thing you've shown me is that the captain of the homicide unit is a drunk and a bigot. And go ahead and report me to IRS and FCC. I'll take my chances."

"See? You're just like the others—you're a phony."

"Why do you say that?"

"Because you haven't even asked me the most important question. And why is that? Because you don't care. All you care about is putting the police on the hot-seat just like all these other non-writing chumps."

It was very difficult for me to not walk out right then. But I have to admit, I was piqued by what he'd suggested. "All right. What's the question I didn't ask?"

"Come on, you went to college, didn't you? You're a smart guy." Jameson drained half of the next beer in one chug, then lit another cigarette off the last stub. "When you've got a string of related murders, what's the first thing you've got to do?"

I shrugged. "Establish suspects?"

"Well, yeah, but before you can do that, you have to verify the common-denominators of the modus. Once you've done that, you gotta pursue a workable analysis of the of the motive. Remember, this is a *serial killer* we're talking about, not some bootlip PCP-head punk knocking over 7-Elevens. Serial killers are calculating, careful. Some guy all fucked up on ice goes out and rapes a girl—that's easy. I'll have the fucker in custody in less than forty-eight hours and I'll send him up for thirty years. But a serial killer?"

"All right, I don't know much about this kind of stuff," I admitted. "After all, this is Seattle, not Detroit."

"All right," he said. "So we establish the m.o., and with that we can analyze the motive. Once we've analyzed the motive, then we determine a what?"

"Uhhhh...."

"A psychological profile of the killer."

"Well, that was my next guess," I said.

"Only until we've established some working psych profile can we then effectively identify suspects."

"Okay, I'm following you."

Shaking his head, he crushed the next cigarette out in an ashtray that read *Yoo-hoo, Mabel? Black Label!* along the rim. "And? From the standpoint of a journalist, the most important question in this case is...what?"

The last guy in the world I wanted to look stupid in front of was Jameson. I was stressed not to say the wrong thing. "Why, uh, why is the killer...cutting off their hands?"

"Right!" he nearly yelled and cracked his open palm against the bartop. "Finally, one of you ink-stained liberal press schmucks has got it! The police can't do squat until they've established an index of suspects, and we can't do that until we've derived a profile of the killer. Why is he killing these girls and taking their hands?"

"But..." My thoughts tugged back and forth. "If he cuts off their hands, they can't leave fingerprints, can't be identified, and if they can't be identified, your investigation becomes obstructed."

"No, no, no," he griped. "In my office I *showed* you the ID list. We ID'd more than half of the victims already. A lot of the girls still had their ID's on their bodies when we found them. So what's that tell you?"

"The killer doesn't–"

"Right, he either thinks he's hidden the bodies so well that they'll never be found, or he doesn't care if they're ID'd. And, from there, the most logical deduction can only be?"

"He's...taking their hands for some other reason?" I posed.

"See? I knew you were smarter than these other bozos." Jameson actually seemed pleased that I'd figured some of it out. "That's what we've done. We've put more man-hours into this investigation than fucking Noah put into the Arc. The killer's *collecting* their hands. And when we find the reason, we'll get our suspects. Here, take this," he said, and reached down to his floor. What he hauled up was a briefcase. It felt heavy enough to contain a couple of cinder blocks.

"What is this?" I asked.

"The entire case file."

I sat back down, put on my glasses, and opened the case. "This looks like over a thousand pages of data."

"More than that," Jameson said. "Sixteen hundred so far. You want to be an honest journalist–"

"I *am* an honest journalist," I reminded him.

"–then do your homework. Read the fucking file, read the whole thing. And when you're done, if you can honestly say that me and my men are being negligent, then tell me so...and I'll resign my post. Deal?"

I flipped through the fat stack of paper. It looked like a *lot* of work. I was fascinated.

"Deal," I said.

"I knew you wouldn't walk out on this." Jameson, half-drunk now, rose to his feet. "I'll talk to ya soon, pal. Oh, and the beers are on you, right?" He slapped me hard on the back and grinned. "You can write 'em off on your taxes as a research expense..."

¤ ¤ ¤ ¤ ¤

Jameson was afflicted by the very thing he condemned: alcoholism. That much was clear. But in spite of his hypocrisy, I had to stick to my own guns. I'm a journalist; to be honest, I had to be objective. I had to separate Jameson's drunken hatred and bigotry from the task. Not a lot of newspaper writers do that, they jump on the easiest bandwagon–and I've done that myself–to please their editors by increasing unit sales. The Green River Killer is the best example in the Pacific Northwest...and it was all a sham, it was all hype. Everybody jumped on the state's favorite suspect...and it turned out to be the wrong guy. I knew I was better than that, so I decided that it didn't matter that Jameson was a reckless racist prick. All that mattered was the quality of the job he was doing.

And it looked like he wasn't doing half-bad.

That briefcase full of paper he gave me? He wasn't exaggerating. It was the entire investigatory file on every victim, going back for three years. Jameson and his crew had left no stone unturned, no evidential hair uncombed, and no speck of evidence unexamined. Of the victims who *had* been identified, the few who'd had traceable living relatives, Jameson had personally made the notification. Not an informal letter or a soulless phone call. The Captain himself, as the major case investigator, had traveled to locales as far of as Eugene, Oregon; Los Angeles; Spokane; and in one case, San Angelo, Texas, to notify the next of kin. All departmental expenditure invoices were included in the case file; Jameson had made these trips on his own time and at his own expense.

The evidence was another thing. Jameson had cut no slack whatsoever on pursuing even the minutiae of the crime-scene evidence. Even thoroughly decomposed and mummified victim's bodies had been analyzed to the furthest extent of forensic science. From things I'd never heard of like particulate-gas chromatographs, iodine and neohydrin fingerprint scans, atomic-force microscopy assays to simple gumshoe door-to-door canvassing. Sure, when Jameson had a load on, all of his hateful pus came pouring out, but from what I could see, when he was sober, he was a state of the art homicide investigator. The guy was doing everything in his power to solve this case. It didn't matter that he was an asshole. It didn't matter that he was a raving caustic racist. Jameson was doing it all. He was working his ass off and getting no credit at all from the local press.

Then I had to weigh my own professional values and I had to be honest. I didn't like this guy at all, but that wasn't the point. So I told it like it was when I wrote my piece for the *Times*. I reported to the readers of the biggest newspaper in the Seattle-Metro area that Captain Jay Jameson and his veteran homicide squad were doing everything humanly possible to catch the "Handyman."

The writers for the other papers about shit when they saw the detail of my article. My article, in fact, made the others look uninformed and haphazard. It made them look like the same exploitative tabloid hacks that Jameson accused them of being. But that didn't mean I was letting Jameson off the hook. If he slacked off or screwed up in any way, I'd write about that too. I gave the guy the benefit of the doubt because he deserved it. The rest was up to him.

Another thing, though. The case file contained several hundred pages of potential psychiatric analyses. I'm not stupid but I'm also not very well-versed in psych-speak. On every profile prospectus, I saw the same name: a clinical psychiatrist in Wallingford named Henry Desmond. I needed more of a layman's synopsis of these work-ups, to make my articles more coherent to the average reader.

So I made an appointment to see this guy, this Dr. Henry Desmond.

¤ ¤ ¤ ¤ ¤

"I appreciate your seeing me on such short notice, Dr. Desmond," I said when I entered the spare but spacious office. A pencil cup on his desk read: *Thorazine (100 mgs) Have A Great Day!* One the blotter lay a comic book entitled *Dream Wolves,* with cover art depicting what appeared to be sultry half-human werewolves tearing the innards out of handsome men.

"So you're the journalist, eh?"

"Yes, sir. I've got a few questions, if you don't mind."

"My last patient claimed to be about to give birth to a litter of extraterrestrial puppies. Her question was would I prefer a male or female. So I can assure you, any questions you might have will be more than welcome considering the usual."

Extraterrestrial puppies? I wondered. I took a seat facing the broad desk. Dr. Desmond was thin, balding, with very short blonde hair around the sides of his head. The dust-gray suit he wore looked several sizes too large. In fact, he looked lost behind the huge desk. A poster to the side read: *Posey Bednets And Straitjackets. Proven To Be The Very Best Three-, Four-, And Five-point Restraints In The Industry.*

Some industry. "I've got some questions, sir, about the–"

"The so-called 'Handyman' case, yes?"

Jameson must've talked to him, but that didn't make a whole lot of sense because I never told Jameson I'd be coming to see Desmond. "That's right, sir. I'm fascinated by your clinical write-ups regarding–"

"Potential profiles of the killer?"

"Yes."

He stared at me as of chewing the inside of his lip. "What you need to understand is that I don't officially *work* for the police. I'm a private consultant."

"So it's not cool with you that I mention your name as a consultant in any future articles I may write?"

"No, please. It's not...*cool*."

Great, I thought. *A cork in a bottle.*

"But I'd be pleased to answer any questions you may have on an anonymous basis. The only reason I must insist on anonymity is probably obvious."

"Uh," I said. "I'm sorry, sir, but it's not quite obvious to *me*."

The doctor let out the faintest of snorts. "If you were consulting with the police about a serial-killer case, would you want *your name* in a newspaper that the killer himself could easily read?"

Stupid! I thought. "No, sir. Of course not. This kind of thing is new to me, so I apologize for my naivete. And I guarantee you that your name won't be mentioned."

"Good, because if it is, I'll sue you and your newspaper for multiple millions of dollars," he said through a stone cold face. "And I'll win."

I stared back, slack-jawed.

"I'm kidding! My God, can't anybody today take a joke?"

I nodded glumly after a long pause. *A funny guy. Fine. Just what I need.*

"I trust it was the good Captain Jameson who sent you?"

"No, sir, he didn't *send* me. He gave me the case file to examine, and I saw your name on the prospective profiling data, so–"

"What do you think of Captain Jameson?" Desmond asked. "He's quite a character, isn't he?"

I opened my mouth to answer, but only my lips quavered.

"Come on, son. Tell me the *truth*. I'm forbidden by law to repeat anything you say."

I guess he was right. Doctor-client privilege and all that, even though I wasn't a patient. So I said it. "I think Captain Jameson is a clinical alcoholic with enough hatred in him to burn down the city.... But I also think he's probably a pretty effective homicide investigator."

"You're correct on both counts," Desmond acknowledged. "He's a tragic man in a tragic occupation. You'd be surprised how many of my patients are veteran police officers."

This struck me as odd. As a psychiatrist, Desmond could not legally verify that Jameson was a *patient*. And I'd never suspected that he was.

Until now, perhaps.

"Your profiles," I said to move on.

"They're not profiles, not as of yet. Think of them as *possible* profiles."

"Er, right. I've read every page of the case load compiled thus far, but I'm still a little shaky on a lot of it. These are highly clinical terms, I need layman terms."

"All right. Understood. So go on."

I must've sounded like I was babbling. "Well, er, sir, it seems that you've, uh–"

"Compartmentalized the potential clinical profiles into three groups?"

"Yes, and–"

"And you don't know what the *hell* I'm talking about."

My shoulders slumped in the chair. "You hit the nail on the head, doctor."

Dr. Desmond stroke his bare chin as if he had a goatee. "What's the first question a paramount journalist such as yourself might be inclined to ask after examining to full details of this case?"

I'd already learned this one the hard way. "Why is that killer taking the hands? It can't be to obfuscate fingerprint discovery because he's clearly demonstrated a total lack of concern as to whether or not the authorities positively identify the victims or not."

"Excellent," Desmond said.

"Which means that the killer is *collecting* the hands, for some unknown reason."

"Well, not *unknown*. There are several *suspected* reasons detailed in the case file."

I nodded. "That's what I'm not clear on, sir."

In his hand, Desmond was diddling with a small pale-blue paperweight that said PROLIXIN - IV & IM on it. "Consider the most obvious symbological reference. There's been no evidence of semen or prophylactic lubricant in the vaginal barrels or rectal vaults of any of the victims, which indicates a sexual dysfunction. He's picking the women up and strangling them, then he's cutting of their hands. This is a strong evidence signature; the crime describes an inner-personal pathology. So you're right. He's *collecting* their hands. Possibly as trophies. The same way Serbs severed the heads of so many Bosnians. The same way the T'u Zhus removed the penises of invaders from nearby tribes. Yes? Taking parts off the enemy. *Offending* parts."

Suddenly, I was beginning to see. "But who's the enemy in *this* case?"

"Clearly, the mother. The first profile possibility indicates someone who was severely abused as a child by the mother-figure. A woman who beat the child, with *her hands*. A woman who molested the child, with *her hands*. The mother who invaded the child's private parts–*with her hands*."

It made some sense...but there were still more possibilities. "And the second profile?" I asked.

"The converse. The polar opposite, in a sense. No abuse in this instance but simply a *lack* of the necessary primal need to be touched–by the mother. We're talking about the sheer lack of the facilitation of the nurturing touch. All babies *need* to be touched by the mother. If they're not, the incidence of subsequent sociopathy is increased by one hundred percentage points. Put a newborn hamster in a cage by itself, and it dies in a few days. Even if it's regularly hand fed by a human. Put it in a cage with a dummy mother, and it lives but later in life it becomes violent, anti-social, homicidal. It's never *touched* by the mother. Any mammalian species that aren't nurtured by the mother never grow up right. Then put this in *human* terms. Humans–the most complex mammalian species. They bear the most vulnerable newborns, which require constant attention by the mother to survive. The mother's touch. Infants who aren't sufficiently touched by their mothers suffer numerous psychological disorders. Theodore Kaczynski, the world-famous Unabomber, never became socially adjusted in adulthood in spite of his high IQ and expert propensity for mathematics. Why? Because complications shortly after his birth required him to be incubated for several weeks–separated from his mother's nurturing touch. It's something that all babies need, and he didn't get it. Look what happened later."

The office sat just behind the McDonald's on Stone Way; all I could smell were french fries and Big Macs, which kind of threw me for a loop: smelling fast food while listening to psych profiles seemed bizarre. "Both of those descriptions make sense," I said. "But I'm wondering–just how crazy is this guy?"

"In Profile #1, the perpetrator may be quite 'crazy,' to use your term. He may be psychopathic or merely sociopathic, but more than likely the former. He's probably in the mid- or late-stages of a hallucinotic syndrome, and has long since experienced a mid-phased episodic reality break."

Christ, I thought. *You need a doctorate in psychiatry just to talk to this guy. Talking to him's worse than reading his write-ups.* "The clinical terms are way over my head, Dr. Desmond," I admitted. "If you could dumb this down a little?"

"Clinically, we would call Profile #1 a graduated bipolar symbolist. The effect of his illness has a tendency to switch off and on at times relative to his delusion, and to put it in general terms, when he's *off,* he's able to function normally in society, but when he's *on,* he is indeed 'crazy.' He becomes overwhelmed by some facet of his delusional fixation to the extent that he hallucinates. The women he murders are symbols. He *sees* his victims as his mother, as the self same person who so heinously abused him as a child."

"Jeeze, that sounds pretty serious."

"Well, it is given the gravity of the crimes. It's unusual, though, that someone could maintain this level of bipolarity for three years. If there's anything 'promising' about the diagnosis, it is the graduated aspect. He's gradually becoming more and more insane; eventually–soon, I would say–he'll lose his ability to maintain social functionality. And he'll get caught rather quickly."

Promising? I thought. *Odd choice of words, but then he's the shrink.* "What about Profile #2?"

"More complicated, and less predictable," Desmond began. "Profile #2 is functionally similar in that the killer is suffering from a symbolic bipolar personality disorder. But he's not experiencing any manner of hallucinosis and his delusions are conscious and quite controllable. The fantasy element takes over. It's probably quite like a dream. When he's murdering these women–and severing their hands–he's immersed so deeply in the delusion that he's probably not even consciously aware of what he's doing. It's a fixation disorder that's run amok. Am I losing you?"

"Well, a little, yes." *A little, my ass.*

"He's dreaming of something he never had. Only, regrettably, he's acting out the dream in real life. Is that synopsis *cool* with you, young man?"

But I still didn't get it. "A dream...of cutting off hands?"

"No, no. Be intuitive. The perpetrator doesn't see it that way. He sees it as claiming what he never had as a child. Remember–the facilitation of the mother's nurturing touch. All infants need to be touched; the perpetrator was not. That should answer your question about what exactly he's *doing* with the hands."

I stared at him, gulped. And the implication was disgusting. "You mean he's... taking the hands–"

"He's taking the hands home," Desmond finished, "and putting them on his body. His mother is at last touching him. Nurturing him. But now, in adulthood, the delusion is so thoroughly contorted and transfigured—he's probably masturbating with the hands too."

What a screwed up world, with screwed up people. "Christ," I said. "That's...sick."

"But so is our perpetrator," Desmond added. "There's quite a bit in our world that's sick, twisted, wrong. And quite a few people in it who don't see it that way."

"But the third," I said, "the third profile." I put my glasses on and looked back at the marked pages of the case file. "You called it a 'fixated erotomanic impulse'. What's that mean?"

Desmond's pate glimmered in a sun-break through the window. He shrugged his shoulders. "It means that in the case of this third potential profile, the killer is simply a sociopath with a hand fetish."

Simply a sociopath with a hand fetish, I thought. The terms just rolled off this guy's lips like me talking about baseball.

"It's the most remote possibility but also the worst as far as apprehension is concerned."

"Why's that?" I asked.

"It's remote because sociopaths rarely engage in mutilation crimes. But they're infinitely harder to apprehend because sociopaths, as a rule, aren't insane; therefore they're less likely to make a mistake that could lead to arrest. Sociopaths are skilled liars. They've had their whole lives to practice. Their amorality isn't a result of mental defectivity. They know what's right and what's wrong, but they choose wrong because it suits them."

They choose wrong, I thought. But Desmond had said this profile was the least likely. "If you had to make a choice yourself," I asked him, "which of the three would you put your money on?"

Desmond tsk'd, smiled a thin smile. "Abnormal psychiatry isn't an objective checklist. Profile indexes exist only through the documentation of known information. So it stands to reason that there's quite a bit out there that we *don't* know yet. It would be of little value for me to make a guess. All I can say is it's probably one of the three. But you should also consider a sexual detail that should also be obvious."

Dumb again. Dumb me. "And that would be?"

"The absence of evidence of rape. No semen in any orifice, no evidence of sexual penetration. Considering any of my three profiles, the possibility should properly be addressed that the killer is at the very least unable to achieve erection in the presence of a woman, or he may be sexually incompetent altogether."

"This is a lot of data you've given me, sir, and I'm grateful," I said, pushing my glasses up the bridge of my nose. The insights he'd given me would make for a great, comprehensive series of articles on the killer. "I really appreciate your time."

"My pleasure, young man."

I grabbed my stuff to leave, but then he held up a finger to stop me.

"One last point, though," he said. "In the cases of Profiles #1 and #2, there's a considerable formative likelihood that the killer's mother was either a prostitute, a drug addict, or both."

"That'll help my article too. Maybe if the killer reads it, it'll scare him into making a mistake, or stopping."

Desmond creaked back in his padded chair. I'm not sure if he was smiling or not, just nodding with his eyes thinned and his lips pressed together. "Perhaps it will," he said so softly it sounded like a flutter.

"Thank you," I said. But then something caught me–two things, actually, both at the same time. Behind Desmond's head, the late-afternoon sun burned, an inferno. And then my eyes flicked down to the doctor's desk blotter.

It was one of those calendar blotters, each top sheet a different month. The Tuesday and Thursday boxes for all four weeks had this written in them:

J.J..—1:30 P.M.

J.J., I thought.

Captain Jay Jameson.

¤   ¤   ¤   ¤   ¤

That's when I knew Jameson was the one. It hit me in the head like someone dropping a flowerpot from a high window. There were still a few holes, sure. But it was one of those things where you just *knew.* It was a presage. It was something psychic.

I just knew.

I knew I had to go see him. I knew I had to get him out. But before I could even make a plan, Jameson walks right into my cubicle the next day.

"There he is. The lib journalist."

I glanced up from my copy, stared at him.

"Hey, I'm just joking," he said. "Lighten up, you'll live longer."

"You come here to bust me for my descrambler?"

"What's a descrambler?" he said. "And tax evasion? Never heard of it."

"Why are you here, Captain? You want to square up with me? Those four Old English tallboys cost me $3.50 a pop. Us lib journalists don't make much."

"Good," he said. He rubbed his hands together. He grinned through that weird lined, tanned face, the shock of blond-gray hair hanging over one eye. "Let me make it up to ya. Dinner at my place. You ever had broiled langoustes with scallop mousse? My wife makes it better than any restaurant in the city. Come on."

This was a great opportunity but… "I've got a deadline. I'm a crime writer, remember? I'll be here at least two more hours writing up the robbery at the Ballard Safeway. My boss won't let me out of here till it's done."

Jameson jerked a gaze into the outer office. "That's your boss there, right? The fat guy in suspenders with the mole on his neck bigger than a bottlecap? I already talked to him. Safeway can wait. You're off early today, boy."

"What are you talk—"

Jameson lit a cigarette, then tapped an ash on my floor. "Your boss has sixteen parking tickets he thought his brother in the public safety building buried. I showed him the print-out from the city police mainframe."

That'll do it. I looked through the door at my boss, and all he did was frown and flick his wrist.

"All right," I said. "I guess Safeway can wait."

¤   ¤   ¤   ¤   ¤

"Honey? This is my good friend Matt Hauge," Jameson introduced. "This is my wife, Jeanna."

I cringed when he said *good friend,* but I also knew I had to play along now. "Pleased to meet you, Mrs. Jameson," I said and shook her hand. She looked about mid-forties but well tended. Bright blond hair, good figure, probably a knockout in her younger days. *What's a good-looking woman like this doing with a busted racist drunk like Jameson?* I wondered. They didn't fit together at all. They both looked out of place standing there together—a shining Waterford figurine next to a rubber dog turd.

He'd driven me from the paper to his Belltown condominium. Nice place, clean, well appointed, which didn't look right either. It was easier to picture Jameson living in an unkempt dump with smoke-stained walls, dirty dishes in the sink, and cigarette burns in a carpet that hadn't been vacuumed in years.

"Hi," she said with kind of a wan smile. "Jay hasn't stopped talking about you."

"Oh, really?" I replied.

"God, since your article in the *Times* came out, he's been like a kid at Christmas."

So that's what this was all about. The red carpet treatment. Jameson's ego and pride wouldn't let him say it, so he let his wife do it. This was his way of thanking me for giving him a good shake in print. *Or maybe it's just his way of continuing the bribe,* I considered.

"From what I can see, Mrs. Jameson, your husband's doing a topnotch job in investigating this case," I told her. "The other writers in this city have chosen not to acknowledge this—and that's wrong. I'm not doing your husband any favors here; I'm just writing it the way I see it."

"Well," she went on, "we're really grateful to you."

"No need to be, ma'am. Because if your husband drops the ball now…I'm going to write about that too." Then I shot Jameson a cocked grin.

"I don't *drop* the ball," Jameson told me and immediately lit a cigarette. "Don't believe me? Check my performance ratings."

"I already have," I said. "And you're right." Then I glanced over at the tv in the corner. "Say, is that a descrambler you've got there?"

"Funny. I like a lib journalist with a sense of humor," he said, slapping me hard on the back and showing me into the dining room. Warm, exotic aromas swam around the room. "What would you like to drink?" Jameson's wife asked.

"A Coke would be fine."

Another hard slap to the back. It was getting old. "Come on, have a drink," Jameson insisted. "You're off duty."

"Maybe later," I said, half lost of breath.

"Dinner'll be right up," Jeanne said, then disappeared into the aromatic kitchen.

Jameson and I sat down at the table simultaneously. I knew I had him pegged, but I also knew I still needed more. This was the big league. He was a decorated city detective, I was just a reporter.

"Look, man," he said. "I ain't too good at, you know–expressing gratitude? But your article really helped me out . Not just me but my whole squad. So…thanks."

"Don't thank me yet," I said. "Like I just got done telling your wife, your step on your dick, I'm gonna make you look like Laurel and Hardy on the front page."

"I hear ya–"

"And it's not just one article, you know. I'm writing a *series* of related articles about the killer," I informed him.

"Oh, yeah?"

"Yeah. This isn't just some fly-by-night crime piece. It's a comprehensive serial-killer story. People want to know, so I'm gonna tell them." It was time to play the card. "I've already talked to Dr. Desmond, and he gave me a lot of clinical info on the case. It'll be a highly informative series."

Jameson's jaw dropped so hard I thought his lower lip would slap the dining room table. "You-you've talked to Dr. Desmond?"

"Yeah, sure. I saw his name on those profile write-ups you gave me. My next articles' going to detail his first profile: the killers who's cutting off his victim's hands out of a symbolic and hallucinatory act of revenge. Then I'll write another about the second profile: the homicidal fantasist whose taking the hands to facilitate what he never got as a child. The nurturing touch of the mother." I paused for a moment, just to gauge his reaction.

All he did was look at me *real* funny.

"Yeah, he gave me all kinds of insights for my series," I added. "It could get national notice."

"Uh, yeah, sure," Jameson said. Was he faltering? Did I throw him a hard slider? "Desmond's an odd cookie, and talk about ego? Shit. He can barely walk into a room 'cos his head's so big. But he does know his shit. That guy can slap a profile faster than the president can whip it out in front of a twenty-year-old."

"I wouldn't put it in quite those terms, Captain," I said, "but Dr. Desmond does seem to be a qualified expert."

Jeanne brought out the drinks, then smiled bashfully, and said, "It'll be just another minute."

I nodded as she scurried back to the kitchen. "So what are we having?" I asked Jameson. "Linguini and something?"

"Langoustes. Petite lobster tails from Britain. Flash-broiled in garlic and lime butter and topped with scallop mousse." Jameson half drained a can of Rainier Ice. "I hope you're hungry."

"I'm starving. Missed lunch."

"Oh, yeah. Bet'cha hate it when you have to put in ten hours."

"Ten? Are you kidding me? Ten's a short day."

Each time Jameson dragged on his cigarette, I watched a third of it burn down; then he'd light another. "Look, I'm sorry about all that shit I said a few days ago. I didn't mean it–it wasn't me. I was just having a bad day, you know?" He grinned. "Even racist police-state cops have bad days."

"Thank God I never pulled up my sleeve. Then you would've seen my Maryland Mansion tattoo."

"Oh, you've got one too?" Jameson exploded laughter, a bit too loudly. "Wanna see my nipple ring?"

Dinner was served, and I have to admit, I've probably never had a better seafood meal in my life. The scallop mousse melted in my mouth, and those langouste things tasted better than any lobster I've ever had. During the meal, we tried to talk openly, but Jameson–the more he drank–dominated the conversation with cop talk. After a while, I could see that his wife was getting uncomfortable, even embarrassed, and after a little more time, she just gave up. I felt sorry for her.

"So we're all standing around the morgue slab with the M.E.!" Jameson bellowed after his fifth beer, "and the corpse cracks a fart! I kid you not!"

Yeah, I felt *really* sorry for her.

"So then Dignazio says, 'Damn, he must get his chili dogs at Schultze's 'cos that fart smells just like mine!'"

The poor woman just wilted where she sat.

"This was a fantastic meal, Mrs. Jameson. Thanks very much," I said. "But I guess I better get going now."

"Bullshit!" Jameson said. Then he put his arm around me and shook me, all the while looking at his wife. "Honey," he said. "I gotta take this boy out for a nightcap, all right? I gotta teach this man to drink!"

"No, really–" I started.

"Come on, don't be a candyass!"

"Just be careful," Mrs. Jameson said.

I'm no big drinker but I still had a few things to snuff out. Bar-hopping with Jameson would provide the perfect opportunity.

We got up to leave. That's when I noticed some framed pictures along the fireplace mantle; there were just a few.

I put my glasses on and looked.

A wedding picture of a much younger Jameson and his wife. Some snapshots of old people: relatives, I presumed. Aunts and uncles, grandparents, like that. A freeze-frame of a beautiful cheerleader wagging pom-poms and doing a split—it was obviously Jameson's wife back in high school days. Then–

A framed picture of a dark-haired adult with his arm around a cock-eyed kid with a bad haircut.

Jameson, I thought. *The kid's Jameson...*

"No kids yet, I see," I said and took my glasses off. I suspected this might be dangerous ground but I had to go for it.

"No," Mrs. Jameson peeped.

"Not yet," Jameson piped in. "We're still waiting for the right time."

Man, you're fifty and she's gotta be forty-five, I thought. *Better not wait much longer.*

Jameson jangled his keys. "Come on, Iib. Let's go have some fun."

I turned to his wife. "Mrs. Jameson. Thanks very much for the excellent meal. You could get a job at any restaurant in town; you'd blow all of those master chefs out of the water."

The woman blushed. "Thank you. Come by again soon."

"Later, babe," Jameson bid and yanked me out of there. He guffawed all the way down the stairs to the parking garage.

"So where you wanna go?" he asked. "A strip joint?"

"And all this time I thought you were gonna take me to hear bald lesbians read poetry," I joked.

"Aw, fuck that shit," he answered, beer fumes wafting out of his mouth. "Let's see some *meat.*"

"Pardon me if I'm misinformed, Captain, but there really aren't any strip joints in Seattle. The girls all gotta wear bikinis via county code, and the only thing you can drink there is orange juice or sodas."

Another loud guffaw. "Pal, you don't know the strip joints I know!"

I'm sure I don't, I thought. When we'd just stepped into the elevator into the parking garage, I slapped my breast pocket. "Oh, shit."

"What's wrong? You just shit your pants?"

"I left my glasses in your condo," I admitted.

"Well go on back up and get them and I'll get the car." He elbowed me. "And no funny business with the wife…or I'll have ta kill you."

He burst more laughter as I jogged back up the stairs.

"I'm sorry," I said to Mrs. Jameson when she answered my knock. "I left my glasses here."

"Oh, come in," she said. I could smell from her breath that she'd already had a stiff one since we'd left. "Were would they be?"

"The table, or maybe the mantle when I was looking at the pictures," I said.

I scanned the table–nothing.

"Here they are," she said, picking them up off the mantle.

"Thanks."

"I apologize for the way Jay gets sometimes," the words stumbled from her mouth. "He has a little too much to drink, and…well, you know."

You ain't kidding I know, I thought.

"But you should also know that your article really pumped him up," she went on. "I haven't seen him happy in years, but your article really made him happy. He's worked hard for so long. It's wonderful to see someone give him recognition in the press."

I shrugged. "He's doing a good job on the case. That's why I wrote the piece."

"Well, anyway, thank you," she said.

The look she gave me then? Christ. She brought her arms together in front, pressed her breasts together. Her nipples stuck through her blouse like golf cleats. *Fuck,* I thought. *Is she offering herself to me…for the article?*

"If you don't mind my asking," I changed the subject. "What's this picture here?" I pointed to the man with his arm around the boy. "Is that your husband, the child?"

"Yes, that's him with his father," she told me. "Jay was seven. His father was killed a few weeks after that picture was taken."

"Oh…I'm sorry." My eyes scanned the photos. "Where's his mother?"

"Jay never knew his mother," she said. "She ran out the day he was born."

¤   ¤   ¤   ¤   ¤

The facilitation of the mother's nurturing touch, I thought as Jameson squealed his Grand Am out of the parking garage. Everything I'd observed so far backed up everything Desmond had told me…

"So how'd you like the grub? Better than the cafeteria at the *Times?*"

"It was fantastic. Your wife is one dynamite cook."

"Yeah, she's a good kid," he said. "She's hung with me through thick and thin, and believe me, there's been a lot of thin. Too bad I can't do more for her."

"What do you mean?"

He steered down Third Avenue. "It didn't help when you brought up kids. Last couple of years, it's been like playing pool with a piece of string."

"Sorry," I said.

"But that's my problem, not yours," he perked up. "Let's go have some fun!"

"Look, I don't really want to go to a strip joint."

"All right, fine. We'll just hit a bar. This city's a kennel anyway. I swear something in the water makes most of the female pop uglier than hemorrhoids on an elephant's ass. All these women with big faces full'a pock marks, tits swingin' down to their knees, and so much hair under their arms it looks like they got Don King in a fuckin' headlock."

By now I was well used to just shaking my head at Jameson's comments. We rode a ways. The streetlights shimmered as the warm air roved down the avenue. We stopped at a red light at third and Marion, and several homeless people approached the car.

"Shine your windshield for a buck, mister," a decrepit man said.

"Get the *fuck* away from the car!" Jameson yelled. "I just had it washed!"

"Hey, mister, relax. We was just askin'."

A woman in rotten clothes approached the passenger side. Toothless, staggering.

"Tell that junkie bum bitch to *get away* from my car!" Jameson yelled.

Then he yanked his gun out of his shoulder holster.

"Are you nuts?" I shouted at him.

The two vagrants scampered off, terrified.

"Yeah, you *better* get out of here, you pieces of shit!" Jameson yelled. "Christ, you people smell worse than the bottom of a fuckin' dumpster!"

"What the hell is wrong with you, man?" I said. "You can't be pulling your gun on people for shit like that."

Jameson reholstered his pistol, chuckling. "Cool off. I just wanted to put a scare in 'em. Bet they shit their pants, huh? See, I just saved the city a clean-up fee. Usually they shit in the street."

"They're homeless, for God's sake. They got nothing."

"Fuck that pinko shit," he said, then bulled through the red light. "Why don't ya go out there and wipe their asses for 'em?"

It occurred to me then that Jameson had a harder load on than I thought. "Hey, look, Captain. You're pretty lit. Why don't you let me drive? You're gonna get pulled over at this rate."

Jameson laughed. "Any cop in this city pulls *me* over, he's transferred to the impound lot in the morning. What's up your ass?"

"Nothing," I said. I knew I had to grin and bear it. But I still had a few more questions to ask. *Just be careful,* I told myself.

"Fuckin' junkies, fuckin' bums." Jameson's eyes remained dead on the street. "Everybody asking for a handout. I never asked for no handouts."

"Some people are more fortunate than others," I said.

"Oh, don't give me that liberal pantywaist *bullshit,*" he spat, spittle flecking the inside of the windshield. "I never had nothing. My father died when I was seven, died in a fuckin' steel mill when an ingot fell on him off of a lift-clip. After that I got hocked into the fuckin' foster care system. So I don't want to hear no shit about poor people from poor environments. I got out of that hellhole, graduated high school, got my degree, and now I'm running the fuckin' homicide squad in one of the biggest cities on the west coast."

But I was still remembering what his wife had said. "What, uh, what about your mother?" I asked.

Jameson lead-footed it through another red light. "My mother? Fuck her." Beer fumes filled the car. "My mother beat feet the same day she dropped me. That dirty bitch wasn't nothing but a junkie whore. She was street-shit. She was walking garbage just like that whore who just tried to smudge up my windshield. Far as I'm concerned, I never had a mother."

¤ ¤ ¤ ¤ ¤

It got to the point where almost anything Jameson did or said would support some facet of Dr. Desmond's profile. A prostitute for a mother, who abandoned him at birth. No nurturing touches as an infant, no mother-figure in the formative years. An ability to control his symbolic delusion to the extent that he can function in society and maintain steady employment. A man who is probably married but probably doesn't have children. A man with a mounting inability to perform sexually.

I also found it interesting that Jameson's favorite places to drink were bars in the derelict districts, bars in which any of the sixteen previous victims might easily have hung out. I wondered what Dr. Desmond would think about that?

Oh yeah, I knew he was the one. But what was I going to do about it?

The next couple of hours were pretty paralyzing. Jameson dragged me around to three more dive bars, getting drunker in each one, his hatred boiling. Loud, obnoxious, belligerent. At one point I thought one of the barkeeps was going to throw him out, but I prayed that wouldn't happen. Knowing Jameson–and as drunk as he was–he'd probably yank out his gun, might shoot someone. But before that could happen, I got him out of there.

Then the end came pretty fast after that.

¤ ¤ ¤ ¤ ¤

"I'm a crime reporter for the *Times*." I flashed my press ID to the two doctors in the ER. "Earlier tonight, I was with Captain Jay Jameson of the city police homicide unit–"

One of the doctors, a balding guy, squinted over at me from a scrub sink. "You know that guy?" The doctor's nametag read PADUANA.

"That's right. I was drinking with him in some area bars," I admitted. "When his name was logged in as an in-patient, the night-editor at my paper contacted me."

"Fuck, the guy was drinking," another doctor said. This one was big, with a trimmed beard; his nametag read MULLEN. He was taking instruments out of an autoclave. "No wonder his blood was so thin. He damn near bled to death right in front of us. He took three pints before we could stabilize him. What happened?"

"I was dragging him out of a bar about two hours ago," I told them. "He was pretty drunk. I was about to put him in the car when he bolted. The guy just ran off across Jackson and disappeared under the overpass. I couldn't find him. The biggest reason for my concern is Captain Jameson said some things to me tonight that lead me to believe he may be–"

"This psycho who's been killing girls and cutting off their hands," Paduana finished.

I stared at them, slack-jawed. "How–how did you know?"

Dr. Mullen snickered. "When the EMTs brought him in, he had a severed hand in his pants."

"Jesus," I muttered. "What happened to him?"

"Looks like after he ran off from you," Paduana explained, "he must've picked up a hooker, then made his move, but she shot him. He was lying in the middle of Jackson when the EMTs found him. But it must've been his second girl of the night 'cos he already had one hand on him."

"Shit," I said. "I called the cops the minute he bolted, told them my suspicions, but they didn't take me serious."

"We'll show 'em the hand we found in his pants," Mullen said. "*Then* they'll take you serious."

"So you said his condition is stable?" I asked.

"We stabilized the blood loss and ligged an artery. But the x-rays showed a cranial fracture–hematoma. He's prepped for more surgery but I wouldn't give him more than one chance in ten of making it."

"Where is he now?" I asked. "I really need to talk to him."

Paduana pointed across the ER. "He's in the ICU prep cove. Second floor'll be down to take him up in a few minutes. You want to go see him, go ahead. But don't hold your breath on him regaining consciousness."

"Thanks," I said, and at the same moment several paramedics burst through the ER doors with what looked like a burn victim on a gurney. "Great!" Paduana yelled. "My relief's two hours late, and now I got a spatula special…"

I rushed to the prep cove and there he was: Jameson. Tubes down his throat, tubes up his nose, strapped to a railed bed. An IV line ran from a bag of saline to his arm. He looked dead.

"Hey, hey," I said. I patted his face. "I guess you're in a coma, huh, Captain? Well you know what? They got you for the whole thing now. I knew you were the one."

His slack, lined face just lay there like a bad wax mask. "Once Dr. Desmond finds out the details, he'll realize that his profile fits you to a tee. He's a smart man. He'll back up my allegation one-hundred percent."

I patted his face a few more times. No response.

Then I took the needle-cover off the hypodermic I'd brought along. "Yeah, I knew you were the one. I knew you were the perfect dupe to take the fall." The hypo was full of potassium dichlorate. It'd kill him in minutes and wouldn't show up on a tox screen. I injected the whole thing into his IV connector.

Then Jameson's eyes slitted open.

"You're a pretty damn good cop, Captain," I gave him. "You got any idea how hard I worked burying those bodies over the last three years? And there are twenty-one, by the way, not sixteen. You did a great job of keeping 'em out of the papers…until those last three. Just dumb luck for me, huh?"

He began to quiver on the bed, veins throbbing at his temples.

I leaned down close to his ear, whispered. "But that really screwed up my game when the victims started making the press. I thought I was gonna have to lay low now, get the junkie bitches from out of town. But you solved all that for me."

I grinned down at him. His eyes opened a little more, to stare at me.

"Yeah, I knew you were the one, all right. The minute Desmond explained those profiles, and when I saw that picture of you with your father. No mother, just a father who died the same year. And, Christ, man! You were Desmond's patient! The press'll eat that up! Homicide cop seeing a shrink—homicide cop turns out to be the killer. It's great, isn't it? It's perfect!"

See, after I dragged him out of that last bum bar, I shoved him in the passenger seat of his car. The drunk bastard had already passed out. I drove down Jackson when there was no traffic, cracked him hard in the head with the butt of my own piece, then shot him in the groin. I was aiming for the femoral artery, and I guess I did a damn good job of hitting it. He bled all over the place; I knew the fucker was going to kick.

Then I stuck the hand in his pants and shoved him out of the car.

The whole thing worked pretty well, I'd say.

"Don't die on me yet, asshole," I whispered, pinching his cheeks. "See, Desmond had it right with his profiles. Only it turns out the real killer was the least likely of the bunch—just a sociopath with a hand fetish."

It was hard not to laugh right in his face.

Jameson's hand raised an inch, then dropped. He was tipping out but I gotta give the old fucker credit. He managed to croak out a few words.

"They'll never believe it," he said.

"Oh, they'll believe it," I assured him. "What? You're gonna tell them what *really* happened? Not likely. In two minutes you'll be dead from cardiac arrest."

"Lib motherfucker," he croaked. "Pinko piece'a shit..."

"That's the spirit!" I whispered. "Go out kicking! But—"

His eyelids started drooping again. This was it.

"Not yet! Don't die yet," I said, squeezing his face. "There's still one more thing I haven't told you, and it's something you gotta know."

Spittle bubbled from his lips. I could see him struggling to keep his eyes open, fighting to keep conscious just a few more seconds.

"Remember when I went back up to your condo to get my glasses?" I said. "What do you think I did to your wife, dickbrain? That hand they found in your pants? It was your *wife's*."

Jameson tremored against his restraints. He shook and shook, like someone had just stuck a hot wire in him. Down the hall, I could hear the elevator opening, the crash team coming to take him up to surgery. *Don't bother, guys,* I thought.

But just before Jameson died, I managed to tell him the final detail. "That's right, I stuck her right hand in *your* pants, Captain. And her *left* hand? I got it safe, right here with me."

Then I patted my crotch and grinned.

They took him up, and his obit ran the next day...along with everything else. Homicide captain investigating the Handyman Case, found with his own murdered wife's hand in his pants? The same shrink he was seeing for alcoholism and sexual dysfunction corroborating that Jameson fit the profile?

Case closed.

And don't forget what Desmond said about sociopaths. They're skilled liars. They've had their whole lives to practice. They know what's right and what's wrong, but they choose wrong because it suits them.

That sounds good to me.

I'll just have to bury the next bodies deeper.

HANDS
AFTERWORD

In June, 1997, I moved from Crofton, Maryland, to Seattle, Washington, thanks to the generosity of my good friend and collaborator John Pelan. (He and his wife Kathy rent me their basement.) One of the first things I noticed about Seattle was its influx of homeless. I can't walk down the street without feeling a spike in my heart for these people. And walking down those same streets, I've seen an inordinate amount of prejudice and abuse. I've seen men in business suits spit on pan-handlers. I've seen middle-class folk shove the homeless away, shouting, "Get a job!" too stupid to realize that many of these people can't *get jobs. They're mentally ill, malnourished to the point of physical dysfunction, or genetically habituated to drugs or alcohol. They* want *to work...but they simply can't. Too many learning disabilities from atrocious childhoods, attention spans too low from decades of malnourishment. Yet the "haves" continue to frown down on the "have-nots." It makes me sick.*

Anyway, I'd always wanted to write a story about a genuine "signature" killer, per se, so I devised this plot and used it to channel a lot of that same prejudice I've witnessed.

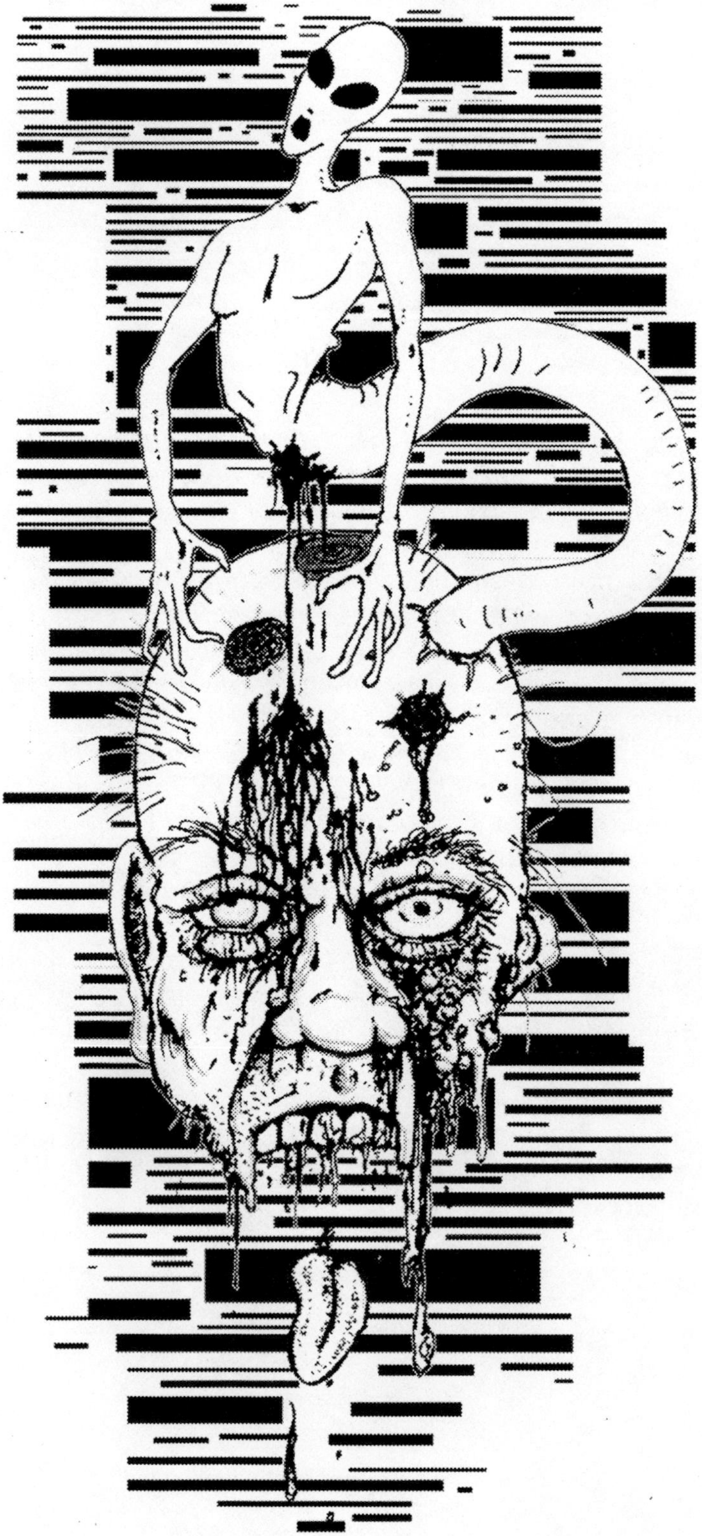

Secret Service

"VICTOR FOUR, SIX, forty-six delta, romeo nine, nine, forty-nine tango, echo eight, seven, forty-seven sierra," the old man muttered.

He looked up, however briefly, and caught Karen's eye, one of his own eyes long since obscured by cataracts. He smiled shakily, deepening the furrows of age.

Garand took Karen's arm, then loudly bid to the old man, "Ms. Lavender will be back shortly, Mr. President. She still has some processing to finish."

"It was, uh, nice meeting you, Mr. President," Karen said.

The old man held his smile on Karen. "Yes, yes, nice meeting you too, young miss. We'll watch tv?"

"Sure, Mr. President, all the tv you want," and then Garand pulled her aside and took her back into the house.

Some President, Karen thought through a smirk.

To be more correct: a *former* President. It was difficult to believe that this broken, half-blind old man sitting in a lawn chair, one Rowland Wilcox Raymond, had served two terms as the Chief Executive of the United States of America. *What a ripoff,* Karen thought.

"You see what we mean?" Garand said.

"Alzheimer's and a half," Karen said. Former President Raymond had been diagnosed several years ago—she remembered hearing it on the news. He was ninety-two now, and in otherwise perfect health.

"He just seems so...I don't know. Like someone's grandfather."

Garand chuckled dryly. "Well, in that case, granddad has a big mouth."

"A big mouth?" Karen inquired. "What do you mean?"

Garand shrugged. "He used to be the President, for God's sake, privy to the most sensitive information in the world—and now he's got Alzheimer's. Talk about a classified nightmare. Anything he might say, right off the top of his head, could jeopardize our national security."

"Oh, come on," Karen scoffed. "He can't remember anything important, can he? He's ancient."

"Ancient?" Garand shook his head. "Those numbers he was reeling off? They were permissive-action suffixes. You know. ICBM launch codes."

¤   ¤   ¤   ¤   ¤

Fuck, Karen Lavender thought. However profane, it was a pale thought, and a hopeless one. Almost ten years on Uniform Branch— night duty at the goddamn Oman Embassy on Massachusetts Avenue. The closest she'd ever gotten to the White House was seeing it on a post card. All right, so her performance ratings weren't that high, and the 2.5 at Maryland probably didn't help, but— *It's because I never slept with the right field supervisors,* she felt sure. *That's why I never got promo'd to White House duty. Sexist pigs. Their brains are in their jockeys.* The only reason she'd joined the Secret Service in the first place was to guard the President—the *real* President—a critical service, a job with prestige and honor. *And because I didn't fuck and suck every pantload in the upper office, I get ten years of night shifts for a bunch of Arabs.*

It was true, at least, that Karen did not agree to carnal activities with *every* "pantload" in the upper office, just the wrong ones. It was mostly oral sex–Karen, of course, on the performing end, and with every ejaculation into her mouth came a similar promise: Certainly she would be transferred to White House duty very soon. She could count on it. Don't worry, Karen. You're there any day now.

Yeah.

But, lo, for all those years, the only thing transferred was semen from some guy's piss-slit into her mouth. *All those years,* she thought ruefully. *Sucking the dicks that didn't matter.*

And now...this.

Well, at least she got out of Uniform Branch, and the 2000-acre ranch in Sacramento was nice. But when she'd asked for the Presidential Security Detail...this wasn't quite what she'd had in mind.

"I can fly anything God can make," the President said. "I should've put USAEUR on Defcon One. Fuck 'em. The ice-cream—*that's* the answer."

"Senile *and* crazy," she whispered to herself.

"What's that, missy?"

"Nothing, Mr. President. I was just saying that it was very *hazy* today."

"Ah, yes, you're right. It was the Texas Mafia. LBJ knew all about it. And I can tell you this. There were four shots total but two of them came from the Dal-Tex Building."

Karen wiped spittle off his chin, refilled his anti-spill cup with Kool-Aid. After two days, she'd stopped being appalled. What was the point?

"All you gotta do is stay with him until eight a.m.," Garand, the Case Agent In Charge, had instructed. "Feed him, change channels for him, like that. Since his diagnosis, his sleep schedule's changed, a typical contraidication of Alzheimer's. He's awake all night long, likes to watch tv."

Great, Karen thought. *My illustrious career forges on...with reruns of Three's Company and Gilligan's Island.*

"But *don't* let him out of your sight. He's crafty, there were a couple of times when he got out of the house at night. We don't want the President getting off the property and winding up on Route 40. Can you imagine if someone picked him up? He'd be spouting off our MIRV targets, or telling someone that Brezhnev was actually murdered with Prussic acid contact poison administered by a U.S. Army field operative."

Karen's spirit felt like a stone dropped in a well. *Plunk..*

"Cheer up," Garand said. "At least he can go to the bathroom by himself. Well...usually. Oh, and you don't mind cooking, do you?"

This couldn't be worse—or could it?

Garand stroked his chin as if he had a goatee. "That's all cake, but...there's one more thing."

"Yeah?" Karen asked.

"See, he's on all kinds of medication—you know, for his Alzheimer's—and some of these meds are new. Vascular dilators, mainly. They increase his blood supply to the brain...but they also increase his blood supply to—"

"Yeah?" she repeated.

"Well, you know. To *other* parts of the body. Sometimes he goes into fits, and we don't want that. He needs to be...taken care of."

Karen's jaw dropped at the words.

"Look, if you don't want the job, I understand," Garand augmented. "We'll send you back to the Oman embassy and get someone else." Another stroke to the invisible goatee. "But if you *do* want the job...I can guarantee you White House duty after he dies. I mean, come on. How much longer can he live?"

Garand had a point. And if she was interpreting him correctly, he was asking her to sexually service a ninety-two-year-old ex-president. *That old?* she asked herself. Vascular dilators be damned. She seriously doubted a man that age cold sport much of a hard-on. And the fits? She could hack it.

"All right," she dismally agreed. "I'll do it."

"Great!" Garand rejoiced. "I knew you weren't a quitter! Thank God we've finally got a gal with some gumption!"

Karen was surprised by the level of his approval. Had other women been offered this assignment, and turned it down once they were informed of the fine print?

"But you *do* guarantee me that I'll get White House duty when–"

"When the old fuck dies, yeah. Guaranteed one hundred percent." Garand grinned sheepishly. "But, uh, there is one more, uh, little thing, ya know?"

Karen smirked. "What's that?"

Garand shrugged. "Just three or four times a week. No big deal, right? I mean, it's not like you haven't done it before, right?"

Karen's eyes thinned. "And that would be?"

Garand unfastened his belt and lowered his trousers and boxers. "I come real fast. Promise."

Karen stared at Garand's face, then his crotch.

Then she got down on her knees. *At this point,* she considered, *what's one more dick in my mouth?*

¤ ¤ ¤ ¤ ¤

She quickly learned, though, that it wasn't *one* more dick–it was two. Karen actually didn't mind blowing Garand–he was right, he was fast–but he wasn't kidding about those vascular dilators. She hadn't been on her new duty for more than a couple of hours before former President Raymond, sitting on the couch, extracted an erection from his pants.

"Missy? I'm ready."

At first she thought it was a joke; she thought it was fake. But when he pulled back the abundant foreskin, she knew it wasn't rubber.

No fucking way! she thought. *Get the fuck out of here!*

The President's genitals were immense. Testicles the size of Szechuan dumplings depended in the wizened scrotum above which throbbed a penile shaft that looked like a peeled, foot-long plantain. With veins.

Karen hoped her stockings wouldn't run when she knelt down. A swallow, a blink, then a deep breath, and her face moved forward. She thought about the most unsexual things when the President's member docked with her mouth; she thought about Hummel figurines, the Telebubbies, and the engine grease under her very first boyfriend's fingernails.

Up and down, up and down, her well-practiced lips glissaded over the ex-President's sexual organ. He made peculiar noises from his throat as she commenced. *I'd have better luck blowing a french bread!* she thought in complaint. His crabbed hands feebled at the back of her head, pushing down, stuffing the immensity of turgid meat past her tonsils and down her throat. Up and down, up and down, seemingly forever. Those vascular dilators, indeed, did the job, but–

Would you hurry up and come! her thoughts wailed.

"Ah-ah...*oogie!*" he mumbled, his old convalescent legs trembling. Then, after an easy half-hour of fastidious sucking, the biggest cock she'd ever had in her mouth vomited plumes of semen down her throat. Karen hitched; at first she thought it might shoot down her windpipe into her lungs. Her nostrils flared for air, and when she finally pried her mouth off the fat prong, a last dribble spilled onto her tongue.

It was easier to swallow than to spit.

The executive penis deflated to something that reminded her of a slack ground-chicken sausage. With veins.

"Booglidoo, Missy," he complimented. "That was better than Nancy."

Drool dangled from Karen's lips as she kneed backward, dizzy. She supposed it was a compliment.

"All right," he said. "Now I'm ready for dinner."

¤ ¤ ¤ ¤ ¤

Garand had the audacity to give her a card file of the President's favorite dishes. "Did you enjoy your dinner, Mr. President?" Karen asked, taking up the empty plate.

"Oh, yes, I'd like dinner very much. I would like corned beef and cabbage, and potato rolls please. And the Green Giant brand lima beans. The fordhooks."

Which was what he'd just devoured in a considerable portion only moments ago. Karen sighed.

"Tv, tv! Magnum!"

Not a professional notion but an honest one: she saw herself wringing his old neck. At least then her life would be interesting, not this busy-work executive nanny blow-job administrator bullshit. At least she only had to blow Garand; she didn't have to change channels for him, or fix his meals, or wipe his ass. *My life is a wasteland,* she thought. Porridge was more interesting. A ten-pound bag of fertilizer was more interesting than this inept tragedy that was her existence.

Shortly after dinner:

"I have to poo," President Raymond declared to her.

If I kill him...at least I'll go down in history, she thought. Instead, she walked him to the bathroom, dropped his pants, and sat him down. He defecated noisily, in blurts.

"Wipe," he ordered.

Mom, Dad, see how I'm carrying on with my career?" she thought. Grimacing, she slid the pad of toilet paper up his crack.

"Ooo," he commented.

Then got hard again.

It flipped up like a police nightstick.

With veins.

"Sit on Mr. Happy," he said.

How about if I cut Mr. Happy off? she thought. She could envision the fat stream of blood draining into the toilet, mingling with his Oval Office shit. She staid the impulse, though, remembering Garand's promise...and hoisted her skirt, rubbed spit into her majora, and sat.

"Sit on Fido. Wuff-wuff!"

Fido about skewered her. She could've sworn she felt the fat glans butting against her abdominal wall. *Goddamn it, would you hurry up and come!* she thought in a painful fury. Big dicks were fine, but not on ninety-two-year-old Presidents. He defecated some more, during the action, ribbons of excrement falling loudly into the toilet water as she rode him.

Then—

"Oogily!" he exclaimed. "Foogily moogily!"

How can an old mummy like this come so much! she though in rebellion. Her vaginal vault flooded. When she finally pulled off, there came a sound like a cork popping, then a snake of hot semen ran down the inside of her leg.

"Gar-hoogily. Fido *liked* that."

Yeah, I'll bet he did... "Go watch tv, you fuckhead!" she yelled, dragging his pants up, shoving him out the door. "I've got to clean up!"

"Magnum!" he celebrated. "Magnum's on FX channel!"

This guy comes in quarts, she thought, wading up more toilet paper and running it up her leg. It took several wads. And when she plopped them all into the toilet and flushed, the toilet backed up.

¤   ¤   ¤   ¤   ¤

Weeks went by, then months. Every Monday, Wednesday, and Friday, like federal clockwork, she sucked Garand's small penis and swallowed his ejaculant. But so many more times than that she was forced to service the ex-president's trout-belly-white tubesteak. Twice a day, sometimes three.

Thank God for those vascular dilators.

One night she'd done the dishes after dinner, and when she was returning from the kitchen, she found the President finnicking with the lock on the french doors.

Pain in the ass. "Just where do you think you're going, Mr. President?"

Secret Service

"I'm meeting North and that ghoul Casey at the Old Executive Office Building. I've got to tell them to shred everything." He blew spit bubbles as she guided him back to his chair. "Casey wants one of his ops to hit Woodward. George thinks we should, and frankly, you'd need a crow bar to get into Hayworth's pants. God knows I tried."

Her mind blankened back in her seat. These slips of senility weren't even funny anymore; by now she'd heard it all: senseless prattle laced with startling utterances. "No, no, it was *Bobby* who did it, I heard Hoover's tapes. She was pregnant. Peter Lawford watched the door." "The *Thresher* was sunk by a Soviet nuclear torpedo." "It was Teddy and Dodd—Remember? The waitress at La Brasserie?—we told them we'd pay the girl off if they abstained on the Companion Bill to H.R. 214." All this and disturbingly more. Undisclosed missile sites, top secret radio frequencies, a White House nuclear self-destruct device, Mach 7 aircraft, secret listening posts, electro-magnetic-pulse beams aimed at a row of townhouses in Reston, Virginia, C.I.A. heroin routes into Burma, and Vince Foster was really executed in Crystal City. On and on.

She didn't even care anymore. The system seemed to work for everyone else, leaving her with the shaft. What, a pissant COLA raise every year and a 401K? That's what life was all about? *I'm a Secret Service Agent in good standing and they make me be a baby-sitter! A have to wear an apron. I do dishes and fuck and suck a brain-rotten president!*

Sometimes she could just lump it all. Forget about duty and service. Do something for herself for a change. At 35, she wasn't getting any younger. Her once-plump breasts were starting to sag. Her vagina looked like ground pork.

Fuck, she thought.

They were watching tv. "Ooo-yeah," some ludicrous pro wrestler yelled. "Step into a Slim Jim!"

"What's a Slim Jim?" the President asked.

"I don't know," she dismissed, waving a hand. "Beef jerky or something."

"Well jerk this beef, bitch."

Karen turned at the slight. The President had already dug his penis from his pants. The gargantuan thing throbbed upward, tapping him on the belly.

Why don't you just die? she thought, but that thought hardly conformed to reality. The reality, instead, involved something else.

She grabbed the warm erection as if grabbing a cucumber. She began to jerk it. She jerked hard. *Christ, am I pumping up a fucking tire!* Eventually, a pearl of pre-ejaculatory fluid formed at the tip of the glans. "Fido's ready for you to sit on him," he informed.

That's just fucking great, Mr. President, she thought. *I couldn't be more elated to know that Fido's ready...*

She sat on Fido nonetheless; the President blew mindless spit bubbles as she fucked his lap. She rode him hard, hoping to get it over with quick, but then he shivered.

"Drew-hoogily! Suck Fido now! Suck him!"

Karen supposed if she smothered him with a pillow, she might get away with it. She supposed that if she just jammed his mouth closed and pinched his nostrils shut, he would die and no pathologist would bother to make checks.

But Karen didn't quite have the guts for that.

She lifted her ass off his penis–another cork unpopping–then resolved to finish the task. She knelt between his ancient, knobby legs, and sucked. The flavor of herself on his dick tasted salty, bitter, sort of like bad fish, and as she sucked more vigorously, her nose detected the clear evidence that the 3-11 shift hadn't bothered to wash the President today.

Kill me, God, she begged. *Just kill me now.*

The President's orgasm shot repeatedly into the back of her throat in thin, hot threads. It reminded her of egg drop soup: thin as water, salty, with immoderate mucoid lumps.

"Glew-googily," he exclaimed. "There's one for the Gipper."

Karen's teeth clacked together. It was just easier to swallow.

¤ ¤ ¤ ¤ ¤

The clock ticked on like her life: without event. This was it. Change channels. wipe his ass, cook his meals, and fuck him and suck him whenever the electorate crane rose. On the limited occasions, when she'd simply refused the latter, Garand's warning rang true. President Raymond had launched into a fit of maniacal inanity, spouting CIA crypts, the names of directors he hated, and choice samples such as "Fuck Congress, we'll take up the slack by selling TOW missiles to Iran," "So what about Mena Airport! Bill's in on it, and so was George!" and "I fucked the shit out of Jayne! That blond bitch was *unconscious* when I was done with her!" It was an Alzheimer's circus tirade.

Easier just to suck and fuck him.

But what of her *life?*

There must be more to life than this, she considered.

When she looked, the President was picking his nose with one hand and scratching his crotch with the other.

Yeah, to hell with this, she gave serious consideration. *Start over again. Do something for me.*

"Alexander Haig was Deep Throat," he babbled. "Rogers assured me we could hide all our ADMs and W-79s from SALT II and the Russians would never know."

"What's that, Mr. President?"

More spit bubbles. "I was just saying, I had sex with Faye Ray once. They invented AIDS at Fort Dietrick in 1976, said it would wipe out the ghettos in five years."

Jesus.

Occasionally she nodded off and caught snatches of plush dreams. Lying on a beach in Cancun. Traveling Europe. Making love and having babies.

"You know the protocol. I need the SAC commander to authenticate confirmation of hostile intent. I don't *care* if our air-space hasn't been violated yet. What, I'm supposed to wait? Give me the discriminators! I'm the President!"

Her eyes fluttered open. She moaned. Now he was fervently pressing buttons on the remote as Tom Selleck switched to Jay Leno, then Jerry Springer, then Beavis. "Goddamn Andropov! I'll bury him! Watch me! See if he doesn't die of a heart attack!"

Yes. A real life instead of this farce. A nice house, a two-car garage. A white picket fence and a dog in the yard. Hubby mowing the grass on lazy Saturdays while she baked cookies... She was nodding again, words rupturing the sweet dreams.

"—million dollar offer posted last year, but so far, no takers."

A million dollars would be nice too, to make the dream just perfect.

"—verifiable evidence. How do you *prove* something like that?"

A handsome husband who never cheated on her... Attractive well-mannered children who earned good grades and didn't get into trouble...

Yes, it would be so nice...

The dream morphed into the face of a stuffy show host and a gaudy background made to look like a tv news room. The dream was gone. She was awake again...

"From Ubatuba, Brazil to Roswell, New Mexico, the mystery may never end, even with countless thousands of eyewitness reports. What's really happening out there? And just *what* is the government trying to hide from the public?"

Great. Now it was this UFO claptrap. One hokey flop after the next. At least Magnum was good-looking, killer butt, gorgeous pecs. And those eyes!

But when she turned her head to check her charge...

"Oh my God, no!!"

The President was gone.

I can't believe it! I fell asleep! How could I be so stupid!

She dashed to the kitchen, then the den, then the south hall. Nothing, and they were all locked accesses. If he'd wandered down to the foyer, the recept team would've seen him right away. Just as she would hit the elopement alarm—

snick-snick-snick

An odd sound to her left. Toward the bedroom. *Maybe the President's finally decided to take a shit on his own.* From the tv, more words droned on: "Fantasy-Prone Syndrome, systematized hallucinosis, shared delusional ideas of reference, and, of course, the primal human instinct to *believe* that we are not alone in the universe. The same can be said of every religion to ever exist. It's a functional mythology..."

Karen winced as a heel snapped off her shoe when she turned toward the bedroom, then a sudden pinching cramp reminded her that her period was starting and it felt like a gusher. This was not her day. But then she heard the sound again, another *snick-snick-snick*. followed by an even stranger wet, crackly peeling noise.

She limped into the bedroom, stopped, and frowned. "What are you *doing!*"

"The tv. Didn't you hear?" He was on his knees, his tongue licking the corner of his mouth as he dug at the floor with a pocket knife. He was peeling a tile off the floor!

"Mr. President, would you *please* give me a fucking break?"

He didn't hear her, removing the rest of the split tile. "Now I remember! LeMay gave it to me when he was Chief of Air Force Operations. I thought I better hide it."

Karen peered over. There was a deep hole in the floor, beneath the tile, and from the hole the President had removed a white one-foot-square metal box.

"Give me that," she said, exasperated. She wrenched it from his crabbed hands. "Oh, yes," came more blabber, "we knew the Walker spies were selling our sub frequencies. Army INSCOM people found the mail drop. It was in Odenton, Maryland."

You dick. "Come on." She guided him back to the tv room, sat his ass down. "It was a phone pole they'd mark with white tape," he continued with his tale. "Our men would take the Walker material and switch it with disinformation and fake codes."

"Shut up," she said. She sat with the box in her lap. Red letters warned: RESTRICTED, DO NOT REMOVE UNDER PENALTIES IN ACCORDANCE WITH THE INTERNAL SECURITY ACT OF 1950, USC 790. Her eyes narrowed in curiosity when she opened the box and withdrew an old, yellowed document:

Secret Service

T-O-P S-E-C-R-E-T

HEADQUARTERS, ARMY AIR FORCES
WASHINGTON

06 JULY 47

SUBJECT: Issuance of Classified Orders

TO: Commanding General
Air Material Command
Wright Field, Ohio

1. Notification of confidential orders to be received by the following USAAC and cleared civilian personnel:

Lt. General Ryan Harding, O-12366, AC
Major General Geoff Cooper, O-14963, AC
F.B.I. Director J. Edgar Hoover
F.B.I. SAC Paul Mausbach

2. All above personnel will report to Air Material Command, Foreign Technology Division, in compliance with Emergency Orders via AR-200-1.

3. These orders will be assumed by all personnel as expeditiously as possible.

RE: Confidential material to be transported to AMC, FTD, via USAAC 1st Air Transport Unit, from 509th Bomb Group, Roswell Field, New Mexico.

BY COMMAND OF THE PRESIDENT OF THE UNITED STATES

FM:
DAVID BARNETT
Lt. Colonel, Air Corps
Executive Military Dispatch
Office of AC/FS-1
THE WHITE HOUSE

Hmm, she thought. The tv rambled on: "...the incontestable fact remains, with all the countless thousands of abduction and eyewitness reports, not one single shred of evidence exists to verify the existence of extraterrestrial visitations to our planet. If these things were really happening, someone, somewhere would've produced genuine proof by now."

She picked up another document.

TOP SECRET
SPECIAL ACCESS REQUIRED/EYES ONLY
TEKNA/BYMAN/UMBRA/SI

DEPARTMENT OF THE AIR FORCE
WASHINGTON DC 20330-100

OFFICE OF THE SECRETARY

25 May 1974
SAF/AAIQ
1610 Air Force Pentagon

TO: THE COMMANDER AND CHIEF

SUBJECT: CLASSIFIED REQUEST PER MEMORANDUM (GAO Code 701034); AFR 12-50 (CLASSIFIED) Volume II, Disposition of Air Force Records and Material

(a) Identify pertinent directive concerning crashes of air vehicles not of terrestrial origin, investigations, wreckage/debris/dead bodies - retention, recovery, and evaluation.

:Dear Mr. President:
Per your request relative to the above memorandum, i.e., the incident concerning the Low Frequency Radar Array (LFRA) detection on 18 April 1974 and disposition thereof. The most notable debris and, of particular sensitivity, all anatomical and post-autopsied remains, have been properly redeposited amongst selected sites within protected districts of the Army, Air Force, Navy, and Federal Reservations, via recent amendments to AFR-200-1, and so ordered by the MJ-12 Directorate.

Secret Service

Attachment (TO): -MILNET
-U.S. Air Force Joint Recovery Command
-NSA (Interagency Liaison Office)

Signed,
Timothy M. McGinnis, Major General O-7
Commander, Air Force Aerial Intelligence Group
Fort Belvior, Virginia, MJ-12/Detachment 4

Karen's eyes felt pried open by hooks. *This can't possibly be for...for...for...*
Real.
"And so ends another edition of *Extraterrestrial Border Line*. Until next time...keep watching the sky."
Next was not a document but a strange wedge of heather-gray material. Thin as newsprint yet sturdy as sheet metal. It wouldn't even bend when she pressed against its corners, nor could she scratch it with the President's boy scout knife. When she held the flame of her cigarette lighter to it, it didn't warp, melt or even blacken, and it didn't conduct any heat. A yellowed sticker, barely readable, stated: PROPERTY OF U.S. ARMY AIR CORP, AIR MATERIAL COMMAND, C/O WATSON LABORATORIES, RED BANK, NEW JERSEY. Another sticker read: EVIDENCE: CORONA, NEW, MEXICO, 198NE, 224S, 5 JULY 47.
Holy...shit...
A song, now, in the background: "With pizza on a bagel, you can have pizza every time!" She snatched the remote. "Turn that shit off, you asshole!" she said to the President.
"Mr. Gorbachev?" he replied. *"Bring down this wall!"* He blew some spittle bubbles as if in contemplation. "Oh, my. I-I think I've got poop in my pants."
Karen may have been able to make a similar claim when she looked back in the box.

¤ ¤ ¤ ¤ ¤

"Point Six, this is Team Leader!" Garand shouted into his walkie-talkie. "Report!"
"Team Leader, this is Point Six. We're clear."
"Team Leader, this is Point Four. Clear."
"Team Leader, this is Point Five. Clear. He ain't in the friggin' house."
Garand's mind raged as he fumbled to jack back the slide of his P-226 9 mm pistol. The elopement alarm blared like an air raid siren.

"Point One, you better get me a fly line to Edwards on the priority band. We're gonna need a tac team out here, and a couple of choppers."

"Roger, Team Leader."

There it all went, like smoke right before his eyes. *My whole life! Twenty years in executive protection and I'm gonna go down in history as the guy who lost President Raymond. With my luck, the old fucker probably got picked up hitchhiking out on Route 40 and he's halfway to L.A. by now. He'll be walking into the Hard Rock Cafe telling everyone about the Aurora spy plane, and how we broke Syria's star-net cipher codes and never bothered to tell the Israelis!*

Another thought just then, a strangely reassuring one.

Maybe I oughta just put this roscoe to my head right now and drop the hammer…

But before any such consideration could become more transitive, his radio barked. "Team Leader, this is Rover Point. We've got him. He looks okay."

Thank you, God. Thank you thank you thank you…

"Oh, man! You're not gonna believe this! He shit his pants! You should see this, Cap! President Raymond's standing here shaking shit out of his pant leg!"

"Maintain proper radio acumen, goddamn it," Garand said.

"He's got a hard-on too! I shit you not! Stickin' right out his fly!"

"Put a lid on it!" Garand demanded, but he had to admit the image was a doozie: the former two-term president sporting a boner while simultaneously shaking excrement from his slacks. "What's your loke?"

"Past the west lawn. Talk about close. He was hitchhiking along Route 40."

Thank you, God, thank you! "Bring him in. Is Lavender with you?"

"No sir," the radio replied.

What? That ditzy head queen—where could she be? "Well look around," Garand ordered. "She's got to be out there somewhere.".

"No sir," the radio repeated. "No sign of her anywhere."

¤   ¤   ¤   ¤   ¤

"My name is Karen Lavender of the United States Secret Service," the woman said. Billiings glared up. *Another kook but…not a bad looker.* Nice figure under the businessy dress, nice hair, nice legs. *Wouldn't mind pumping one in her,* he mused. *Slick up her slot.* "Look lady, I'm in makeup right now, we're taping in five minutes and I'm on a tight shooting schedule. You wanna be on the show, fine. Go talk to the line producer."

Secret Service

The woman looked flushed, dizzy, out of breath by some weird kind of excitement she was trying hard to suppress. Her eyes shone hard, steely. Very serious. "I don't want to talk to the line producer, I'm talking to you."

Huffy bitch, ain't she? "Yeah?" Billings challenged. *Maybe she needs to have her ass plumbed. Bet that's what she really wants. The good ole spunk enema...*

"Yeah. I'm here to collect the million dollars you're offering for incontrovertible proof of the existence of extraterrestrial life."

Then, onto Billings' makeup table, she set down a big white metal box about the size of a portable television. *Looks like one of those military courier cases, and very official looking markings.* Then he checked out the documents, and the best piece of "debris" he'd yet seen. *Fuck, this is damn good work.* But still, in this day and age? Forgery had been honed to a state of the art.

"Look, lady, there's hackers out there who can make documents with their PageMaker that look better than this. And this piece of crash debris? *You* may think it's part of a UFO, but I can tell you, it ain't nothing but treated titanium. Believe me, I've seen it all before a million times. Where'd you get this stuff anyway?"

"I stole it from the private residence of former-President Rowland Raymond."

Billings chuckled. *She's good.* "Uh-huh, and I just rode the Merry Go Round with Hillary and Bill. Bill asked me for a hand job."

"There's one more thing in the box," she said. "Take it out. Look at it."

Yeah, she's a huffy bitch, all right. Sort of reminded him of his wife. Only difference was he had no desire to see his *wife's* tits. He'd seen those busted bags too many times. But *this* bitch?

He'd wring milk out of 'em.

Billings peered in the box. She was correct. An acrid redolence, like formaldehyde maybe, seemed to eddy from the open lid.

When he reached in, it was a heavy-duty clear plastic bag that he removed. A sizeable parcel, with some heft to it.

Billings' guts sunk. All thoughts of sex with this woman sunk just as quickly.

Something slack and fat drooped at the bottom of the bag. Kind of a mottled gray color, like slug skin–about a foot long. Billings didn't have to be told that the thing in the bag was a severed alien penis.

Secret Service Afterword

I'm not saying I believe in UFOs; but I must admit a fascination regarding the avalanche of eyewitness testimony involved with the so-called Roswell Crash. Keep in mind, in 1947, Roswell Field was essentially the only atomic weapons depot in the world. Consequently, the only people stationed at that base, at that time, were people who had been investigated as thoroughly as any person could BE investigated, given the necessary security clearance required for such a post. In other words, Roswell Field, in 1947, was a military base full of people who would be less inclined to lie than any other per-capita perimeter in the world. Were ALL of these people lying?

Doesn't matter; it's just something that's always interested me. And when I was invited to submit a story to Daw's THE UFO FILES, I wrote this. The next day, though, I reread the piece and realized that it was too sexually explicit to make the cut. I wanted to be in this anth in a big way. So I trimmed down the story rather significantly, and it sold.

The uncut version is the version you've just read.

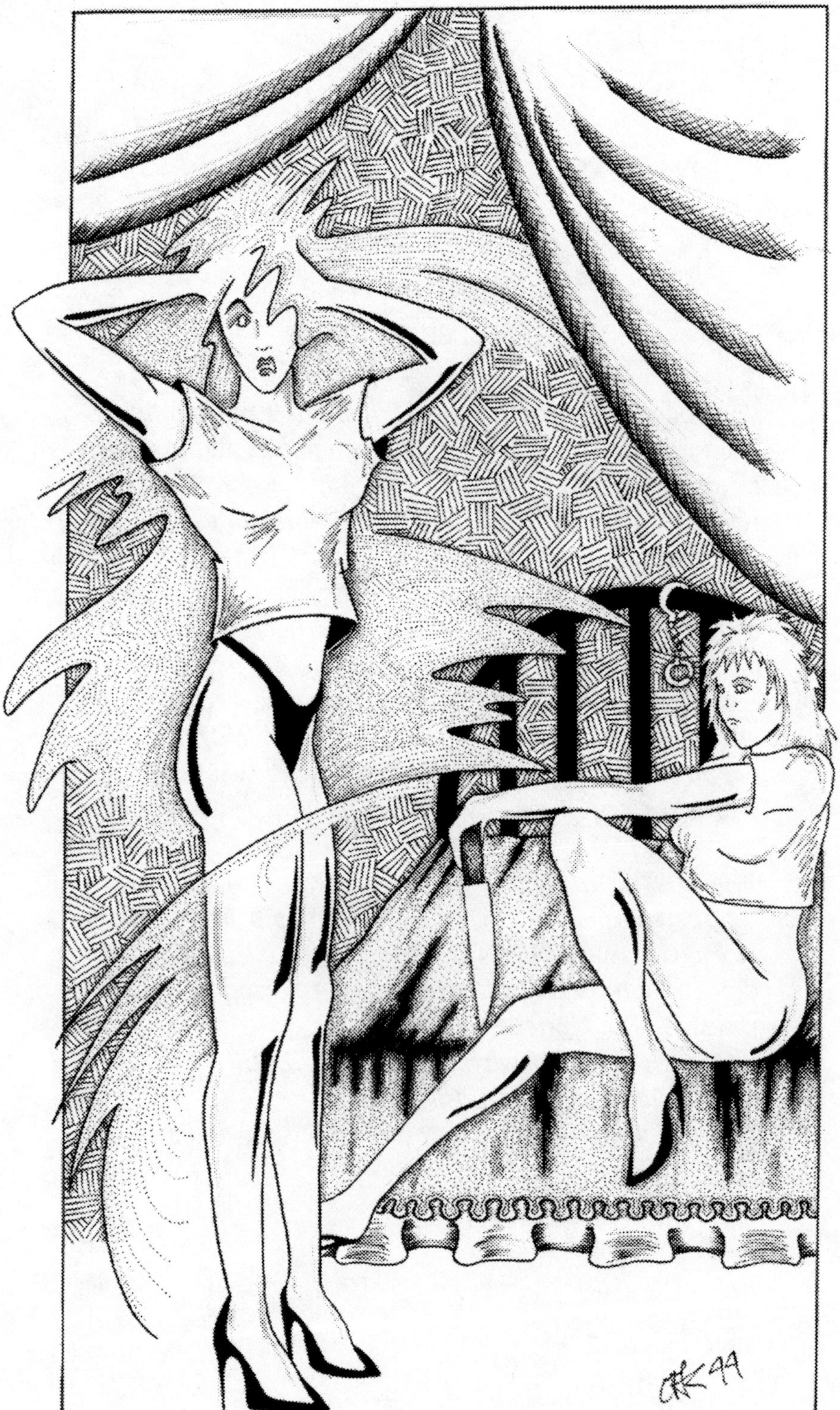

THE WRONG GUY

"WE SURE MADE a mess of him," Wendlyn remarked.

Rena cut a wicked grin. "Yeah. Neat, huh?"

Neither woman, by the way, wore panties. As they each leaned over the big opened trunk of the clay-red 76 Malibu, this fact would be obvious to any onlooker. Not that there would be any onlookers in proximity to the old Governor's Bridge at close to 4:30 in the morning. Nevertheless, the further over these two women leaned, the more of their backsides, i.e. rumps, i.e. glutius maximi, i.e. asses peeked out from beneath their shortish skirts. Rena wore tight blue leather. Wendlyn wore a more mature Ralph Lauren navy chino wrap.

"This one was fun," Rena said.

"Yeah," Wendlyn agreed. "A real scream, pun intended."

Rena giggled, "One less pretty-boy motherfucker to affront the society of women."

Moonlight dappled their well-lined backs and legs, wavering through high trees. An owl hooted. Below them, the gentle stream burbled over stones.

They both wore latex gloves as they tended to the corpse; just because they were impulsive didn't mean they were stupid. They'd read all about the state police carbon-dioxide lasers and special resin treatments that could lift fingerprints off human skin. No way these two gals were going to get caught. Wendlyn couldn't imagine anything more dreadful: doing life in the state slam, the dike wing. She was not adverse to the pleasures of a woman, but eating some 300-lb. cellblock mama's crusty cooze every night did not strike her as a pleasure. No, indeed.

"Shit!" Rena suddenly fretted. "Where's his—"

Wendlyn paused with the pliers, glaring. "God, you're so careless sometimes, Rena! You better find it! Did you leave it at the house?"

"Uh—" Rena blinked. "I don't think so."

"What about your purse? Did you put it in your purse?"

"Uuuuuuuuuuuh..."

"Rena, you should stand in front of a fan to change the air in your head! Honestly!"

"Well I'm sorry!" Rena whined, close to lacrimating. "I don't remember *what* I did with it!"

Wendlyn shook her head. *Kids,* she dismissed. *So unaware.* Rena was only 23, and quite flighty sometimes. Wendlyn, six years older, viewed her in a sense as a sister, that is at least when they weren't licking up each other's vaginal grooves. Sisters didn't generally partake in such practices. This was more an esoteric thing, a psychical/social bond, perhaps. They were sisters of the ether.

What had this one's name been? *Will?* Wendlyn thought. She'd never been good with names. *Walt.* There. That was it. They'd picked Walt up, without much effort, at Kaggies, one of the ruckus danceclubs downtown. Walt was one of those guys too good-looking for his own good. Rena and Wendlyn weren't too shabby themselves, mind you; they had the tackle to drag them in just as pretty as you please. Rena stood slim, trim, and alabaster-skinned, with short-cut shiny black hair. Wendlyn appeared more robust, a big, sturdy, curvaceous frame of plush flesh, with silken-straight white-blond hair, gem-blue eyes, and crisp tan lines. They rarely had trouble making a mark, and were always meticulously careful not to be seen leaving with a victim. Which might be worth pointing out now that not only were Wendlyn and Rena diverse, voracious, attractive, and highly sexualized women, they were also what psychiatrists would clinically label as systematized stage sociopaths with acute erotomanic impulses. Sex killers would be a less articulate label. Murderesses. Pure ass crazy psycho bitches...

Their philosophy was societal and rather militant in its feministic design. Never mind that they were fucked up in the head: abused, malnourished, and locked in closets as children, maladapted via unbridled drug and alcohol use and hence damaged of certain critical brain receptors, and, in general, rife with a plethora of environmentally- causated personality disorders and biogenic amine imbalances. They saw themselves instead as philosophers of the new dark age of sexual terror, chameleon siren songs of the nihilistic '90's. They did not perceive men, for instance, as individuals but as a cyclic and conspiratorial consortium bent on the total subjugation, exploitation, and sexual abuse of womanhood. They were pioneers of a sort, social guerrillas. Their manifesto was thus: since the beginning of civilization, man had freely and unconscionably exploited women. It was high time, therefore, that someone started exploiting them back.

Which led them, in their zeal, to some particularly brow-raising extremities. Walt, for example. Guilty by association. No doubt he'd exploited dozens, in not hundreds, of women with his looks and his phony charm. They'd taken him back to the house, for a "nightcap." Rena had his penis out before they even made it to the bedroom, her deft little hand exploring away on the burgeoning meat. That's all men were to them. Meat. They shared the remote little rancher Wendlyn's father had left her after his unfortunate "suicide" back in 88. He'd passed out drunk at his desk one night, after which Wendlyn had helped him along into the netherworld via a vintage Webley .455 revolver. Talk about a mess! And *loud?* Dad's brains looked like bloody chicken salad slopped across the fine lime and avocado print wallpaper. Anyway...

"Kinky babes, huh?" Walt had commented when Rena produced the four sets of handcuffs from the box under the bed. "You game? They're just for atmosphere," she'd assured him. "Trick cuffs, see?" She put one on and demonstrated that a simple tug would release the locking ratchet. These cuffs in truth, however, were not trick cuffs at all but Peerless Model 26 police-issue detention cuffs, the Real McCoy, and what she *hadn't* shown the snide, cocky-smiling, and now fully erect Walt was the tiny shim she kept pressed against the ratchet during her demonstration. In other words, unbeknownst to Walt, once they got him stripped down and cuffed to the big brass bed, he was in there for the long haul.

Rena and Wendlyn stripped each other then, while Walt watched ga-ga-eyed from his low comfy vantage point. He looked quite silly now, handcuffed to a bed with his penis sticking up like a pulsing, tumescent root. "Yeah, this is hell, ain't it?" Walt joked next when his two suitors commenced with the tongue bath. "Yeah, some tough life, I'll tell ya." *Shut up, Walt,* Wendlyn felt like saying, alternately licking his testicles. Rena gave Walt's mouth something to do besides jabber, inserting a nipple into it and instructing, "Suck, Walt. Just keep quiet and suck." Walt sucked, with no reservations. Rena's breasts, i.e. hooters, i.e. rib melons, i.e. tits, were smallish yet quite interesting: pointed, with bounce, and ornamented by big distended brownish cones, while Wendlyn proved more conventional in regards to the mystic thing known as the human mammarian carriage—a formidable rack of firm buoyant 38D's with large pink areolae and nipple ends akin to thimbles. An equal distinction existed, respective of the manner in which they maintained the outer geographies of their sexual real estate. Rena had spent serious money electrolocizing the entirety of her pubis, while Wendlyn preferred a more unruly state of affairs, displaying a big, dense, extruding light-blond bush.

And it was into this same bush that, next, the shaft of Walt's sexual architecture eagerly disappeared. Wendlyn very articulately responded "Oooooooo…," to this gesture, as Rena masturbated to the frictive and delicious sensation of having her coney nipples sucked.

Wendlyn rode him awhile, then queried, "Ready, Rena?"

Out popped the nipple from Walt's lips. "Yeah," she said.

"Ready for what?" Walt breathily inquired as Wendlyn's gorgeous broad bottom continued to rise and plunge. It was her own curiosity that founded this latest escapade. During a short stint as a nursing assistant, she'd read in the *American Journal of Psychiatry* an article about sexual response during that ever rare occasion of Female-to-Male Rape. This article claimed that, when threatened by death or grievous injury, the human body would respond to any demand that might increase the likelihood of survival. In other words, for instance, if a man with a gun to his head was told to fuck, by golly, those libidinal hormones would make damn sure he was able to, maintaining an erection in spite of the undeniably non-arousing circumstances.

Only it was not a gun that Rena produced from the macabre toy box under the bed.

It was a pair of tin snips.

"Holy fucking shit!" Walt yelled, as would most any man in this same predicament.

"Quiet, Walt. And listen." Wendlyn eased all the way down on Walt's cock, adroitly flexing her vaginal muscles as she explained the details of this latest sociopathic supposition. "It's this simple. I'm going to fuck you, and if you go soft on me, Rena here will cut off your cock with those tin snips. Is that perfectly clear?"

About the only thing *perfectly* clear to Walt just then was that he was in some shit of monumental depth. He responded quite stupidly, as men often do, by avoiding the question. He jerked his wrists against the cuffs and with great befuddlement exclaimed: "These aren't trick cuffs!"

"No, Walt, they're not," Rena replied, displaying the hard-steel heavy-gauge snips. "And it doesn't look to me like there's a whole hell of a lot you can do about that."

snip-snip, whispered the tin snips in the air.

Wendlyn, with lewd grin and narrowed eyes, soon found that the *American Journal of Psychiatry* was quite accurate in their claim. Walt's cock, despite this freight of human terror, did not surrender one iota of its spongal turgidity. If anything, it grew even more stiff within the damp, excited confines of Wendlyn's reproductive channel, i.e. vaginal pass, i.e. birth canal, i.e. pussy. Rena, meanwhile, opened and closed the tin snips before Walt's bulging eyeballs, explicating, "We're killers, Walt"–*snip-snip-snip*–"we're psycho-sexual *killers*"–*snip-snip-snip*—"and we've murdered over a dozen men in the last year." *snip-snip-snip*. "I'll bet that makes your cock just want to go limp as an overcooked noodle, hmmm?"

Walt's cock did no such thing, remaining stiff as a polished night-stick. Wendlyn leaned forward in her greedy straddle, accelerating the pace of the congress until her flexing, well-lubricated loins gave way in luscious throbbing thrumming orgasm...

"There," Rena consoled, smiling down between her unique, elongated breasts. She patted his tummy.

Wendlyn climbed off. "You did it, Walt. You're a standup guy."

"Yuh-yuh-you're gonna let me go now, right?" Walt asked.

"Nuh-nuh-no, Walt," Rena answered. "We're going to cut your cock off."

Walt was quite understandably outraged by this bit of information, and he began to snap his ankles and wrists madly, and quite uselessly, against their stainless steel fetters, blubbering: "Buh-buh-but you said if I didn't guh-guh-go soft, yuh-yuh-you wouldn't—"

"Don't be a doe-doe, Walt," Rena suggested, delighted by his state of prostrate and inescapable horror. "Don't be *stupid*."

Wendlyn's pretty face grew alight in the knowing grin. "We just got done telling you that we're killers, and if we're killers, it only stands to reason that we're probably liars, too."

The tin snips slowly opened, like jaws.

Walt began to scream, as Rena began to snip.

¤ ¤ ¤ ¤ ¤

Which left them now in their current quandary, at precisely 4:26 in the morning, parked on the old Governor's Bridge. Rena desperately rummaged through the Malibu's cargo-hold-sized trunk. Where was it? Where was Walt's dick?

Rena started crying.

"Oh, now," Wendlyn tried to soothe her, rubbing her back. "Don't worry about it. It's not like he can be identified by his *cock*."

This was true, unless of course the police had some secret new system of genital identification. Wendlyn smiled to herself. Perhaps one day she'd open the fridge and see a picture of Walt's *dick* printed on a milk carton. There were, however, some other things that Walt definitely *could be* identified by, thirty-two of which Wendlyn now went to considerable effort to take care of. Before the nursing job, she'd been a dental technician, but that didn't make the task of extracting Walt's teeth any less laborious. The pliers were difficult to manipulate in such limited oral space. Eventually, though, she managed to get them all out of Walt's dead maw, whereupon she placed them all into a small cloth sack.

Rena was still crying, rummaging. She was checking the tool box, for God's sake, and the plastic cooler they used when they went to the beach. "Oh, Wendy, I'm sorry! Where could it be? Did I leave it on the dresser with the keys? The kitchen counter?"

"Rena, I told you. Forget about his cock. Here. Help me get him out."

They travailed then to lifting out the plastic dropcloth in which the deader-than-dogshit Walt had been carefully becloaked. Rena hammered the little bag of teeth against the asphalt with a four-pound sledge, until all were sufficiently pulverized. Wendlyn, meanwhile, removed the glass flask (one of many perks of working in a hospital) and emptied its teeming contents onto Walt's remaining identifiable features. The concentrated nitric acid made short work of the hands and feet, fizzing away any and all ridge prints, loops, whorls, and bifurcations. Walt's face, too, bubbled away with equal steaming vigor.

The unappreciated separation of his genitals from his groin, by the way, had not of itself spelled Walt's demise. He'd screamed loud and hard as a horn on a semi-rig, thrashing amid his Peerless-handcuff trap, but had surprisingly not died. Nor had Wendlyn's delvings with the Clay Adams brand bivalving scalpel done the trick. It got quite ugly, Walt screaming like that, and thrashing away with no penis. Blood gushed like Great Falls. Eventually Rena had stuck a knitting needle up his nose, driving it back with her palm deep into the meat of Walt's parietal lobe. She'd jiggled it around a few times, until he checked out.

"Ashame about his face," Rena lamented now, looking down in the moonlight. "He could've been on the cover of *GQ*."

"Not anymore. *Fangoria,* maybe. Say goodnight, Walt."

They hefted up either end of the dropcloth and rolled it over the rusty metal bridge rail. *Ka-SPLASH!* The moonlight rippled spectacularly.

Then they were driving away, off into the warm, star-chipped night. "Wendy, look!" Rena celebrated, bending over in the passenger seat. "I found Walt's dick!"

So she had; somehow, Walt's severed member had found its way to the footwell. "Now I remember. I brought it along to diddle with while we were driving out." Rena picked it up and, ever the comedian, slid back her blue-leather skirt and held Walt's now seriously shriveled cock to her clitoris, spreading her trim legs. "Look, Wendy! I've got a penis! I'm a man!"

Wendlyn rolled her eyes behind the wheel. "You're so silly sometimes. Honestly." She took the wizened thing and flipped it out the window, where eventually it would be eaten by possums.

¤   ¤   ¤   ¤   ¤

Wendlyn expertly plunged the dual Doc Johnson vibrators in and out of Rena's off-pink vulva and rectum, licking the swollen clitoris. Rena squirmed, sighing through her grin, as Claudius, the largest of her three pet hognose snakes, slithered about her belly and pointed breasts. Rena was possessed of some rather left-field eccentricities, several of which Wendlyn was hard-pressed to tolerate: Heineken douches, Bull Frog Stuffing, electric ben-wa balls up her ass whilst in public. Plus snakes. They'd met at North County General, where Rena was a floor receptionist. Wendlyn, a Class I nurses' aide, caught Rena masturbating in the janitorial closet one night, with a polypropylene Bacti-Capall culture tube and hemostats clipped to her nipples. "Ooops," Rena had said. Instead of filling out an employee negligence report, Wendlyn had sealed their friendship by immediately planting her big blond pubis in Rena's face. Their careers, though, had ended rather expeditiously. Rena had been fired for stealing an array of controlled pharmaceuticals from the nurses' station, while Wendlyn, shortly thereafter, had received her walking papers for "gross sexual misconduct upon the hospital premise." A staff doctor had pulled back a privacy curtain in an end ICU cove, to discover the ever-curious Wendlyn fastidiously fellating a male critical coma patient. "I wanted to see if a brain-dead person could come," she'd explained. "You're fired," the doctor had replied.

Oh, well. Nevertheless, their friendship remained, and to make a long exposition short, they soon found a vivid compatibility in their ravenous sexualities as well as their sociopathies. In no time at all, they were murdering men at about a rate of one a month, through all manner of demented imagination: gastric lavage with Clorox, non-anesthetic live dissection, brain surgery with power tools, and acts of genital mayhem that copuld only be described as "bigtime." Once they'd catheterized a bartender and filled his bladder with 5W 30-grade motor oil, then ice-picked his lower abdomen to watch the oil ooze out. Another time Wendlyn was blowing some dolt they'd picked up at the races; Rena had clipped off his testicles at the precise moment of his climax. Once they'd even dissected a penis, on a living "patient," removing all the skin and the entire scrotum, after which Rena had clipped off the raw shaft a quarter inch at a time. This guy had screamed so loud they'd had to put cotton in their ears! One pickup had gotten rude with them, actually hailing such invectives as: "Bitches! Lesbos! Psychopaths!" Wendlyn had opened his anus with a pair of rectal retractors stolen from the hospital, while Rena, with more than a smidgen of difficulty, had inserted Tiberius, one of her pet hognose snakes, into the offender's bowel. Tiberius had churned away for quite some time in there, before finally giving up the ghost, while their unmannerly companion had screamed shock-eyed and blue in the face. "Poor Tiberius," Rena regretted. She'd finished the man off by carefully drilling a shallow hole in his skull with a l/4-inch carbon bit, then slowly inserting long carpet needles and autopsy pins into the hole. Genital electrocution, ground-glass and/or boiling bacon grease enemas, ice picks in the ears and/or eyes, Coca-Cola blood transfusions, total body flensing, and, of course, what Rena referred to as "dick-scarfing." Nothing would get a fella screaming faster and louder than having his pride and joy and family jewels nimbly chewed off by a pair of crazier-than-shithouse-rats militant feminists. No, sir. You name it, Wendlyn and Rena did it, much to the disconsolation of many a man, and all in the name of their righteous ideology, to vindicate roughly seventy centuries of subjugation.

Plus, it was fun, at least from the standpoint of a clinical sociopath.

One thing they never considered, though, was the possibility that sooner or later they might pick the wrong guy…

¤   ¤   ¤   ¤   ¤

Larry seemed a little fat and doty; pickings were slim some nights. He provided at least the necessary prerequisites: your typical gaping, gawping, lustful cockhound/ nutchase/Feel-'Um- Fuck 'Um-And-Forget-'Um Man. At the bar, Larry's eyes had been all over them, and eventually so had his hands. He'd plied them with drinks and smothered them with overtly suggestive remarks, foremost of which was: "What say we get outa this gin joint? I could show you two babes a really hot time." He'd actually winked then, and gave Rena's little rump a pat. Wendlyn smirked. *A hot time?* she thought. *We'll see who shows who a hot time.* She got wet just thinking about it.

Back at the house, Larry had offered no protestations whatsoever to Rena's "trick" cuffs. "I'm easy," he'd chuckled as they'd cuffed him down. Naked, he looked like dough stretched out on the bed, beer gut, no muscles, but…*Hmmm,* Wendlyn considered, appraising his works, which, despite their flaccidity, looked very promising. Rena sat at once on his face, her sleek back to the wall, as Wendlyn perked him up with her hand. "Jesus Christ!" Rena delighted. "You're gonna need a shoe horn to sit on all of that!" *You ain't kidding,* Wendlyn thought, plying the hardening tube of flesh. Larry's genitals bloomed; Wendlyn smiled giddily. "This looks like something that should hang in a smokehouse." Larry easily sported a twelve-inch root, with the girth of a pony bottle. Wendlyn reveled in its shape, its colossal well-formed glans, fat veins, and a urethral ingress big enough to admit her pinkie. Even his testicles were monsters: heavy and hot, and large as Jumbo Grade-A eggs. Wendlyn wasted no time in mounting this wonderful gorged pole, which actually nudged the cap of her cervix each time she rode down. She and Rena faced each other now, both murmuring and rolling their eyes at Larry's oral and copulatory prowess.

"His tongue must be as big as his cock," Rena was very happy to relate, gritting her teeth through a lascivious grin. "Feels like it's going right up my fuckin' uterus!"

"He can fuck too," Wendlyn assured, grinning much the same. This was so good—so slow and luscious and *hot*; she was actually drooling. *Fucking, my foot,* she thought. *This isn't fucking, it's deep-well drilling, and Larry Boy's about to tap the pool.* Indeed, Larry's penis felt more akin to one of those extra-long tubes of chocolate-chip cookie dough; this thing was squeezing her g-spot her flat against her anterior wall. Shit, she didn't even know she *had* a g-spot until now. Wendlyn's reproductive orifice was no stranger to phalli of above-average proportions, but this—*this*—was ridiculous! That Miller Pony-Bottle ~ Girth stretched her vulva out to a tight delicious bright-pink rim, plowing steadfast as a derrick wheel, while the length continued to plumb the absolute extremities of the tract of her womanhood. She felt skewered: Wendlyn-ka-bob. Quaking multiple orgasms went off deep in her loins like subsurface demolition. Her vagina pulsed and pulsed, wringing pleasure out of her nerves much the same as a hand wringing milk out of a cow's gorged teat. Exhausted, then, she switched positions with Rena, who immediately exclaimed "It's like fucking a rolling pin, Wendy!" as she inserted the elephantine penis into her slick bald snatch. Wendlyn found no exaggeration in Rena's previous affirmation; when she pressed her own downy-blond snatch to Larry's face, a tongue of utmost dimensions delved at once up into the beslickened furrow. She came again in minutes, leaving Larry's face shiny as wet shellack, and then Rena, too, tensed up and shuddered in wave upon wave of deepest orgasm, at which time Larry's own crisis unloosed, warm gouts of semen fat as worms rocketing up into the squirming purse of flesh. Rena's face strained, her hands opened on his belly, as she squealed in glee, "He's coming in me like a fucking garden hose!"

"Whew!" Larry replied, laxing back against the handcuffs. "That was one dandy nut. I knew you girls were hot."

"And we're gonna get a lot hotter," Wendlyn promised. Larry didn't notice Rena leaving the room, too engrossed via the next distraction: the application of Wendlyn's mouth to the flaccid, veined penis. It didn't remain flaccid long, though. In only minutes, back to turgid life it sprang. Wendlyn 69'd him, already anxious to feel that long tongue slide back up into her groove's salt-wet depths. To her surprise, however, and in an ultimate display of male bravado, the tongue bypassed this usual fissure and forced its way instead into the tight, flinching button of her rectum. It took quite a man to offer his tongue to this less-dainty orifice and, likewise, it took quite a woman to sufficiently perform fellatio upon a cock like Larry's. She could scarcely get the glans in her mouth much less the tumid shaft—she'd have better luck sucking a summer squash! Eventually she took to drawing her pinkie in and out of the big peehole, the sensation of which Larry tittered at as his visage remained vised in the cleft of Wendlyn's buttocks.

But when Rena reappeared, she climbed off. "You said you wanted a hot time, right, Larry?"

"Oh, yeah, oh, yeah," Larry concurred. His penis bobbed, like a ludicrous puppet.

"Well how's this for hot?" Rena stepped into the light, wearing sunglasses, for a reason that would become apparent in another moment. In her left hand she held a match. And in her right hand she held—

"OH, MY GOD!" Larry justifiably screamed.

—a blowtorch.

"This should be *real* hot, Larry," Wendlyn proposed. She pressed her breasts together in sheer, erotic delight. "And I mean *real real* hot…"

Rena lit the blowtorch and adjusted its flame down to a hissing, white-blue point. "Hot enough for you, Larry?" she inquired, applying the 1200-degree-plus flame to the tip of his dick. The tip shriveled at once, like a smoking marshmallow. Ditto as for the big testicles. Rena languidly roved the torch flame back and forth across the crisping scrotum, while Larry screamed so hard the whites of his eyes turned red in hemorrhage, and thrashed with such force the bed rocked up and down on its legs.

Wendlyn waved away at the stinking smoke, laughing along like a naked blond cheerleader from hell. Rena next bore the flame down on the center of Larry's flabby chest, straddling him as he bucked horselike in agony better left undescribed. The flame burned down down down, disintegrating flesh and bone alike, opening up a great black smoking pit in which Larry's heart cooked, then broiled, then collapsed to ash.

So much for Larry.

"Yeah," Wendlyn remarked, grinning down through the odiferous smoke. "I think that was hot enough for him."

¤   ¤   ¤   ¤   ¤

Wendlyn sauntered nude to the garage, to fetch a dropcloth.

Her big orbicular breasts bounced quite nicely with each step, and her big smile made no secret of her satisfaction. *Chalk up another one for womanhood,* she thought. *One more greedy, lustful, pussy-hungry woman-exploiter for the deep six.*

Back in the bedroom, though, she froze.

"What the...*fuck?*"

The bed lay empty. At first she thought Rena must already have unlocked the corpse, but a closer glance invalidated this suspicion. Each set of handcuffs remained secured to the bed's brass rails, yet each set was clearly missing its counterpart. In other words, the cuffs had been broken...

And above the lingering smoky stench of fried human flesh, Wendlyn smelled something deeper, more pungent. Like fresh sewage enlaced with something else...

Then she glanced to the left—

Glanced down—

And screamed.

Out of the room's shadow, Rena lay sprawled in the corner, glassy-eyed in death. Some heinously sharp instrument had lain open her abdomen, and from this gaping insult most of her lower g.i. tract had been yanked out. Shiny pink intestines formed squiggles on the floor, like queer garlands. Kidneys, spleen, and pancreas glistened. Worse, though, was that Rena's adorable, pointy little breasts were...gone. Bitten off. And the same too for that silk-smooth hairless pubis: gnawed out from betwixt the askew legs.

Beady eyes glinted. From the shadow, the huge angular head lowered as similarly huge jaws spread, baring white teeth the size of masonry nails. Rena's face was then eaten off the skull as a child might eat the icing off a cupcake.

A cascade of warm amber pee flowed freely down Wendlyn's plush legs. Her mouth froze open. She couldn't move. Then the voice croaked, but it was no human voice at all—just a ragged, unearthly suboctave, a succession of rasps, rattling like phlegm.

The voice said this: "You picked the wrong guy to fuck with tonight, baby."

By now Larry had transformed to near completeness, and this ancient and mystical metamorphosis had fully repaired Rena's earlier handiwork with the blowtorch. Three lone facts stood before Wendlyn now which, despite their impossibility, she could not deny. One, Larry was alive. Two, he was pissed off. And, three, he was a werewolf.

Wendlyn gulped.

Correction. He was a *big* werewolf, and in more ways than one. No reckoning would save her now, nor would any defensive action, and certainly no plea. Despite her understandable horror, however, and the paresis from which she could not release herself, the cogent agreement sparkled in her mind. *Yes. Yes, you're right. We definitely picked the wrong guy to fuck with tonight.*

So much for counter-exploitation.

The creature rose, the vulpine face grinned. Well-hung as a man, Larry was even bigger as a lycanthrope, the evidence of which now bloomed in obviousness, the doglike sheath sliding back showing glinting, shiny pink. Poor Wendlyn easily acknowledged the deduction: Now that Larry had eaten, he was ready to get down to some serious exploitation of his own.

THE WRONG GUY
AFTERWORD

As I write this afterword, it's 3:30 in the morning, and I'm watching Three's Company. *Jack is putting oranges into his sweatshirt, as breasts. Cool show, huh?*

The above story, however, I wrote in 1988, shortly after my first "Edward Lee" novel GHOULS was published. Can't really define any creative impetus on this one, just that I felt compelled to take one of horror's most overdone clichés–the "Wrong Guy" formula–and punch it up to a comedic max. When I finished, I had the balls to send it to a mass-market editor for an anthology. His rejection was simple: "You've got to be kidding me. I'd get fired if I bought this." Eventually, the story was published first by Cyber-Psychos A.O.D. *and* Into The Darkness. *Both of these wonderful mags saw to fantastic illustrations. I couldn't have been happier. Later, some astute reviewer was kind enough to point out that this story was "PLB," that is, Pre-Lorena Bobbitt, when it was first published in* Cyber-Psychos. *I added a Bobbitt reference when Dave Barnett reprinted it several years later.

I've always gotten a kick out of this piece, and I hope you do too. But I gotta tell ya:* Three's Company *is still on, and all of a sudden, Wendlyn and Rena remind me an awful lot of Chrissy and Janet. Now I kind of feel sorry for Jack.

Picture it.

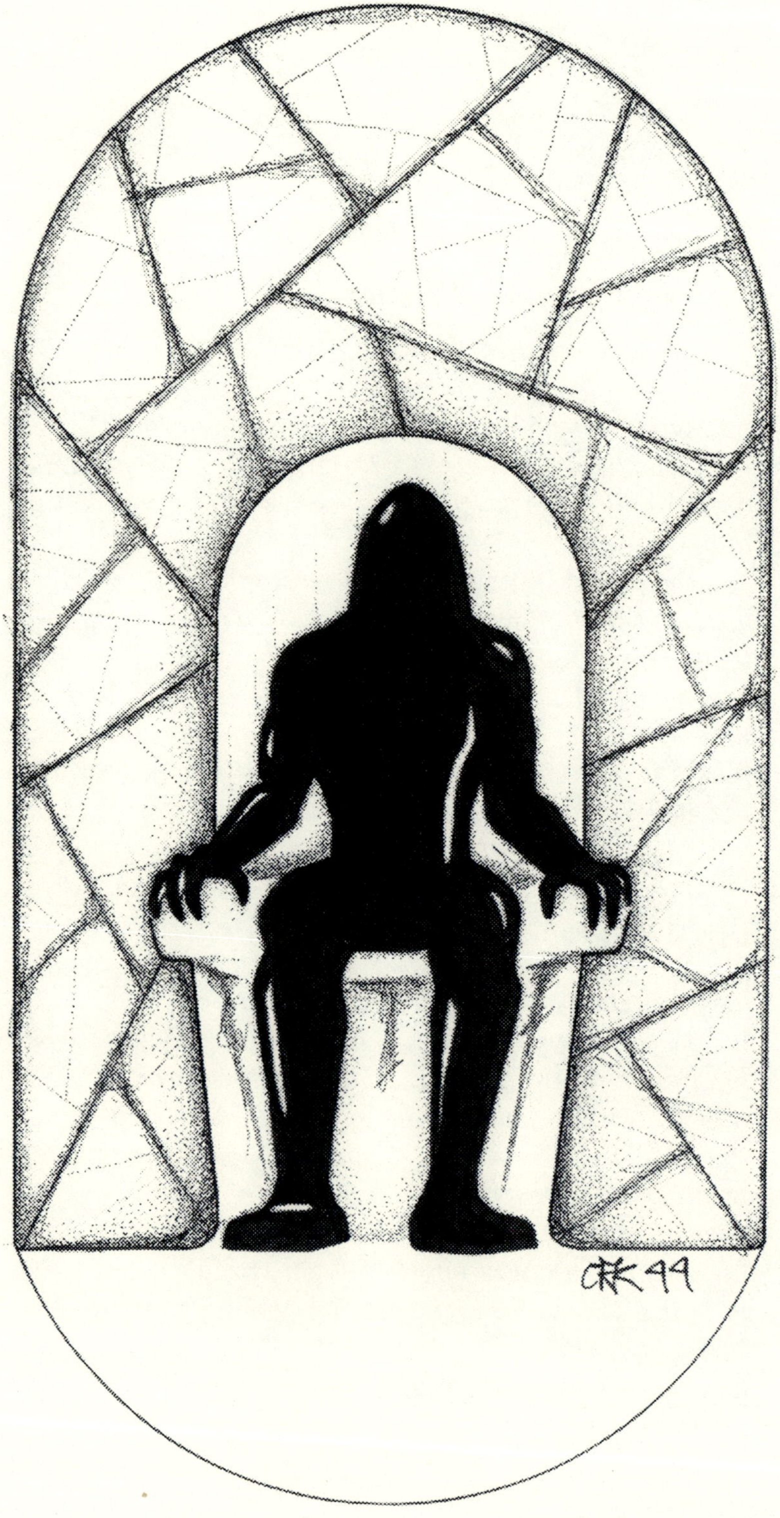
CRK 99

The Decortication Technician

YOU EVER SHIT your pants? I did a couple of days ago, first time in my life, but, see, at the time I wasn't wearing just pants, I was wearing a pair of sealed Class III EUDs. That's plat-talk for environmental utility dress—a spacesuit, to creamcake earth-loving non-hackers like you.

The recovery platoon brought it in at about 0300 zulu, *it* clearly being a hyper-velotic vehicle of extraterrestrial origin. Heel-shaped, twenty meters long, thirty wide. A dull-gray finish just like the old "UFO" fables from a quarter of a millennium ago. No viewports, no passive vid-lenses—no windows of any kind.

No doors.

Obviously this space-canoe came from a technology far superior to the Federated World's. Since I was the plat's decort tech, the OAC ordered me to assist in the r-dock, and, no, that's not when I shit my pants. I was jazzed just like the rest of the crew. This was the find of all of human history, and we were part of it. We'd all be famous. Our names would be in the history chips for as long as humankind endured, and with successful colonies on fifty-seven planets now, it's a good bet that humankind will endure for quite a while.

I open things, that's my job. I open things very carefully. That's why the OAC ordered me to the dock and no one else. Lotta sour grapes there, I can tell you, but to hell with 'em. When the OAC talks, you jump. Once the grunts brought this thing into the retrieval dock, we scanned it every which way but couldn't find any seams, no signs of any kind of entrance. We could only presume it was pressurized but God knew with what, so that ruled out a hot cut. And another thing: when we p/a/a'd the hull, it told us it was made of a non-metallic element as yet undiscovered.

"Burn the fucker open," SSG Yung said. "*Blow* it open with some C-11."

"Yeah, yeah!" the rest of his bohunkers shouted.

Just like ground-pounders, I thought. "Have you boys been drinking the cooling-tube effluvium again? Any gas inside the craft could be flammable. We could blow up the whole plat, you mallet-heads."

"Well then how are we gonna open it?" Yung grumbled. "We *gotta* open it!"

"Yeah, yeah!" the rest of his platoon shouted.

"We don't *gotta* do anything of the sort," I told the idiots. "We don't know anything about it. We start fucking around with it, we could destroy it–and ourselves. Smartest thing to do is secure it in one of the hold-warrens. Take it back to earth when the mission's done."

"That's three years!" Yung bellowed. "We got a fuckin' *alien spaceship* here, and there might be a fuckin' *alien* inside. We're supposed to wait three fuckin' years before we find out what's fuckin' inside the motherfucker?"

"You speak with the eloquence of kings," I remarked, but then, just as I'd voiced my objection, the OAC appeared on my head's-up-display.

:-cE jONSIN, dT1163: aTTEMPT tO eNTER tHE oBJECT-:

"Yeah, yeah!" Yung and his whitewalls shouted.

Orders were orders, so that was it. "You guys got what you wanted. Evacuate the r-dock."

"No way," Yung took some exception. "We busted our balls hauling this tin can aboard. We're damn sure gonna be here when you open it."

I shook my head. "It's for your own safety. You guys gotta leave."

Six grinning meat-racks in EUDs surrounded me.

"*Make* us leave, civvie."

"Suit yourself," I said, getting the point. "Prep me. I want this victor covered with lexlar blast blankets. Keep the dock de-preshed. And charge me up a nute-drill and a quarter-inch blackie-pete bit…"

¤ ¤ ¤ ¤ ¤

I guess I should back up a little, huh? Set things off right? I mean, I got no idea when this log-chip might be found, and I guess it's highly probable whoever finds it won't know what the hell this is all about.

My name's Dug Jonsin, twenty-nine earth years old. Mission ID: DT1163. It's Tuesday, 25 May 2202. I'm a civilian astro-entomologist attached to the Federated World's Academy of Galactic Studies. I examine and catalogue insects by academic design, but what I really do is cut them open. Officially, I'm a FOS 95C20 Decortication Technician.

Sounds fancy but…I'm a light-weight by earth standards. My college GPA was only 3.89. Couldn't get a good job with the Academy earth-

The Decortication Technician

bound, so here I am on this tub which they call a Deep Space Analytic and Collection Platform, vessel tag CW-DSP-141. Fourteen-man crew: six Army grunts for the retrieval platoon, one Jarine security ape who doubles as a corpsman, two more civvies like me on the Technistics Unit, and five Naval Space Corp dupes who run the plat.

And me.

The job's a cake walk, really. We hit different star clusters, ID planets, planetoids, moons, and asters with nitrogen-oxygen atmospheres, and then we check them out. Fauna and flora, for the Academy's zoological indexes. The FW's been running survey missions like this for over a hundred years, since the invention of I-grav drives. That's inverted-gravity propulsion. A simple cadmium laser electrically charges a Palladium/Peridotite ceramic plate and harnesses one-half of available interspacial gravity as a force of propulsion. The lasers provide specific photon wavelengths to pass or dissipate the electrical charge through a gallium isolator. Cadmium for ON, Helium for OFF. Simple. It proved that the Twentieth Century eggheads were right. You can't beat the speed of light, but you can sure as shit bend it. That's how we can move our platforms far out of the Milky Way. So much for universal invariants.

Each mission is a ten-year gig, but they say you only age about three and a half. Nobody wants this shit so there's a pay off. Early retirement on the fed lamb. I figured it was worth it. No wife, no kids–could never afford that stuff. But when I get back to earth I can have it all. Phenothiazines keep you from going insane, and tetra-amine implants kill your sex drive. A lot of the crew don't believe it at first, so they sneak on porn chips, but after the implant, man, you can look at a cyberpegs of Miss Defense Corp buck naked but it's about as erotic as looking at your own turds in a gravity toilet. I haven't had a hard-on in seven years, wouldn't know what to do with it if I did. Every month the OAC orders you to sit on a rectal bolus, a sub-static charge that makes you ejaculate so you don't get prostate cancer down the road.

Oh, and the OAC? That stands for Operational Analysis Computer. There's no captain on this rowboat, just the OAC. When it gives you an order, you do it. If you don't, you get cryo'd, and when you get back to the World, you get no compensation, no retirement, no nothing. Just ten years of your life down the drain and sometimes a full nickel stint on the Lunar Detention Facility.

So if this crap-pot full of microchips tells me to stand on my head and cluck like a chicken, I don't ask why, I just do it.

But back to my FOS–that's Federal Occupational Specialty. Astro-entomolgy is the fancy way of putting it, bug-cracking is the more realistic way. I'm a decorticator. One thing we found out fast after we started searching other solar systems for signs of life is that there were *all kinds* of life on a lot of these rocks.

Just nothing interesting.

Nothing mammalian. Usually just microscopic stuff like entozoas, chlorophiles, trimeciums–space germs–and we'd cryo the samples and that was it. Same thing with vegetation, thallophytes, and fungus. Tag it and freeze it.

But another thing we found a lot of were what could be categorized in earth terms as *insectas*: hexapods, anthropods—aquatic and terrestrial–anything with an exoskeleton. And a lot of them were pretty big.

Ever seen a cockroach the size of a 55-gallon drum? Ever seen a moth the size of a bald eagle? We'd get so much stuff like that–alien insecta phylas–that you wouldn't believe it. For an entomologist, it was exciting as hell.

For about a month.

Then it all got to be the same. When the exploratory surveys started, there was this idealistic hope that someday one of the missions would find mammalian life, would even find something akin to the human species. But that never happened.

All we found were bugs.

Big bugs. Insects that had evolved for millions or even billions of years and had genetically adapted a physical size that could accommodate longevity. Heavily shelled creatures that could withstand hostile environments, drastic fluctuations in atmospheric pressure and content, neutrino and meteoric showers and volcanic debris.

Big bugs. Big bugs with hard shells. That's pretty much what the rest of the galaxy had waiting for mankind to discover.

So that was my job.

As the mission's decortication tech, I had to take two samples of each sex of any insecta we discovered. One sample I'd cryo immediately. The other sample I'd autopsy if the creature's size was deemed by the OAC as practical. Some of these things had three or four sexes. And a lot of them were huge.

I had to establish the most effective way to decorticate the insect while still alive. In other words, I had to cut off its hull, shell, carapace, exoskeleton, or whatever, and autopsy the bug while digigraphing the entire procedure for the Academy's archives.

Yeah, yeah, I know what you're thinking. How hard can it be to cut the shell off a bug?

Space bugs? It's a bitch. See, I gotta do it without destroying the bug. You don't use scissors. You don't use a knife–not for this job. You don't

The Decortication Technician

pin the goddamn thing to a board. Some of these things are as big as men, bigger. If you try to open 'em with an ectine torch, all you'll do is fry the damn thing. And if you fry it, the OAC logs that into your service file as a demerit.

You should see some of the shit that these bugs got inside of them. Black slop, brown slop, green slop. Slimy organs whose purpose you couldn't even guess at. Hell, one time I decorticated an octopod from P31 on the Ryan Cluster—I cut the sheath off the groinal trap and this thing had something that looked just like a human cock! No lie! This thing didn't have an ovidpositur—it had a dick!

So, anyway, that's my ten-year gig. Decorticating bugs.

I never would've imagined that, one day, I'd be ordered to decorticate something else.

¤   ¤   ¤   ¤   ¤

It was the MADAM that picked it up first—that's Mass-Activated-Detection-Alarm-Mechanism. It's a souped-up spheric-pulse radar, picks up anything in the scan field that the OAC calculates can't be organically or naturally formed.

We'd just hypervelled through the Zuby System, using grids piped to us from the Hubble 6 matrix, and we weren't thrusting through this white-dwarf system for more than an hour before the MADAM went off. THE OAC called General Quarters, and all we could do then was wait. Wait for the tri-wave scans to bounce back to the sensor-slats and tell us what was out there.

The OAC told us this:

:-mADAM cOORDINATES vIA hOME pLATFORM aS zERO: sEVEN-sIX-tHREE dEGREES sIX mINUTES oN mENISCUS cHART. pROBABLITY cOMPUTATIONS iNDICATE nINE-nINE-pERCENT lIKELIHOOD oF eXTRATERRESTRIAL vEHICLE oF hIGHER tECHNOLOGY dERIVATION tHAN iS pREVIOUSLY iNDEXED-:

I'd been sitting in the chow hall, eating gengineered monkfish-steak when that call came through. The Army grunts were scrambled, and thrusted out on a retrieval skiff in less time that than it takes to fill your piss bag. About an hour later, they were redocking and asking for ingress countercodes. The OAC passed them through, and that's when I was ordered to r-dock.

¤   ¤   ¤   ¤   ¤

You're still wondering what this has to do with me shitting my EUDs, right? Well, I'm getting to that. I'm standing on the lock-rails in r-dock when the grunts bring the victor in and tack it down to the stulls. They close the dock door but wisely don't represh; we all keep our CVC helmets on with defoggers set on high. This victor—vehicle—looked stunning, a perfect crescent with no seams, no doors, no visual outlets or propulsion vents, no indication even of a gravity-amplification node.

Just a thirty-meter-wide crescent, a giant boomerang.

The laze scales put the thing in at just under two-hundred pounds. Something that big? It should've weighed at least a couple of tons. Which meant that whatever unknown element it was made of had very little weight, very little photon mass. It was at the least a kick to have the grunts following my orders. Federal Military didn't like it when civilians told them what to do. But I was the expert here, at least the best that this mission could provide. My expertise involved cutting bugs open. Therefore I was the best candidate to cut open an alien vehicle.

"Pop this can," one of the field privates muttered, wide-eyed behind his glexan visor. "Crack it open."

"Do it," SSG Yung said.

"What do you think I'm going to do? Play paddycakes with it?" I strapped on the force harness, then closed the chuck on the Black & Decker neutron drill; the treated black-phosphorus bit would make a million-and-a-half cycles per minute but it wouldn't get hot. No heat conduction, no sparks. "And if this doesn't work, I'll try the nuclear spanner." I raised the massive drill on its waist-bracket, then planted my nanoboots on the floorwall and pressed the bit against the victor's hull.

"Hardcore," someone said.

"Last chance to evac, guys," I reminded them. I winked at SSG Yung.

"Just rev that fuckin' thing up and go!" Yung yelled.

Suit yourself. I toggled down the charge lever, flipped open the safety. Just as I was about to hit the power detent—

"Wait a minute!" a platoon Spec 4 shouted. He was standing on the other side of the victor, running a hand-held photon-activation-analysis scan on the hull.

"What?" I said, the drill harness weighing down on my hips.

"You ain't gonna believe this…but I've got double-pozz poroscopy on the hull, and residual chloride ions."

"*Bull*shit!" I practically spat into my mic.

"I shit you not, man," the Spec replied. "Ain't nothing else this could be."

It's got to be a mistake, I thought, but I unstrapped the drill anyway.

"What the fuck are you fuckin' talkin' about?" Yung complained. "Chloride *what?*"

"Chloride *ions,*" I said. ""It's part of a typical sebaceous amino acid secretion, unless the OAC's glitching. Your man just found a *fingerprint* on the hull."

The Decortication Technician

Yung eyes opened wide as condenser slugs behind his visor. "The *fuck?*"

"It looks overlayed a bunch'a times," the Spec 4 observed, focusing the p/a/a screen. I checked it out myself and he was right.

"No ridge patterns," I said more to myself than to him. "The pore pattern's relatively intact, but that's it. Then it looks like..."

"A smear?" the Spec ventured.

"Yeah, I think so. Digigraph it a couple of times and save the files in the OAC," I said. Then I turned to SSG Yung, who still didn't get it.

"Someone or some thing touched this victor, Sergeant Yung. And whoever touched it, touched it repeatedly in the same place."

Behind the glex visor, Yung's face twisted up. "You mean a *human?*"

"Well, something clearly human*oid,*" I corrected. "Something that has sebaceous secretions similar to ours."

"All right...uh– Just get back on that drill and cut this fucker open," he said.

Be as dumb as you can be–in the Army, I thought. "The nute-drill could take hours or days. Let me try something. If it doesn't work, then I'll power the drill back up. Is that square with you?"

Yung smirked, reached up and tried to scratch his chin before he remembered he was wearing a sealed CVC. "Yeah, fuck, all right."

"Represh the dock to six-five," I told the Spec. Yung nodded consent. It took a few minutes but I needed enough PSIs in the dock to take my EUD mitt off. Then I grabbed an SV probe off the hardware lock.

"What the fuck are you fuckin' doin'?" Yung asked.

I didn't bother answering. The sub-violet lume element would show me the same spot where the hull was touched. "There it is," I muttered. It was a downward streak. Someone had pressed his or her or its fingertip against the hull at this precise point. Then they'd dragged their fingertip down in a straight line...

With my mitt off, then, I did the same thing. I pressed my fingertip on the same spot, then dragged it down.

A small ingression in the high quadrant of the hull formed. And for you earth-loving non-hackers who don't know what that means... It means a doorway opened.

¤   ¤   ¤   ¤   ¤

"He did it!" Yung barked. "The candyass civvie fuck *did* it! First Platoon! Lock and load." Yung shoved me back out of the way as his troops charged their Colt M-57 Squad Assault Systems. "Cole, Alvirez, take firing positions at the bulkhead! Filips and Bensin, cover the entrance at one-five meters! Come on, Roburts! It's me and you."

"Sarge, Sarge," I interrupted. "The G.I. Joe stuff isn't going to be necessary." I showed him my fileflat which was now out-indexing the atomic chromatography specs from the p/a/a scan. "Check this out."

Yung frowned at the readouts, his trigger finger twitching. "The fuck am I supposed to know what that shit is? I ain't no wirehead–I'm a fuckin' Army Ranger!"

Tell me about it. "This is a radio assay and carbon-date of the fingerprint. It's over 2,100 years old, Sarge. Any life form inside that victor is long dead."

"Balls," the platoon sergeant replied. "Cover me, Roburts!" Then he raised his weapon and entered the craft. I guess these guys had their games to play, so what the hell. They had to go through the motions, I guess to maintain their identities. And I guess I did the same thing, in my own way, too.

But when Yung entered the victor with his wrist-light and rifle–it seemed like a whole lot of time went by with all of us just standing there staring at the doorway. Yung didn't respond. We couldn't even see his shadow moving in there.

"Hey, Sarge?" I called out.

Nothing.

"Sergeant Yung! Relay your status!" Roburts cracked.

Nothing.

Then—

"Holy everlovin' motherfuckin' shit…"

It was Yung's voice that carried back to our CVCs. I turned to the SGT E-5 next to me. "You're next in command, pal. You better send someone in there."

"I-I-I—," he stammered.

What the hell, I thought. I grabbed the SGT's wrist-light and stepped into the victor. The cabin walls were black but somehow tinged with silver. I saw no evidence of an operator's seat, instruments, or controls. Just the weird silver-black, which sucked up the 1000-candle-power sodium light I was carrying.

"Down here," Yung's voice drifted to me.

It was like walking through black fog. I seemed to take many more steps than the depth of the craft would allow, but eventually Yung's form came into focus. He'd dropped his weapon on the victor's floor and was just sitting there on a starboard protrudement.

"Guess I just wasn't ready for it," he said. He sat there with the rim of his helmet in his palm. He looked out of it. He looked whacked.

"What's that, Sarge?"

"Seen a lot of fucked up shit in my time. Seen guys die, my own men, seen whole transport plats blow up 'cos some mech jockey forgot

The Decortication Technician

to close a vent-line. I saw the P-4 quake split the whole planetoid in half and swallow fifteen thousand colonists five minutes after my thruster took off. It's fucked up shit, man."

"Straighten up, Sarge," I said. For whatever reason, he was going down memory lane, and the scenery wasn't too great. "Get your shit square. Sure, we're standing inside an alien spacecraft–the first one ever discovered–and you're right, it's fucked up. But we gotta keep it together. We got our jobs to do. You got men out there shit-scared. They're counting on you."

His CVC turned toward me. Through the glex visor, I could see his blank eyes in the light. "Since I was a little kid," he droned, "I always thought that this would happen someday. But it was just a fantasy, you know? Some kids fantasize about being president, some kids fantasize about seeing an alien… Man, this is fucked up."

The tone of his words wrapped me up. "Seeing…a what?" I said. But now I guessed his point. We knew there must have been something inside this ship, however long dead. What else could it be but an "alien?" A "spaceman?" Something every man, woman, and child in the Federate had thought about, dreamed about, but something, by now, that nobody really believed in anymore. Like afterlife, reincarnation, spirituality. Just myths now. Mankind in the 23rd century no more believed in spacemen than they believed in Santa Claus.

Yung's voice cracked like tinder. "Take a look, civvie," he said.

I let my light follow his gaze. Some kind of a molded object rose from the floor, something like a chair, and sitting in that chair was the victor's obvious pilot.

¤ ¤ ¤ ¤ ¤

An ecstatic chaos filled the plat, everyone running around like meth-freaks. Time seemed to stand still. The OAC ordered most of the crew to analyze the victor. As for the dead pilot, of course we couldn't analyze *him* until we got his suit off. That was my job: to decorticate the pilot, so to speak. To remove his environmental suit and extract the body for digraphy and autopsy.

We'd moved the body to the medcove, lain it out on an exam table under the lumes.

"Twenty-one May, 2202," I said into the mission recorder. "Jonsin, Dugliss, FOS 95C20 decortication technician for mission survey on DSP-141. The Operational Analysis Computer has ordered me to attempt to extract the body of the victor's apparent operator for analysis and archives indexing. For this record, the victor's operator will be referred to as VO from here on…"

Oh, damn. Some story teller I am, huh? I forgot to tell you what the guy looked like. Humanoid and bipedal. Two pronating arms, two pronating legs, and a head. Each hand showing four fingers with three phalanges, and an opposable thumb. One hundred and forty-six point four pounds via mean-specific gravity, and seventy-one inches long in extemis. For all intents, it was a guy in a spacesuit with a general surface anatomy similar to ours.

But it was still an alien, and it was the ev-suit that kept reminding me of that. Same color, same hue as the ship: a flat silver-black. To the touch, the material felt like something polycron or cloth, but if you pressed down on it, it wouldn't give at all. I tried a particle vise on the right thumb and *nothing happened*. The vise broke at 7,000,000 psi. But if you grabbed the hand, you could bend the fingers in their natural direction. Same with the rest of the body. The suit was pliable...but then again, it wasn't.

The head was the weirdest part. Not a helmet, nothing like what you would think of as utility headgear. Just a bullet-shape extending from the shoulders. No visor, no visual ports, no bumps where the ears should be. Just imagine dipping a doll in wax enough times that only the basic shape remained.

This was my company for about the next seventy-two hours. First thing I tried was a standard scan of the suit, same way I'd scan a bug before cutting it open. But this was no bug. X-rays, V-rays, triax tomography, nuclear-resonance scans—all negative. And it was no big surprise that, like the victor, the VO's suit showed no signs of any sort of opening. No zipper on this spaceman. And I tried touching the suit, like I'd touched the ship, but...no such luck.

The only way to see what was inside was to do what I did best. Cut it open.

I didn't sleep for days; I only ate when the OAC ordered me to. I became obsessed, but then everyone else was too–*obsessed* with their particular mission assignments. This was history, this was *it*. And we were all a working part.

But for *my* part–failure.

Section lasers, nuke-picks, impact-bezels, the sub-cabundum bandsaw, the ectine torch? All of them failed. Whatever material it was that the VO's suit was constructed of, none of these tools touched it. I couldn't dent it, couldn't melt it, couldn't even scratch it. Detcord failed too, and so did beta-fluoric acid. Nothing. The most invasive and corrosive substances and tools known to man did *nothing* to the VO's suit.

In the meantime, though, I learned from the OAC updates that the rest of the crew were having the same bad luck trying to take the victor apart. Every single testing and analysis method available could determine absolutely nothing about the composition, structure, or engineering of the craft. And since no propulsion system could be detected, God knew how this thing got to the Zuby system. Where was it coming from? Where was it going?

Eventually, though, a half-answer blipped over our HUDs. Since no engine, fuel, or propulsion structures were discovered on the victor, the OAC, after almost three earth days of computations at half a trillion cycles per second, told us this:

:-cALCULATIONS fOUNDED iN aLL kNOWN qUANTUM pOSTULATION eSTIMATES tHAT fOREIGN vICTOR mAY bE pROPELLED bY sOME dESIGN oF rELATIVISTIC mOMENTUM-eNERGY rELATION bASED oN pROPOSED 20th-cENTURY tHEORY. *E = pc aND mo [momentum] = 0*. iF a pHOTON cEASES tO mOVE aT tHE sPEED oF lIGHT, iT cEASES tO eXIST. tHEREFORE, tHERE iS a hIGH pROBABLILITY tHAT tHE vICTOR iS pROPELLED bY pHOTONIC wAVELENGTH eQUALIZATION. hIGH bERYLLIUM vAPOR-pHASE tHROUGH tRACKED pROXIMITY oF zUBY sTAR sYSTEM wOULD dISABLE sUCH a pOWERPLANT-:

So there it was. The most off-the-wall theory of motion and yet the simplest. All of a sudden it made sense. And so did the fluke. Evidence of gaseous beryllium in space was almost ziltch, but gaseous beryllium would be the only elemental substance that could shut down such an engine. Beryllium deflects photons. Like an old prop plane from the 1900s suddenly entering a vacuum.

Beryllium would shut down the engine. One chance in a hundred million. And that chance happened.

An accident.

The grunts and the techs and the swabbies pulled their hair out over the victor just like I pulled mine out over the VO. Both were puzzles that couldn't be solved. All we had was the OAC watching over us. In all its calculative power, it could not make a single suggestion on how to analyze the victor or how to remove the suit.

But on the third day...

¤ ¤ ¤ ¤ ¤

Particle beams can be focused into ancipital-shaped fields. Two edges joining to a point on a plane one electron wide. It was a theory of my own (not even the OAC came up with it) whereby random particle projections could be agitated with cyclically fluctuating laser streams. In theory, it would produce a pinpoint of heat maxing out at 180,000 degrees. If I could just put one pinhole in that suit....

I might be able to get a foothold to cutting it all off.

I didn't know what I expected, even if it worked. I wasn't thinking about it. None of us were. We were only thinking about the present task, one step at a time. And in three days, nobody on the plat had even made a hair's width of headway. Even if I got the suit off...what would be waiting inside? After over twenty centuries?

Just bones? Dust? Karyolitic rot? But the suit, by all evidence, was hermetically sealed. So maybe the body inside was perfectly intact. But once exposed to air pressure, would it implode? Dissolve? I didn't know the answer to any of these questions. It wasn't my job to ask, it was my job to *do*.

I put on an oxygen recharger and a full EUD hazmat suit. If I *did* punch a hole in this stuff, I didn't want toxic gas or alien liquefaction squirting in my face. When I began to upcharge the particle generator, I expected the OAC to shut me down because of the danger margin, but that never happened. I cranked the beam nozzle over the right thigh; I had a depth marked, by one-tenth of one millimeter that would scroll down to a max of five. I punched in my pass-crypt and then turned on the power.

The General-Quarters alarm sound immediately after I pressed the DISCHARGE switch. Even through my rebreather, I could smell burning metal. I began to get sick. The beam jumped to its max of 180,000 degrees in a split second but it shut down after penetration was achieved; the material of the VO's suit was only one-tenth of one micron thick.

As the beam powered down, and as the GQ alarm blared, I just stood there, frozen, looking down at the VO. Then the VO began to convulse: arms and legs and back flip-flopping on the analysis table.

Like it was still alive.

And that's when I shit my pants.

¤   ¤   ¤   ¤   ¤

See, at the same instant I burned that hole into the VO's suit, all kinds of powerups starting happening on the victor. Lights came on. RAD displays began to appear: instrument readouts. Some kind of humming began to reverberate, like an engine starting. What I mean to say is...I wasn't the only guy on the plat who shit his pants. Damn near everyone did.

But they were all in R-Dock. I was all alone in the medcove, the VO still convulsing on the table.

I asked the OAC what to do but there was no answer. Just me standing there, my brain ticking, warm shit running down the back of my leg.

Penetrating the VO's suit was some kind of trigger. It turned things on in the victor. And one of the things it turned on was a 2D map projection. No doubt there were computers laced into the victor's hull, but there was no way the OAC would ever be able to get into them, and even if it did, what language would such programs be written in?

But seeing is everything, right? And when we digigraphed those map-projection displays, the OAC instantly recognized the astronomical reference points.

It matched those points to our own recorded star charts.

Everything happened so fast after that...I'm not sure about the order. But it was the OAC that determined the victor had powered up *because* I had finally penetrated the VO's suit. It had occurred at the same microsecond. It was as if I'd pulled some kind of a switch, but none of us could guess why.

And I didn't have time to wonder, not then. The body convulsed on the table for maybe five seconds but to me it seemed like an hour. Once it fell limp again, though, I got back to work. It took me three days to put a microscopic hole in the suit—how long would it take me to cut the whole thing off?

Not long, I found.

I managed to sink a kinetic needle into the puncture hole, then I connected the needle to a maletric field amplifier. From there it was cake. It was like cutting the carapace off a sextapod. It probably didn't take me two minutes to cut the rest of the suit off the VO.

The material fell off the limbs and torso like cheesecloth; what lay there afterward was an intact humanoid male. Sturdy, well-formed physique, unblemished skin, long hair and beard. When I weighed the naked body on the spec-grav scale it came up the same: one hundred forty-six point four pounds. Which meant the suit had no perceptible weight. But even before that, I hooked the body up to the sensor monitors.

It was still alive.

Those initial convulsions hadn't been a reactive exposure to air pressure or heat; they hadn't been autonomic or the result of perimortal nerve conduction. The body maintained a regular heartbeat of about a sixty-five pulses per minute and registered systolic/dystolic blood pressure in the normal range for humans. Pulmonary expansion and collapse was normal too; the VO was *breathing*.

But the encephalopeg readout was the kicker. Alpha, beta, and theta four-wave brain patterns indicated a 1.0 synaptic coma.

But with slow-gradual improvement.

The VO wasn't dead. He'd been floating in the victor for more than twenty centuries...but he wasn't dead.

How could that be? No food, no air, no climate control?

Would he come out of the coma? If so, when? Everything was an avalanche of questions now. The victor was generating power. The operator was alive.

What next?

We didn't know.

"We should vector back to earth now," Yung suggested that night in the chowcove. He was drunk on synthbeer and so were most of his men. At least the Navy guys weren't around; they were passed out on byhydrognine in their doms. "Fuck the rest of the mission," Yung blurted. "This is more important."

We both lit up Premier Menthols, sucked in the nicotine-laced steam. "The OAC would never allow it, Sarge," I reminded him.

He leaned closer. "Yeah, but maybe we can override the fucker."

"No way—too many safeties. It's a fuckin' federated crime. We try something like that, we lose everything. The only reason the OAC didn't overhear you saying that is because—"

"Because its programs are too busy processing all this new data—I know that. That's why I'm talking to you now. We just made the find of all of human history, and that goddamn motherboard is gonna make us finish the survey. That's three more years, pal."

"Yeah, and it's also operating orders," I said. "We can't beat the program, Sarge. You and I both know that. We all signed on for the dime—we do the dime."

"Aw, fuck all that fuckin' protocol shit," he said, waving a hand. "Christ, we've got an intact alien victor, we've got star charts from an extraterrestrial databank, and we've got the goddamn pilot in a coma. That's enough to override the fuckin' operating procedures."

I was about to beg to differ but then the OAC blipped onto our HUDs.

:-mAINFRAME pROGRAM aNALYSIS iS nOW cOMPLETE. BASED oN cURRENT iMRPOVEMENT cALCULATIONS, tHE vICTOR oPERATOR wILL REGAIN fULL cONSCIOUSNESS wITHIN fORTY-tWO mONTHS. tHE sURVEY pLATFFORM iS oNE hUNDRED aND sIXTEEN lIGHT yEARS fROM eARTH. EMERGENCY gUIDELINES dICTATE aN aLTERNATE mISSION iTERNARY-:

"The fuck is that shit!" Yung yelled.

:-sTAR cHART cONFIGURATION cONFIRMED oNE hUNDRED pOINT zERO pERCENT. fOREIGN vICTOR'S pREVIOUS tRAJECTORY cONFIRMED. fOREIGN vICTOR'S fUTURE tRAJECTORY cONFIRMED -:

"Yeah!" I shouted and hugged Yung like a brother.

"The fuck?"

"The OAC knows the victor's final plotted destination! And it also knows its debark point!"

The Decortication Technician

Yung clearly wasn't a brainchild, but even before he could mouth another gripe, the OAC shot him its orders:

:-sSG yUNG, pS mOS 11E40. rEPORT tO r-dOCK aSAP. dO nOT cONTEMPLATE aCTIONS wHICH tHE jUSTICE cORP mIGHT dEEM aS mUTINOUS-:

"Don't you get it?" I asked Yung. "The OAC input those star charts into its own program files. It determined where the victor was coming from and where it was going to before the beryllium flux depowered its engines! Get to your post!"

Yung rubbed his face, blinked hard, then he got up and left the cove. The OAC cut him a big break.

:-cE jONSIN, dT1163-: the OAC told me next. :-tHIS iS aN iNSULATED mESSAGE. MOST oF oTHER cREWMEMBERS aRE cLOSE tO mUNTIOUS aCTION. THEREFORE i aM cOMMUNICATING tHIS mESSAGE tO yOU aLONE-:

"I understand," I said.

:-aTTEMPT tO cOERCE rEST oF cREW nOT tO mUTINY. THIS iS oF pARAMOUNT iMPORTANCE-:

"All right," I agreed. "But why?"

:-oAC aNALYSIS cOMPUTATIONS cOMPLETE. yOU mUST mAKE a mORE dETAILED eXAMINATION oF vICTOR oCCUPANT-:

I ran back to the medcove. The naked body still lay on the table. I'd run every kind of scan possible on the nude body, and everything was coming up humanoid. But there were five anomalies that the OAC had indexed that I didn't know about yet.

I stared at the TRI graph, and then I knew what the OAC was talking about. We couldn't go back now. We had to go on.

We *had* to.

:-mAKE tHIS iNFORMATION aVAILABLE tO tHE rEST oF tHE cREW. cONVINCE tHEM oF iTS iMPORTANCE. tHEY wIll nOT tRUST mE bECUASE i aM nOT hUMAN-:

"Will do," I said.

See, what the OAC had been doing all along was not only analyzing displayed star charts in the victor and all the other displayed info, it also analyzed all of my triax-tomes and resonance scans of the VO's body once I cut the suit off. I didn't see these things, but the scans did.

I read the output data over and over, all the while staring down at the naked and comatose body on the table. The long hair, the beard, the glazed eyes.

Then I read the tome scans a last time.

Healed-over wounds were present between the navicular and cuboid bones of the feet. Healed over wounds were present just under the pisiform and tubercle bones in the wrist. And one other healed over wound was present between the fourth and fifth rib bones on the thoracic cage.

Then I knew.

A fingerprint on the hull over twenty-two hundred years old? The OAC analysis of the victor's star charts left even less doubt. The victor's debark point had been verified by gauss trails: they'd been from earth somewhere between 29 and 33 A.D. from a place in the ancient Middle East referred to in Late Latin from Aramaic, a word meaning *gulg_ ltha,* or Golgotha.

When I explained to the rest of the crew exactly what this might mean…the strangest thing happened.

The men who'd been raised as Christians quickly became atheists. And the men, like Yung, who'd been raised as atheists converted to the ranks of Christendom.

But me?

I guess I fall somewhere in between.

This all happened on the third day. Seven more have passed since then, and I don't know how much planar space we've folded since then, not with the i-grav engines running full tilt half way into the redline. Someday, yes, the VO will probably regain consciousness. But who knows how long that will take? Months? Years? Decades?

Doesn't matter.

The star charts that were activated when I cut open the suit—they didn't just indicate the debarkation point of the victor. Those charts also showed the *final destination grid.*

We're taking our passenger back to where he came from, and I want to see what's waiting for us when we get there.

THE DECORTICATION TECHNICIAN
AFTERWORD

I'm frequently asked if there are any "lines" I won't cross, and generally my answer is always no. But that's a little bit of a lie. One reason I wrote this story is because my dutiful publishing magnate, Matt Johnson, specifically asked me for a piece dealing with the, uh, subject matter, and he really dug what I originally proposed, a story idea entitled "The Witness of Thomas." But, lo, when it got down to the brass tacks, I changed my mind and refused to write the piece. Why? Because it crossed a line I deemed as unacceptable.

I wrote this one in its place, and I chose the sci-fi angle because I've never really read sci-fi before; I felt challenged to try and write it. I hope to write more down the road.

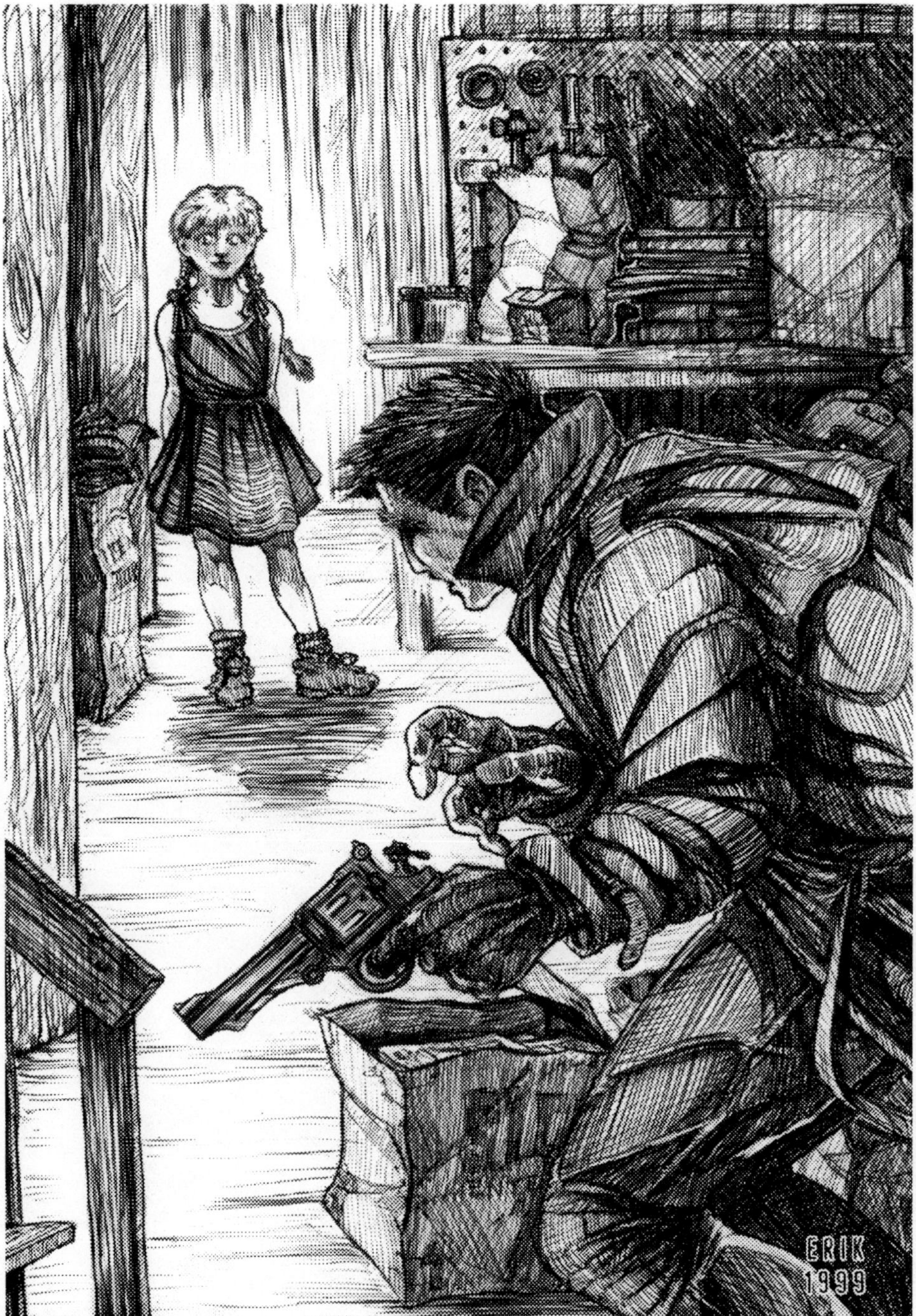
ERIK
1999

Almost Never

CRUNCH

    Katie took another step, then froze, listened.

crunch

    Just a tiny sound, from the trees behind her. Perhaps she'd imagined it; Grandpa always said she had a big imagination. But then—a rustle? Did she hear a voice? Katie's heart fluttered.

crunch, crunch

    She broke briskly down the narrow, tree-lined trail, taking long strides over fallen branches and gnarled roots. Around her, the woods seemed too still, too quiet. The moon, just rising, dappled her little face in white light. The grocery bag under her arm felt like a satchel of dead weight.

    Those two men, she realized. She'd noticed them several times, following her around in the store. Now, the faster she walked, the more aware she became of the soft, quick crunching behind her that could only be footsteps...

¤   ¤   ¤   ¤   ¤

    "Someone's been following me, Grandpa." The flimsy screen door snapped shut. Katie rose on her tiptoes to set the bag of groceries on the counter.

    "What's that, honey?" Grandpa wheeled forward, keen at the sudden question. "You say someone's been—"

    "Two men. I've seen them in the grocery store a few times, and I think they've been following me down the trail." Her small confused face turned to the old man. "Why would two grownups want to follow me?"

    Grandpa's aged visage seemed to twitch; his knuckly hands tightened on the rungs of the wheelchair. *Blast it,* he thought. *Two men.* Jesus. He and his granddaughter didn't bother anyone. Why couldn't people leave them alone? "You just steer clear of them, honey," he said. "From now on, I'll do the shopping. You just stay here where it's safe."

"Grandpa!" she little girl scoffed. "You can't get to the store in your wheelchair. The trail's not big enough."

"I'll get on all right, don't you worry. I'm not as useless as people might think," Grandpa complimented himself. "What you got to understand, honey, and it's a sad thing, but, see, there're a lot of bad people in this world, evil people." He gulped thickly at the thought. "People who'd want to do bad things to a little girl like you."

Katie began to put the groceries away, oblivious in her innocence. "What kind of things, Grandpa?"

"Never you mind about that." God, what a question! How could he explain something like that to a little girl? *There shouldn't be no need to explain,* he retorted to himself. *'Cos such things just shouldn't be.* "You just do like your old granddad tells ya. I'll be able to get this blasted chair down the trail. Might take awhile, but I'll manage. Old duff like me could use the exercise."

"*Grand*pa." Katie stretched the word. "That's dumb. I can get there in ten minutes."

"And I don't want no more said about it, you hear me, miss?" No, he could never explain. Never. Child molesters, pedophiles. *Creatures,* he thought. They were out there, everywhere. His disgust seemed to percolate in his head, like pitch bubbling. He watched Katie bend to place the steaks and nonesuch in the refrigerator. She seemed radiant in her naivete, springy and slim in the simple avacado dress and flipflops. She was a lone flower in a vast field of parasites. Bright white-blond hair hung long and straight to the middle of her back, several strands of which swayed before her unblemished face. The old man's heart felt squashed, in the sure knowledge that it was her innocence that made her such easy prey for all the evil in the world.

¤ ¤ ¤ ¤ ¤

"We shoulda nabbed her tonight," Binny said, peering forward through low branches. "Why piss away time? The sooner we get her upstate, the sooner we got our scratch."

Cementhead, Rocco concluded. "I told you, it's supposed to rain tonight. That's a dirt road we're parked on back there. The van'd leave treadmarks. And you left your damn gloves on the console, as usual."

Binny shrugged, as though the observation were of no significance whatsoever. "So what? We're gonna torch the place. What I need gloves for?"

Almost Never

Rocco was no crime tech but he wasn't stupid. In the joint, you hear about the latest. "They got lasers now, man, and special lights, and some new resin stuff that can lift prints ten years old off charred wood and metal. Our mitts are both on file and you know it. We'd be boy-cunt before we could even blink. We'd both have size-11 assholes by the time we got out." Rocco had already done a nickel in the cut; an abduction rap would put him away for twenty, easy. Binny must've lost half his brain the last time he took a shit. *No way I'm going back to the cut on account of this numbskull.* It wasn't something he ever talked about, but during his nickel, he'd taken it up the backway a few times himself–it felt like taking a Thanksgiving shit in reverse—and he'd sucked more his share of balony ponies too. Half the guys in a fed cut were buttons for the big families in Philly. You fuck with one of *those* guys, you're dead before chow call.

"Yeah, talk about a cake walk," Binny assessed, ignoring his partner's cautions. They'd staked the place out good a couple of times already, and had the routine down pat. Just about every night at seven sharp the kid would take the trail around the woods to the Safeway, pick up groceries, and walk back. A cute little girl, real young, like eight or nine. *The old guy in the chair must have some real dogshit for brains letting a kid that age walk the woods at night,* Rocco speculated. Some people just didn't get it, did they?

Rocco had run up some high markers at the wrong places; even bad guys had bad days. He'd taken five large from shylocks to win back his dump, and hit a losing streak. The shylocks had been Vinchetti's men. They gave him a choice, since he was from the neighborhood and only had one stint on his rap sheet. "You can feed the fish, or you can work for Vinchetti." Rocco didn't like the water. They'd set him up with Binny, to run errands for Vinchetti's lieutenant in Maryland, and to "make grabs." They'd pulled a dozen so far. Malls seemed best, and the safest, but this... Even Rocco had to agree. A cake walk. They couldn't ask for an easier grab. *Almost too easy,* he thought, hunkering down beside Binny, who roved the lit windows with a small pair of Bushnell's. The squat little house sat way back in the woods, off one of the old county logging tracks. No car, no outside lights, no neighbors. From what they could make of the place, there wasn't even a telephone, and it was just the old guy and little girl. Probably the usual story; the kid's folks croak in a car wreck, or maybe mom leaves town with the plumber, and dad takes a bullet in the Gulf thing, so now the geezer's taking care of the kid. And the kid...

Rocco's belly squirmed.

"Would you gander that little peach, man," Binny remarked. The scumbag actually licked his lips. "Vinchetti'll pay double for that kind of soft stuff."

"Why?"

"She's blond. The Yaks pay big money for blond kids that aren't beat."

Yaks referred to the Japanese mob, and beat, in this business, meant that the kid wasn't over twelve. He'd seen some of the shit himself once or twice; sometimes they helped Vinchetti's crew set up when they made a delivery. Rocco had about puked. He was no saint, sure—a pinch, a fence, he'd even run skag in the 70's—but this shit drew the line. Rocco, after all, was born Catholic.

"I was thinking of getting out," he said.

Binny shot him a funky look. "Getting out of what?"

"This whole gig, man. I don't like it. I mean, we're talking about kids, for Christ's sake."

"You ain't getting out of nothing." Binny went back to the binoculars. "Your marker's clean only for as long as you grab for Vinchetti, so don't be stupid. You walk out on him, paisan, and they'll find you the next day in some apartment project laundry room looking like a platter of cold cuts, and they'll blow-torch your cock off for starters."

Rocco frowned. This was probably true. He'd never met Vinchetti—aka Vinnie Shorteyes, on account of he had an eye for short stuff. Vinchetti ran the kiddie porn circuit all along the east coast. What they did was they grabbed kids and used them for videos, then they'd sell the kids to their dope honchos overseas, the Japs, the Burmese. They'd flick the kids on 1/4-inch masters, then dupe the masters and send them out to their lab mail-drops for mass-reproduction. The feds called it "The Underground," and it was a big market. Lot of times, Rocco couldn't sleep. He'd seen the kids' faces, the terror in their eyes, the innocence. He couldn't bear to think of what went on in their heads while Vinchetti's crew set up the cameras and the lights...

"Kids," he muttered. "Christ. Kids."

"Shut up, man," Binny sniped. "You're starting to sound like a stool. If we don't do it, someone else will—fact of fucking life. Besides, we'll bag five grand a pop on this little nookie." Binny looked up, grinning in the dark. "Five grand. That's righteous bucks if you ask me. Shit, we'd be on the street taking down candy stores if Vinchetti hadn't dropped this gig in our laps. And you remember the last guy who tried to book on him? They picked him up in Jersey, autopsied the guy alive in a Red Roof Inn. Then they cut off the fucker's face and fed-exed it to his mother..."

Rocco's mouth went dry. That would be some party. *Thank God my mother's dead,* he thought.

Almost Never

Binny rambled on, "Plus I gotta feeling we're gonna bag more than five large on this one. The old fucker gives the kid cash whenever she goes to the store. You ever see her stop at the bank? He's probably one of these old-fashioned cranks who doesn't believe in banks. Keeps his life's savings in a gym bag under the bed or some shit. We're gonna be walking with some green here, paisan."

Rocco felt distant, barely hearing the words. All he could see just then, and all he could think about...were the kids...

"And I say we take them out tonight, right now."

Rocco ground his teeth. "No way they're sending me up on a kiddie porn bust. I told you, it's gonna rain. We'll leave evidence all over the place."

Binny opened his mouth, to complain further, when suddenly the sky broke. A moment later, it was teeming.

"Okay, man," Binny gave in. "So we do it tomorrow night, then. No ifs, ands, or buts. Got it?"

¤   ¤   ¤   ¤   ¤

"Grandpa?"

Katie leaned over, gently nudged the old man.

"Hey, Grandpa?"

He sat sound asleep in the chair, his head lolled to one side. Katie didn't have the heart to wake him; he was old, he needed his rest. Yesterday, he'd forbidden her to go shopping, but... *I'll go,* she decided. *He can't go. In the chair? It'd take hours!*

Grandpa kept his money behind the kitchen baseboard; Katie plucked out a $20 bill and replaced the board. A long time ago, he'd turned his money into T-bills, whatever they were, and once a year a special cab came out to the house and took him to town where he cashed in some interest. Katie wasn't sure what interest was, either, not that it mattered. Grandpa was a good man, and he always made sure there was enough money for things.

It was already dark when she embarked, dressed in her Smurfs shirt, flipflops, and spangled pants. It would be getting cold in a month or so, and Katie worried about that. Grandpa had some problem where his hands hurt in the cold. With that, and the chair, he had enough problems. The least Katie could do was go to the store.

She moved briskly down the narrow trail through the woods. An owl hooted; moonlight shimmered in the trees. As she quickened her pace, her fine blond hair rose behind her like an aura.

Her big eyes fixed ahead. She remembered what Grandpa said, about how there were some people who would want to do bad things to a little girl like her. Katie didn't understand what those things could be, but that only distressed her more deeply. *Why can't everybody be good?* she ineptly wondered. She and Grandpa never did bad things. *Why would people want to do bad things to us?*

At the grocery store, her heart quickened as she wandered the aisles. She always checked for the things that were on sale. A special on ground beef. Window cleaner two for the price of one. And laundry detergent. She chose the store brand because it was a quarter cheaper than Tide. She knew she was hurrying. She felt antsy and weird in the express line. She wanted to get out of there, and back to the house before Grandpa woke up.

On the way back she failed to notice the big white windowless van parked just off the utility road.

She felt watched all the way back down the trail. She knew she hadn't imagined those two men. Several times when she'd been shopping, they'd followed her around the store, always stopping and turning when she looked back. But they weren't there tonight, she happily realized. Nor did she hear any sounds behind her as she walked the trail. Katie suddenly smiled. They must be gone! Yes, the two men must've gone away, gone to follow someone else.

Katie's smile widened. She skipped back to the house, happily toting her bag of groceries.

¤   ¤   ¤   ¤   ¤

"Blast it, Katie!" Grandpa railed, leaning forward in the chair. "I told you not to go to the store! I told you—"

"Don't worry, Grandpa," Katie cut in.

"Don't worry! How am I supposed to not worry with that pair of weird ones followin' you around?"

Katie closed the door and began to put away the groceries. "You were asleep, Grandpa. I didn't want to wake you up. And besides, those two men are gone."

Grandpa's stern visage laxed a bit, and he eased back into the chair. "You mean they weren't followin' you tonight?"

"Nope," Katie was happy to inform. "And they weren't at the store either. They're gone."

Grandpa considered this. "Well. Hmm. Maybe they are, but you still shoulda woke me up. Can't be too careful, not these days."

Katie's young face beamed at her grandfather. "Don't worry, Grandpa. I told you. Those men are gone. I'm sure of it."

¤   ¤   ¤   ¤   ¤

"Yeah, I'm sure of it," Binny acknowledged, focusing the binoculars from their low lookout in the trees. "It's a gas stove, all right. Makes the place easier to torch."

Almost Never

Rocco's face felt like a mask of wood. He had the timer ready to go, a simple rig yet an ever-reliable one—a metal-case watch with a plastic face strapped around a six-volt drycell battery. You tape the positive lead to the watch casing, and the negative to a thin nail melted through the plastic face. A piece of Jetex had been tied between the leads. When the minute hand made contact with the nail (the watch had no second hand) the circuit was made, the Jetex burned off at 800 degrees, and BOOM!

Rocco, however, wasn't thinking of pyrotechnics at this precise moment. He'd dreamed again last night, of the bleak faces of the children, of their vacant thousand-yard stares. *This is some bad shit,* he very simply thought. In a queer moment of vertigo, he looked at the back of Binny's head. God, it would be so easy. Rocco packed a Smith Model 49 in a clip holster under his shirt. It would be so easy to slip that hammerless snubnose baby out and pop Binny a nice .38 semijacket right in his sick skull...

And in the next moment, Rocco found that his right hand had moved to the revolver's slim grip.

"I called Vinchetti's crew and told them about the girl." Binny never took his eyes off the binocs. "Guaranteed them we'd have her in Jersey by morning. This time tomorrow night, we'll be partying hearty, paisan, with green in our pockets and neck-deep in snatch."

Rocco's fingers trailed off his piece. Vinchetti. Rocco knew he'd have to be very careful. Popping Binny right here would be suicide. He'd never beat Vinchetti's hawks without a plan. He needed papers, and cash. There was a printer he knew in Davidsonville who did good work; for a couple of grand he'd set Rocco up with a phony driver's license, SS number, birth cert, and an MVA record that would wash right up to a fed-level check. Good fake ID was the only way he'd get away from Vinchetti. There was only one option: *Just one more job. I'll do this one last job, take the cash, get my papers. Then I'll cap this evil fucker and disappear for good.* There was no other way. To buy good papers, he'd have to do this job on the old man and the girl first.

"Aw, God," Binny remarked. "Check it out."

Rocco took the glasses and focused up. The old man was sitting in the lit kitchen, at the table. "Big deal. He's eating dinner."

"No, no, man," Binny corrected. His breath was hot on Rocco's neck as he leaned over. "The bathroom. Tell me that ain't the sweetest stuff you ever saw. Vinchetti's gonna love us. That right there is pure angel food cake, partner."

You fuckin' slime, Rocco thought when he moved the binoculars. The kid stood buck naked, her blond hair tied up as she stepped out of the tub. She began to towel herself off under the bright light.

"Yeah, man." Binny grinned. "I could eat that myself."

Rocco reserved comment, electing instead to think, *I can't wait to take you down, Binny.* It provided a glorious fantasy. *Once I get my papers, I'm gonna put your fucked-up brains all over the floor.*

Binny chuckled. "Let's hit it."

They emerged from the trees, breaking off. Rocco's head pounded with each step. His last job, sure—but that didn't do the kid any good. She'd still be meat on Vinchetti's porno slab, and they'd have to kill the old man. *Just don't think about it,* he commanded himself. It was the lesser of two evils, that was the only way he could look at it. The back window popped open with just one press of the crowbar. Rocco climbed in.

A bedroom. Dark, but the door was open, and down the hall he could see the kitchen light, and the old man at the table.

Rocco set down the timer to free his hands; he moved into the hall. The kid was still in the bathroom—the light glowed under the door. Binny already had a cord around the old man's neck by the time Rocco made it to the kitchen.

A pitiful sight. Binny grinned as the old man squirmed in the wheelchair, gagging. "Let him talk," Rocco complained.

"Just havin' a little fun first."

The old man's crabbed hands roved to and fro like a drunk conductor; his thin chest heaved. Just as the aged face began to turn blue, Binny loosened the garrotte.

"Blasted bastards!" the old man wheezed, hacking and bringing his arthritic fingers to his throat.

Binny grinned down. "Get to work, Roc. Me and Grandpa here have some talking to do."

"Get the hell out of my house, the both of you!" gargled Grandpa. "Ya got no right!"

"Sure we do, Gramps." Binny tightened the garrotte a bit. "We know you got cash stashed in this cozy little dump our yours." A little tighter. "So how about it, Gramps? Where's the money?"

Jaundiced eyes bulged in their sockets; the wizened mouth struggled. "Let him talk!" Rocco yelled. "You're killing him!"

"Relax." Again, Binny loosened the cord. The old man slumped, sucking breath and pointing to the floor. Eventually he was able to croak, "Baseboard. By the stove. Take it."

Binny knelt and pried out the board. "Christ, Roc! It's the fuckin' motherlode!" He slid out bands of bills, twenties and fifties. "There must be ten or fifteen grand here, man!"

"Closer to twenty," the old man coughed, waving a worm-veined hand. "Take it and get out of here. Leave us be."

"Oh, we will, Gramps." Binny chuckled and rose. "After we're done killing your tired ass. Huh, Roc?"

Rocco smirked, then suddenly jerked around. Feet pounded. A little blur swirled and at once small hands were dragging at him. The little girl jumped up onto Rocco's back and yanked his hair, shrieking: "Leave my grandpa alone!"

Binny laughed uproariously. Rocco turned in hunched circles, trying to keep the kid's fingers out of his eyes. When he flipped her to the floor, she sprang right back up and socked her little foot square into his groin. Rocco went down.

"Look at this!" Binny laughed. "One of Vinchetti's bulldogs is getting his ass whipped by a little kid!"

Rocco tried to wrestle the girl down, but she slipped out of his grasp like a greased lizard. *Shit!* Rocco thought. The girl banged through the door to the basement and scampered down.

Rocco got up, sputtering. At least there were no windows in the basement. No way the kid could go out.

"Go get her, killer," Binny mocked, then got back behind the old man, who futilely whipped his hands around. "Ya blasted punks!" he rasped. "Don't you hurt that little girl, I'm warnin' ya! Why, goddamn it all, if I wasn't in this blasted chair—"

"But you *are* in the chair, Gramps, you *are* in the chair," Binny ripped off that great old Bette Davis line.

Now the old man pleaded, his fine white hair sticking up as his face strained in the most desperate despair. "I'm beggin' ya not to do this. I got more money in the bank. I'll give it to ya, all of it. Just leave us alone…"

"This'll do us just fine, pops," Binny said. "See, we gotta deliver that sweet little girl of yours upstate tonight, so our friends can take some pretty pictures of her. And that means it's time for you to say good-night."

The old man lurched, then hacked. Binny deftly brought the blade of his Gerber Mark IV straight across the throat.

Blood gushed, pumping. The old man hitched twice in the chair, gargled a final invective, then died.

Rocco felt enslimed. *Look at us,* he thought. *Two back-alley thugs fucking up little kids' lives and killing old men in wheelchairs. Christ almighty.*

"Don't just stand there, man," Binny complained, scooping up the banded cash off the floor. "Go get the girl. I'll get the joint ready to torch."

"Timer's in the back room," Rocco said. His heart felt sunken as he slid out the flask of Roche Pharmaceutical chloroform. "I'll bring her up now."

"Fuckin'-A. And be careful. That little hellfire's probably down there waiting for you with a pitchfork."

Or maybe a gun, Rocco mused. He almost wished it. He almost wished the kid would blow both their asses away.

"Get a move on!"

Rocco descended the creaky wood steps. Light wobbled from a suspended bulb. The little girl sat sobbing in the corner, her face long with despair and glazed by tears. Rocco poured some chloroform into his handkerchief.

What could he say? What could he tell this innocent little child? The chloroform wafted up, sickly sweet. "Come on, kid. You gotta come with us."

"You're the two men who've been following me," she sobbed.

"Yeah," Rocco said.

"But why?"

Why? The question haunted him. "I don't know why, kid. It's just the way things are sometimes."

The tears streamed. Strands of fine blond hair stuck to her face. "Grandpa said you wanted to do bad things to me. We haven't done bad things to you. Why do you want to do bad things to us?"

Rocco gulped. A simple question with no answer. He stared at her as her wet face peered up, her little feet tucked under her legs as she crouched in defeated terror and confusion. She wore a long flannel nightgown with rabbits on it. *Rabbits,* Rocco thought. *Bunny rabbits. She's just a little innocent kid, and I'm gonna deliver her to a bunch of child pornographers tonight. What kind of a monster am I?*

But he had no recourse, did he? The specter of Vinchetti's hatchetmen loomed behind him, a dark surging shape.

"I'm sorry, kid. I really am. But I got no choice."

Rocco moved forward, leaning down, and reached for the girl.

¤   ¤   ¤   ¤   ¤

Binny rolled the dead old man out of the way, into the corner, then bagged the rest of the cash. *What a fuckin' haul!* Not only would they walk with decent scratch for the kid, but there was this in the baseboard. *Binny could use a beer,* he thought. *Yeah, a tall cold one. All this hard work makes a guy thirsty.* But when he opened the fridge all he found were some steaks and hamburger. Not a can of Bud to be found.

Rocco, he thought next, walking to the back bedroom. It was a sour thought. The guy was losing his edge, and this wasn't good. A job like this you don't bring your conscience. What was the big deal? It was like anything. When somebody wanted something, you got it for them, so long as the money was right. Supply and demand. That was the American Way, wasn't it?

He came back to the kitchen with the timer. Yeah, piece of fucking cake. "Hey, Roc!" he yelled. "Sometime this year, huh?" Christ. The gas range looked ancient. He figured they'd set the timer for a couple of hours, give the dump plenty of time to fill up. So what if he started a forest fire? That wasn't his problem. Smoky the Fucking Bear could worry about that.

What the fuck? he thought. He'd turned on the gas knobs, but no pilots came on, and no tell-tale hiss. He put his ear to the burner. Nothing. Then he slid the range out to take a peek.

The gas lines weren't even hooked up. *This thing hasn't been used in years,* he realized. And that didn't make a lick of sense, did it? A busted range and a fridge full of meat. He noticed no hotplates, no microwaves. What the hell did they cook their meat on?

This was a good question, not that it really mattered. What *did* matter, though, a moment later when he turned to the corner, was this:

The wheelchair was empty.

¤ ¤ ¤ ¤ ¤

"Why?" the little girl sobbed just as Rocco stooped to press the handkerchief to her mouth. "Why? We haven't done anything bad to you!"

Rocco stared at the little thing. For a moment, he couldn't move. *What am I—* Then he dropped the chloroform-soaked rag.

The little girl was right.

"Fuck it," he said aloud. "I ain't doing it any more. The old man was already dead...but the kid? *It ain't gonna happen. What I do right now is I go back upstairs and I pop Binny. Then I take the cash and split, and Vinchetti never gets his paws on the girl. If she ID's me in a mugshot, then that's my tough luck.*

"Relax, kid," he said. "Your grandpa's dead, and I'm really sorry about that. But ain't nothing gonna happen to you. Things won't be that bad."

"It's-it's too late," the little girl said.

What did she mean by that? Rocco squinted at her. "Look, kid. I'm giving you a break here. I know it's hard but–"

—then his words were severed, cut off cleanly as a knife through yarn. Cut off by the wavering, high-pitched scream that exploded next from upstairs:

"HOLY JESUS CHRIST GET THE FUCK AWAY FROM ME!"

Rocco shucked his five-shot snub. His heart hammered as he raced up the stairs. Binny continued to scream, loud and hard–a sound more like a bad flywheel at high rev—when Rocco three-pointed into the kitchen. The first thing he saw made his eyes bulge.

The old man's wheelchair with no old man in it. No way the guy could've lived! Binny'd cut his throat clear to the bone.

And the second thing he saw...

Binny flailed frenetically on the floor beneath a dark form. It was not a dog which vigorously yanked out his partner's lower g.i. tract; it was a wolf. A big wolf.

Rocco emptied his bladder while he simultaneously emptied the Smith snub into the animal's side. Binny flinched, blood bubbling from his mouth. The huge animal paused only a moment at the shots, bit off Binny's face, then turned. Its great angular head rose, lips peeling back to show rows of crooked teeth the size of masonry nails. Jet black eyes bore into Rocco's stare. The eyes seemed mocking, even amused. Then the creature lunged.

Rocco missed having his throat bitten out by all of half an inch. He jerked back into the basement entrance, pulled the door closed, and fell head over heels to the bottom of the steps.

The little girl was standing now, her arms crossed over the rabbit-printed nightgown.

"See?" she said defiantly. "I told you."

Rocco's head spun. Upstairs he could hear the wolf return to its meal, bones crunching like potato chips. The image of the little girl bobbed back and forth like something floating.

"Your grandfather's a—"

"He's been that way for a long time," the girl said. "But he's always been good. You should've been good, too."

Rocco stared at her. Upstairs, the crunching went on and on.

"Nobody has to be bad. It's better to be good," the little girl philosophized. "I'm the same way. Just little animals and things." She pointed to the corner of the basement, to little piles of animals that looked dried as husks.

"Never people," she said. Then her face seemed to flutter, as if adrift in an intricate confusion. "Well, almost never."

Rocco felt paralyzed. He couldn't get up. He couldn't even look away from the big, glittering eyes.

Almost Never

"You're just like your grandfather," Rocco croaked.
"No I'm not," the little girl said.
Did she smile?
"I'm a lot worse."
She moved forward very slowly. Her twin incisors glinted like nails.

Almost Never
Afterword

An elemental trimming of "Almost Never" may seem familiar. It's always seemed to me that the very worst aggregate evil that the human species can take credit for is child pornography. Not just child abuse but child abuse as spectacle for profit. "Xipe," in this collection, involves this topic, so does my novella "The Pig," my collaborative novel (with Elizabeth Steffen) Portrait of the Psychopath as a Young Woman, *and my short story "ICU," which will appear in Avon's* 999: A Millennium Anthology. *You ask me, anyone involved with child pornography should be executed in public. Televised. Better yet, drain all his blood for the Red Cross and confiscate his organs for transplant needs. Then grind up what's left for crop fertilizer.*

Nevertheless, "Almost Never" is a piece I'd been dying to write for a long time, something that bisected traditional genre elements with modern evils. I didn't want it to be too hard, though, because, to be honest, I wanted very much to get a second story into Cemetery Dance. *I kept a slightly lighter edge in mind here, because Rich Chizmar, the magazine's award-wining editor, had previously told me that he didn't particularly dig my harder core stuff. So I wrote this one and was honored to receive my second acceptance to his cool mag, then was doubly honored that Rich included it in his mammoth anthology* The Best of Cemetery Dance.

Rich is a great guy; the only thing I can say bad about him is he doesn't like the Yankees. Come on. How can anyone *not like the Yankees?*

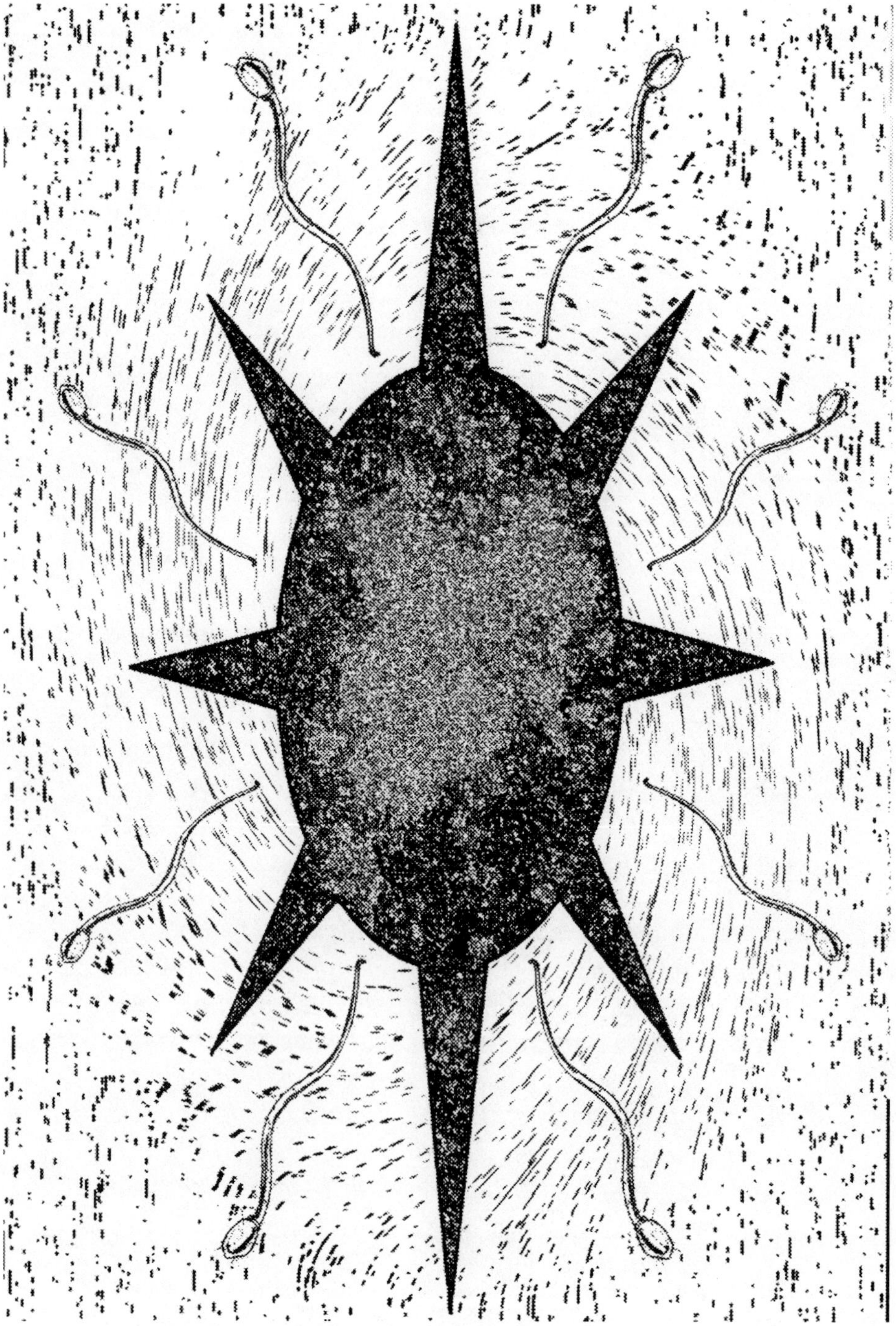

THE HOLE IN THE WALL

FOR FIFTY YEARS she lived with me in the house.
 I never knew her name.
 I only saw her twice—
 —through the hole in the wall.

¤   ¤   ¤   ¤   ¤

I'd inherited my uncle's estate when I was twenty-five. Never had to work again. Computer games all day, beer and tit flicks all night.
 Tough life, huh?
 That first day, half-drunk, I moved in. There was a hole in my bedroom wall, and when I looked in it…

¤   ¤   ¤   ¤   ¤

D.T.s already? I wondered. *Hallucinations? I'm looking in a hole in the wall and seeing a beautiful woman…*
 Slim, naked, 34Cs and hourglass curves. It was crazy, but there she was, holding up a candle in the crawlspace.
 "Who are you!"
 "Put it in," she whispered.
 Yeah, I'm drunk, all right. I'm seeing things. Now her mouth was at the hole.
 The hole just under waist-level.
 No…
 The wet tongue licked full, pouty lips.
 "Come on."
 I'm crazy, I reasoned. *So what's the harm?*
 Right?
 What would *you* do?

I put my cock in the hole and let her blow me.

The best blowjob of my life, and the first of countless thousands.

¤ ¤ ¤ ¤ ¤

I never told anyone. What? Hey, guys, a beautiful naked girl blew me through a hole in the wall?

Nope.

I figured I'd sleep off the D.T.s, but her silken whisper tickled me from sleep.

"Promise to never look in here again, never ask any questions, never tell...and I'll do it whenever you want."

"Sure," I chuckled. "You got a deal." Since I was hallucinating, I decided to seal the promise. I stumbled up and did it again. Wham. Right down the hatch.

Then I passed out.

¤ ¤ ¤ ¤ ¤

Next day, the hole was still there. So was the succulent mouth. All I could do was laugh at my madness when I put it in again. And again and again and again.

And that's how it went...

Three or four times a day–*every* day—for fifty years.

¤ ¤ ¤ ¤ ¤

Never got married, never even went on a date.

Who needs love when all you gotta do is stick your John Thursday in a hole in the wall for the best action in town?

Soon I realized that she was no hallucination, she was real. I figured she must be sneaking downstairs every night for food and water. Probably some trapdoor I didn't know about. I never even tried to find it.

And I never broke the promise. I never asked, and I never looked.

Just kept sticking my pecker into that hole and getting head like you wouldn't believe.

¤ ¤ ¤ ¤ ¤

Sure, I was *tempted* to look. I remembered how beautiful she was—a Penthouse Pet—and I'd think about that image whenever she was doing it. Even after years, after decades.

But after decades, I didn't *want* to look. I was old, and so was she. A shriveled old headqueen on the other side of my wall. Breasts sagging, wrinkles, varicose veins.

No, that first image was enough.

Not bad for an old man, either, huh? Still getting it up three, four times a day, still popping a wad every time?

Never got sick of it either, not even after all those years. That's how *good* it was.

The Hole in the Wall

That and the image of her that I knew I'd take to my grave.

¤ ¤ ¤ ¤ ¤

Which I'm one foot out of now. Cirrhosis. Too old for a transplant. Fuck.

But you want to know what happened, right?

¤ ¤ ¤ ¤ ¤

Couple weeks ago, I put the Captain in the hole but—
Nothing.
"You can look now," came the silken words
So I did...
Her face was as youthful and beautiful as that first day.
"I'm full now," the lips spake. "I'm a vessel."
Then she backed away to show me her body.
Bulbous. Obese. Breasts like feedbags, a stomach large as a medicine ball. Jiggling amid a *sloshing* sound.
A vessel.
Full.
Full of *me*.
White light bright as the sun filled the crawlspace, then she was gone, taking fifty years of *me* with her.

¤ ¤ ¤ ¤ ¤

Think what you want, I don't care. I'm dying. My life is over and so is this.
No regrets, though.
I mean, this was *really good head*.

THE HOLE IN THE WALL
AFTERWORD

All right, yeah. I wrote this one while I was drinking. Isolationism mixed with primal male existential sex-fantasy by way of the Heineken brewery. There was an anthology soliciting "short-shorts," so I tapped this out only to discover the anth had been closed for months.

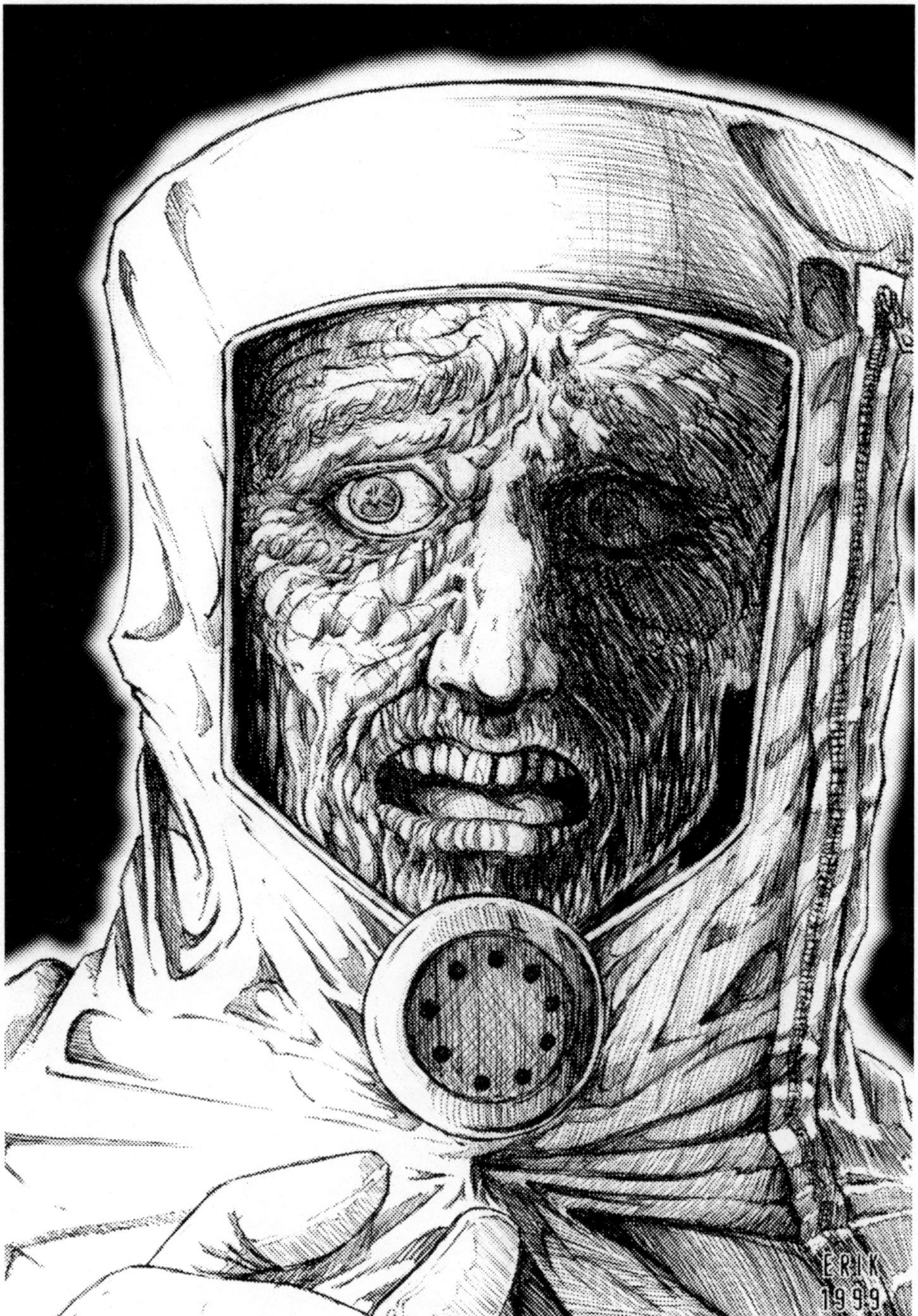
ERIK
1999

THE SEEKER

BOCK'S EYES FLICKED up. "Something buzzing the hopper, Sarge."

Balls, SFC John Ruben thought. He unlocked the alert safe behind the driver's compartment and removed the CEIC binder which contained today's prefixes and code dailies.

Then: "Victor Echo Two Six, this is X-ray One. Acknowledge."

Bock stalled over the radio and AN/FRA shift-converter. "Who the fuck's X-ray One, Sarge? Division?"

Ruben checked the codebook. "It's Air Force Recovery Alert Operations. Gonna get shit on by fly boys again. Answer it."

"X-ray One, this is Victor Echo Two Six. Go ahead."

"Proceed to incoming grid. Target perimeter positive."

Bock held the mike away from himself like a chunk of rancid meat.

Ruben could not believe what he'd just heard. The pause hovered in static, then Ruben grabbed the mike. "X-ray One, this is Victor Echo Two Six Tango Charlie. Repeat your last transmission."

"Proceed to incoming grid," the radio answered back. "Target perimeter positive."

His memory struggled with the reality of fright. The sequence seemed miles away. "Status white. Progress code?"

"Red."

"Recall code?"

"None."

"Directive order?"

"Directive order is standby at target perimeter. This is NOT a drill. This is NOT an exercise. Assume SECMAT alert state orange."

"Orders logged," Ruben droned. *Holy mother of shit,* he thought.

"Victor Echo Two Six, this is X-ray One. Out."

Ruben hung up the AN's mike. Bock was sweating. Jones, the track's driver, craned back from the t-bar. "What gives, Sarge!"

"Calm down," Ruben eased. But he could not calm the thought: *This has never happened before.*

"We're at war," Bock muttered.

The alert had sounded at 0412; they'd been in the field nearly a day now. Victor Echo Two Six was a modified M2 armored personnel carrier, fully CBN equipped, and its crew was what the U.S. Army Chemical Corps termed a hazmat field detection team. Their primary general search perimeter was familiar open scrubby land; they'd tracked this terrain dozens of times on past alerts. Ruben, the TC, hadn't been worried until now—until he'd heard the magic words: *Target perimeter positive.*

"What are you guys, a bunch of dickheads?" he countered. "This is a CONUS alert. If we were at war, the whole state would be a clusterfuck by now, and the op stat would've been jerked up a lot higher than a CONUS. We'd be at Defcon Two at least. Think with your brains instead of your asses. If this was war, why would they recall every unit in the division except us?"

"This is shit, Sarge!" Jones was not appeased. "Something's really fucked up!"

"Calm down. We're not at war."

Bock was shaking, muttering, "It fucking figures. I'm two weeks short, and this shit happens."

"You guys are shitting your pickles for nothing. We had four of these last year, remember? One of the early warning sites probably picked up something in our telemetry line. It's probably another meteor, or a piece of space junk. Relax, will you?"

"Here it comes," Bock announced.

The XN/PCD 21 began to click. The hopper freqs shifted through their 5-digit discriminators. Then the mobile printer spat out their destination grid.

Bock slid out the map book, teeth chattering. Jones' face was turning to paste. They were just boys, and they were shit-scared, but Ruben had to wonder if he was too.

He put his hands on their shoulders. "We gotta get our shit together, girls. We're hardcore Army decon ass-kickers, and we don't piss in our BDU's every time an alert directive goes up. We ain't afraid of nothin'. We eat napalm for breakfast and piss diesel fuel, and when we die and go to hell, we're gonna shove the devil's head up his ass and take the fuck over. Right now we gotta job to do, and I gotta know if you guys are with me."

The Seeker

Bock wiped sweat off his brow with his sleeve. "Hardcore, Sarge. I'm no pussy. My shit's tight, and I'm with you."

"Jonesy?"

Jones gave the thumbs up. "Hell on fucking wheels, man! Nobody lives forever, so let's roll!"

"Hardcore," Ruben approved. "Squared-fucking-away goddamn die-for-decon outstanding."

"Let's kick ass!" Bock yelled.

"Decon!" Jones chanted.

Ruben handed Jones the grid. "Get this twin-tracked Detroit coffin rolling, Jonesy. Hammer down."

Jones revved the throttle, whooping. The track's turbocharged Cummins V8 roared. Bock strapped in behind the commo gear. Ruben had enlivened them, but for how long? What was happening out there? *What's waiting for us?* he wondered.

"Proceed to target perimeter positive," he said.

¤   ¤   ¤   ¤   ¤

How powerful is the power of truth?

It was more a motto than a question. It was all that motivated him.

The writer didn't believe in God, for instance. Now, if he *saw* God, then he'd believe in Him. He believed in nothing he couldn't see, but that's why he was here, wasn't it? To see? Behind him, the bus disappeared into darkness. *I see that,* he thought.

Ahead, the sign blazed in blue neon: CROSSROADS.

"I see that, too. A drink, to help me think."

But then he heard a word, or thought he did. It was not his voice, nor a thought of his own. He heard it in his head:

SUSTENANCE.

So he was hearing voices now? Perhaps he'd been drinking too much. Or, *Not enough,* he considered, half-smiling. *All great writers drink*. He could not dispel the notion, however, that he was entering something more than just a small-town tavern.

Dust eddied from the wood floor's seams when he trod in and set down his bag. Yes, here was a real "slice of life" bar: a dump. Its frowziness, its cheap tables, dartboards, pinball machines—its overall *Vacuus spiritum*—delighted him. This was reality, and reality was what he sought.

Seek, he thought, *and ye shall find.*

"Welcome to Crossroads, stranger," greeted the rube barkeep. The writer mused over the allegorical possibilities of the bar's name. The keep had a basketball beer belly and teeth that would compel an oral hygienist to consider other career options. "What can I get ya?" he asked.

"Alcohol. Impress me with your mixological prowess, sir."

Only three others graced these eloquent confines. A sad-faced guy in a white shirt sat beside a short, bosomed redhead. They seemed to be arguing. Closer up sat an absolutely obese woman with long blond hair, drinking dark beer and eating an extra-large pizza. Her weight caused the stool's legs to visibly bend.

You're here to seek, the writer reminded himself. *So seek.*

"May I join you?"

The blonde swallowed, nodding. "You ain't from around here."

"No," the writer said, and sat. Then the keep slapped a shooter down. It was yellow. "House special, stranger."

It looked like urine. "What *is* it?"

"We call it the Piss Shooter."

The writer's brow rose. "It's not, uh… *piss,* is it?"

The keep laughed. "'Course not! It's vodka and Galliano."

The writer sniffed. *Smells all right.* "Okay, here's to—what? Ah, yes. Here's to formalism." He drank it down.

"Well?"

"Not bad. Very good, actually." He reached for his wallet.

"Uh-uh, stranger. That there's a tin roof."

"What?"

The keep rolled his eyes. "It's on the house."

"What'cha want in a dull's-shit town like this?" inquired the fat blonde, chewing. Her breasts were literally large as human heads. "Ain't nothin' around for fifty miles in any direction."

Isolatus proximus. "I'm a writer," the writer said. "I travel all over the country. I need to see different things, different people. I need to see life in its different temporal stratas."

"Stratas," the fat blonde said, nodding.

"I come to remote towns like this because they're variegated. They exist separately from the rest of the country's societal mainstream. Towns like this are more *real.* I'm a writer, but in a more esoteric sense… I'm…" He thought about this. He thought hard. He lit a cigarette and finished. "I'm a seeker."

"You've got to be shitting me!" the guy in the white shirt shouted to the short red-haired girl. "You've slept with FIVE OTHER GUYS this week? Jeeeeesus CHRIST!"

She sipped her Tequila Moonrise reflectively, then corrected, "Sorry. Not five. Six. I forgot about Craig." She grinned. "His nickname's Mr. Meat Missile."

"Jeeeeesus CHRIST!" White shirt exploded.

"He must be in love with her," the writer remarked.

"He don't get her pussy off," the fat blonde said.

The Seeker

The keep was polishing a glass. "What's that you were sayin'? You're a *seeker?*"

"Well, that's an abstraction, of course. What I mean is I'm on a quest. I'm searching for some elusive uncommon denominator to perpetuate my aesthetic ideologies. For a work of fiction to exist within any infrastructure of resolute meaning, its peripheries must reflect certain elements of truth. I don't mean objective truths. I'm talking about ephemeral things: *unconscious* impulses, *psychological* propensities, etc.—the *underside* of what we think of as the human experience."

"I've never heard such shit in my life!" White Shirt was still yelling at the redhead. "Those other guys don't love you! *I* love you!"

The redhead doodled indifferently on a napkin. "But I don t want to be loved," she said. Then she grinned as intensely as an indian devil mask. "I just want to be fucked."

"*Jeeeeeesus Chriiiiiiiiiiiist!*"

"You gotta tune 'em out," advised the fat blonde, now halfway done with the pizza and starting her third dark beer. Grease glossed her lips and chin.

"The seeker," said the keep. "I like that."

"But what exactly do you write about?" asked the blonde.

"*What* I write about isn't the point, it's *how* I write about it." And then, with no warning, the thought returned: *How powerful is the power of truth?* The writer smoked his cigarette deep. "Honesty is the vehicle of my aesthete. The truth of fiction can only exist in its bare words. Pardon my obtuseness, but it's the *mode,* the *application* of the vision which must transcend the overall tangibilities. Prose mechanics, I mean— the structural manipulation of syntactical nomenclatures in order to affect particularized transpositions of imagery."

"Oh," said the fat blonde. "I thought you meant, like, fucking'n shit like that."

The writer frowned.

He swigged another Piss Shooter, another tin roof. The fat blonde's pizza lay thick with extra cheese, anchovies, and big chunks of sausage beneath a sheen of grease. Her stomach made fish tank noises as she voraciously ate and drank.

"Why, why, why?" White Shirt looked close to tears, or a schizoaffective episode, staring at the redhead. "At least tell me why I'm not good enough anymore?"

"You don't want to know," she nonchalantly replied.

White Shirt hopped off his stool to stalk around her. Anger made his face appear corrugated. "Go ahead! Tell me! Spit it out! I WANT TO KNOW!"

The redhead shrugged. "Your dick's not big enough."

Oh, dear, thought the writer.

White Shirt's low moan issued out like that of a just-gelded walrus. He stumbled away crosseyed, and staggered out of the bar.

The keep and fat blonde ignored the outburst. The redhead looked at the writer, smiled, and said, "Hey, he wanted the truth, so I gave it to him."

Truth, thought the writer. Suddenly, he felt empty, desolate.

"But if you're a seeker," posed the keep, "What'cha seekin'?"

"Ah, the universal question." The writer raised a finger, as if to preamble a scintillating wisdom. "And the answer is this. The true seeker never knows what he's seeking until he finds it."

The fat blonde's wet eating noises ceased; she'd finished the entire pizza. "Here's something for you to write about," she said. She leaned over and kissed the writer on the mouth.

Her lips tasted of grease and cheese. But actually the kiss inspired him. Her mouth opened and closed over his, tongue probing unabashed. The writer found himself growing aroused. *Truth,* he thought frivolously. *Ephemeral reality.* This was it, wasn't it? Spontaneous human interface, inexplicably complex yet baldly simple. Synaptic and chemical impulses of the brain meshed with someone's lifetime of learned behavior. It was these simple truths that he lived for. They nourished him. *Human truth is my sustenance,* he thought, and remembered the voice he'd heard. Yes, sustenance.

The fat blonde's kiss grew ravenous. Then—

urrrrrrp

She threw up directly into the writer's mouth.

It had come in a single, heaving gust. He tasted everything: warm beer, lumps of half digested sausage and pizza dough, and bile—lots of bile. Utter disgust bulged his eyes and seized his joints. Then came a second, and larger, gust, which she projected right into his lap.

The writer fell off his stool.

"There," said the blonde. "Write about that."

"Ooooo-eee!" remarked the keep. "That one was a doozy, huh?"

The writer, flat on his back and in shock, could only groan, staring up. The heavy, hot blanket of vomit lay thick from chin to crotch; it oozed down his legs slow as lava when he got up. He spat immediately, of course, and incessantly, and out flew several chunks of sausage and strings of flecked slime. Almost blind, he staggered for the door.

"Come again... seeker," laughed the keep.

"Hope you liked the pizza," bid the fat blonde.

The writer grabbed his suitcase and stumbled out. The dusk in the

The Seeker

sky had bled to full dark, and it was hot outside. He reeked, drenched. He was mortified. *Human truth is my sustenance?* he thought. *Jesus.* The awful tinge in his mouth seemed to buzz, and he could still taste the sausage.

Then he heard the voice again, not in his ears, in his head.

What was it?

He stood stock-still in the empty street, sopped in vomit.

¤ ¤ ¤ ¤ ¤

The power of truth? He'd come here seeking truth and all he'd gotten was puked on. And he was hearing voices, too. *Great,* he thought. *Fantastic.* But he had to find a motel, get showered and changed.

He strayed up the main drag, aimless. Shops were closed, houses were dark. The bus station was closed too, and in his wandering he found not one motel.

Then he saw the church.

It sat back quaintly behind some trees, its clean white walls lambent in the night. What relieved him was that it looked *normal.* The front doors stood open and, within, candles could be seen.

He entered and crossed the nave. The pews were empty. Ahead, past the chancel, a shadow lingered, mumbling low words like an incantation.

It was a priest, reading rites before an open coffin.

"Excuse me, father," the writer said. "I need to know—"

The priest turned, chubby in black raiments. He was glaring. In the coffin lay the corpse of an old woman.

"What!"

"I'm new in town. Are there any motels?"

"Motels? Here?" the priest snapped. "Of course not!"

The writer's eyes flicked to the open coffin. "Do you by chance know when the next bus arrives?"

"How dare you come in here now!" the priest outraged. He pointed abruptly to the coffin. "Can't you see my mother's died?"

"Sorry, father," the writer groped but thought, *God!* He hurried back out. In the street he felt strange, not desolate as before, but woozy, disconnected. *Is it the town, or is it me?* A sudden and profuse flash of sweat made his vomit-drenched shirt feel like a coat of mucus.

The sweat was a herald, like a trumpet—

Oh, no.

—for the voice:

SEEKER. SEEK!

A block down, the sign glowed over the transom: POLICE

His footsteps echoed round his head like a halo as he trotted up.

Surely the police would know about the next bus. He pushed through the door, was about to speak, but froze.

A big cop with chopburns glared at him. "What'cha want, buddy? I'm busy."

"I…" the writer attempted. The cop was busy, all right. He stood behind a long-haired kid who'd been handcuffed to a chair. A tourniquet had been fashioned about the kid's neck via a cord and nightstick.

"Okay, punk," warned the cop. "No more bullshit. Where's them drugs?"

The kid, of course, couldn't have answered if he'd wanted to. He was being choked. The mouth moved in panic within the strained, ballooning face.

"Still not talkin', huh?" The cop gave the tourniquet another twist.

"What the hell are you doing?" shouted the writer.

"Police business. This kid's got drugger written all over him. Sells the shit to kindergarten kids probably. All that crack and PCP, you now? We gotta rough 'em up a little; it's the only way to get anything out of 'em."

Rough them up a little? The writer stared, flabbergasted. The cop twisted the tourniquet all the way down, until the cord creaked. The kid's body stiffened up in the chair, his face turning blue.

"Talk, punk. Where's your stash? Who's your bagman?"

"How can he talk!" the writer shouted the logical question. "You've got a tourniquet around his fucking neck!"

"Scram, buddy. This is a police matter." The cop paused and looked down. "Aw, shit, there he went." The kid twitched a few times, then fell limp, swollen-faced in death.

Madness, the writer thought.

The cop was unwinding the tourniquet, taking off the cuffs. "Just a drugger, no loss. No point in wastin' it, either." The cop gave the writer a comradely look. "Girl pussy, boy pussy, s'all pink on the inside, right, buddy? Help me get his pants off so's we can poke him 'fore he's cold."

A sign on the wall read *To Protect and Serve.* The writer, brain thumping, teetered out of the station.

Phone, he thought dumbly. He abandoned his suitcase in the street and staggered on. *Something's happened here. Got to call someone, get some help.* The houses set back off the street looked harmless. He knocked on the first door. A middle-aged man answered it—

"Yes? Can I help you, young man?"

"I…" the writer attempted. The man wore eyeshadow and cherry-red lipstick. He also wore panties, garters, and stockings. Stainless-steel clamps were screwed down on his nipples, distending the fleshy ends.

"Sporty, wouldn't you say?"

The Seeker

"Huh?"

The man lowered his frilled panties, revealing a penis and scrotum glittery with safety pins. One pin pinched closed the end of the foreskin.

"Uh...sporty, yes," the writer said.

"Would you care to touch it?"

"Uh, well, no–"

The writer jogged off. At the second house he peered through the storm door and saw a beautiful nude woman chasing a giant St. Bernard, and a man at the third house stood grinning on his porch rail, a noose around his neck. "Fly, Fleance! Fly!" he quoted Shakespeare, and stepped off the rail. Heavy, tonerous thuds greeted the writer at the fourth house. WHACK-WHACK-WHACK! WHACK-WHACK-WHACK! In the kitchen window, he saw a man very contentedly cracking open a baby's head with a large meat tenderizer while an aproned woman prepared a fry pan in the background. The man pried the cranium apart and began to spoon the tender brains into a bowl. "Olive oil or canola?" the man asked the wife.

The writer foundered away, gagging, and tripped back into the street. The impact of vision made him feel sledgehammered in the face. He'd seen enough; he didn't want to be a seeker anymore—he just wanted to go home. Then the sweat rushed again, and the voice, like a raddled chord, fell back into his head:

BUT THERE'S SO MUCH, SO MUCH FOR US TO SEEK.

Whatever did that mean? Without reservation, the writer bent over and threw up. This seemed the logical thing to do, an obligation, in fact, after all he'd seen. *Madness,* he repeated, urping it up spasm after spasm like a human sludge-pump. Ropes of saliva dangled off his lips as his stomach rocketed out its contents. The wet splattering crackled down the street.

Oh, what a day.

Done, he felt worse, he felt decamped. The particulate mush of his last meal glittered nearly jewel-like in the frosty glow of streetlamps. He felt empty, not just in the belly, but in the heart. Had he thrown up his spirit as well?

Do I even have a spirit? he thought.

Too many things cruxed him. The town's madness, of course; and the voice—most certainly. Hearing voices in one's head was not generally an indication of well being. What cruxed him most of all, though, was simply his own being here. Why had he come? For the truth, for shards of human realities to nourish his writing, but now he wondered. It made no sense, yet somehow he felt the opposite: that actually a *lack* of truth had evoked him. Vacuities, not realities. Wastelands.

Lies.

Absurdly, he sat beside the puddle of vomit, to reflect. Was throwing up catalytic to subjective conjecture? He felt rejected, but by what? By the mainstream? By society? In a sense he was—all writers were, and perhaps it was the backwash of his rejection that had instigated the summons, chosen him somehow. *Human truth is my sustenance. How powerful is the power of truth?* But the more he plied the speculation, the harder he laughed. The quest had backfired, leaving him to sit gutterside as his vomit spread into strange shapes between his feet. *Seeker, my ass,* he concluded. *Bugger truth.* All he cared about now was the next bus.

"Mother!" he heard.

The plea had sounded impoverished, a desperate whine like a lost child's.

Then: I SHOW YOU TRUTHS, SEEKER. SEEK. SEEK OUT THE SUSTENANCE OF TRUTH. SHOW ME YOUR WORTH.

The writer smirked. *What else have I got to do?* He could feel the churchfront as he approached, as one might sense a particular face in a crowd. Candlelight caused the nave's darkness to fitfully shift, populating the pews with a congregation of shadows, worshippers bereft of substance.

"Mother! I'm here!"

Aw, God, the writer thought, and it was the palest of thoughts, the bleakest and least sapient. What he saw numbed everything that he was. He stared toward the chancel as if encased in cement.

The coffin stood empty. Its previous tenant—the dead old woman—had been stripped of her last garments and lay stiff across the carpet, all gray-white dried skin and wrinkles, and a face like a dried fruit. Between the corpse's legs lay the priest, black trousers at his ankles, copulating furiously.

"I'll bring you back!" he promised, panting. His eyes squeezed shut in the most devout concentration. Sagging bags for breasts jiggled at the corpse's armpits.

"You're having sex with a corpse, for God's sake!" shouted the writer.

The fornication ceased. The rage of this ultimate coitus interruptus focused in the priest's eyes as sharply as cracked glass. "What?" he shouted.

"You're fucking your *mother's corpse!*"

"So?"

The writer shivered. "Correct me if I'm wrong—I'm not an expert on modern clerical protocol—but it's my understanding that priests

The Seeker

aren't supposed to have sex, especially with their mothers, and more especially when their mothers are DEAD!"

The priest faltered, not at the writer's objection, but at some inner query. A sad recognition touched his face as he withdrew and straddled the embalmed cadaver. "I can't bring her back," he lamented. "No, not like this." His erection pulsed upward, a parodical stiff root. Forlornly, he picked something up.

The writer's guts shimmied. What the priest had picked up was a pair of heavy-duty roofing shears.

"There's only one way, I'm afraid," mourned the priest. The writer shouted "No no no! Holy shit! Don't do th—"

—as the priest unhesitantly clipped off his glans with the shears.

The obligatory scream shot about the nave; the glans fell to the carpet like a gumdrop.

The writer was backing away, his ears ringing. *I do not need to see this,* he thought. But something forced him to look, and by now he had a pretty good idea what that something was.

Blood jetted freely from the priest's clipped member—yes, freely as water out of a garden hose. "Mother, oh, Mother," he muttered, shuddering as the blood poured forth.

TRUTH, banged the voice in the writer's head as he plodded in shock back out onto the street. *Something's made everyone in this town crazy,* he realized.

NOT CRAZY. BLOOMED IN TRUTH, THE *REAL* TRUTH.

He ignored this; he had to. *So how come I'm not crazy?*

YOU'RE THE SEEKER, came his answer.

He gazed emptily down the street. He didn't feel crazy, he felt fine. So why was he hearing voices?

AH, YES, he heard. SUSTENANCE!

Was it really madness, or was it susceptibility, as the voice seemed to infer? All his deliberating over truth, and what truth really was, had skirted one very important consideration. Perhaps truth was mutable. Like philosophy, art, technology— like life itself—perhaps old truths died and were replaced by new ones.

So the truth had changed? Was that it?

The writer banged through the swingdoors of the Crossroads.

"Look, he's back!" said the fat blonde. "It's the writer!"

"The *seeker,*" corrected the keep. "Ready for a shooter?"

"Cram your shooters, rube, and you," he pointed violently at the fat blonde, "Stay the hell away from me." She burped in reply, halfway done with her next pizza. The redhead was still at the rail too; on a bar napkin she absently doodled stick figures with inordinately large genitals.

"What brings ya back?" asked the keep.

The fat blonde ripped off another belch, which sounded like a tree cracking. "Maybe he wants more pizza."

"You haven't seen my hopelessly inadequate boyfriend wandering around, have you?" the redhead asked.

Jesus, thought the writer. "All I want to know is when the next goddamn bus comes into this goddamn town."

"Call Trailways," invited the keep. "Pay phone's by the john."

Finally, a phone!

"But hold up a sec." The keep slapped a yellow shooter down. "Drink up, seeker. And don't worry, it's a—"

"I know, a tin roof." *Can't hurt, can it?* The writer shot the shooter back, froze mid-swallow, then spat it out. "What the fuck was that!"

"A Piss Shooter, partner." The keep's fly was open. "The house special. Bit more tasty than the last one, huh?"

"You're all a bunch of psychopaths!" screamed the writer.

"Crank up one of them Snot Shooters," suggested the fat blonde.

"Good thing I've had a cold all week. Makes 'em thicker, meatier." The keep applied an index finger to his left nostril, then loudly emptied his right one into a shooter glass. "Yeah, there's a beaut. Go for it, seeker."

The writer's head was reeling. "No, thanks. I'm trying to cut down."

"Cheers," said the fat blonde. She tossed it back neat, swallowing it more or less as a single lump. "Nice and thick!"

It just never ends, does it? The writer wobbled back to the pay phone, dropped in some change, and waited.

No dialtone.

"Goddamn this fuckin' shit-house piece of shit crazy-ass motherfuckin' town!" the writer articulated to the very best of his refined and erudite vocabulary. "Suckin' fuckin' redneck shitpile town ain't even got a fuckin' *phone* that works!"

"Phones haven't worked since last night," he was informed. It was the guy in the white shirt, who'd just come in the back way. He was hefting a shiny 44-oz aluminum softball bat. "Shh," he said next. "I want to surprise her." He snuck up behind the redhead, assumed a formidable batter's stance, and swung—

Ka-CRACK!

The impact of the bat to the redhead's right ear sent a big spurt of blood from her left. She flew off the stool like a golf ball off a tee and landed on the floor.

"How about *that?*" White Shirt softly inquired. "I'll bet *that* was big enough for you." The keep and fat blonde applauded. The writer just stared. White Shirt dragged the redhead out the back door by the throat.

The Seeker

"Still ain't found what'cha seek, huh, seeker?" commented the keep. "Still ain't found the truth. Well lemme tell ya somethin'. Truth can change."

The writer peered at him.

"I know what the truth is," claimed the fat blonde.

"Yeah?" the writer challenged. "Tell me then, you fat hunk of shit redneck walking trailer-park puke-machine. What is the truth?"

"It's black!"

Great. The truth is black. Wonderful. The writer started for the back door, but the keep implored, "Don't go yet. You'll miss my next one." He was lowering his trousers.

"Jizz Shooters!" cried the fat blonde.

Laughter followed the writer out the door. It made him feel rooked. Perhaps in their madness they knew something he didn't. Perhaps madness, in this case, was knowledge.

In the alley, White Shirt was eviscerating the redhead with a large hunting knife. Less than patiently, he rummaged through wet organs like someone looking for something, cufflinks maybe. "Give it back!" he shouted at the cooling gore. "I want it back!"

The writer leaned against the wall and lit a cigarette. "Buddy," he asked quietly. "Could you please tell me when the next bus comes through town?"

"There aren't any busses anymore. Things have changed."

Changed, the writer thought.

THE TRUTH HAS CHANGED, elaborated the voice. YOU WERE RIGHT. IT HAS BEEN REBORN, THROUGH *ME*. I LIVE ON IT.

The writer gave this some thought.

"I'm looking for my love," White Shirt remarked and gestured the redhead's opened belly. "I gave her my love, and I want it back." He scratched his head. "It's got to be in there somewhere."

"Love is in the heart," the writer pointed out.

"Yeah, but this girl was heartless."

"Well, the patriarchal Japanese used to believe that love was in the belly, the intestines. They believed that the belly was the temple of the soul on earth. That's why they practiced ritual suicide by disembowelment—to release the soul and free the spiritual substantate of their love."

"Intestines," White Shirt contemplated. "So...if I gave *my* love to her..." He stared into the tilled gut, fingering its wares. "To get it back, I have to bring it into me?"

The writer shrugged. "I can't advise you. The decision is yours."

White Shirt began to eat the girl's intestines.

The writer's sweat surged. The redhead was as dead as dead could be, if not deader. Nevertheless, as her ex-lover steadily consumed the loops of her innards, her eyes snapped open and her head turned.

She looked directly at the writer.

"He's taking his love back," she giggled.

"I know," said the writer.

"It...tickles."

"I would imagine so."

The moon shone in each of her eyes as a perfect white dot. "Real truth sustains us, just in different ways."

Sustains, considered the writer. *Sustenance.*

"The end of your quest is waiting for you."

The writer gulped. "Tell me," he pleaded. "It's very important to me. Please."

"Look for something black," she said, and died again.

The writer leapt the alley fence. The fat blonde had said the same thing. Black. But it was nighttime. How could he hope to find something black at night?

Then he heard something—a stout, distant *chugging.*

A motor, he realized.

The he saw...what?

A glow?

A patch of light that was somehow, impossibly, black.

He was standing in a schoolyard–ironically a place of learning. The light shimmered in a rough trench-like bomb crater. *It's black,* he thought. In the distance sat the source of the motor noise: a squat U.S. Army armored personnel carrier.

The writer looked into the dropped back hatch.

"Don't go out there," warned a crisp yet muffled voice.

Murky red light bathed the inner compartment like blood in a lighted pool. A sergeant in a gas mask and full decontamination gear slouched at a console of radio equipment. Very promptly, he pointed a 9mm pistol at the writer's face.

The writer urinated in his pants, just as promptly. "Don't shoot me. I'm only a novelist."

The masked sergeant seemed very sad. "Bock and Jones. I had to send them out. It's a DECON field order. The lowest ranking men go into the final exclusion perimeter first."

Final exclusion perimeter?

"I think it got them," the sergeant said

It, the writer reckoned.

In the mask's portals, the sergeant's eyes looked insane. "When my daughter was an infant, I'd rock her in my lap every night."

"That's, uh, that's nice, sergeant."

"It gave me a hard on.... She's fourteen now. I drilled a hole in the bathroom wall so I can watch her take showers."

"They have counselors for things like that, I think."

A dark suboctave suffused into the words. "At midnight, the wolf howls."

The writer winced. "What?"

"I never knew my father."

Then the sergeant shot himself in the head.

Sound and concussion hit the writer like a physical weight. *BANG!* It shoved him out of the rumbling vehicle as the sergeant's mask quickly filled up with blood.

I HUNGER FOR TRUTH TOO, loomed the voice. BUT TO SEE IT, IT MUST BE REVEALED. DO YOU UNDERSTAND? YOU *MUST* UNDERSTAND.

The writer strayed into the yard. Yes, he thought he *did* understand now. Here was what his whole life had been leading him to. All that he'd sought, in his absurd pretensions as a *seeker,* had brought him to this final test. There could be no going back. His preceptor awaited, the *ultimate* seeker.

A second decon soldier lay dead in the grass. There were no hands at the ends of his arms, and the stumps appeared burned. Some colossal inner pressure had forced his brains out his ears.

"Get out of here, you civvie fucker!" someone commanded. A third soldier strode through shadows, a kid no more than twenty. "The light! It's mine!"

"Are you quite sure about that?"

"It's...God. I'm taking it!"

A TEST? WATCH.

"Watch!" the boy cried. "I'll prove it's mine!" He ran manic to the trench, his young face in awe above the radiant black blur. "Hard-fucking-core, man! I'm taking *God!*" He put his hands into the light, eyes wide as moons, and picked it up. But in only a second the light fell back to its resting place, melting through the boy's hands. He stood up stiff and convulsed, a silent scream in his lips.

The voice trumpeted. ALAS. FAILURE.

This disconcerted the writer, for he knew he was next. For the last time in his life, then, he asked himself the ever important query. *How powerful is the power of truth?*

I'LL SHOW YOU.

The boy's innards prolapsed through his mouth in a few slow, even pulses; the writer thought of a fat snake squeezing from its hole. Lungs, liver, heart, g.i. tract—everything that was inside now hung heavily outside, glimmering. Then the red heart, amid it all, stopped beating, and the boy fell dead.

ONLY FAITH CAN SAVE YOU NOW.

"I kind of figured that," the writer admitted.

THE TRUTH IS MY SUSTENANCE. I EXIST TO EXPOSE IT, TO GIVE IT FLESH. I DRAW IT OUT SO THAT IT CAN BE REAL AND, HENCE, SUSTAINING. DO YOU UNDERSTAND? TOO OFTEN THE TRUTH HIDES UNDERNEATH. WITHOUT REVELATION, WHAT PURPOSE CAN THERE BE IN TRUTH?

Good point, the writer mused.

WE'RE BOTH SEEKERS, WE BOTH HAVE QUESTS. LET OUR QUESTS JOIN HANDS NOW IN THE REAL LIGHT OF WHAT WE SEEK.

"Yes," said the writer.

WILL YOU MINISTER TO ME?

"Yes."

THEN THERE IS BUT ONE DOOR LEFT FOR YOU TO ENTER. GLORY OR FAILURE. TRUTH OR LIES. THE TEST OF *YOUR* FAITH IS UPON YOU.

The writer looked into the shimmering trench. This would either be the end or the beginning; it was providence. To turn away now would reduce his entire life to a lie. He began to reach down, softly smiling.

I am the seeker, he thought.

He put his hands into the light.

YES!

He picked it up. He looked at it, cradled it. The glory on his face felt brighter than a thousand suns. The test was done, and he had passed.

Was the black light weeping?

CARRY ME AWAY, it said.

He took it into the Army vehicle and closed the back hatch.

THERE'S SO MUCH, SO MUCH FOR US TO SEEK.

In the driver's compartment, the writer lit a cigarette. *Looks simple enough,* he observed. A t-bar, an accelerator, and a brake. Automatic transaxle, low and second. The fuel gauge read well over half.

He thought of sustenance, the first pronouncement of the light. This town had been too small; that was the problem: tiny, dry. There weren't enough people here to provide the truth its proper flesh. But that was all right. He knew it wouldn't take long to get to a really big city.

SUSTENANCE, SEEKER, whispered the light like a lover.

The seeker put the vehicle into gear and began to drive.

THE SEEKER
AFTERWORD

In 1989, I was romantically involved with a woman named Mary. Things didn't really work out, to say the least. It was a violent relationship: she punched the crap out of me many a time. Nevertheless, I loved Mary—too oblivious to realize the incompatibility. I was blind. Much like the protagonist of this story, I felt I was searching for something, and when I found it, it was already a heap of ashes. It had changed. Something I felt was a certain truth had changed into something else. Nevertheless, my involvement with Mary provided a tremendous creative impetus for which I will always be grateful. She was a "formalist"; she was a ballerina–she manipulated the strictures of art with her body. Then one day she simply gave it up. She stopped searching for whatever it was she sought.

There should be some obvious symbolism in this piece. Too often the things we think are most important to us are supplanted by something altogether opposite. A philosophical writer seeking "truth" finds out that the real *truth is little more than a gross-out B-movie!*

OBEDIENCE IS VIRTUE

Grub Girl in the Prison of Dead Women

SURE, HON, I GOT some time. I'll tell you the whole thing while you make up your mind. And this is no bullshit, either. You can read about it in the papers.

You know about Grubs, right? No? Shit, man, you from overseas or something? I'll make a long story short. "Grubs" are what they call us, same way they call black people niggers. Nice tag, huh? But I guess we *are* a little on the pasty side. But, look, don't get freaked out. I heard somewhere there are over ten thousand of us total. It all started with that ramjet thing, I don't know, a couple of years ago. Christ, I'm sure you heard about *that*. NASA and the Air Force were testing some new kinda plane, remotely piloted, they called it, flying it a hundred miles off the coast over the Atlantic. It was a nuclear ramjet or some shit, could fly indefinitely without fuel, no pilots, ran by computers. The idea was to have these things flying around all the time real high up. Cheap way to defend the nation. "The ultimate deterrent," the President said when they announced that they were gonna spend billions developing this flop. What they *didn't* announce was that plane kicked out a trail of some off-the-wall kinda radiation wherever it flew. The government wasn't worried about it 'cos it flew so high, the shit would go right out of the atmosphere. Well, something fucked up during one of the test flights, and one of these things wound up flying up and down the east coast at treetop level on something they called an "emergency urban alert bomb mode" for something like five days before they could veer it off course over the sea and shoot it down. Thing was flying over *cities,* for shit's sake. And I was one of the ones lucky enough to get rained on by this thing.

I'd just come up from the docks down there, you know, by the Market Square, and I was walking up toward Clay Street. 'Rome, my pimp, he usually picked me and his other two girls up at about four a.m. Best time for us alley girls to turn tricks is after two, after the bars are closed 'cos then the cops stop buzzing the street to bust our chops. Fuckin' cops, nine times outa ten when they catch you, all they do is make you give 'em a blowjob, then let you go. Anyway, here I am, hoofing it up to Clay after turning about five tricks, and then there's this rumble way down deep in my belly and this sound like slow thunder, and I look up and see this ugly motherfuckin' thing flying about hundred feet over my head. Didn't know what to make of it. It looked like a big black kite in the sky, and when it passed, I could see this weird blue-green glow coming out of the back of the thing, its engines, I guess. I died a couple hours later, and the next day I woke up a grub.

There was a big whupdeedo for a little while. All of a sudden there were ten thousand dead people walking around and not knowing what the fuck hit them. President called an emergency meeting or some shit. Oh, you should've heard all the fancy talk they were spouting. At first they were gonna "euthanize" us "to safeguard the societal whole from potential contraindications," until some egghead at CDC verified that we weren't psychotic or contagious or radioactive or anything. Then some asshole Republican senator made a big pitch about how we should be "socially impounded." "Protean symtomologies," see, that's what they were worried about. These shitheads wanted to round us all up and put us on an island somewhere! It all blew over, though, after the activists started gearing up, and they let us be. After all, grubs are people too.

It didn't hurt really. Just felt sick for a few minutes, got a headache, puked, and died. Woke up the next day feeling pretty much the same as I always did. Woke up a Grub, and that's my story.

We call live people "pink" or "pinkies," and they call us Grubs. Only fair, they got names for us, we got names for them. 'Rome didn't get it, the prick, he stayed pink, and so did his other two hookers. The shit from the plane wouldn't get you if you were in a car or under a roof. About a dozen other hookers got it, though, 'cos they were out on the street just like me when that fucked up plane flew by, and now every pink hooker in the city hates us. See, johns want Grubs more than pink girls 'cos we're cheaper and we ain't got diseases. AIDS, herpes, and all that shit, I had it all when I was pink, but not no more, and a john knows that if he buys himself a nut with a grub he ain't gonna catch nothing.

Here's why I killed 'Rome, though. After I got grubbed, he got this brainstorm that he could really cop a bundle off me with the kinks. He'd work me right out of his crib, hitting johns up for a couple hundred bucks an hour! These sick fucks'd come in and do anything they wanted, and I mean *anything*. Bondage, S&M, scat, that sort of shit. 'Rome's only rule was that they weren't allowed to break any bones or cut off any parts. These kinks were a trip, let me tell you. You'd be surprised how many really sick motherfuckers there are in the world. They'd tie me up, jack me out, stick needles in my tits, shit in my mouth, you fuckin' name it.

Well, I started to get sick of this shit real fast. Here's this scumbag making cash hand over fist offa my ass, and I don't get shit out of it. So I...

Well, if you wanna know the details, I busted a toilet tank cover over his head one night, cut his belly open, and ate his guts.

Sometimes a girl's gotta do what she's gotta do.

¤ ¤ ¤ ¤ ¤

See, grubs can only eat raw stuff. You eat regular food like the pinkies and the shit don't come out, you bloat up. There was this one gal named Sue who got grubbed just like me—blonde, kinda heavy set, *really* big tits—and she just goes on eating the regular shit that the pinkies eat, and one day I saw her walking past the hotel and, I swear, she's big as Jabba the Hut, and before she could make it to the bus stop, she, like, *exploded* right there in the street, made one holy hell of a mess. And this shithead Republican senator I was telling you about, you should've heard the guy, like because we can only eat raw stuff, that means we're gonna go on some zombie rampage eating people in the streets like some horror movie so that was his case for "socially impounding" us. Glad that asshole's shit didn't fly. Of course, it probably sounds pretty hypocritical of me, since I just got done telling you I chowed down on 'Rome insides. I just figured it was the thing to do, that's all. I got tired of being used by this scumbag, so I did the job on him. It wasn't like his guts tasted any better than anything else—grubs don't have a sense of taste.

One good thing about being a grub hooker, though, you start to stick up for yourself. You get a case of the ass and you don't take shit anymore. The rule had always been no girl works solo. You wanna work the street, you gotta have a pimp. Ask any hooker in any city in the world. You try to work solo, you get your face beat to mush or wind up in some dumpster with your throat cut. We'd always be too afraid to fight back, stand up for ourselves, you know? Shit, most girls are strung out anyway. I was. Back when I was pink, I was firing up scag four times a day, had to shoot up into my foot 'cos the veins on my arms all collapsed and turned black. I'd turn over my take to 'Rome every night like clockwork, and he'd keep me in junk, and that was all I cared about. When you're strung out, you really don't have a soul anymore. Yeah, turning my tricks, keeping 'Rome happy, and getting my fix—that's all there was for me. It was hell, let me tell you. But after I got grubbed, I didn't need the scag anymore, and it finally dawned on me that I didn't need 'Rome, either. All the other grubs working the street got the same gist, and all of a sudden a lot of pimps were winding up in body bags. The pink girls, sure, they're all still in their stables, but their pimps don't fuck with us grubs 'cos they know that if they do, they'll wind up just like 'Rome.

Fuck 'em.

¤ ¤ ¤ ¤ ¤

And this fuckhead senator? He starts this shit about we'll destabilize the work base, how we gotta be segregated because employers will be hiring grubs instead of pinkies 'cos we can work round the clock, but then the congress passed a law against it. Of course, prostitution's still illegal but around here at least, the cops don't fuck with the grubs. It's a real laugh. We give 'em the creeps, so they just let us do our thing and leave us alone.

Er, I should say, they *used* to. But the new congress changed all that and fast. Now it's roundup time, hoss. If you're a Grub and you so much as spit on the sidewalk, there'll be some John Law motherfucker waiting to lock you up.

It was a plainclothes U.S. Marshal that busted me. Just my luck. "You're under arrest for sexual solicitation," he was nice enough to tell me only *after* he came in my mouth. "You motherless dickcheese ballbag-stinking pig motherfucker!" I yelled back. I was gonna bust his coconut right there in the unmarked but before I could—PAP!—he hit me with a round from his track-operated spicule pistol, and that was it for me.

Regular weapons don't work on Grubs—we're dead, you know? So the pigs started making new kinds of guns that would paralyze us. Tubocurarine darts, electromagnetic-pulse nets, milliwave disrupters. When I came to, some fat DO —stands for Detention Officer—a guy named Stryker, he was finishing up a body-cavity search while I was chained to a wall. The fucker had his hand so far up my ass I thought he was trying to stick his fingers out my mouth.

"I want a fucking lawyer!" I screamed.

"Lawyer? Don't you watch the news? You're dead, bitch. Civil rights don't apply to dead people anymore. Thank God the Republicans are back in office. We can do anything we want to you grub scumbags."

When he finished fishing in my bowels, he jerked off on my ass, then let a half dozen more DOs gang-bang me right there against the wall. The last guy pissed up my ass, for posterity, I guess.

Grub Girl in the Prison of Dead Women

¤   ¤   ¤   ¤   ¤

So that's it in a nutshell. The new administration dropped all the previous non-discrimination laws. Grubs weren't considered people anymore, so we were no longer entitled to humane treatment. That $10 blowjob got me a five-year sentence in this stone motel they call the Alderton Federal Rehabilitation Center. We'd heard rumors about this joint on the street; it was a Grubs-Only prison. Torture, slave labor, experiments. I learned the score here real quick; any Grubs that were good-looking got assigned to the Behavioral Segregation Wing. They called it the Fuck Farm. Gang rape was the order of the day, and so were kink jobs. In the old days, if the pinkies fucked with us we'd just pop their heads open and scarf their brains—Grubs are a lot stronger than pinks. But we couldn't fight back anymore because all inmates were fitted with UV nodes.

I remember the day I went in for my "fitting."

¤   ¤   ¤   ¤   ¤

The sign on the door read: OBEDIENCE IS VIRTUE, but below that was another sign:

IMPLANTATION UNIT.

Stryker and some egghead tech had me strapped down to a padded table. The tech slit each of my nipples with a scalpel, stuck something about the size of a marble in each tit, then sewed me up. Then he slit open my clitoris and repeated the procedure. Sounds nasty but it was really no big deal: Grubs don't feel pain...er, at least that's what I'd always thought.

DO Stryker grinned down. "From now on, Grub, you do everything we say."

"Don't count on it, pig," I told him. "Oh, and by the way, your mother blows farm animals."

"What we've done, inmate," the tech informed me, "is surgically implant Bofors Model 250 ultraviolet-wave transponders into your most sensitive mammarian and genital nerve clusters. Upon activation, each transponder node will become energized with 20,000 nanounits of collective ultraviolet-band energy. In spite of the fact that you're clinically dead, this energy will flood the target dendron/axon ganglia, replenishing all electrical synaptic impulses—hence, causing pain that can only be described as incalculable."

"Drink my zombie piss," I replied.

"Mouthy little whore, ain't she?" Stryker chuckled, unstrapping me. I got up off the table, still groggy from the tubocurarine darts they'd been zapping me with. "But she'll soon learn that silence is golden."

"The only thing golden is the shower I'm gonna give you when I get out of this cement Ramada. Too bad your pappy didn't pull out early and leave his peckersnot on the floor. World'd be a better place."

"I'd take the officer's warning under serious advisement," the tech said. "The Bofors Model 250 is decidedly effective."

When you're a zombie, your life is bad enough. Grubs don't like to be intimidated.

And I guess I always did have a big mouth.

"How about I cut your cock off and fuck you in the ass with it?"

"You think this is a joke?" Stryker whipped out the sending unit, like a tv remote. "If I tell you to shit on the floor and eat it, you'll shit on the floor and eat it."

I dragged up a big chest oyster and hocked it in his face. "Eat that."

Ever heard of the Chicago Fire? That's what I felt like when the ever dutiful Detention Officer Stryker tapped my ID number into that sending unit. First my tits and pussy felt warm, tingling...then—WHAM! I felt alive again, all right, and that tech geek wasn't kidding about the pain. Like a brand-new Red Devil razor blade being slowly dragged through the middle of my clit, and a channel-lock on each nipple, a sewing needle in each eye, and a drill bit in my brain—that's what the pain all added up to when Stryker "activated" me.

"Gonna be a good girl now?" Stryker asked.

The ultraviolet waves surged through me. My spine arched back like a u-bolt, and I hit the floor. There was a sound somewhere that reminded me of squealing tires, but eventually I realized it was me—screaming.

"Here's your golden shower, bitch." I just lay there flopping like a fish on a hot plate. Stryker must've pulled a ten-beer piss on me, which upped the current transfer...and doubled the pain.

"Be a good girl now and do what I told you."

More needles, more channel-locks, more razors sliding... Just when it felt like my eyeballs would rupture, I...well.

I did it.

Shrieking like a baby in a furnace, I shit on the floor and ate it.

¤ ¤ ¤ ¤ ¤

Stryker and his boys ran the Bev-Seg unit. Since Grubs don't sleep, they'd work us pretty much round the clock. First thing every morning they'd take us to the "Dining Hall." Brother, this was no Four Seasons. What they'd feed us was this goulash of what they called "rendered livestock." Mostly diseased pigs and chickens that wouldn't pass USDA, they'd get the shit from local farms and grind it up in hoppers. Um-um good.

After that, General Work Block. Cleaning up this federal outhouse, whatever needed to be done: swabbing toilets, mopping floors, cleaning the dumpsters and greasepits. Along the way me and the other girls'd sometimes catch glimpses of the other wings. Males Grubs, and any Grub girls who weren't good-looking, they'd be used for CDC research and Defense Corp experiments. But it was mainly curiosity when you get right down to it. The government still didn't know a whole lot about Grubs, so they'd do all these experiments to see what happened when you fucked with one. Starvation, for instance, wouldn't kill a Grub; you'd just get down to literally skin and bones. They had an entire wing full of Grubs who hadn't been allowed to eat for over a year. Then there were the transplants: putting live organs into dead people, usually animals guts and shit like that. There was a rumor that the R&D techs had successfully transplanted two heads onto a single Grub. Ordnance Development was worse: the military using Grubs to test new bullets, landmines, and rockets on. When things got too hot, they'd send us in for the cleanup—Jesus. It was mostly pieces we carried out of there. The Ectogenics Lab was reserved for Halfers—a Halfer is a Grub who'd only partly turned: half dead, half alive, and they'd fuck around with the ovaries on these Halfer chicks, knock them up, and see what came out.

You name it, these sick fucks did it, anything for a kick: microwaving, broiling, freezing. Brain transplants, lobotomies, transfusions. Whatever turned them on. It was enough to turn even a dead girl's stomach.

Next was RT—Rehabilitative Therapy. They'd make us sit in a room four hours a day and watch snuff films, live S&M, executions, car-wreck and ER footage. This was supposed to "cure" us, showing us what a life of crime would lead to. Gimme a fucking break! One time they showed this flick of a bunch of stoners with ten-inch herpetic cocks pulling a train on some junkie chick eight-months' pregnant. They fucked her so hard she breaks her water and miscarries right there on the floor. So I look in the back of the room and half the DOs are so boned up watching this flick they're jerking off! If anybody in the slam needed rehab, it was them, not us.

After that was another Work Block, then a trip to the Hygiene Unit; the DOs'd watch while we soaped each other down, then they'd hose us off and get us ready for LockDown. See, they'd want us squeaky clean before the fun began. They might as well've put a revolving door on our cells with all the men coming in and out. First shift was for VIPs: big-wheels in the state government, Prison Admin chiefs, staffers, Public Safety officials, the Warden and his suits. One hard tubesteak after another. Then the guards themselves would get their turn, and that was worse. These guys were real kinks and psych-jobs, especially Stryker.

Ass-fuck parties, fletch parties, scat, gang-bang face-fucks. One girl threatened to bite the next cock someone tried to stick in her mouth, so they activated her UV implants and left them on all night. Then they took us to the Med Unit the next day and pulled all our teeth just to be safe.

Stryker particularly had it in for me: ordering other girls to shit on me, piss in my mouth, fist-fuck me. His favorite move was to buttfuck another chick and make me suck his jizz out of her ass. And what could I do about it? Jack shit. Any time I pitched a fit, he'd whip out his sending unit and activate my UV nodes. You learn fast in this place....

But don't worry. No way in holymotherfucking hell was I gonna take this shit for my whole hitch.

See, I had a plan.

¤   ¤   ¤   ¤   ¤

A three-part plan. I had to do it just right, and it took months to get ready. Busting out of this shithole wasn't good enough. I had to get the rest of the Grubs out too, not to mention a few scores to settle.

Once a week it was my job to empty the trash in the Booking Unit. There were a lot of used tubocurarine darts in bottom of the can. Any chance I got I'd pinch a few, hid 'em in my cell later. Why? Because there was still a little curare left in cartridges...

Next was the geek in the Implantation Lab—and when I say geek I mean GEEK. This wuss made Mr. Rogers look tough, and it was a good bet he'd never been laid. Next time I got mop duty in the IL, I put the make on him hard. I mean, I ain't bragging but ya gotta admit—am I good-looking or what? Once I stepped out of my cellblock overalls, I had this guy worshiping me, wound up fucking his brains out. Wore his virgin pecker out, I did.

And when the asshole wasn't looking, I pinched one of his scalpels...

¤   ¤   ¤   ¤   ¤

Part Three was the toughest part. See, in 2003 the NRC authorized liquid-plasma isotope reactors for industrial use, and they had one of these little Three Mile Islands providing all the power for the prison.

If I could get a key to the Fuel Core Station...

¤   ¤   ¤   ¤   ¤

At night, when the gang bangs and kink parties were over, I'd just sit in my cell and dream. Even dead people dream. I'd think back to the way things were when I was working the street. Didn't ask for much, and I never ripped off a john in his life who didn't have it coming. Sure, I killed some pimps and baddies, but they had it coming too. All I ever wanted was to do my thing, mind my own business, and live my life.

But the Feds and the pigs and the U.S. Marshals came along with their Dr. Strangelove Big Brother bullshit. What I ever do to them? And—what?—it's my fault their fuckin' nuke-powered plane crashed and turned 10,000 people into Grubs? Fuck that.

And fuck them.

I knew I had to make my move just before LockDown. I wanted as many government bigwheels in here as possible. But I knew I had to get Stryker alone.

So when they were taking us to chow before LD, I hocked a lunger right into Stryker's face and said, "Your mother sucks cocks in hell."

Stryker grinned. He was glad I did it. "You're a ballsy little whore, ain't ya? Like to run that cocksuck zombie-whore mouth of yours."

"Your daddy must've had shit on his dick when he knocked your mama up with you."

His grin turned demonic. "Baby, I'll cut your head off and jerk off in your mouth."

I cracked out a laugh. "Man, all you can *do* is jerk off. Can't lay any *serious* dick on a woman to save your life."

"Think so?"

"Gimme a break? A peter-licking, panty-wearing, no-hard-on little candy-ass like you?"

"Yeah, maybe I'll activate you till your tits pop and your hair burns off. See how the smart-mouth Grub Girl likes *that* action."

"Talk is cheap. You can light me up with that pissant UV thing all you want. I *like* pain, pig. Gets me horny, you know, for a *real* man? Too bad there ain't any in this armpit. I'll bet you ten bucks your dick wouldn't last a minute in my pussy."

He stared me down, nodding. "You're on, bitch. I'm gonna fuck you so hard your brains'll be squirting out your ears, and when I'm done I'm gonna throw your whore ass into Isolation and leave your transponders on for a month."

"I hear ya talking, Liberace."

"Get the rest of these dead bitches to chow," Stryker barked to his sergeants. "I'll be taking this one here back to her cell for a private consultation."

He dragged me by the hair to my cell, and then I knew I had him.

By then, see, I'd collected enough curare from the used cartridges to fill an entire dart. Stryker didn't even have time to get his pants down before I had that baby stuck right in his fat red neck.

¤ ¤ ¤ ¤ ¤

"What...what did you...do?"

He came to about an hour later, and an hour was plenty of time to do the job. I held up the scalpel I jacked from that nerd tech. "See this, asshole? I cut the UV implants out of myself."

Eventually his crossed eyes began to focus, incomprehension on his face.

"Whaaaa...."

"Then I sewed them back up in your nutsack."

Now the incomprehension turned to slow horror. He reached down to his ballbag, felt around, and then moaned. You could hear the little nodes clicking in there. "God in heaven...please don't—"

"Guess we better test 'em huh?"

"Noooooo! Pleeeeeease!"

I tapped my own ID into the sending unit and lit DO Stryker up like the fucking Fourth of July. Yes sir-ee. 60,000 nanounits of ultraviolet-band energy right smack-dab into his family jewels.

The fat fuck screamed louder than a truck horn, and I gotta tell ya, it was fun watching him flop around on the floor like a tadpole out of water. I had a mind to just leave him there like that, but...

There was still work to do.

¤   ¤   ¤   ¤   ¤

"Punch in the passcode," I ordered.

I'd marched him down to the Utility Wing. Shiftchange was over so the halls were clear.

"No way," he said. "I can't. It's a security breach. The core's running—"

"Punch in the passcode and open the door, motherfucker, unless you want me to cook your nuts again. By the time I'm done, they'll look like a couple of fried chicken gizzards."

He was crying now, blubbering like a baby. I showed him the sending unit, and that was all it took. He plipped in the code and the vault door sucked open.

WARNING, one sign read. NUCLEAR FUEL CORE IS *ON*. FATAL RADIOACTIVE DOSE AFTER TWENTY MINUTES.

Fatal? Sure. But not to somebody who's already dead.

I threw Stryker aside and jacked the fuel rods right out of the core chassis. The evac alarms went off immediately. "Don't leave me in here!" Stryker bellowed. "I'll die!"

"Buddy," I said, "five minutes from now you'll be *praying* to die." Then I activated him again. It was tempting not to stay there and watch awhile—no, the meltdown wouldn't hurt *me*, but I had the other Grubs to get out. I took one last gander at Stryker: screaming, shitting and pissing himself, blood leaking out his eyes, ears, and mouth, his hair baking off and his crotch smoking. Man, it was sweet.

Grub Girl in the Prison of Dead Women

Then I left and closed the door.

The reactor cooked-off about a half-hour later; the radiation took out every pinkie in the joint before they could reach safe distance. As for the rest of the Grubs, I used Stryker's block keys to open their cells and we all waltzed out of that shitpit like we owned the place. Out front I could see the Warden and a bunch of twerps from the Governor's Office crawling across the asphalt with their skin running off their bodies. So long, chumps.

* * * * *

So that's the story, pal. Don't believe me? Read about it in the papers. Oh, and that plainclothes U.S. Marshal who busted me in the first place? You probably read about him in the papers too. I spotted the motherfucker the first week I was back working the street. Yanked his cock and balls off then pulled his intestines out his ass. The fucker looked like he had a *tail* when I was done! I mean, come on, he had it coming. I never fucked with no one who didn't fuck with me first.

But how about you, pal? Made up your mind yet? You're kind of cute, if you don't mind me saying so, and—holy Christ—is that Godzilla in your pants or are you just happy to see me? Ten bucks, partner, best blowjob of your life, and if I'm lying, I'll give you your money back.

So what do you say?

Good man!

GRUB GIRL IN THE PRISON OF DEAD WOMEN AFTERWORD

This story is actually Part II of my first piece about this character. The first, entitled simply "Grub Girl" was published in Pocket's HOT BLOOD V, which was a particular trip for me because I'd sold "Mr. Torso" to their previous anthology. (Two more stories would sell to the HOT BLOOD series, a collaboration with Gary Bowen entitled "Dead Girls In Love," and another collaboration with my best friend Jack Ketchum, entitled "Love Letters From The Rain Forest.")

At any rate, shortly after the first Grub Girl story sold to HOT BLOOD, a very cool guy named Rex Miller called me and tipped me about a comic company in LA called Verotik, and he told me they were looking for horror stories to adapt for their line. So I sent them "Mr. Torso" and "Grub Girl" and in less time than it takes me to suck the guts out of a crab, Verotik bought the stories ("Mr. Torso" can be found in Verotika Issue #6; *"Grub Girl" in* Issue #8). *HOT BLOOD paid a decent word-rate for the prose stories, and Verotik paid even more. But for some reason, my Grub Girl character intrigued me, and I knew I had to continue her plight, so I wrote the above story, which was kindly published by Paula Guran in her excellent magazine Wetbones. At roughly the same time, though, Verotik asked for more material, and they purchased the adaptation of my novella Header (which appeared in* Verotika Issue #14) *and the adaptation of the above (retitled "Grub Girl Returns," in* Verotika Issue #15).

The response was so positive that Verotik then expressed interest in a Grub Girl comic mini-series. Book #1 was released in August 1997, and was absolutely wonderful. But between Book #1 and Book #2, the comic market regurgitated hard. Even though Book #1 sold out, Verotik couldn't release Book #2, so it never happened. That sucks because I'm really happy with the scripts I wrote for #2 and #3. Someday down the road they may happen. However, an adorable Grub Girl plastic figure is available from Verotik, Inc.

Buy one! It's cool!

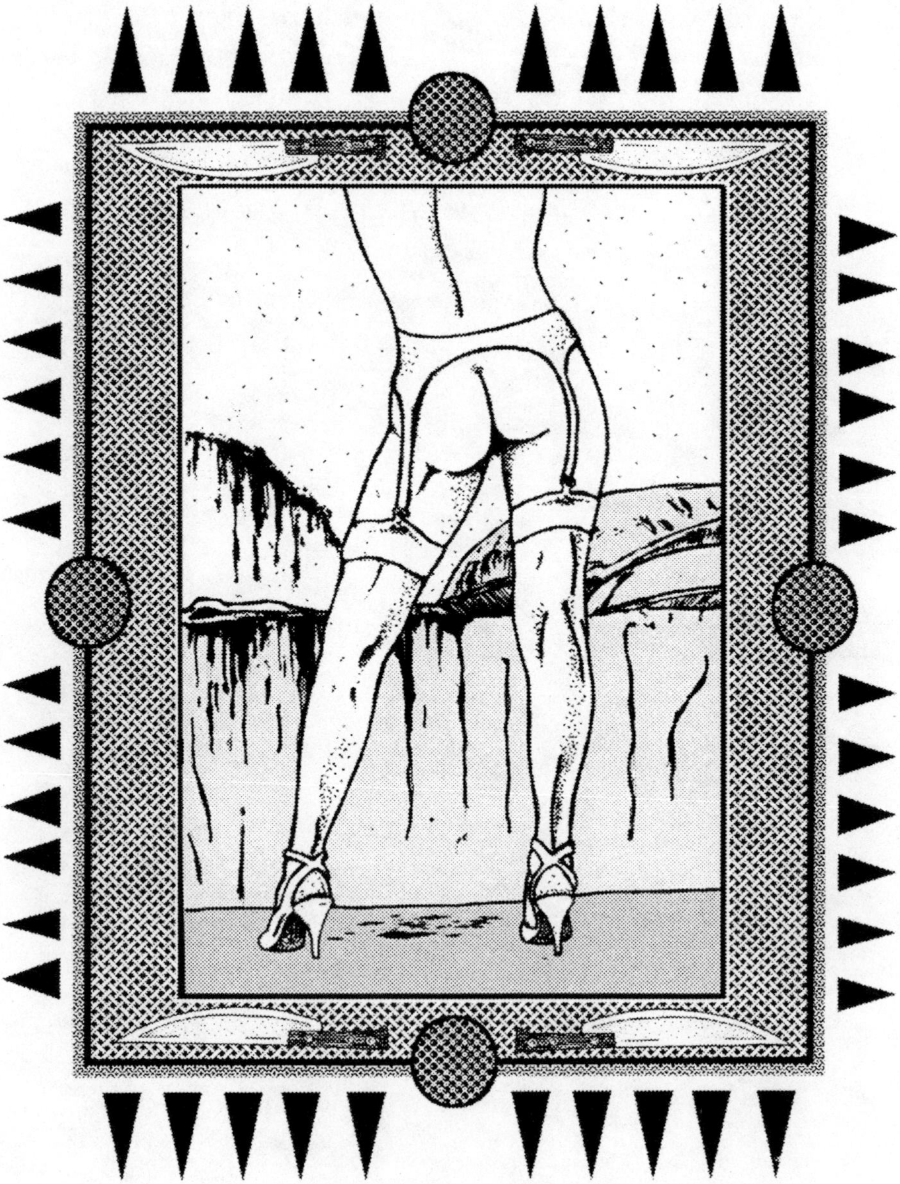

Please Let Me Out

"WHAT'S A WOMAN to do?" Dee posed the question past her Packard-Bell computer. Her bleached-blond hair looked like bright straw. "Liars, cheaters—all of them. I've never in my life dated a guy who didn't run around behind my back."

Marianne, the redhead with a face reminiscent of a pugnosed Meryl Streep, lamented in agreement. "Goddamn men, they got their brains in their pants. I mean, I never cheated on Willy, and let me tell you, I had plenty of opportunities. I gave that bastard my heart and soul, and next thing I know he's playing musical beds with half the barmaid staff."

Joyce Lipnick couldn't help but overhear these vocal ruminations: the CSS bug in Dee's intercom speaker was Joyce's ear to the outer office. She didn't consider this eavesdropping; she was just being careful. When you were a managing partner at the number-three law firm in the country, you *had* to be careful.

But the girls (Dee, her paralegal; and Marianne, the floor receptionist) were right. *What's a woman to do?* Joyce reflected in the plush, cherry-paneled office. Czanek, the sleazy P.I. she'd hired, had proved Scott's rampant infidelities. With full-color glossies, no less. How could Joyce ever erase those images? Scott, the love of her life, servicing his secret bevy via every conceivable sexual position. He left her no choice.

"I couldn't believe it," Marianne rambled. "I came home early one day, and there's Willy with that hussie from the first floor, and he's going at it like a lapdog."

Like a lapdog, Joyce pondered. Has Scott performed likewise? Czanek had verified at least five "steadies," but suspected four more. "Your man gets around, Ms. Lipnick, a real nutchase," he'd eloquented upon receipt of his $200-per-day fee. "Of course, a good-looking boy like that, it stands to reason."

Stands to reason. Joyce could've spit. *I give him a car, a beautiful home, money, credit cards, not to mention all my love, and he repays me by sewing his oats with a bunch of bimbos!*

"Yeah, you tell me," Dee reiterated over the hidden bug. "What's a woman to do?"

Joyce sympathized... But she herself had *done* something.

She pressed her intercom. "Dee, I forgot to tell you. File a health insurance termination for Scott. Right away."

The pause yawned over the speaker. "A termination, Ms. Lipnick? But I thought Scott was on vacation."

"No, Dee. He was fired. What good is a copy boy who's late every other day? And I want those deposition digests for the Air National case on my desk in an hour. I'll look pretty idiotic if I can't go into court and cross examine those grapeheads on prior testimony. Oh, and remember, we only have a week to get out the preliminary jury instructions for the JAX Avionics appeal."

"Yes, Ms. Lipnick."

Joyce switched off and listened to the bug.

"Did you hear that shit?" Dee whispered to Marianne. "She fired Scott!"

"And he was so cute," Marianne lamented. "That face, and—Christ, did he have a body."

"Tell me about it." Dee's whisper lowered. "That guy could go all night. It was unreal."

"Dee! You mean you... With *Scott?*"

"A bunch of times," she giggled. "Let's just say that all my sick leave's used up for the year, and there're a lot of worn out beds at the Regency Inn."

"Dee!"

But even this news didn't dishearten Joyce. Not now. Not ever again, she resolved. *What's a woman to do, girls? I wish I could tell you, because I did it.*

And as for Dee... *Giddy little slut.* Joyce would trump something and fire her next week.

¤ ¤ ¤ ¤ ¤

"Darling?" Joyce set down her litigation bag and unlocked the steel-framed bedroom door. She supposed it was fitting: that Scott's prison be a bedroom. Poetic justice with a twist.

He was waiting for her in bed. "God, honey, I missed you." His strong arms reached out for her. *He's just so sweet,* she thought. *How can I be mad at him?* She decided not to even bring up the business with Dee. That was over now. All of his infidelities were over. Instead, she kicked

Please Let Me Out

off her shoes, climbed into the luxurious four-poster, and was embraced by him at once. "I missed you more," she whispered.

"Uh-uh." His kiss devoured her: it took all the stresses of the day and banished them. It made her forget everything. In just seconds, she was so *hot*. His tongue roved her mouth. His hands—strong, assured, insistent—shucked her right out of the charcoal cardigan, then stripped off her white Evan-Picone silk blouse. Nimble fingers released her breasts from lace bra and stroked her nipples. *Oh God, oh my love,* came the helpless thought. His mouth sucked her breath out of her chest.

"Baby," he murmured. "Please."

Her own kisses descended then. Scott's hands peeled away her skirt as Joyce played her tongue over his nipples, then licked ever downward. "Sweetheart..." His fingers finnicked in her coiffed black hair, pushing. "Do you love me?" she asked and admitted his penis into her mouth before he could answer. He squirmed, moaning. She sucked slow and hard while her fingers explored testicles that felt large and heavy as hen's eggs. "Do you love me?" Again. "Do you love me, darling?" Again, again. "Yes," he panted. Her tongue traced around the gorged dome, teasing the tiny egress. This only heightened his squirming, as Joyce squirmed herself to get shed of her panties.

"Joyce—honey... I love you *so* much."

"Do you? Do you really?"

"Yes!"

"Then show me." She crawled up to poise herself, then placed her sex right onto his mouth. Her eyes rolled back at the instant flood of sensation.

"You taste lovely," he murmured.

¤ ¤ ¤ ¤ ¤

Later—many, many hours later—Joyce lay sated and deliciously sore. She sipped Perrier-Jouet and watched him sleep. So beautiful, so loving. Czanek's photographs reared in her mind. And Dee? *Don't think about it. The little tramp.* Joyce could scream thinking of Scott with someone else. Those strong hands, the broad sculpted chest, shoulders, and back, and that gorgeous curved cock. *With someone else?* she pondered. *No, never again.*

Who could provide for him better than Joyce? Four hundred thousand a year, a spacious house on the water, and anything else he'd ever need. *And love,* she thought. *Real, mature, guiding love.*

She'd never been with a man like him: so passionate, so deft.

His ability to sense her—her moods, her needs, her desires—was nearly psychic, and the orgasms he gave her—a dozen hot thrumming gifts each night—wrung pleasure from her nerves like warm water being twisted from a sponge. Often he'd make love to her till she simply couldn't move.

And he would understand the rest, in time. When he was older and realized that Joyce knew what was best for him. That's all that mattered. *The truth,* she thought.

Later, his whispers woke her. "Darling?" His hands traced her warm flesh. "Darling?" He nuzzled her breasts, stroked her back and buttocks. "Once more," he whispered.

Joyce's heart pattered against her fatigue. "I don't think I can do it again, honey. You wear me out!"

"Yes," he insisted. "Yes." He rolled over on top of her, pinned her arms above her head as his erection slid directly into her sex. "I love to make you come." The deep, gentle strokes, like a lovely derrick of flesh, drew expertly in and out of her. Joyce felt electrified. Her breasts filled, her nipples distended to pebbles. Oh, she could do it again, all right. Always. Always. Her hands plied his muscled buttocks as he rocked into her, and his penis—always so hard for her, so large and knowing—tilled her salt-damp depths without abatement. Orgasms like sweet dreams unloosed in her, strings of them, carrying her away with their succulent spasms. *I'm in heaven,* she affirmed. *I'm in heaven every night.*

When he'd finished, Joyce lay immobile, shellacked in sweat and afterglow. His semen ran out of her, so much of it. Scott coddled her, soothing her inflamed breasts, kissing up and down her throat. "Joyce, I know I was bad before," he whispered.

No, she thought. *Please.*

"But I really do love you. I would never want anyone else again, ever. Please believe me, darling…"

Please don't…

"But it drives me crazy, sitting here by myself all day waiting for you. Each hour you're gone feels like a week."

Joyce was wilting.

"Oh, please, honey. Please let me out."

She stroked his hair, touched the side of his handsome face. "I will," she promised. "I will."

But the promise, like many made among lovers, was a lie. She knew she could never, ever let him out.

¤   ¤   ¤   ¤   ¤

Their morning ritual: breakfast in bed. Nude, they fed each other languidly—Eggs Benedict, Iranian caviar on toast points, chickoried coffee—as their bodies pressed. Then she showered and began to dress. She always dressed slowly, knowing his fascination for watching her. It

Please Let Me Out

made her feel sexy, delightfully lewd.

"You're so beautiful," he said. His clear baby-blue eyes fixed on her from the bed, "I might have to touch myself."

"Don't you dare," Joyce said behind a sly grin. Of course he touched himself; all men did. But did he think about her when he did it? Facing him, she snapped her bra, then teasingly drew her stockings up her legs. "I want you to save it for me, all of it. Every drop."

"Well..." His grin cut into her. "I'll try."

She fastened her floral waist-skirt, then buttoned up the placketed Jacquard top.

"Give me something," he said.

"What?"

"Give me your panties."

Joyce blushed. "Scott, I can't go to work without—"

"Yes you can. I want them with me, so I can think about you sitting there at the office with nothing underneath. I'll think about your beautiful pussy all day, and how bad I want to taste it."

God! Joyce's blush deepened. When he talked dirty like that, she was helpless. She slipped off her panties and tossed them to Scott, who plucked them out of the air and held them fast to his chest.

"I love you," he said.

"Not as much as I love you," she assured him, and then she assured him even further when she left the bedroom and locked the heavy hardwood door behind her.

¤   ¤   ¤   ¤   ¤

It was for his own good, anyway. Cruel, yes. Extreme, certainly.

But left to his own devices, Scott would cheat on any woman he became involved with. *What kind of life is that?* Joyce inquired. *What would he become?* All Scott had were his looks. Little education, and less drive. Without Joyce's guidance, he'd be a drifter all his life. *I'm saving him from himself. He'll thank me someday.*

Joyce idled the Porsche into the firm's underground lot, then strode, Bali heels clicking, to the elevator. *Of course, keeping a man locked in your bedroom presents some legal problems.* But why worry? The windows were Lexan set into steel frames, the doors were all locked, and the great waterfront house stood so remote he could yell till his face turned blue and no one would hear him.

"Good morning, Ms. Lipnick," Dee and Marianne greeted in unison when Joyce entered the front office.

"Good morning, girls." She repressed the urge to frown at Dee, whose large breasts threatened to erupt from her blouse. *If she ever has a child,* Joyce postulated, *it'll overdose on milk.* "Don't forget those Delany 'rogs, Dee. I want them out today."

"Yes, Ms. Lipnick."

"And those JAX instructions—today."

"Yes, Ms. Lipnick."

Blond ditz. Thinks she can steal away any man with those big boobs. In her office, Joyce contemplated her own breasts in the mirror. They looked fine now—the $5,500 implant job had taken care of the sag. And as for her dreaded cellulite, good old Dr. Liposuction had made short work of it. Scott being so handsome, Joyce felt the maintenance of her own appearance was an obligation. *You're fifty-one now, Joyce, and you're not getting any younger.* Soon would be time for another lift, or a chemical peel. Thank God for plastic surgeons.

But the two fresh young girls outside inhibited her. She pressed her intercom. "Marianne, come into my office please."

"Yes, Ms. Lipnick?" said the receptionist a moment later.

"Come in please, and close the door." Joyce stood up, mildly befuddled. "This may sound silly, Marianne, but I'd like your opinion about something. Your honest opinion."

"Sure."

"Am I..." The question drifted. "Do you think..."

"What is it, Ms. Lipnick?"

"What I mean is, do you think I'm pretty?"

The young receptionist fidgeted at the question, "Well, of course, Ms. Lipnick. You're a very attractive woman. In fact, I heard some the associates talking the other day, and they were saying how they couldn't understand why a woman so attractive wasn't married."

Joyce brimmed. "Ah, well. Thank you, Marianne. It's very nice that you related that to me. But please don't tell anyone I asked."

"Of course not, Ms. Lipnick."

Marianne left. Joyce reseated herself and thought, *There, see? Nothing to be paranoid about...* Nevertheless, she turned on the bug.

"Dee! You'll never guess what the Ice-Bitch just asked." Joyce's jaw set. *Oh, so it's the Ice-Bitch is it?* "She asked me if I thought she was *pretty!*"

Dee chirped laughter. "What did you say?"

"I'm not stupid, I told her she was very attractive." Marianne chirped a bit of her own laughter. "I even made up a lie about how the associates thought so too."

"I still can't get over that boob-job she got. Thinks no one noticed. One day they're like pancakes hanging to her waist, and the next day she's Dolly Parton."

Please Let Me Out

"What an old bag!" Dee whispered.

An old bag, huh? Joyce smirked back her ire. Pancakes. She'd trump something up on Marianne and fire her next week, too. Then the two little airheads could stand in the unemployment line together. See if their youth put food on the table. See if their big tits paid the rent.

¤   ¤   ¤   ¤   ¤

That night Scott spread Joyce Lipnick out like a feast. A feast of passion. A feast of warm flesh. Her orgasms rushed out of her, each a torrid spirit unleashed by her lover's ministrations. It was like this every night now: any pleasure Joyce could imagine was made manifest in the locked room's gossamer dark.

Via mouth, hand, or genitals, Scott left no orifice untended, no anticipation unslaked. Time passed not in minutes, nor hours, but in the repeated pulses of her bliss. His love consumed her, it carried her away on angels' wings to a demesne of passion and indefectibility that was theirs and theirs alone.

It would be like this, she knew, for the rest of their lives. Till death do them part. Scott's imprisonment was really his salvation, his *freedom* to love and to be loved to the ultimate limit of truth. What could be more wonderful, or more real, than that?

Later, they embraced, laved in sweat, lacquered in joy. Joyce fell asleep, content by the feel of his copious semen in her sex, and the trail of its aftertaste glowing down her throat. But she also fell asleep to his whispers, and the night's ever-faint plea:

"Please, Joyce. Please let me out."

¤   ¤   ¤   ¤   ¤

Weekends unfolded in sheer hedonism. Rich meals in bed, between frenetic bouts of love. Once Scott ate Steak Tartar out of the cleft of Joyce's bosom. Another time he'd poured an entire bottle of Martell Cordon Bleu over her body and licked it off. Salmon roe was daintily eaten off of genitalia. Sashimi was lain out on abdomens. Once Scott had even filled her sex with baby Westcott oysters—flown in fresh from Washington–and plucked each one out with his tongue.

Was this so bad, so cruel, to share with him life's delicacies? To enjoy each other in unbridled abandon? What difference did it make that the door was locked? Between hard and heavy love-making, they'd loll in the jacuzzi, sipping champagne from Cristal d'Arques flutes. Swirls of warm bubbles cosseted them. Joyce couldn't resist; any proximity to Scott lit a lewd fuse in her that never went out. Frequently she'd fellate him beneath the water, gentling stroking his buttock's groove. Scott shuddered amid the luxurious swirls, then Joyce would coax out his climax with her hand and watch the precious curls of sperm churn away in the foam...

Week mornings shared the same feasts of the palate. "I've got to keep my baby well-fed," she'd say. "You'll need the energy tonight." Then he'd watch her shower and dress—in total adoration. Giving him these images of herself kept her aroused all day. To hell with what those silly tramps thought? If Joyce wasn't really beautiful, then why was Scott always so hot for her? Sometimes she'd make love to him just before leaving: fully dressed but for panties she'd straddle him amid the covers, and just ride him until his climax answered the demand of her loins. Or she'd service him orally, and swallow up his need. "That should tide you over till I come home, hmm?"

This particular morning, though, he repeated his former request just as she would leave. *My darling fetishist,* she thought.

"Give me something," he said.

"Hmmm?" Joyce coyly replied.

"Your bra," he decided. "Give me your bra."

"Oh, so it's my bra this time?"

"That's right. Take it of f right now and give it to me." His smile teased at her, his awesome pectorals flexed as he lay with his fingers laced behind his head. "So I can think about you sitting at your desk all day long with your bare breasts rubbing against your blouse. I'll think about your beautiful nipples getting hard, tingling. I'll think about kissing them, licking them...all day..."

Joyce's face flushed. She'd get excited just listening to him! She removed her blouse, tossed him the sheer, lacy bra, and redressed.

Scott held the bra like an icon. "I love you," he affirmed.

"I love you too, and I'll show you how much when I come home."

And when she left, and locked the sturdy door behind her, Scott's eyes squeezed shut so hard that tears leaked out. His hands mangled the bra, twisting, twisting, as though it were not a bra at all, but a garrote.

¤   ¤   ¤   ¤   ¤

Joyce's guilt frequently presented itself by midday. So she did what all good lawyers did with guilt: she rationalized it out of existence. *Look at what I'm absolving him from,* she attested. Shallow interludes, bogus relationships, disease. What she'd done was actually an act of love—a superlative one—and she knew that already he was beginning to realize that. Her mere sleeping with him was proof, wasn't it? At night Joyce locked herself in with him. She was open to him, vulnerable; in a sense, she was at his mercy every night. Scott easily had the physical capability to kill her if he wanted to. But not once had he even threatened violence.

Because he loves me, she realized, braless and musing at her desk. *Because he's finally beginning to understand.*

Without me, he knows he's powerless against the seductions of the world. *If I hadn't taken the necessary steps, he'd still be out there cheating on me, wasting his life and disillusioning himself. Causing pregnancies. Catching chlamydia, herpes, AIDS.*

He knows now. This is the only way.

Between deposition rewrites, Joyce turned on her bug. Dee and Marianne, the magpies, chattered away as always.

"Gary was such a dream. I mean, we were perfect together."

"Dee, Gary was a conniving, treacherous *cockhound*. He was putting the make on your mother, for God's sake."

"Yeah, and both my sisters, too. I hate to think how many women he went to bed with while we were engaged."

"They take everything for granted... The minute they find a good thing, they're snuffling around every skirt in sight."

"Men. Sometimes you could just lock them up."

Joyce nodded a curt approval. *Ladies and gentlemen of the court, the verdict is in, and the judgment is unanimous.*

She thought about Scott all day, her tingling nipples an interminable reminder of her bralessness. She imagined Scott's adroit tongue gingerly encircling the tender areolae, his heavenly mouth sucking them out. She imagined his hands describing the contours of her breasts—adoring them, worshiping them. And she imagined much more, till the urge to masturbate overwhelmed her. *No!* she demanded. *Wait.* Why touch herself when in just a few hours *he* would be touching her?

Marianne buzzed. "Ms. Lipnick? There's a man to see you.."

A man? Probably some counter-lit bozo from the JAX Avionics appeal. *Wants to settle now for five or ten mil. Don't hold your breath, pal.* "Send him in, please," she said.

Past the threshold stepped a tall, well-postured man in a fine pinstripe suit. Short sandy hair, blue eyes. *Handsome,* she thought. But something bland like a stoic chill set into his face. "Ms. Joyce Lipnick?" he queried. "My name is Spence."

Joyce stood up, hard-pressed not to frown. "Well, what can I do for you... Spence?"

"Oh, I'm sorry. I should say *Lieutenant* Spence."

Lieutenant?

"...District Major Case Section."

Joyce felt forged in ice—

Spence continued, "You are under arrest, Ms. Lipnick, for first-degree sexual misconduct, abduction, and sexual imprisonment, and those are just the trifling charges."

"Now see here, Lieutenant!" Joyce erupted. "What in God's name are you talking about?"

Behind the policeman, Dee and Marianne could be seen peaking in, their faces pinched, inquisitive. Spence looked like a well-dressed golem as he paused to assay Joyce's expression.

And then it dawned on her. *God, no. Somehow Scott got—*

"He got out, Ms. Lipnick," Spence informed her. "It must've taken him hours to pick the lock on the door—he did it with two bent bra-clips. Then he got to the phone and called us."

Joyce's nipples instantly lost their arousal. She could only stand there now, opposing this brazen cop as she felt all the blood run out of her face. "I—" she attempted. But the words dissolved. In fact, her entire being felt as though it were dissolving right there before the witness of the whole world. Eventually she was able to croak, "I had no choice. He was cheating on me."

"Well, you certainly took care of that inconvenience." Spence, for only a moment, spared a smile. "And it gives me great pleasure, Ms. Lipnick, to inform you that you have the right to remain silent, and that anything you say…"

Joyce paid no attention to the rest of the policeman's obligatory mirandization. Instead, paling, she thought in scorn, *The goddamn ungrateful bastard got out. I should've know he'd try something like this. How could I be so stupid?*

And what was that Spence had initially said?

—and those are just the trifling charges—

Spence, at least, had a lawyer's wit.

Dee and Marianne looked on, aghast. Joyce's face felt like pallid wax as Spence handcuffed her. "Don't you have anything to say, Ms. Lipnick?" the policeman inquired. "In my experience, criminals generally have a comment or two upon arrest."

"I think I will observe my right to remain silent," Joyce blandly replied.

"A commendable decision."

But as Joyce was ushered out, she couldn't escape the inscrutable image—-Scott, travailing down the hall for the phone. Nor the final consideration: *I guess I should have out his arms off too,* she thought.

Please Let Me Out
Afterword

Here's another piece from my "Torso Period." (Oops, I hope you're reading the stories before you read these afterwords!) I couldn't have been more thrilled when John Maclay bought it for his anth "Voices From The Night," for it marked my first appearance in a hardcover book.

The Horror of Chambers
Foreword

I'm doing a foreword here instead of an afterword because, well, this story stinks! Hence I feel the need to preface that it's my first published story, so PLEASE bear that in mind. Please! W. Paul Ganley–clearly more out of charity than anything else–was kind enough to include it in his Weirdbook *offshoot* Eerie Country. *I think I was 19 when I wrote it, got it published three years later. It's included in the collection as a curio, and to serve as an example of the imitative–and often laughable–roots most would-be writers try to dig up when they first start out. Robert W. Chambers, like Lovercraft and Machen, was the first horror I read in any serious fashion. Of course, this is an inept pastiche, but I think is projects my love for Chamber's infamous "The Yellow Sign," which to this day strikes me as one of the creepiest stories I've ever read. And I'll forever remain grateful to Mr. Ganley for publishing this and giving a kid the necessary encouragement to continue.*

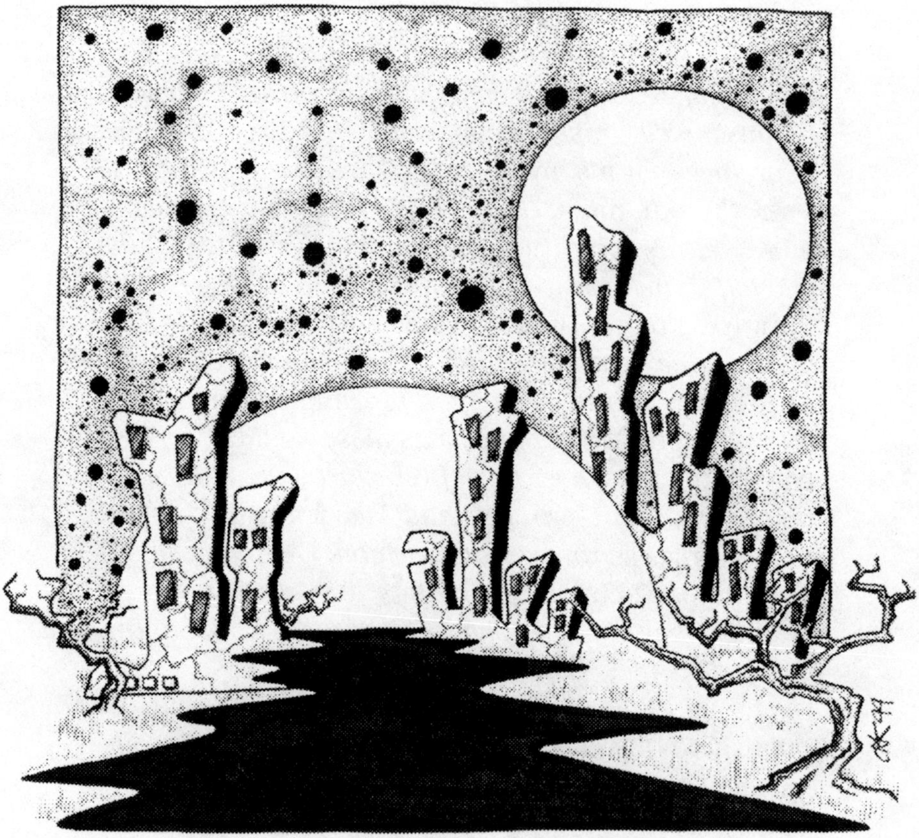

The Horror of Chambers

"MORE WINE, CHARLES?"

"Thank you, Edward," Charles replied with his usual actor's charm. Edward had always admired Charles. He was a real classic of a man. Well-read, well-educated, well-spoken, and well-cultivated. He was an authority on the arts. All arts: media, painting, and literature especially. Not only was he a patron, but also a participator. A published author, a pastel artist, and, most important, an actor. An actor of most intense magnitude.

Edward poured more wine and asked:

"So how are the rehearsals coming?"

"Splendid! And today I had a marvelous audition for a movie part! I was one of five chosen from five hundred!"

"Charles, you'll never cease to amaze me," Edward smiled.

Charles changed the subject, so as not to appear pompous in front of his friend. "Tell me, Edward, are you still engrossed with reading all that morbid literature?"

"Not morbid. Realistic."

"Indeed. I was wondering, have you ever read anything by Robert W. Chambers?"

Edward's face lit up with elation. "Why, yes! Chambers was a brilliant author! So versatile, and such culture! He wrote over seventy books, you know. Unfortunately, I haven't read much of his work. It's quite hard to find nowadays."

"Last week I read one of his books called *The King In Yellow*. Have you read it?"

"No," Edward answered sadly, "I'm afraid not."

"Well, I must say, it was a masterpiece of horror. Scared the dickens out of me! I thought you'd be interested, since you seem to favor that sort of stuff."

"Why yes!" Edward replied. "Go on!"

"All right. You see, the book itself is a colletion of horror stories; ten stories in all. They loosely correlate toward the same subject, the King in Yellow."

Edward projected a puzzled look and asked:

"Who is the King in Yellow?"

"In this case," Charles returned, "not who, but what. According to Chambers, The King in Yellow is a play. And a very bizarre one at that. So bizarre, in fact, that all who read it become hopelessly insane. And like I said, all the stories in this book relate to this play, this King in Yellow."

"But what does the play consist of?"

"Ah! That's the fine part. Chambers tells that the play concerns a land called Carcosa. Lost Carcosa. Its twin suns hide behind the lake of Hali and the black stars rise. Carcosa's inhabitants are called the Hyades, and they sing to their ruler, the King in Yellow. The king whom emperors serve."

"I see. Science fiction."

"No, not really. Though Carcosa is not on this earth, all of Chambers' stories are. They only tell of how earthly men react to their discoveries in the play. I choose to call it not science fiction, but instead, theological horror. Chambers makes scores of religious allusions, the greatest of which is that Carcosa is a hellish heaven, it's ruler an evil god. But even more paramount is the Man in the Pallid Mask."

"The Pallid Mask?"

"Yes. Once the king's favorite counselor. However, the Man in the Pallid Mask becomes envious and ambitious, and dares to question the rule of the King in Yellow. For this, he is banished from Carcosa—to earth. And he shall not return until he has made all the people of earth bow down and worship the King in Yellow. So, you can easily see that the Man in the Pallid mask is Chamber's version of Satan: a fallen angel."

"How does this Pallid Mask fellow get the people of earth to worship the King in Yellow?"

"By trickery! Hook or crook, you might say. You see, each earth man turns his soul over to the Man in the Pallid Mask, then he accepts the emblem of the King in Yellow. The emblem is called the Yellow Sign. The Yellow Sign is in the form of a black stone on which the Yellow King's sign is engraved. Once a man possesses the Yellow Sign, his soul is forever lost to the Pallid Mask. The story gets a bit confusing here, as the possessor must be killed by a previous lost soul. Apparently the Yellow Sign must be collected by someone who is physically dead, but

The Horror of Chambers

still contains a will. Though his body rots to the bone, he still moves like a zombie until he has found the Yellow Sign. He then murders the current possessor, and thus, his soul is released to wicked Carcosa. The murdered man, in turn, then becomes the new physically dead assassin. What you might call a gruesome game of tag, in which the cycle continues on and on."

"So Chambers' stories are about men who have fallen prey to this Yellow Sign, and its consequences?"

"Precisely."

"What if a man doesn't accept the Yellow Sign?"

"He has no choice. Once the man in the Pallid Mask has given it to him, even if it be by tricking him into taking it, or by planting it on him, all is lost."

"This play," Edward inquired, "The King in Yellow—I assume it's imaginary."

"Chambers claims," Charles returned, "that it does, in fact, exist, and is quite real. But I'm sure it's just a hoax; totally fictional, like Lovecraft's Necronomicon."

"I see," Edward reflected. "Sounds rather grim, but interesting nonetheless. I'll have to read it sometime."

"Indeed. Chambers proves himself a very formidable fiction writer."

The two men chatted in that vein for a while longer. At midnight, they shook hands and Charles departed, leaving Edward alone for the evening.

Edward had not a worry in the world, for he was independently wealthy. He didn't have to work, like Charles, in order to secure a living. He could come and go as he pleased. As he ascended the stairs to his bedroom, he decided that he would drive to the city in the morning and do a little shopping.

Edward rose at ten. After getting cleaned up, he got in his car and headed downtown.

When he arrived, he parked in the usual pay lot, and stepped out into the cold light of day. Lazily, he strolled down 52nd street and watched the hustle and bustle of the big city. At times like these, he was glad he didn't have to work. Being rich was so much easier. No boss, no office, no stress. Edward smiled with contentment and satisfaction, musing at the virtues of the good life. He could do anything he wanted. Listen to music. Occasional writing. And yes! Reading. Reading horror stories all day long. His life was a horror story—and he loved it.

Edward decided to browse through some bookstores. New York has some lovely bookstores. He especially loved the used bookstores. They were treasure houses of forgotten literature.

He walked into the first one he saw and enjoyed the tell-tale signs. Books stacked vertically up and down every wall. Dimly lit. Ladders standing like stick figure sentinels, reaching out with long wooden arms to touch the darkest corners, the most inaccessible shelves.

Edward browsed around for awhile until he noticed he was the only person in the store. Not a single customer in the place. *How lovely,* he thought. He had the store to himself.

He found some old Hitchcock paperbacks he had never seen before. And some even older anthologies. He was especially surprised at finding an ancient volume of Clark Ashton Smith's *The Double Shadow*, thought by most to be extinct; a particularly rewarding find.

Edward continued digging for more. Books were stacked behind more books. And more books. He searched frantically through the obsolescent shelves, raising a great cloud of dust that seemed to diffuse the entire shop. Then he discovered a thin black hard-covered volume. He looked curiously at it. The cover and binding had no title.

Its cover made a crackling sound as he opened it. He mused at the fact that he was probably the first to open it in many years. The copyright was 1895. He turned the tattered page and cast his eyes upon the book's title. It read:

The King in Yellow.

Marvelous! It was the book of short stories that Charles had told him of. But oddly enough, he didn't notice the name of Robert W. Chambers. *That's strange,* he thought. The author's name wasn't even on the title page. Edward then turned to the second page. He froze; his mouth dropped open wide as he read:

The King in Yellow
Act 1 Scene 1

Edward couldn't believe his eyes. It wasn't Chambers' book of short stories, but instead, the play itself! Charles had dismissed it as fiction, but he was wrong! It did exist! It was real! What a discovery!

Dumbfoundedly, Edward ran to the cashier, leaving the Hitchcocks and the Smith volume on the shelf.

"Miss!" he snapped. "Might I ask where you came upon this book?"

"What is it?" she inquired.

Edward handed her the book and she inspected it.

"Hmm," she muttered. "I've never heard of it. It's probably been in here for ages. I have no idea how we got it."

"I see. What is the cost?"

"Oh, I think two dollars is a fair price."

The Horror of Chambers

"Excellent!" he exclaimed, as he handed her a twenty. "Keep the change, my dear!"

The girl stood, astonished, as Edward exited the shop with a mammoth grin on his face. Without delay, he galloped to his car and paid the attendant. Then he sped home with his prize.

"Wait until Charles hears about this!" he said aloud.

Before he knew it, he was pulling up his drive on Hawberk Avenue. In a flash, Edward was sitting in his bedroom with the book before him on his desk. He couldn't wait to read it. Like a child at Christmas, he opened the book to page one.

The King in Yellow
Act 1 Scene 1

And the reading began. As Edward delved deeper into the play's pages, he began to read faster—then frantically. He absorbed every word, every letter. Soon he found himself reading the words aloud.

"Lost Carcosa! Dim Carcosa! The Lake of Hali! The Yellow Sign! Carmilla's screams! The King! The King! The King in Yellow!"

Edward finished the play. He read it again, and again. And again. He laughed. He cried. He shouted. Tears streamed down his laughing face. He ranted and raved, for his words he read were sacred and spellbinding.

He read until midnight. Then he sat in the dark with a hideous grin on his tear drenched face; exhausted and drained. Soon, he went to bed, thinking of the hallowed words he had read. Later, he flicked off the lone lamp and went to sleep. He dreamed.

He dreamed he was walking down unknown streets. He found himself in a place he had never been before. Looking up at the horizon, he noticed that the suns were setting behind the lake. Passers-by cast long black shadows on the cobble road. He walked and walked. The clouds were black. The stars were blacker.

A man walked by and Edward asked:

"Excuse me, sir. Where am I?"

"Why, you sir," the man answered, "are in Carcosa, the land of the King. The land of mirth and frolic."

"But alas," Edward returned sadly, "I am not happy. I see no mirth."

"Then come with me, my friend, and I shall show you mirth."

Edward followed the man.

"Where are you taking me?"

"To a party!" the man replied. "To a masquerade party!"

"A masquerade party? But lo, I have no costume."

"Fear not, my friend. We shall get costumes now."

The man took Edward into a shop. A costume shop. It was filled with filled with gay costumes of every sort.

The man approached and handed Edward a plastic mask.

"Here, my friend, is your costume."

"But alas, sir, I have not money to pay for it."

"There is no money in Carcosa, land of the King."

With that, they left and proceeded down the strange street.

"At the masquerade party," the man said, "we must exchange gifts with the others."

Edward sighed, "I have no gift to exchange."

"Fear not, my friend, for I shall provide. Here is a gift for you to exchange."

The man handed Edward a gold locket. Edward opened the locket and saw that it contained a photograph of a twin sunset.

"This is a lovely gift," Edward said. "Whomever I exchange with shall be pleased. Thank you."

"My pleasure, sir. We shall soon be at the party. It is time for us to put on our masks."

With that, the two men donned their masks. They were happy smiling masks, and they made Edward happy.

They approached a large stone building.

"We are here."

The two masked gentlemen entered the given building and climbed down a dark column of granite steps filled with people, all wearing happy smiling masks.

"Behold!" the man said. "Mirth! I shall leave you now, to enjoy yourself among the Hyades!"

"Thank you."

Edward walked amidst the crowd of cheerful partiers. They were all wearing masks. However, in the distance, Edward noticed one mask that wasn't smiling. Instead, it was an ugly, frowning mask. It was repulsive and Edward turned away from it.

Cheerful music reverberated in the ballroom, along with laughter. Edward walked into the middle of the crowd, in attempts to mingle. But for some reason, the happy partiers didn't notice Edward. They ignored him.

As Edward stood wondering, he, again, noticed the person with the ugly mask. He was closer this time and saw that the mask was even uglier than he had thought. It was disgusting and pale, and possessed a frighteningly radiant quality. Edward quickly turned away, the evil mask making him uneasy.

The Horror of Chambers

Just then, one of the masked partiers stepped onto a podium and gleefully announced:

"Hyades! Hear me out! The time has come to unmask and exchange gifts! So, seek out a partner. Unmask!"

Edward searched frantically for a partner, but all were taken. Then, someone came up behind him and asked:

"Do you, sir, have a partner to exchange with?"

Edward turned, and was startled in finding that it was the man wearing the ugly mask.

"Why, uh...no," he answered.

"Wonderful!" the stranger exclaimed. "Here is my gift to you."

"And mine for you," Edward returned, as he handed him the locket. In the corner of his eye, Edward noticed that the frolicking crowd had now exposed their true, smiling faces. Everyone had taken off their masks, so Edward did the same.

Then he inspected the gift from the stranger. It was a pendant; a polished black stone on a string. The stone had a geometric figure etched on it.

"Thank you very much," Edward said to the man.

"And I thank you."

Edward then noticed that the man had not unmasked. Wincing, he noticed the sickening details of the man's hideous mask. It was a visage of bellicose abomination. Sickly-pale. Grotesque and waxen. It was horrible; a revolting sight.

Edward exclaimed in objection:

"Why, sir, do you not unmask?"

"Unmask?" the stranger said.

"Indeed. The time has come. All here have put aside their masks but you. I, sir, insist that you unmask."

"But lo," the stranger returned, "I wear no mask."

With that, he walked away and Edward stood, bewildered.

"You wear no mask!" he stammered. "Wait! You say—no mask!"

But the man was gone, as was everyone else. Still aghast by the experience, Edward left the ballroom and stepped out onto the street.

There, he was again stunned.

Stunned, because the street was not of cobble, but of asphalt. A street sign at his side read Hawberk Avenue, the street where he lived. He looked up at the white clouds and the bright stars. The sun was setting at the horizon. He walked up his drive leading to his front door, still fondling the black stone that the stranger had given him.

Edward heard the footsteps behind him. In the distance, he saw someone walking in the fog. It was a man wearing a dark overcoat with the collar turned up. He proceeded toward Edward. Yearning for the company, Edward put a cigarette to his lips and approached the man.

"Excuse me, sir," Edward asked. "Might you have a light?"

The man did not answer. Instead, he glared at Edward with an odious, abhorrent look on his face. Edward saw that the man's face was sallow with pallor, as if diseased; like the face of a slug, plump and slimy.

Edward was nauseated, and said:

"Same to you, you fat crud! Worm!" the man shuffled away.

Disgusted, Edward lit his cigarette and stood at the end of his driveway, thinking of the man at the party

As he blew the cigarette smoke from his lungs, he heard more footsteps. It was the same man in the dark overcoat walking back. Again, Edward caught the man glaring, with that same hateful look about him. Edward leered back into the loathsome, puffy face; like the countenance of a corpse. The man stopped and muttered something over and over. But with it came a sick, gurgling sound, unearthly and deep. It sounded like:

"Do you have the Yellow Sign?

"Do you have the Yellow Sign?

"Do you have the Yellow Sign?"

Edward dropped his cigarette and retreated in disgust, not knowing of what the man spoke. He paced hurriedly up his driveway, and swept through the front door, after which he locked the door securely. Still holding the pendant, Edward climbed up the stairs to his bedroom. The moment he entered the telephone on his nightstand began to ring violently.

"Hello—" Edward said.

"Do you have the Yellow Sign?" a far-off voice asked in a gurgling tone.

"What? Who is this?"

"Do you have the Yellow Sign?"

"What on earth are you…"

"I must have the Yellow Sign."

"Now listen here! I demand that you iden—"(click)

Edward stood shaking in his room, frightened out of his wits. Not a second after the mysterious phone call, he heard something. Yes… he heard footsteps. Sharp, clapping footsteps. Outside. Footsteps. Edward ran to the window and looked out. Someone was walking down the street toward the house.

"Oh my God."

Edward watched in horror as the huddled man in the dark overcoat turned and shuffled up the driveway, slowly making his way to the front door. Edward pushed up the window and shouted:

The Horror of Chambers

"Go away! I'll call the police!"

Edward then sighed in relief; the front door was locked. The man couldn't possibly get in.

Then he heard a loud sound coming from the foyer, from the front door. It was a loud slam, followed by the sound of cracking wood.

In a panic, Edward locked his bedroom door and listened.

More footsteps, slow and plodding. Someone was in the house. It was *him*. The steps were coming closer. The intruder was coming up the stairs.

"No!"

The intruder was now on the landing, dragging feet toward the bedroom.

"Stay away!" Edward shouted.

The doorknob rattled and turned. Edward ran to his dresser and withdrew a revolver.

"Go away—I have a gun! I won't hesitate to use it!"

Outside, he heard a sick, gurgling sound. In a split-second, the bedroom door barrelled out with a great boom. The trespasser was throwing himself against it. Then again. And again.

Slam!

The door burst open as the wretched man with the puffy white face stepped toward Edward.

"I must have the Yellow Sign," he drooled.

"Stay back, or I'll shoot!"

In a rapid series of thunderous claps, Edward fired five shots into the intruders belly.

"I must have the Yellow Sign!"

The room permeated with a ghastly stench, like that of a dead dog that had spoiled in the sun for three days.

Shrieks of horror came from Edward's gaping mouth, as the man with the detestable face came closer.

Edward aimed, ever-so-carefully, and squeezed the trigger of his pistol. The last shot caught the stranger square in the forehead. Something vile gushed out of his cracked skull. But it wasn't blood. Like a fountain, the wretched liquid spilled onto the floor, forming a puddle of squirming things. Not blood, but maggots. Writhing maggots. Coffin-worms. A pool of moving-putrescent-liquidity.

Still, he nudged closer.

"Give me the Yellow Sign."

Edward could only think of the pendant in his pocket, as the grotesque, decomposed figure pawed at him with rotting hands.

The man grinned nefariously; his lips, wet and oozing with organic bilge. "I must have the Yellow Sign!"

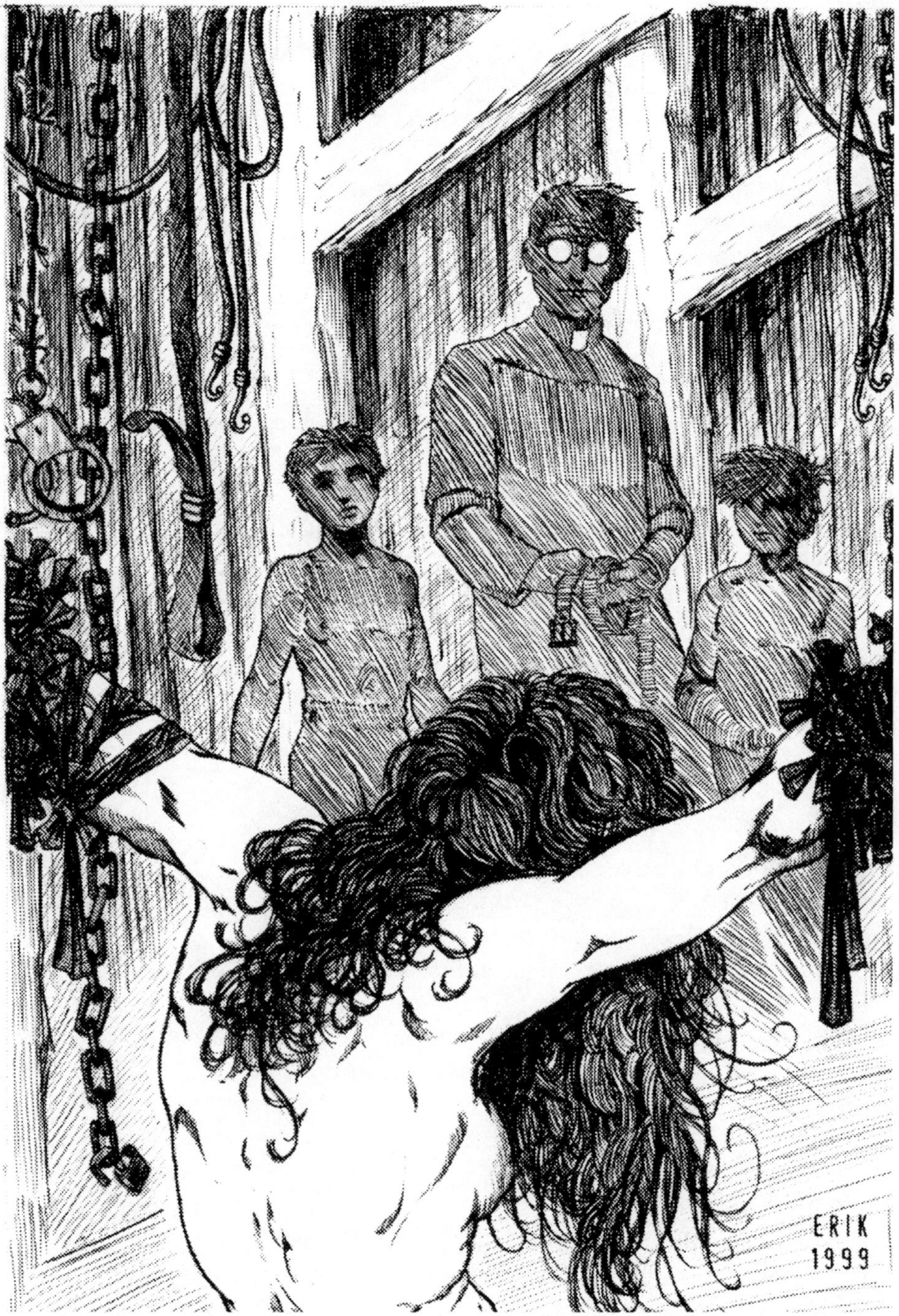
ERIK
1999

SCRIPTURES

MY FATHER WAS an Episcopal minister. He would always inject the heroin into my mother's arm for her. "'Thou shalt rejoice in every good thing which the Lord thy God hath given unto thee,'" he would quote. Then, to my brothers: "Boys?"

"Deuteronomy!" Mark and James would shout.

Mother would collapse on the bed, grinning before the opiate bliss. "'A merry heart maketh a joyful countenance,'" Father would say next, taking down his black trousers.

"Proverbs!" my brothers would shout.

"Right, boys. You've studied well, and I'm proud." His uncircumcised penis looked like a snout. "And, also from Proverbs, 'A wise son hears his father's instructions.' Now, take your mother's clothes off and turn her over onto her belly."

They always made me watch first. Father would spit into my mother's buttocks and slowly sodomize her. "Watch, Ruth," he'd say to me. "The price of wisdom is above rubies."

My mother's head lolled in her stupor.

"And it also says," he'd continue, pumping her, "'a whore is a deep ditch, but love covers all offenses.'"

Then he'd pull out and instruct Mark or James to masturbate him. "Good boys, such fine, good boys," he'd mutter. He'd ejaculate onto my mother's back and make me lick up the semen.

But this was just the beginning, like the opening prayer he'd read before the sunrise service.

¤ ¤ ¤ ¤ ¤

It all started, I guess, when I was about four, but I didn't really become aware of it till I was ten or so. By then Mark and James were fifteen and sixteen. The sex was never mentioned outside of the bedroom; Father had long since programmed us to regard it as "one of God's little secrets." We went to school, did our chores and homework, played with the other parish kids. No one ever knew.

We lived in the big house the diocese provided; Father had been the pastor of St. Edward's for as long as I could remember. Each night before bedtime, we'd all sit together in the living room and read the Bible, and he was always quizzing us on the quotes. Then he'd take us upstairs...

He'd met my mother when he was still in the seminary, doing volunteer work at the halfway house sponsored by the district diocese. He'd counsel the drug addicts and prostitutes that the court paroled there. When he got assigned to St. Edward's, he married her, and maintained her habit with collection money.

Mark and James were perfect little boys, always trying to out-do each other in school and Bible study. My grades were just as good but that never seemed to matter; Father wanted sons, to go on to become ministers, to follow in his footsteps. He'd often beat my mother for giving birth to a girl. Her sins, he'd say, her days of "whoredom," disgraced him in the eyes of God. He'd tie her up a lot and whip her with his belt, and he'd make me watch. "Mother of harlots!" he'd exclaim, cracking the belt across her buttocks and back. "'I come not to call the righteous, but sinners to repent!'" Often he'd slap her in the face too, choke her, spit in her mouth, things like that. He'd grab her hair, twisting her face to my eyes. "Say it!" he'd shriek. "Ecclesiastes! 9:18!"

Eventually, racked by pain and withdrawal, my mother would have no choice but to gasp, "'One sinner destroyeth much good.'"

"There! See!"

Only then, after her confession so to speak, would he give her her heroin. She'd throw up and pass out.

Then it was my turn. The boys would strip me and tie me down to the bed. Sometimes the belt hurt so much, I'd pass out too, but Mark and James would always throw water in my face to revive me. They'd take turns sodomizing me, and my father would celebrate by reciting, "So sayeth in Psalms: How good and pleasant it is when brothers dwell in unity!"

They'd take little breaks in between, watching me flinch each time hot candle wax dripped onto my buttocks or nipples. "The ways of sin are an easy route for the traveler, but only through pain and travail is the route of love revealed."

Sometimes my father would masturbate as he watched Mark and

James having sex with each other. "'Be kindly affectioned to one another with brotherly love.'"

"Romans!" Mark would announce.

"And 'A new commandment I give unto you: That ye love one another.'"

"John!" James would exclaim.

All the while, I'd lie there, usually on my belly, bound and gagged. Then my father would sit on the bed, hold my head over his groin, and make me fellate him. When he came he'd always say, "'Thy lips drop as the honeycomb, honey and milk are under thy tongue.'"

"'Greater love hath no man than this,'" Mark would say when he was done. But he was always ready again soon. They all were. And eventually, my father would always get back to me, with his belt. By then I was trained well.

"Say it!" Father commanded me between the pauses of his belt. His voice sounded like an echo in a mountain rift.

"Psalms! 51:5! Say it!"

I knew that if I didn't say it, they'd burn me some more with the candle. And they'd do more things to my mother.

"Say it!"

"'I was shapen in iniquity,'" I'd sob as the belt cracked down, "'and in sin did my mother conceive me...'"

"The Word of the Lord," Mark and James said together.

They were all completely insane.

¤ ¤ ¤ ¤ ¤

"Leave, Ruth," my mother croaked to me on my sixteenth birthday. "He's killing me, and when I'm gone, he'll do the same to you. You've got to get away from him, from both of them."

Both, she'd said, excluding Mark. He hadn't made it into the seminary; he'd failed the psychiatric interview. My father hadn't been happy. So Mark had joined the Army, the Chaplain's Corp. He was killed in the field during a training accident; a transport helicopter he was on had crashed. No more Mark.

But that still left my father and James. James had actually managed to graduate college, and the diocesan seminary had admitted him. The seminary was so close that James lived at the house, helping my father with the parish, and commuting to school. And during this time, the nightly rituals never stopped. They got worse.

I knew my mother was right; I had to get out or else I'd die. Eventually they'd kill me, like they were killing my mother every day. After Mark's accident, my Father used some of the money from the G.I. insurance policy to make certain "improvements" to the little room upstairs. Whips and chains. An iron-framed bed equipped with manacles. Rectal and vaginal retractors, a shock baton, pins and needles and nipple-screws. Blindfolds, rubber-ball gags, leather wrist and ankle restraints. They even had this weird leather mask they'd zip onto my head sometimes. No eye-holes, no hole for the nose, just a black plastic tube to keep my mouth forced open. It was medieval.

¤ ¤ ¤ ¤ ¤

That last night was a real send off. They had me gagged with the rubber ball, and shackled to the wall in the corner. They liked to make me watch what they did to Mother first. They'd blindfolded her, and lashed her wrists to her knees. She was in withdrawal, convulsing, as James sodomized her vigorously from behind.

"'Love covers all offences,'" my father said, standing aside stroking himself.

"Proverbs!" James exclaimed.

When James was finished, my father whipped her right there on the floor, leaving long, red weals across her back and buttocks. "'Get thee hence!'" he shouted. Then, to James: "'My son, help thy father in his age.'"

"Ecclesiasticus," James said and then took my father's penis into his mouth. All I could do was hang there against the wall and watch. "And from John," my father went on when he'd become aroused enough. Now it was his turn to sodomize my mother. "'Those that loveth not, knoweth not God, for God is love.'"

James wrapped a length of rope tight around her breast, waiting for a vein to bulge. "And Proverbs. 'Love covers all offenses.'"

"Good, good, son," Father complimented, thrusting. "And, now, from Luke. 'Her sins, which are many, are forgiven…'"

"'For she loves much,'" James finished. Then he injected heroin into the vein in my mother's breast, released the rope. She shuddered as my father, next, ejaculated on her buttocks, grunting like some mammoth animal.

James was hard again; he could go six or eight times a night if he wanted to. I saw his solemn face approach from out of the candlelight. "'Thy two breasts are like two young fawns,'" he recited from the Song of Solomon and placed the silver screws on my nipples. He screwed them down till I whined against the rubber ball. "'They are a perverse generation,'" my father added, "'the child in whom there is no faith.'" James took off the ball-gag and zipped the eyeless black mask over my head.

Suddenly the world turned as black as the abyss they had warned me about for my whole life. He took me down from the wall and lay me

Scriptures

out on my back, on the bed, tying my wrists to the iron headboard as my father did the same with my ankles. They stretched me out so tight I thought my arms would pop out of the sockets.

"'Create in her a clean heart, oh God,'" James said, opening my vagina with retractors, "'and renew a right spirit within her.'"

Then he slipped the lubricated shock baton into me, deep.

"'The way of transgressors is hard,'" I could hear my father's voice flutter beyond the black wall of my vision. "'Harken, oh daughter, and consider, and incline thine ear.'"

The baton clicked, then hummed for a second, and a second later its electric pain shot from my sex to my brain. My eyes bulged open inside the black mask. I wanted to scream but the plastic tube in my mouth wouldn't let me.

"'A silent woman is a gift from the Lord.' James?"

"Ecclesiasticus!"

"Good, good. Now… Again."

The baton hummed. The searing pain ran through me again, and my whole body went rigid. I kept trying to scream but all that came out was a weak choking noise.

"'Let your women keep silent, for it is not permitted unto them to speak.' 'There is no fear in love, for perfect love casteth out fear.'"

"'God hath not given us the spirit of fear,'" James continued. He took the baton out, and mounted me. "'But of power and of love…'"

They took turns, taking little breathers in between to zap my breasts and vagina with the baton. For every second of this, I thought I would die—I had to struggle not to. I was whipped until I was numb, sodomized over and over. Then Father stuck his penis into the tube in my mouth and came. "'Out of the mouths of babes and sucklings hast though ordained strength.'"

"Psalms!" shouted James.

The hot sperm slid down my throat. Then—I guess it was James—someone spit into the tube, then urinated into it, and there wasn't anything I could do but swallow. I felt dead and buried, smothered in blinding blackness, and when they began whipping me again, and zapping me with the baton, I didn't even feel it anymore.

No, I couldn't feel, I couldn't see. All I could do was hear.

That's when my father got on top of me again, tightened the nipple screws some more, wringing out blood, and said, "'Come, let us take our fill of love till the morning!'"

¤ ¤ ¤ ¤ ¤

The morning, yes. It was just before dawn when they untied me and put me to bed. I waited a little while, then put on some clothes and snuck downstairs. Father kept some cash in an old alms box in his desk. I was taking the money when the light clicked on.

It was James.

You should've seen him staring at me with that pious, solemn face of his, and if you looked hard enough, you could see the quiet madness raging behind his eyes. Just like Father.

"The thief in the night," he whispered, then he quoted, Job, I think, "'In the dark they dig through houses, which they had marked from themselves during the daytime.'" His hand was at his crotch as he said this. I knew what he was going to do.

"'Thou shalt not steal,'" he said, then grabbed me by the shoulders.

It was a crazy feeling. For the first time in my life I wasn't afraid of him. A sound seemed to buzz in my head.

His face turned into a fish-face when I stuck the letter opener up under his jaw. I could see it digging into the roof of his mouth, and then I quickly slammed a bronze bookend of Thomas Aquinas up against the haft, which drove the opener's point into his brain. He didn't make a sound.

"Yeah?" I said, leaning over. "'Cain rose up to rebel against his brother. And slew him.'"

¤ ¤ ¤ ¤ ¤

I wound up in the city, at the bus station. I didn't know what I was going to do or where I was going to go. I merely put my trust in the Lord. *'We walk by faith, not by sight,'* I told myself in the words of the second letter to the Corinthians. I wasn't afraid. I knew that God would not abandon me.

I got raped twice the first night. My money got stolen. Soon I was sleeping in alleys and picking food out of garbage dumpsters. Within a month, I guess I was probably dying. I prayed and thought of heaven but dreamed of devils and hell. One night I woke up under the cardboard, and a man was sodomizing me. "Gonnas ass me this bitch," he said. "Gonnas fuck you up." *'Blessed are they that put their trust in Him,'* I thought. I did not despair. Then he grabbed my throat, put his penis before my lips. "Goes on, bitch. Lick the shit offa that stick, 'else I'll'se kill you." "'Ye have heard of the patience of Job,'" I said and then did what he told me to do. But his hand never came off my throat. He chuckled in the dark. "Gonnas kill you anyways," he promised. Then he began to strangle me.

"Yeah, gonnas kill you good."

"'Let me die the death of the righteous,'" I managed to choke out.

"Gonnas kill you, an' fucks you again."

I was blacking out then. I thought of Job, *'There the wicked cease from troubling, and there the weary be at rest.'*

Scriptures

"Haves me another nut up yo' dead ass..."

'Come to me all ye who travail and are heavy laden, and I will refresh you...'

His hand on my throat was squeezing my life out like water out of a sponge...

'He shall send His angels with a great sound of a trumpet—'

ka-CRACK!

The man fell off me after the sound like a plank breaking. When my vision cleared I looked up and saw the figure that had saved me. He stood there, a black silhouette with the streetlight behind him, like an aura. Like a halo.

Like an angel.

I was saved.

¤   ¤   ¤   ¤   ¤

Streetlife is another world—it changes you. Like about a month after I got turned out—I changed. Fast.

Coke. Skag. Ice. Eight to ten tricks a night seven nights a week. Shit...

And God? I forgot about Him as fast as He forgot about me. At least, that's how I saw it at the time.

Oh, and the "angel?" The dude who pulled that scumbag off me in the alley? He was a guy named Tredell. Hustler, bagman, pimp. Smalltime. He got me fixed up, fed, got a roof over my head. Then he turned me out.

I was a double sawbuck car trick. I'd hang out on U Street in my shorts. Old men mostly was what picked me up. The Blow-and-Go, we called it. Quick headjob in the car, like that. Shit, I bet I've swallowed enough come to fill a milk bucket. Kinda reminds you of raw egg whites going down. But, Christ, twenty bucks is twenty bucks. If I didn't have a hundred in my pussy pouch end of each night, Tredell'd beat the shit out of me. He ran rock for the local Jamakes, too, and every week or so the point guys'd come over to the crib to meet with him. I was the dessert that sealed the deal— trains, you know? They'd gang-bang me for hours, but, shit, I was so high most of the time I could shit care less. The street does something to you; it kind of splits the way you think about things, almost like you're two people. Part of me was the street whore, but there was another part of me that was still my old self, with the same old dreams. *Where did it all go?* I wondered. All I ever wanted was to be like any other girl my age, and here I was sucking come out of a bunch of old guys' cocks every night, and getting the shit beat out of me every other. The beatings, the gang-bangs, all that shit—that was no big deal because my father and brothers broke me in pretty good there. But it was almost like a ghost of myself always reminding me of how bad I got ripped off by life, how because of my father and brothers, I never got the shit that I should've got. I wanted to graduate high school, go to college, be something. Fuck...

Lotta times the heat was on heavy. The pigs started busting johns and printing their names in the papers. Talk about pissing on business. I couldn't get my take, even when I lowered my price to fifteen, even ten bucks a suck. Shit, it got to the point I was begging these old shits, I was giving them full fucks in their cars for ten, letting 'em ass-fuck me for fifteen, and I still couldn't bring home enough take for Tredell. The fucker beat the shit out of me every night, said he was gonna sell me to the Jamakes for a couple of grand, let 'em turn me to "kiddie burger" he told me. He'd always carry around this little peashooter .22, acting like he was Superfly or something. There were two girls in the stable I know of that Tredell snuffed, popped them each with his piece, said they were burned out on boy and ripping him off. One night I came back to the crib with eighty bucks. He'd been smoking flake and he about went nuts, whipped my ass with an empty Carling bottle, started burning me with cigarettes, then he sticks that .22 up my cooze, tells me if I ever come home with fuckin' eighty bucks again, he's gonna give me a .22 douche. Suddenly that other part of me came back, remembered what I did to James, and what Tredell did to those two chicks, and I didn't really even know what I was doing when I grabbed that little piece of shit Saturday Night Special, quoted John, "'He was a murderer from the beginning, there is no truth in him,'" and busted a cap right in his fuckin' head. Fuck him.

That kinda set the stable free, but most of the other girls went straight to other pimps. Me, I tried to swing it solo, and did all right, until one night I was working Vermont Avenue, and it's almost dawn, and I'm walking home when some guy jumps out of an alley. He conks me in the head with something, drags me into a car, and drives away.

¤   ¤   ¤   ¤   ¤

"'That which is crooked cannot be made straight.'"

The voice revived me like a bucket of cold water. *No, no, no,* I thought even before my vision cleared. I woke up on the metal-framed bed, the pain in my head pounding. I was back at the house.

And standing before me in the candlelight was my father.

"But 'the goodness of God leadeth thee to repentance.'"

No, no, no, I kept thinking. *No, no, no...*

I hadn't really been gone that long, but Father looked older, not quite as plump, a few more lines in his face. But the solemn eyes hadn't changed at all, the faithful, reverent eyes burning with madness beneath them.

Scriptures

"'Rescue those who are being taken away to death,'" he quoted Genesis.

"Eat shit and die, you cock-suck sick motherfucker!" I yelled back as best I could.

I could barely move he'd hit me so hard. At least he hadn't tied me up yet. I had to make a move, I had to do something, but by then I was starting to shake and sweat, I was starting to string out. I needed to fire up bad.

Father's voice sounded like rocks grinding when he recited Ezekiel:

"'As is the mother, so is the daughter.'"

"Where's my mother!" I shouted, my head reeling.

"I sent her to heaven," he said. "It was time, just as it's time for you. Now."

I flailed on the bed when he jumped on me. From somewhere I heard this ugly sound—*pap! pap! pap!*—and it took me a few seconds to realize he was hitting me in the head again, with a blackjack or whatever it was he'd used to jack me out on the street. I tried to fight back but couldn't, and the next thing I knew, my vision was going black. Suddenly I was biting down on something hard, a plastic tube, and then I heard the ever familiar *zip!* I was blind again. He'd zipped the leather mask on me.

"'Mother of harlots and the abominations of the earth—'"

I knew this was it. My heart was beating so fast I thought it was gonna bust. In my blindness, I felt him grab my right wrist—

"'I will arise and go to my father, and will say unto him, Father, I have sinned against heaven, and before thee.'"

—and tied it to the bed. Then he grabbed my left hand—

"'Let them know first to show piety at home!'"

—yanked it up, and—

"'Woe to the rebellious children, saith the Lord!'"

It was more impulse than anything else. I raised my foot, kicked out—

Then my father screamed and fell off the bed.

Blind, I untied my right hand, then unzipped the mask and took it off. When I'd kicked out, the spike on my high heel caught my father in the eye. He lay there shrieking now, blood gushing down his face. Like a maniac, I kicked him in the temple a few times, dragged him up on the bed. I was giggling.

I tied him down.

"'Stolen waters are sweet,'" I whispered, "'and bread eaten in secret is pleasant.'"

First I zipped the leather mask over his head, then I grabbed the shock stick.

I worked on him for a good, long time.

¤ ¤ ¤ ¤ ¤

And it all went away. "We speak the wisdom of God in a mystery," it says in Corinthians. I guess that's what it's all about.

I got off the dope easy. I finished school, went to college. And when I graduated from the seminary, they assigned me to St. Edwards.

I've already written my first sermon. The first line, from Job, is this:

"'He discovereth deep things out of darkness, and bringeth out to light the shadow of death.'"

SCRIPTURES
AFTERWORD

Here's a story that demonstrates either the travails of horror's small-press, or simply the level of my bad luck. This piece was accepted by three different magazines, and each one in turn went out of business before it could be published. Oh, and when I referred to "Death She Said" as my most negative story...I guess I lied. But at least this is a happy ending, right?

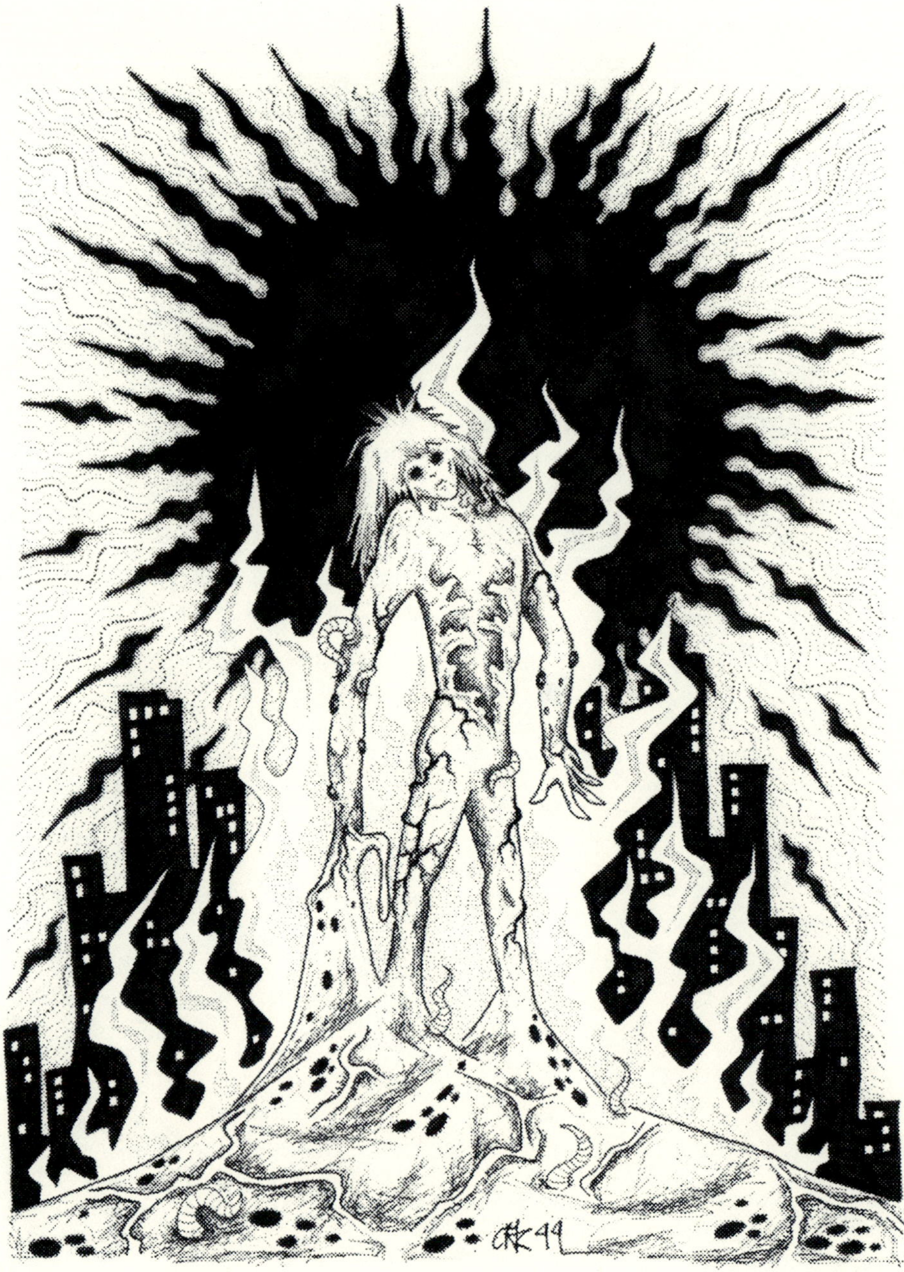

The Goddess of the New Dark Age

"WHAT IS REAL?" he wondered aloud.

Then Smith heard the words: *Revere me. Make me real.* Not his words, but a muffled hiss, like someone whispering on the other side of the wall...

The wall was nightmare: tremoring flesh, skin sweating in turmoil, pain, despair. *So I'm dreaming standing up now,* Smith thought. *Wide awake, in daylight.*

Flecks of mica guttered up from the sidewalk. The sun raged. *Old man,* he thought. City police cruised by, eyeing him, squab faces dark behind tinted glass. "Frog, Ice, Cokesmoke?" a hand-pocketed black man asked him. By a newspaper stand, where headlines blared MAN SETS WIFE & CHILDREN ON FIRE, a raddled prostitute twitched, scratching at needlemarks inside of her thigh. In the mouth of a urine-soaked alley, a woman in rags vomited up blood as rats the size of small puppies boldly approached the emesis, to eat.

Smith hated the sun. It seemed bright with life, which made him feel even older, more depleted. *Where am I going?* The question didn't mean now, today, this minute. *Where am I going forever?* he wondered. *Where have I been?*

The footsteps padded behind him; they had for weeks. Smith had long since stopped looking back. It sounded like someone walking barefoot—a woman, he surmised, a robust, beautiful woman. He also detected the lovely scent—perfume—and some kind of inexplicable heat at his groin and his heart. Whenever he turned, though, at the sound and the lush fragrance, nothing was there. Just a shadow sometimes, just a fleck, like the mica in the cement.

Perhaps it was a ghost, whatever ghosts were. *Ghost, or just halluci-*

nation. Smith's physical body felt like vermiculated meat. Too many artificial sweeteners, cigarettes, alcohol, saturated fats. A body could only take so much vandalism. But Smith didn't care. Why should he, now? Or ever, for that matter?

Or maybe ghosts were real. *Physical residuum,* he speculated. *Interplanar leakage.* Was there really a netherworld, like an anxious tongue licking across pressed lips, desperate for entry? He'd read somewhere that horror left a stain, a laceration through which the tenants of the void could ooze into the world. But if this were true, mankind would surely be smothered by such ooze.

So what was this "ghost?" A spirit? An angel?

Was the ghost real?

Sometimes he could actually see it, via the presage: the longing perfume scent, the warmth. Generally only at night. *Of course,* he thought. *Night.* Dr. Greene had told him to expect as much. But ghosts? "Be prepared for some containdications from the chemotherapy," came the words like a clipped dissertation. "Olfactory and aural hallucinosis. Exodikinesis, immoderate scotipic debris, synaptic maladaption and toxicity intolerance. It's normal." *Normal,* Smith reflected. *Dying's normal too.* Three treatments left him racked for hours, dry heaving bile. His hair had fallen out. "To hell with this," he'd told Greene, on the fourth visit. "Let me die." Cancer seemed an appropriate way for a writer to die. It seemed nearly allegorical. The festering beneath the miraculous veneer of human flesh.

No, the ghost wasn't a side effect. *It must be real.* He thought he could see it, the shadow within the shadow, peering back. A shadow in want of flesh.

Was it Smith's flesh it wanted? *Why should it want me? My flesh's dying. I am essentially a walking corpse.* He could smell the perfume, even over the city's mephitis of carbon-monoxide, stale sweat, and garbage. "You smell beautiful," he whispered. "Whoever you are." He walked on, shriveling against the glare of the sun, but then stopped to look back once more.

"Are you real?" he asked.

¤ ¤ ¤ ¤ ¤

"What is real?" Smith lit a cigarette; it scarcely mattered now. But the question kept occurring to him, like an itching rash. Why should it be so important?

His biopsy analysis—now *that* was real. The single sheet seemed too thin for such a grievous message. It drooped in his hand like something already dead:

The Goddess of the New Dark Age

CYTOLOGY REPORT
NAME: Smith, Gerald E.
AGE: 61, W/M
CLINICAL CONSULTATION:
    Large Cell Coaxial Mass
Specify:
    <u>Right Lung Mass Aspirate</u>
_ Negative
_ Atypical
X Positive

MICROSCOPIC DESCRIPTION: Right Lung Aspirate showing numerous malignant large cells, some of which showing large vesicular irregular nuclei, consistent with non-keratinizing carcinoma, probably large-cell differentiated type of adenocarcinoma.

PATHOLOGY DIAGNOSIS: Positive for Malignant Cells.

    Smith was a realist. *No sense in crying over a spilt life.* He felt he had a mission now, but wasn't sure what it could be. He couldn't stop thinking of the ghost.
    "Are you real?"
    Behind his typewriter, behind his desk, a shadow, or a smudge, seemed to nod. "Who are you!" Smith suddenly yelled. "What do you want from me?"
    Your reckoning, something seemed to hiss. It wasn't even really a sound, more akin to insect appendages abrading. The soft bare footfalls followed him to the bathroom. *A ghost is coming into the toilet with me,* he thought. It was almost funny. He smiled at the lovely perfume-scent, then winced, urinating blood. Of course: by now the disease had bloomed. Dr. Greene had warned him, hadn't he? "Renal malfunction. What happens, Mr. Smith, is that the raging malignant cells become insinuated into the nephrons and the cortical kidney tissue, scleroticizing the calyx cavities." *Charming,* Smith thought now. The pain was extraordinary, like bright light.
    Smith had been a writer for over forty years. *Had been,* he emphasized, pulling up his zipper. He flushed the toilet, and thought of his career. Had he been a good writer? He'd thought so, until Greene had told him the truth. The good doctor had at least been respectful enough of Smith's profession not to mince words. "You're dying," he'd said. "You'll be gone in oh, say, six weeks."
    Gone, Smith considered. He was still in the bathroom. What did *gone*

mean? Did it mean no longer real? The question continued to nag at him, worse than the cancer. "What is real?" he asked.

Find out, the hiss replied. *You haven't much time.*

As a writer, he'd spent his life trying to create realities out of assessments of imagination. *The truth of any story can only exist in its bare words,* he'd heard someone say in a bar when he was eighteen. He'd been a writer ever since, pursuing that. But now, now that he was dying, he knew that he'd failed utterly. Was that why the ghost had come to him, evoked by the knowledge of his failure? What was the hiss trying to tell him?

"I see you," he said. For a moment he had, behind him in the mirror. *Beautiful,* he thought. A beautiful, beautiful woman, an amalgam composed of inverted bits of wallpaper, a prolapsation. It smiled weakly, then vanished. Only its pleasant smell remained.

The television poured forth atrocities. Or were they realities? "Up next," promised the newswoman with a visage of wood, "Florida state supreme court grants local journalists the right to televise executions." Outside the courthouse, a crowd in floodlit darkness cheered. Then, a commercial, a slim brunette in a white swimsuit: "If you're counting calories, here's something you should know..." Smith changed the channel. "...where officials estimate that one thousand children are starving to death daily, while government troops remain free to confiscate relief rations from the United Red Cross, selling what they don't eat themselves to the black market."

And next: "—confessed today to that he knowingly tainted the entire hospital's transfusion supply with AIDS infected bl—"

"—amid allegations of abducting over one hundred children for what the FBI officials have called 'the underground snuff-film circuit—'"

"—strangled slowly with a lampcord while her common-law husband and his friends took turns—"

Smith turned off the set, feeling as confused as he felt disgusted. The newspaper offered more of the same. CRACKMOM TURNS KIDS TO PROSTITUTES read one local headline. The *Post* seemed less blunt: EARTHQUAKE DEATH TOLL EXPECTED TO REACH 120,000. Here was a story. A Tucson, Arizona, woman locked her three children in her attic while she went shopping with a friend. All three children died as the temperature in the attic exceeded 150 degrees. Stray bullets in a drug-related shootout killed three six-year-olds in front of a Detroit apartment project. The body of a thirteen-year old was found by hunters in Davidsonville, Maryland; the police reported that she'd been raped en mass and tortured with power tools. A suitcase was discovered in a dumpster behind a Washington D.C. convenience store, containing a dead newborn baby complete with umbilical and placenta.

The Goddess of the New Dark Age

Smith's contemplations wavered. What could be more real than all of this? *But there must be something.* The ghost was walking around; he could feel it. It seemed to be perusing the bookshelf full of his work. Then it hissed at him, and disappeared.

¤ ¤ ¤ ¤ ¤

The sun felt like a blade against his face as his guest dragged him back out onto the street. He was shriveling. It occurred to him, as he ascended the stone steps, that this was the first time he'd entered a church since he'd become a writer.

An old priest limped across the chancel, his bald head like a shiny ball of dough. He began to change the frontals on the altar.

"Excuse me, sir...er, Father," Smith interrupted.

"Yes?"

"What is real?"

The priest straightened, a frocked silhouette before stained glass. He did not question, or even pause upon, the obscurity of Smith's query. He answered at once: "God, Christ, the kingdom of Heaven."

"But how do you know?"

The priest's bland face smiled. He held up his Bible.

Smith thanked him and walked out. He felt abandoned, not as much by God as by himself. Conviction wasn't proof. Belief didn't validate a *reality.* Next, he took a Yellow to the University, where the static sunlight made everything look brittle and fake. Inside, cool darkness and tile shine led him down the hall. PHILOSOPHY DEPARTMENT. Smith stepped unannounced into the first office. A man—who looked as old—glanced up from a cluttered industrial gray metal desk. "May I...*help* you?"

Smith considered how he must look – a haggard, emaciated vagabond. "Forgive my appearance..." *but it's hard to look good when you're dying from a large-cell metastatic mass.* He had no time for intricate explanations nor cordialities. "I have a question that only a philosopher can answer. The question is this: What is real?"

The professor lit a pipe with a face engraved in relief on the bowl. His eyes looked tiny below the great, bushy gray brows. "That's quite a universal question, wouldn't you say? You want *my* opinion?"

In the window, the campus stood empty in sunlight. "Yes," Smith said after a pause. That's when he noticed the ghost. It was standing just outside, looking at him, an ethereal chaperon. "Yes, yes," he said. "I'd appreciate your opinion very much."

"Ah, what is real?" Pipe smoke smeared the professor's aged face. "Consider, first, the initial tenets of conclusionary nihilism. Truth is reality, and there is no objective basis for truth. Take mathematics for example, which exists only because space and time are forms of intuition; all material qualities are only the *outward* appearances arising from monadistic nexi. See? What is real can only be found in the *imma*terial mind; hence, the solipsistic doctrine. The human self is the only thing, in other words, that can be known and therefore verified. Quite a contradiction, since life is clearly a material, or a physio-chemical, interaction. Being and reality are not found in objects of knowledge but in something accessible only to the free and total self. Man's destiny is a struggle for power, or, in your case, for answers. What I mean is, the real can never be made manifest in our finite minds but in the genetic empiricism beyond the whole. In other words, and I think it should be obvious now, reality is a consistence of a judgment pursuant to other judgements, fitting in ultimately to a single absolute system."

Smith resisted rolling his eyes. He thanked the professor for his time, and left, thinking, *what a crock of shit.*

¤ ¤ ¤ ¤ ¤

So it wasn't truth, and it wasn't spirit. Smith lit a cigarette, pondering the smoke. *Love?* he wondered. Was love real? Did love make something real? He didn't know. He'd been too busy writing to ever love anyone.

These were simply subjectivities trying to be concrete, which was impossible. *Beauty, then?* He leaned back. *Hmmm.* Did beauty — a true subjectivity — make something real? Suddenly Smith felt buoyant with excitement. His kidneys throbbed, and his lung felt like a bleeding clot. Yet the surmise gave him energy.

Beauty.

Wasn't beauty what all writers were supposed to pursue?

He heard a sigh, or no — a hiss. Did it denote relief, or disappointment? "It's beauty, isn't it?" Smith asked aloud to the shadow which now lingered at the closet. Was it inspecting his clothes? The shape sharpened as dusk bled into the room, creeping. What had it said, just days ago, on the street? *Revere me.* Smith knew at once that he must appease the ghost, with aphorism, with comprehension. "I'll show you," he said.

He opened the Yellow Pages, to the E's. ESCORTS UNLIMITED, BEAUTIFUL GIRLS, CONFIDENTIAL, 24 HOURS, VISA, MASTERCARD.

The sigh replayed in his head, and the wondrous scent rose as Smith reached for the phone, to call beauty.

¤ ¤ ¤ ¤ ¤

"Do you believe in ghosts?"

The girl's smile twitched. "Uh, well..."

"Never mind," Smith said. "I was allegorizing, I suppose. I used to be a novelist." He sat behind his desk, behind his typewriter, which was turned off. He would never turn it on again, and this left him dryly depressed. He had nothing to write. But it seemed a suitable place from which to observe: the lap of his failure. *I've written over a hundred books,* he felt inclined to brag. But so what? Why say that? His books had not been real.

"What, uh, what would you like me to do?" the girl inquired.

Smith squinted. "I want to see you. I realize how obscure that must sound, but I'm on a quest of sorts, and I'm afraid I've become subject to a considerable time constraint. I've been made aware of a possibility, though, quite recently, that reality only arrives through an acknowledgment, or a reckoning, of human beauty. Not an objective acknowledgment, but a temporal one. I'm looking for something, the underside perhaps, or what makes something real in our minds and, more critically, our hearts. Use a sentence in fiction as an example. Objectively, the sentence is nothing more than configurations of ink on a piece of paper. But the mechanism of the words, and *function* of the mechanism, in conjunction with the manner by which we define the sequence of the words, affects a transposition of imagery. It makes the sentence real in the process. The *process* – do you understand?" Smith doubted that she did. "The words suddenly become *real,* in some other, ineffable way." He must sound worse than the professor. *You're just a piece of physical meat,* he could have put it, more simply. *But I need to see what you are beyond that, not as just a body but as an image transposed* through *the body.* Would it offend her? Would she understand?

At least the ghost seemed to understand. Smith caught frequent glimpses now, since the call-girl had arrived. He felt certain that the more effectively he strove to conquer the question—What is real?—the more real the ghost would become.

"I smell perfume," the girl remarked.

"Yes," Smith said but did not elaborate. "In other words, I merely need to see you, all of you."

"Ah," the girl said, stretching the word. "Now I get it. Now I know what you mean." She smiled, a manufactured wickedness, and took off the short fuchsia dress. "You just want to watch. That's okay. It's your dime."

Smith's "dime," in this case, had been a $150 escort fee on his charge card, plus "tip." He'd given her several hundred in cash, all he had left in the apartment. What did he need money for? He'd never really needed it in life. What good would it do him now?

"Show me your beauty," Smith said.

Off, then, came the garters, the stockings and frilly lace bra, all the same vibrant, bright fuchsia. She wore no panties. What stood before Smith now was her raw, physical reality. But— *Not enough,* he thought, squinting past his desk. He needed to see her *beauty,* and at first she did indeed strike him as beautiful…

Smith tipped up the desklamp. "Come closer. Please. Closer to the desk."

She sauntered forward like a chic model on a runway, and assumed quick poses, turning before the light. Flesh flashed in cold glare. Glance by glance, the beauty collapsed.

The silken white-blond hair and bangs clashed with the waxed, black pubic patch. The rhinoplastied nose seemed too perfect on the elegant face. Smith's eyes calculated up the sleek supple physique, and snagged. Minute cannula marks pocked along her trim hips and waist, from liposuction, and when she raised her arms, the erect orbs of her breasts easily displayed the hairline implant scars.

She blinked at him, her smile freezing. Even the crystal-blue eyes were a lie, designer contacts.

"Thank you," Smith said. "You may go now."

Her nude, pretty shoulders shrugged. "It's your dime." Then she quickly put her clothes back on and left.

The ghost was laughing.

¤   ¤   ¤   ¤   ¤

On the night he was to die, Smith awakened as if rising from a lime pit. The darkness swarmed. His eyes felt plucked open by fish hooks.

You should have more faith, the hiss whispered.

"I figured as much," he muttered. He walked to his desk, wizened as a dried corpse in the moonlight. *Faith?* he wondered. Smith didn't believe in God. Perhaps he should have. Nevertheless, he doubted that the ghost meant religious faith.

Faith in me. Faith in what is real.

He'd failed again, he'd misconstrued everything. He'd never know reality now, only the reality of death, of being embalmed and buried, of dissolving to slime in a box. But what was he – a writer – really dying of? Cancer, or the failure to recognize what was real? Prevarications were killing him, not disease.

Deserts, he thought. *Wastelands. All the lies of history.*

Only two realities mattered now. His dying flesh, and the ghost.

He saw it more clearly now than ever, which made sense. It faced the window, naked in its oblivion, a razorline shape of inverted oddments of darkness and light. "You're real, aren't you?" Smith stated more than asked.

Only you can make me real, the hiss replied.

The Goddess of the New Dark Age

Smith felt adrift on the scent of her—or its—perfume. But how could he *make* it real? Did it mean that it was only half-real now? Did it mean there was something about *Smith* that could unloose the ghost's full reality?

"Assimilation?" Smith lit a cigarette, his last. "No," he felt. "Transposition." Perhaps he'd been correct all-along, back when he'd been talking to the blonde call-girl. Correct, but on the wrong tangent. It was his trade that had summoned the ghost – he was a writer, a creator, or, more accurately, a *recreator*. Writers re-recreated their own conceptions of images of reality and blended them with abstraction, *transposing* the images, and making both the conception and the abstraction, in a sense—

Real, he thought.

He'd only been partly right. Beauty reflected only a semantic; it was something created, not transposed. Smith stared at the shifting figure and its ebon glint. It seemed to gaze back at him, over the shadow-boned shoulder...

"Too late, though, hmmm?" Of course. His life was over. His face felt sucked in. The old heart began to skip within the sunken cage of his chest. But at least he would die pondering this; at least he would die trying.

Ghosts. Not Dickensian specters flailing chains and moaning amid graveyards. Not transparent apparitions and sheet-shapes. Ghosts would be entities of human backwash, of unfulfillment, of failure. Ghosts would be slivers of the real world. And what was the world, then? A realm, not a sphere of rock, a domain of...transposition—a mutable domain, one that squirmed with each new generation, and each new age.

The ghost turned. Its black-chasm eyes widened.

"Now I've got you going, eh?" Smith felt proud. "The old dying stick in the mud isn't as dumb as you thought."

Make me real, came the hushed reverberation.

"I don't know how," Smith testily replied.

But you do.

Was it weeping? It seemed to be, perhaps as Smith, secretly, had wept over his entire life. He turned on the radio. Vivaldi seemed nice to die to, or a light nocturne by Field. Besides, Smith wanted beautiful music as he confronted the ghost.

He rose, joints clicking, as he crossed the nighted room, atrophied, shrivel-penised, and as pale as death already. He could feel the cancer percolating, and it was a surprisingly neutral sensation. *Transposition,* he considered. *Each new generation, each new age.* Yes, the world was a realm of emotion, of which this queer thing in his room had surely been born. Behind him, out of the dark, the radio squawked another day's unholy news. A bomb had exploded on an airliner, scattering hundreds of bodies across the outskirts of Los Angeles. A coterie of scientists convened in Washington, citing the benefits of using brain tissue from aborted fetuses for genetic research. Terrorists had thrown seven satchel charges into an Israeli maternity ward...

Look. The ghost indicated the window. Smith peered out. At first, what he saw seemed beautiful: a warm endless night chipped by stars, the high, resplendent moon, and man's crisp, perfectly symmetrical monuments. The scape of buildings looked like an intricate carved mesa of flawless black, still with tiny lights.

"It's beautiful," Smith muttered.

But then its reality rose before the vision. Flashing red and blue lights of terror. Sirens. Gunshots. Distant screams. A cool breeze carried in the chaotic stench.

Smith blinked.

Revere me. Make me real.

The ghost shifted. Now he understood.

It's time now, isn't it? Time for a new realm? Your realm is done, isn't it?

It didn't mean his life—of course not. It meant the *age*.

The night lolled. The ghost shifted like black sand pouring, until it was perfect, beautiful flesh. Dark long straight hair and dark eyes. Dark yet lambent nakedness. Poreless indefectible skin smooth as newly spun silk. And it wasn't a woman at all, but a girl, a prepubescent little girl. Nor was it a ghost...

A goddess, Smith realized. *A little goddess...*

The goddess' voice eddied like water running through the bowels of a sewer, or garbage blown in gutters.

The new dark age needs a scribe.

Smith felt on fire inside. He watched his hand reach out, but it wasn't the veined, liver-spotted hand he had known. It was a new hand, forged in truth, in acknowledgment. Smith wept, oblivious to the new hot blood, the fresh skin, strong muscles, and steady heart. He embraced the goddess.

He began to slide down, as if on a greased pole, sloughing off her perfect skin, and revealing her true age. Her horror sang to him, and embraced him back, the flensed figure gleaming in hate, disease, insanity. In despair and in pus. In cruelty. In truth.

Smith knelt in worship, and kissed the little feet, which were now caked by the blood, offal, and excrement of eons.

THE GODDESS OF THE NEW DARK AGE
AFTERWORD

Interchange, transposition, transfigurations. With this story, I transposed a certain aspect of myself into the meld of my fears. The protagonist is me, in some abstract realm. My fear...and perhaps any writer's fear. If fiction can be a real thing, this is as real as I can get. I like this story very much, and I dedicate it to my father who died on Christmas night, 1986.

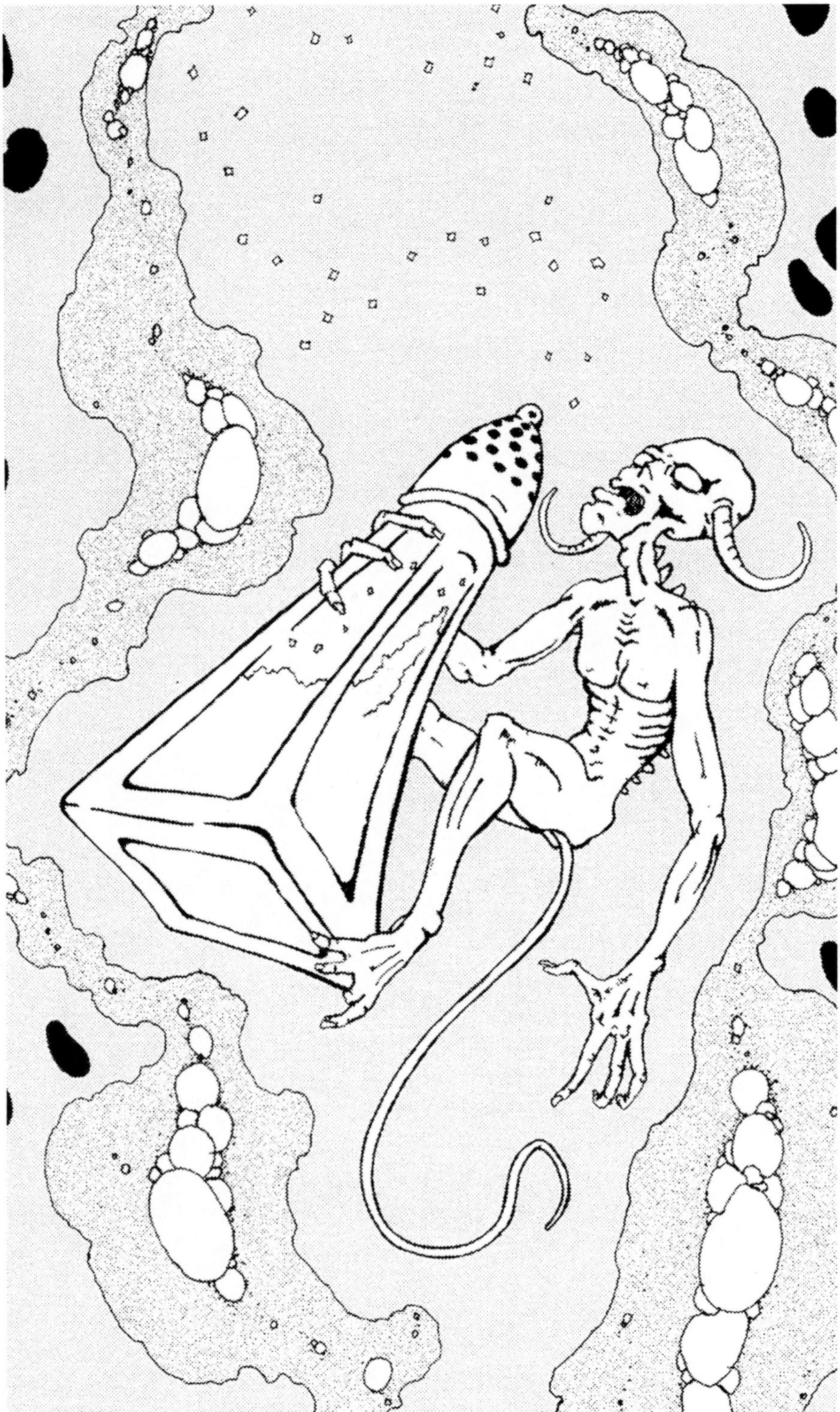

THE SALT-DIVINER

PROLOGUE

THE ONOMANCERS HAD failed, and so had the Sibyllists. The Haruspicators came next, keen-eyed yet solemn in their blood-red raiments. One of them nodded within his flaplike hood, and then the young girl was stripped naked and lain on the onyx slab.

It was one of the geldings, who'd previously had his eyes sewn shut, that clumsily shoved the ivory rod into the girl's sex. The slim naked thing's hips bucked, and the shriek of pain launched out above the ziggurat as though she were shouting to the gods themselves. Blindly, then, the gelding held up the bloody rod for the Synod to see.

No doubt, a true virgin.

The gelding was summarily beheaded, his body dragged off by silent legionnaires. Next, the highest of the Haruspist's slipped the long sharpened hook deep up into the girl's sex. She flinched and died at once, a tiny river of red pouring forth. But the Haruspic priest was already at work, his holy hand a blur as the hook expertly extracted the girl's warm innards through the opening of her sex. Barehanded, then, he hoisted up the guts and flung them down to the ziggurat's stone floor.

The wind howled, or perhaps it was the breath of Ea himself.

But when the Haruspist gazed intently at the wet splay of innards...

He saw nothing.

The King's jaw set; he seemed petrified on his throne. Only one recourse remained, and if it too failed, only doom awaited the King and his domain. He turned his gaze toward the last flank of robed and hooded priests–the alomancers. The King gave a single nod.

One figure stepped forward, face hidden within the hood's roll. From one hand, a thurible swayed, a thurible full of salt.

He depended the thurible over the fire...until the salt began to burn.

Smoke poured from the object's finely crafted apertures, and the figure leaned forth–and inhaled the holy fumes, one deep breath after another, until he collapsed.

The King stiffened in his throne; legionnaires burst forward to render aid. Eventually–thank Ea–the alomancer revived after a distended silence. Even the wind stopped, even the clouds seemed to freeze in the sky.

The alomancer shuddered. Then he gazed at the King with eyes the color of amethyst, and he began to speak....

I

It started when the salt spilled.

The man looked ludicrous. Black hair hung in a perfect bowlcut, like Moe. He stood at the rail, tubby and tall, with a great, toothy, lunatic grin. "Ald, please," he requested. "It's been eons."

Rudy and Beth nursed cans of Milwaukee's Best down the bar, Rudy pretending to watch the fight on the television. They'd made the rounds downtown, hoping to cop a loan, but to no avail. Then they'd retreated to this dump tavern, The Crossroads, way out off the Route. Rudy didn't want to run into Vito–as in Vito "The Eye"—a minute before he had to. He felt like a man on a stay of execution.

"Are you the vassal of this *taberna*, sir?" the ludicrous man asked the barkeep. "I would like some ald, please." "Never heard of it," swiped the keep, who sported muttonchops and a beer-belly akin to a medicine ball. "No imports here, pal. This is The Crossroads, not the Four Seasons."

"I am becruxed. Have you any mead?"

Rudy could've laughed. Even the man's voice sounded ludicrous: a high nasalwarble. *And what the hell is ald?*

"We got Rolling Rock, pal. That fancy enough for ya?"

"I am grateful, sir, for your kind recommendation."

When the keep came down to the Rock tap, Rudy leaned forward. "Hey, man, who *is* this guy?"

The keep shrugged, tufts of hair like steel wool poking out from his collar. "Some weirdo. We get 'em all the time."

Beth, frowning afresh, looked down from the no-name fight on tv. "Rudy, don't you have more to worry about than some eightball who walks into a bar? What if Vito shows up?"

"Vito The Eye? Here?" Rudy replied. "No way." The assurance lapsed. "Hey, maybe Mona could loan us some dough."

The Salt-Diviner

"She barely has money for tuition and rent, Rudy. Be real."

Women, Rudy thought. *Always negative*. He glanced back up at the fight—Tuttle versus Luce, middleweights—but thoughts of Vito kept haunting him. *What will they do to me?* he wondered.

The keep set down a mug of beer before the ludicrous man, but as he did so, his brawny elbow nicked a salt shaker, which tipped over. A few trace white grains spilled across the bartop.

The odd patron grinned down. Focused. Nodded. He pinched some grains and cast them over his left shoulder. "Blast thee, Nergal and all devils. Keep thee behind, and slithereth back into your evil earthworks."

"We ain't superstitious here, pal," the keep said.

"To blind the sentinels of the nether regions," the man went on, "who stand to our left, behind us. Dear salt, a gift from the holiest Ea, and all gods of good things. To spill the sacred salt is to bid ill fortune from heaven. It was once more valuable than myrrh."

"Who'da hell's Merv?" asked the keep.

"Beware the woman infidel," intoned the patron. "Your paramour—"

"What'da hell's a paramour?"

"A lover," Beth translated, for all the good her education had done. "A girlfriend."

"She is so named," the ludicrous man said, ". . . Stacy?"

The keep's pug-face tensed up like a pack of corded Suet. "How'da hell you know my girlfriend's name?"

"I am an alomancer," the odd patron replied. "And your lovely paramour, hair like sackcloth and teeth becrook'd, will be in a moment's time abed with a man unthus known."

The keep scratched a muttonchop. "What'd'ya mean?"

"He means," Beth said over her beer, "that your girlfriend is cheating on you with a guy she just met."

"A man," the patron continued, "too, of a formidable endowment of the groin."

"'At's a load of shit," the keep said. "You're a nut."

This guy's something, Rudy thought. He was about to comment when someone tapped on his shoulder. *Oh...no*. Very slowly, then, he turned to the ruddy and none-too-happy face behind him. "Vito! My man! I was just downtown looking for you."

"Yeah." Vito wore a tan leather jacket and white slacks—*Italian* slacks. They called him The Eye, since only his right eye could be seen. A black patch covered the left. "Your marker's due Friday, paisan. You wouldn't be forgetting that, huh?"

"Oh, hey, Vito," Rudy stammered. "I remember."

"That's six large. The Boss Man ain't happy."

"Barkeep," Rudy changed the subject. "Get my good friend Vito here a beer on my tab, and one for this guy, too," he said, slapping the ludicrous man on the back.

Vito jerked a thumb. "I'll be over at the booth marking my books. Come on over if you got anything you want to talk to me about."

"Actually," Rudy seized the opportunity. "I was wondering if like you could maybe give me a little extra t—"

"I ever tell you how I lost my eye? About ten years ago, I ran up a big marker on the Boss Man's tab, and I made the big mistake of asking him for a little extra time."

Rudy gulped. When Vito disappeared to the back booth, Beth jumped in to complain. "That's great, Rudy. We're nearly broke, you're six thousand in debt to a mob bookie, and now you're buying beers for people. Jesus."

"Guys like Vito like to see generosity. Part of their machismo."

"And now look what you've done!' she whispered.

The inane, toothy grin floated forward; its owner took the stool next to Rudy. "Innumerable thanks, sir. It's not ald; however, I'm grateful to you."

"What the hell is ald?" Rudy asked.

"A high and might liquor indeed, and a favorite of the mashmashus. We invented it, by the way, though your zymurgists of today refuse to acknowledge that. You see, the great grain mounds would accumulate condensation in the sun. The dregs, then, seeped into pools of effluvium, which were squeezed off into the casks." He sipped his beer, crosseyed.. "I am Gormok. And you are called?"

Gormok? What kind of fruitloop name is that? Rudy wondered.

"I'm Rudy. This is Beth, my fiance."

Beth frowned again, and Rudy supposed he could see her point. Nothing he'd promised her had come true. His gambling was like a ritual to him, an obsessive act of something very nearly reverence, and it kept a monkey on their backs the size of King Kong. The stress was starting to show: tiny lines had crept into Beth's pretty face, and a faint veneer of fatigue. She'd lost weight, and the lustrous long caramel-colored hair had begun to take a tint of gray. She worked two jobs while Rudy sweated bullets at the track. And now mob men were calling. *No wonder she's always pissed. I'm gonna get my eye poked out next Friday and here I am buying beers for a shylock and some loose-screw named Gormok.*

"And I affirm," Gormok went on in his creaky, sinitic voice, "that your generosity will not go unrewarded. If I can ever be of service to your benefit, I implore thee, make me aware."

"Forget it," Rudy said. *Nut.* He drained his beer. "Where'd the barkeep go? I could use a refill."

The Salt-Diviner

"Our humble servitor, I believe," Gormok offered, "is at this sad moment seeking to contact his unfaithful paramour."

Rudy spied the keep down the other end of the bar, talking on the house phone. Suddenly the guy turned pale and hung up. "I just called the fuckin' trailer," he muttered. "My girlfriend ain't there. Then I ring my buddy down at The Anvil, and he tells me Stacy left after happy hour...with some guy."

"A gentleman, too," Gormok reminded, "unthus known and of a formidable endowment of the groin."

"Shadap, ya whack." The keep went back to the phone. Beth maintained her terse silence. But Rudy was thinking

"Gormok. How about doing that salt thing for me."

"An alomance! Yes?" came the grinning reply.

Rudy lowered his voice. "Tell me who's gonna win that fight."

"Alas, the gladiators of the new, dark age," Gormok remarked, and peered up at the boxing bout on the bar television. "But have thee a censer? Clearer visions are always begot by fire."

"What's a censer?"

"It's something you burn things in, during rituals," Beth defined. "And don't be idiotic, Rudy."

Rudy ignored her, glancing about. "How about this?" he ventured, and slid over a big glass ashtray sporting the Swedish Bikini Team.

"It shall suffice," Gormok approved. He sprinkled several shakes of salt into a bar napkin and placed it in the ashtray. "A taper, now, or cresset or flambeau."

I hope he means a lighter. Rudy flicked his Bic. He lit the napkin, which strangely puffed into a quick flame and then went out. Gormok's face took on a momentary expression of tranquility as though he were indeed taking part in some ritualistic worship. Then the odd man leaned forward...and inhaled the smoke.

Rudy stared.

"The combatant dark of skin and light of garb," Gormok giddily intoned, "who is called Tuttle, before two minutes have expired, will emerge victorious by a single blow to the skull of his oppressor."

Rudy snatched up Beth's purse.

"Rudy, no!"

"How much money you got?" he asked, rummaging. He fingered through his fiancee's wallet. "*Twenty bucks?* That's *it?*"

"Damn it, Rudy! Don't you dare—"

Rudy turned toward the mob man's booth. "Hey, Vito? A double sawbuck says Tuttle KO's Luce this round."

Vito didn't even look up. "No more credit, Rudy."

"Cash, man. On the table."

Now Vito raised his smirk to the tv. "Tuttle's getting his ass kicked. Don't make me take your green."

"Come on, Vito!" Rudy barked. "Quit bustin' my balls. Are you a bookie or a book collector?"

Vito made a shrug. "Awright, Rudy. You're on."

Rudy jerked his gaze to the tv, then drooped. Luce was dancing circles around his man, firing awesome hooks which snapped Tuttle's head back like a ball on a spring. "You're such a fool," Beth groaned.

"Hark," Gormok whispered, and pointed to the screen.

Tuttle shot a blind jab which sent Luce over the ropes—

"Yeah!" Rudy yelled. Then: 'Yeah, fuckin-A *yeah!*" he yelled louder when the ref counted Luce out and raised Tuttle's arm in victory.

Vito came over. "Good call, Rudy. Just don't forget that six large."

Rudy's smile radiated. "That's five thousand, nine hundred, and eighty, Vito."

"Yeah. See ya next Friday, paisan."

Vito left the smoky bar, while Rudy fidgeted on his stool. Even Beth was rubbing her chin, thinking. And Rudy had a pretty good idea what she was thinking about.

"How'd you do that, man?" he asked aside to Gormok.

"I am an alomancer," Gormok answered through his ludicrous grin. "I am a salt-diviner for the Fourth Cenote of Nergal."

What you are, Rudy thought, *is a nut. But I love ya anyway.* He put a comradely arm about Gormok's shoulder. "So, Gormok, my man. How would you like to come and live with us?"

II

"Who's *that?*" Mona winced when they got home.

Snooty bitch. "This is our very good friend, Gormok," he told the blonde coed. Her 38C's pushed against her blouse. "Gormok, this in Mona, our housemate."

Gormok appraised the attractive, tight-jeaned student. "Men have rown leagues for such beauty, priests have scaled ziggurats."

"Uh...huh," Rudy said. "Mona, how about going to your room to study, huh? Gormok and I gotta talk." Mona made no objection, padding off with her English 311 text, *Pound, Eliot, and Seymour: The Great Poets of Our Age.* "Sit down, Gor," Rudy bid. "Make yourself at home." Gormok did so, his lap disappearing when he sat down on the frayed couch.

Rudy nudged Beth into the kitchen. "Get him a beer. He seems to like beer."

The Salt-Diviner

"Rudy, this might be a bad idea. I don't know if I—"

"Just shut up and get him a beer," Rudy politely repeated. He went back to the squalid living room, bearing an ashtray and a shaker of salt. "So, Gor. Tell me about yourself."

The lunatic grin roved about. "I am but a lowly salt-diviner, once blessed by the Ea, now curs'd by Nergal."

"Uh...huh," Rudy acknowledged.

"I was an Ashipu, a white and goodly acolyte, but, lo, I sold my soul to Nergal, The Wretched God of the Ebon. Pity me, in my sin: my repentance was ignored. Banished from heaven, banished from hell, I am now accursed to trod the earth's foul crust forever, inhabiting random bodies as the vessel for my eternal spirit."

"Uh...huh,"

"Jesus," Beth whispered. Disapproval now fully creased her face when she gave Gormok a can of Bud. *Yeah, we've got a live one*, Rudy thought. The next fight—Jenkins versus Clipper—was on the west coast; it would be running late. "That's pretty, uh, interesting, Gormok. You think maybe you feel like doing the salt thing again?"

Beer foam bubbled at Gormok's grin. "The alomance!"

"Uh, yeah, Gor. The...alomance. I could really use to know who's gonna win the Jenkins-Clipper bout."

Gormok's grin never fluctuated. He knelt on tacky carpet tiles and went into his arcane ritual of burning salt in a napkin, then inhaling the smoke which wafted up from the ashtray. He seemed to wobble on his knees. "The warrior b'named Clipper, dear friend, in the sixth spell of conflict." Then he collapsed to the floor.

"Holy shit!" Rudy and Beth rushed to help the alomancer up. "Gor! Are you all right?" Rudy asked.

"Too much for one day." Gormok's voice sounded drugged. "Put me abed, dear ones. I'll be better on the morrow."

"The couch," Rudy suggested. "Let's get him on the—"

"Deep and down," Gormok inanely remarked. "I must be deep, as all damned Nashipus are so cursed. Get me near the cenotes."

"A cenote is a hole in the ground," Beth recalled from her college myth classes. "They'd hold rituals in them,.sacrifice virgins and things like that."

A hole in the— "The basement?" Rudy suggested.

Beth opened the ringed trap-door, then they both lugged the muttering and rubber-kneed Gormok down the wooden steps.

"Better, yes! Sweet, sweet...dark."

They lay the bizarre man on an old box-spring next to the washer and drier. Dust eddied up from the dirt floor. "He's heavier than a bag of bricks!" Beth complained.

Rudy draped an old army blanket over him. "There."

"Ea, I heartily do repent," Gormok blabbered incoherently. "Absolve my sins, I beg of Thee!" He began to drool. "And curse thee, Nergal, unclean despoiler! Haunter! Deceiver of *souls!*"

"Uh…huh," Rudy remarked, staring down. *Yeah, we've got a live one, all right. A real winner.*

III

In bed, they bickered rather than slept. "I can't believe you invited that *weirdo* into our house," Beth bellyached.

"I didn't hear you complaining," Rudy refuted.

"Well, you do now. He's…scary."

"You don't belive all that mumbo-jumbo, do you? It's just a bunch of schizo crap be made up."

"It's not made up, Rudy. I majored in ancient history, that is, before I had to quit school and go to work to keep you out of cement loafers. Cenotes, ziggurats, alomancy— t's all straight out of Babylonian myth. This guy says he's possessed by the spirit of a Nashipu salt-diviner. That's the same as saying he's a demon."

Rudy chuckled outright. "Somebody hit you in the head with a dumb-stick? He's a flake, Beth. He probably escaped from St. Elizabeth's in the back of a garbage truck and read about all that stuff in some occult paperback. He *thinks* he's possessed by a demon. And so what? Let him think what he wants. What's important to us is the guy's *genuinely psychic*. You heard him, he *predicted* that fat barkeep's squeeze was cheating on him."

"That could be just coincidence, Rudy."

"Coincidence? What about the Tuttle fight? He didn't just pick the winner, Beth, he picked the *round*. He picked a KO by a guy who every bookie in town said was gonna lose."

"I don't care," Beth replied, turning her back to him amid the covers. "He's scary. I don't want him in the house."

"Beth, the guy's a gold mine on two legs. We keep him under our wings, we'll never have to worry about money again. We'll be—"

The scream came down like a guillotine blade. Rudy and Beth went rigid in the bed.

Then another scream tore through the air.

"Thuh-that came from M-Mona's room, didn't it?" Rudy stammered.

"Yuh-yeah," Beth agreed.

"She's *your* friend. *You* go see what happened."

"Fuck you!" Beth shouted. "Inconsiderate coward son of a—"

"We'll both go, then. Here. I'll protect you." Rudy boldly brandished

The Salt-Diviner

one of Beth's nail files. Then, disheveled in their underwear, they crept out of the bedroom.

"Aw, Christ," Rudy muttered when he saw the trap-door to the basement standing open.

Then they padded down the ball, and peered into Mona's room...

"Aw, Christ," Rudy muttered again.

But Beth didn't mutter. She screamed.

Gormok, his face smeared scarlet, grinned up at them in the lamplight. And atop the stained bed lay Mona, naked and quite dead.

She was also quite eviscerated.

The student's trim abdomen had been riven open, and from the rive an array of organs had been extracted and arranged about her as if for some macabre inspection. An outline of slowly seeping blood spread about the corpse like a Kirlian aura.

Gormok was eating something dark and wet out of his hands. *Her liver*, Rudy realized. *He's eating Mona's liver.*

"Friends! Hello!" Gormok greeted, chewing. "How art?"

Rudy bellowed, "What in God's name did you do!"

"Not in God's name," Gormok lamented. "In Nergal's. Lo, and to my eternal shame, behold the freight of my curse. I try to fight it, on my heart. But the blasted Nergal has condemned me to such heinous acts wheneverest I breathe on the salt's divine fumes."

'Uh...huh." Rudy shuddered, feebly wielding the nail file. *Should I kill him*? he debated. But he thought about that. He'd never much liked Mona anyway. Bitchy, arrogant, and always taking cheap shots. Sure, he'd fucked her a couple times when Beth was at work (–no great shakes in bed, either. Like fucking a starfish–) and since then she'd regularly implied that it wouldn't be a good idea for Rudy to ever raise her rent.

"Gormok, wait here a minute. Beth and I have to talk."

"Of course! Enjoy your discourse, dear friends," Gormok invited. "Whilst I enjoy my meal."

Rudy had to about carry Beth back to their bedroom. She was going pasty-faced, pale. "Rudy," she fretted, "we have to get out of here while we still can! We have to call the police!"

"Don't overreact, honey. He's harmless."

"Harmless!" Beth's eyes came close to jettisoning from her head. "He's eating Mona's *liver!* You call that harmless?"

Rudy had a plan, but he had to play it out right. "Listen, Beth," he said in a consoling, quiet voice. "Mona's got no relatives or friends—hell, she doesn't even have a boyfriend. She'll never be missed. And she wasn't doing well in school, anyway—"

"Rudy! You call the police right now!"

"All right, all right." Rudy held up his hands, his hair sticking up. "I'm calling the police. See?" He picked up the phone and began to dial.

But not the police. Instead, he dialed 1-900 Sportsline. He listened a moment, tapping his foo. Then he hung up and smiled.

"Clipper won the bout in the sixth round."

Beth went into a staccato burst of crying and screaming. "Rudy, you're out of your mind! What is *wrong* with you?"

"Baby, it's only because I love you," Rudy, well, lied. "I'm not doing this for me, I'm doing it for *us*. I want us to be married someday, have kids, and all that."

Beth sniffled, looking up. "Really?"

"Of course, honey," he assured her and gave her a hug. "But I need you to have faith in me, okay? I want you to go to bed now. Just trust me." He lovingly touched her cheek. "I'll take care of everything."

¤ ¤ ¤ ¤ ¤

Rudy did exactly that. First, he put Gormok back to bed in the basement. The alomancer, smiling calmly, said, "I'm sated now, dear Rudy. My curse is relieved, and now I can sleep. And I am heartily sorry for any inconvenience I have caused you."

"Hey, Gor, don't worry about it." Rudy winced a bit, thinking of Mona's liver. "These things happen all the time."

"Until the morrow, then! And for now—sleep. For to sleep is perchance–to dream."

"Uh...huh," Rudy said.

When he went back up, this time, he locked the trap-door.

Digging graves was hard work, harder than one might expect. Yet dig Rudy did, maniacally in his boxer shorts. He dug deep.

Inserting Mona's internal organs back into her opened abdominal vault proved a trying task too, but at least it was unique...

And later, in the little moonlit backyard, with the crickets trilling and the grass cool under his bare feet, with the scent of the bay in the air, Rudy buried the fickle bitch.

¤ ¤ ¤ ¤ ¤

But one more task remained. Gormok said he was cursed to commit murder on any day that he performed a salt-divination. *That's a big problem*, Rudy realized. He couldn't very well have Gormok cutting folks up and eating their livers every time he gave Rudy the read on the next fight or ballgame, now could he?

So...

He crept quietly back down into the basement.

Gormok slept on, murmuring sweet Babylonian nothings .

The Salt-Diviner

Here goes, Rudy thought—

—and raised the fire ax.

"Sleep no more!" Gormok quoted Bill Shakespeare as the great blade cut down. "MacRudy doth *murder* sleep!"

Blood flew like spaghetti sauce. Things thunked to the floor. But there was no other way! *Hell, I'm doing him a favor*, Rudy felt convinced as he chopped and chopped.

And chopped some more. Once he'd succeeded in severing Gormok's limbs, he tied off each stump with twine.

What a day, he thought when he was done.

IV

Beth, shrieking, pummeled up the basement stairs the next afternoon. "*What did you do!*"

"Hey, didn't I say I'd take care of everything?"

"Rudy! You turned him into a...a *torso!*"

"Yeah, well, he can't hurt anybody now, can he?" Rudy rationalized. "And he doesn't even care, as long as we keep him happy."

Beth's face crimped. "What do you mean?"

Rudy thought it best to change the topic. "Look!" he celebrated and waved a sheaf of $100 bills. "Our man came through again. Pimlico, baby! Afternoon Tea by a nose in the first! The odds were 32-to-one! Can you believe it?"

Beth, quite reasonably, went nuts. "Rudy! You bet *again?* He's a murderer, for God's sake! We can't keep a murderer in our basement! Much less a murderer who's a *torso!*"

"Sure we can." Rudy placed the stack of bills in her hands.

Beth went lax, astonished. "This looks like about ten-thou—"

"*Eleven* thousand clams," Rudy corrected. "And I already paid off Vito The Eye. We're rolling from here, babe."

Beth's eyes stayed fixed on the money

"But, uh, you see," Rudy commenced with the bad news. His throat turned dry. "There's a catch. Remember when I told you, 'as long as we keep him happy'?"

"Yeah?" Beth replied.

¤   ¤   ¤   ¤   ¤

The catch was this:

That morning, Rudy had shown the head atop Gormok's de-limbed body the racing journal as he held the fuming ashtray under the alomancer's nose.

"Afternoon Tea, dear Rudy," informed the happy head. "In the first tourney."

Rudy didn't argue, in spite of the odds. But since last night, a question had itched at him like stitches healing.

"Hey, Gor? Yesterday you said something like you had to commit a murder any day you do the salt thing."

"Upon any such day I perform a holy alomance, yes," Gormok affirmed. "Nergal, the abyssal prince, has cursed me as such."

"What happens if you, uh, don't commit a murder?"

"Then the gift of prophesy is lost to me. Forever."

Balls! Rudy thought. *Shit! Fuck! Piss!*

"Unless," Gormok's head leaned up and added, "I am, as a substitute, properly relieved of the groin whenever such needs of passion call."

Rudy's gaze thinned. "You mean…"

¤   ¤   ¤   ¤   ¤

"No!" Beth wailed upon the revelation. "No no no!"

"Honey, come on," Rudy urged. "It's the only *way*. If you don't, he can't pick the winners anymore."

"Rudy, read my lips! *I'm not going to have sex with a torso!*"

Ho boy, Rudy thought. *Women.* You ask them to do a little something and they get all bent out of shape. *Time to lay on the heavy bullshit*, he decided. "It's for our future, sweetheart. It's for our *children*."

Evidently, *children* was the magic word. Beth pouted a moment more. She looked at him, pink-faced.

"Our…children," she whispered. "I- I…"

Rudy hugged her, stroked her hair. "It's the only way, honey. I wouldn't ask you to do it, but *it's the only way*. Don't we want our children to have the very best?"

"Our children," she dizzily repeated. "I guess, I guess you're… right."

Then she turned for the basement steps, began to descend.

That's my little trooper, Rudy approved.

¤   ¤   ¤   ¤   ¤

Little trooper was right—and then some. Rudy, being an investigative kind of guy, felt it only fitting and proper to make an observation or two, so he sneaked down a few minutes behind her and peeked through the slight gap in the door…

Good God! he thought.

Most would deem this a reasonable thing to think when witnessing one's finance engaged in the physical act of love with a living torso. Beth wasted no time in the deletion of her garments, and, despite a rather disconsolate look on her face—just as reasonable–she commenced to her task with something that could only be described as a formidable

The Salt-Diviner

resolve. She squatted over Gormok, who lay unsurprisingly motionless atop his blanket. This afforded Rudy a front-on view, and though Beth's discomfiture was plain, she soon began to ease into the brass tacks, so to speak, of the project.

In the dim basement light, her face flushed, and her small, pretty breasts began to sway. Meanwhile, her companion gibbered sweet Babylonian gibberish in response to her attentions. *How does she do it?* Rudy wondered. This was, after all, a torso. Moreover, ha wondered next: *What is she thinking about?*

Now *there* was a question! What would any woman think about while slamming glands with a dismembered salt-diviner? Perhaps it was brute rationalization, but Rudy came up with the only answer his psyche would allow.

She's thinking about me—

Of course. Who else could she be thinking about? Certainly not Gormok. In moments, Rudy became aware of a considerable hardness loitering at his groin. *My girlfriend's humping a torso and I'm getting a woody.* And as he watched further, the image transposed...

He imagined himself in Gormok's place, right there on the basement floor and shuddering in bliss as the slot of Beth's womanhood slid hotly up and down over his cock. His crotch felt smoldering, his heart *raced*. Beth's breasts bobbed vigorously on her chest as she stepped up the momentum. Up and down, up and down, hot and frantic, her hips began to locomote like a machine, until–

Aw, Christ...

"Sweet mercy of Ea!" Gormok exclaimed at the obvious brink of his crisis.

Rudy caught his breath, and realized that he'd had a crisis of his own, his libido relieving itself to the sheer exploitation of his underpants...

I just watched my wife-to-be get it on with a fat torso, he realized. *And I spunked in my shorts.*

He crept back upstairs, as bewildered as he was disgusted. But he did feel convinced of one thing at least: it was all for a good cause...

V

No, a great cause, an absolutely big time *wonderful* cause. Within a week, Rudy was something he never recalled being: debt-free. Exit the '76 clunker Malibu, enter his and hers Mustang GT's. The 35" Sony tv was nice too, and so was the Adcom stereo and the $50,000-worth of new furniture.

And the new house. A spacious, skylighted A-frame off Bay Ridge Drive. It was the nicest house in the area that had a basement.

VI

Gormok remained surprisingly content, considering what Rudy's greed had divorced him of. He jabbered and drank beer through a convalescent straw during the day, propped up behind pillows in bed, while Rudy cashed in at the track. Not once had Gormok's divinations failed, and soon Rudy's biggest problem was what to do with all the money. Beth, of course, had her ups and downs—the freedom to buy anything she ever wanted was a bit spoiled by the constant sexual service she was required to perform upon the libidinous torso in the basement. Eventually, she began to complain...

"That thing downstairs made me give it head today!" she spat at Rudy. "Did you hear me! I had to give *head* to a *torso!*"

Just like a woman, Rudy frowned in thought. *You give 'em a good thing and they STILL bellyache.* "Honey, he's not a *thing*. He's not an *it*. You're talking about Gormok–he's our man."

Beth gaped. "*Our man!* Then you go down there and fuck him! See how you like it! You go down there and blow *our man!*"

Rudy thanked the fates Gormok wasn't gay. "Stop being selfish," he told her. "Don't we have everything we want?"

"Yeah, Rudy, we do, and that's my point. We have enough now, so I shouldn't have to do it anymore."

Rudy looked up reprovingly. "Beth, there's never enough."

"Oh, so that's it, huh?" Beth, who rarely wore anything other than panties these days (due to the mounting frequency of Gormok's need), stomped exasperated around the kitchen table. "You think you're going to spend the rest of your life cleaning out the goddamn racetrack while good old Beth fucks and sucks a dismembered Babylonian alomancer!"

"Don't be vulgar, honey. It's not like you."

Beth's little breasts jiggled as she belted out a bitter chortle. "You make me fuck a torso and tell *me* not to be vulgar! I'm sick of it! You hear me! I'm sick of fucking that disgusting, ridiculous, grinning...trunk!"

Rudy brought a finger to his lips. "Keep your voice down. He might hear you. You'll hurt his feelings."

"God," she lapsed, paling. "He takes forever sometimes, and—" she gulped—"he's—he's—be's just so...*huge.*"

Then quit complaining, Rudy felt inclined to say. *Women always want the big dick—well, baby, now you got it.* At the table, he weeded out the ones, fives, and tens, into the garbage.

"Beth, oh Bethieeeeeeeee!" called out the familiar nasal warble from downstairs. "Wither thee, my sweet beatific vision? My lovely, lovely Beth of the light-brown hair?"

The Salt-Diviner

"Oh, no," Beth croaked.

"Leave me in turmoil no longer, oh, my wondrous angel, so lovely of countenance and sweet of loins. Come! I beg thee! Come assuage my beckoning fancy."

Rudy cocked a brow. "Assuage my beckoning fancy?"

Beth glared at him. "That means he *horny* again, Rudy." Her eyes rolled back in despair. "I don't believe this. All I ever wanted was a nice normal average life, and what do I get instead? A torso with a boner."

"Dearest Beth, *please!* Partake of my desire! My loins cry out for thee!"

Beth's disdainful glare focused. "And you, you fucker. You haven't made love to me in months."

Rudy shrugged. It was not an easy thing for a man to rise to the occasion when he knew his squeeze was doing the bop with a naked torso. *Hey, she's got her gig, I've got mine,* he thought. His bevy of call girls at the track wore him out. Some of those girls could suck the paint off a battleship. Not much lead left in the old pencil after when *they* were done. "It's all the stress, honey," he lied through his teeth. "All this betting everyday—it takes a lot out of a guy. And now the IRS is all over me."

"Wondrous Beth!" the torso whined on, "my passion throbs for you! Oh, let your lovely loins be wed to mine again! Let your angel's lips give succor to my manly love, and drink of my warm and copious seed!"

"You better get down there," Rudy advised, "unless you want me to lose everything on the next race."

Beth stared at him, her shoulders slumping.

"I hate you," she said.

¤ ¤ ¤ ¤ ¤

One thing Rudy had added to the new house, unbeknownst to Beth, of course, was the hidden video camera in the basement. Rudy, after all, was a successful man now, and successful men didn't watch their girlfriends fuck torsos through mere cracks in basement doors. No, they watched with state-of-the-art video equipment. And Rudy had a lot to watch...

Jesus Christ in a hotdog stand, he thought, staring at the screen in his den and adjusting the remote, low-light lens.

Despite his arousal, Rudy could no longer deny that watching Beth's sexual feats maintained in him a necessary level of disdain for her. It didn't matter at all that he coerced her to tend to Gormok–that was beside the point. And so was logic. He needed to hate her as much as he could in order to compel her to continue. In truth it was money, not love, that made the world go round, and Rudy liked the world very much.

Sometimes, though, the things he saw on the screen really bothered him. Like right now, for instance. Beth was performing an act of fellatio on Gormok the likes of which would make Linda Lovelace look like Rebecca of Sunnybrook Farm. "Goddamn! can she smoke a pole," he whispered aloud. And he saw with even more distaste that her earlier claim was no bull. To describe Gormok as huge was sheer understatement. Try hung like a fucking Clydesdale stallion. *That fruitloop motherfucker's got more dick than four or five guys,* Rudy grimly realized, and at the same time he stroked his own endowment which, in comparison, more resembled a Jimmy Dean breakfast link than a penis. And what Beth was doing to Gormok more resembled a freak-show sword-swallowing than simple fellatio. Down her assiduous lips went, all the way to the hilt, a Gormok's legless hips squirmed in pleasure. Where did it all go? *Deep throat, my ass,* Rudy thought. *This is deep stomach. She never sucked my cock like that, the dirty bitch.*

And Rudy's hatred did not abate in the least as his hand assuaged his own beckoning fancy. *I'll bet the little whore is enjoying it,* he convinced himself. *I'll bet she's getting off! And, Christ, she's making more noise than a truck-load of hogs at the slop trough!*

As was his habit now, Rudy pretended it was the pillar of his own manhood that was being so fastidiously gobbled up by Beth's suck-to-wake-the-dead yap; it was the only way he could tolerate this–to fantasize. But when he eventually relocated the wares of his prostate gland and balls onto the Scotchguarded carpet, the fantasy shattered. His own release was a mere dribble compared to Gormok's veritable whale blasts of sperm, which Beth allowed her face to be showered with as the alomancer gibbered in glee...

VII

Rudy knew it would happen eventually, but he had a contingency plan for that too. One night he woke to find Beth staring at the big bay window in the bedroom.

"Honey?" he feigned. "What's wrong?"

"I can't even sleep anymore. I can *hear* him down there. He jabbers all night long."

This in fact was true. Even from the basement, Gormok could be heard mattering inanities in arcane languages, and bubbling nasal laughter. *Well, maybe if you fucked him a little better, he'd simmer down,* Rudy thought. *Ain't my fault you're a dull fuck. Suck his big dick harder–try that, bitch. Suck his ass–that'll keep him happy.*

Beth sat on the bed and began to cry.

"Sweetheart," Rudy offered a phony consolation. "Don't cry."

"You said we'd get married," she sobbed. "You said we'd have children."

"Honey, we will."

"When, Rudy? I need to know when."

"Soon, I promise." He stroked her hair, kissed her teary cheeks. "I've got a plan," he whispered. "The race track, the ball, games and all that? That's smalltime."

"What are you talking about?" she sniffled.

Rudy reached into the night stand. "See this? It'll set us up for life in no time, honey." What he showed her was the NASDAQ Index of *The Wall Street Journal.* "We'll be *millionaires,* Beth. And then, I promise you, we'll get married and have kids just like we planned."

"Please, Rudy, please," she sobbed, hugging him back.

"I promise," he reasserted. "But you've got to give this just a little more time. Okay?"

Beth's sobs began to abate.

"Honey? Okay?"

"Okay," she croaked.

"Oh, Bethieeeeeeeee!" shot the voice from below. "Come hither, please!"

VIII

Within a few months they'd moved out of the A-frame in favor of a waterfront estate. The his and hers Mustangs were replaced by his and hers Lamborghini Diablos. Rudy merely had Gormok perform a few divinations, then laid his money down at a broker's. It didn't take long. Blue Chip stocks. Municipal bonds. T-Bills. Not to mention the thirty-million in 6-month CD's. Even in the highest federal and state tax-brackets, Rudy had enough to keep them pig-shit rich for life. And that bevy of call-girls? Well, now they were *his* girls. He had thirty of them, one for each day of the month, and he put them all up in luxury condos he paid for in cash. Things weren't bad. No, not bad at all.

And Rudy found a great solace in his calendar-month of bimbos; they provided him the escape his psyche needed, the abstract catharsis which relieved the entails of his complicated, high-stress lifestyle. Plus they fucked good, which furthermore relieved the hatred he now harbored wholesale for Beth. Rudy got lost in his women, and this banished the steady and bothersome awareness that his fiance was impaling herself on a "bigger" man than he, limblessness notwithstanding. Becky was his favorite, a slim, sultry blonde, whose specialty was tongue-baths, which made Rudy a great adherent of personal hygiene. Then there was Shanna, the full-tilt brunette with a rack of tits you could use to drydock a Los Angeles-class sub, and a welcome propensity for always asking Rudy to enter through the, uh, back door. And we mustn't forget Chrissy—now *there* was a woman! She had looks that would make Pamela Anderson seriously consider suicide, not to mention a mouth that could suck-start a Ford Tri-Motor.

Yes, Rudy's buxom recreational brigade all proved quite adroit at helping him cope with his problems, to the extent that his only *real* problem was wondering just how much joy juice his vesicles could manufacture. A man could only put out so much, but lo and behold, his girls were always ready to prove that he was possessed of an endless reservoir of love lava. And on those dread occasions when he felt the old crane simply wouldn't rise, his bevy of beauties were always quick, by their sheer expertise to prove a grand synonymy with Jesus—in that they could raise the dead. Rudy loved his women, he *cherished* them. And whenever he grew sick of one, he simply dumped her and found someone else. Just as there was no shortage of beer in Bavaria, there was no shortage of beautiful women who liked moolah. What a life!

In the meantime, Rudy urged Beth to research, as thoroughly as possible, every aspect of Mesopotamian mythology, ancient ritualism, pre-Christian divination, and the like. She even found one book called *The Synod of the Alomancers*, and learned everything about the Cenotes of Nergal, the Nashipus, the Ashipus, the ziggurats, and all the intricacies of the regalia and the ritual. Rudy felt this necessary in order to make Gormok feel more at home. He had contractors make a mock temple out of the basement. He purchased real censers and thuribles, standards and statues and murals etched with the holy glyphs. He even had a clothier make a special hooded black robe and sash, identical to those worn by the ancient alomancers, which he donned each time he asked Gormok The Talking Torso to perform another divination. Rudy wanted the atmosphere to be right for his dismembered bread-winner; he figured it was the least he could do.

On the other hand, though, Beth grew more and more sullen. She rarely even spoke, not that Rudy was around much to talk to—his harem kept him busy, when he wasn't busy himself wheeling and dealing at the broker's. Beth became stoical, morose. Now, the ludicrous head atop the diviner's torso insisted she service him many times a day, amid an array of kinky twists which were better left undescribed.

But more months went by.

And Rudy's fortune increased exponentially.

IX

It was funny, sometimes, how the universe worked. Rudy recalled

The Salt-Diviner

telling Beth once that there was never enough, but actually, now, he found he was wrong. Already he was one of the richest men in the country. What more did he need? So it *was* rather appropriate, in a cosmic way, when Beth walked into his den one evening and dropped the bombshell:

"I'm pregnant," she said.

At first Rudy felt enraged. "Pregnant! You're shitting me! This is a joke, right?"

"It's no joke, Rudy. I'm pregnant."

He gnashed his teeth and jumped up. "You mean you let that goddamn horny torso *knock you up?*"

"I have to fuck him ten times a day," she drily pointed out. "What did you expect?"

"Well—well, goddamn it, Beth! I thought you were on the pill!"

"The pill isn't foolproof, Rudy."

Calm down, boy, he induced himself. *Don't panic.* "Yeah? Well, it's no problem. You'll simply get an abortion."

Her race looked carved in granite. "I'm not getting an abortion, Rudy. I'm having this baby."

"No. You're not." He opened and closed his fists, to quell his rage. "You're not going to have a kid by that *thing's* spunk."

"Thing?" Beth chuckled. "I thought he was *our man.* Forget it, Rudy. I'm having this baby. You won't give me one, so I'll settle for Gormok's."

You evil calculating bitch, he thought. *You did this on purpose, didn't you? You went off the pill on purpose just to put me on the spot.*

"But I'm willing to make a deal," she went on. "I will get an abortion on two conditions. One, you make me pregnant, and two, you kill Gormok." Then she passed a small box to him. "Open it," she said.

Rudy opened the box to find it occupied by a Smith & Wesson Model 65 .357 Magnum.

"You'll do it right now, Rudy. No more lies. No more false promises. You'll dig a grave in the back yard. Right now. And then you'll take that silly thing outside and you'll kill it. And I mean right *now.*"

Rudy didn't care for being dictated to, especially by a woman. *So she's calling the shots now, huh? Beth the little Torso Fucker. Well...* It was all he could do not to smile.

"All right," he told her. "You've got a deal."

Rudy found the shovel. Then he went out back,

¤ ¤ ¤ ¤ ¤

He'd been thinking along these lines for a while now anyway, hadn't he? The shovel bit into the soil. He didn't need any more money, which meant he didn't need Gormok, either.

And there was one more thing he didn't need:
Beth, he thought, and grinned.

He'd gotten what he wanted out of her. And another point: she was starting to look really beat these days. Skinny, pale, dark circles under her *eyes. I'm a high-roller now*, he congratulated himself. *Why's a big time, big-buck guy like me need a little-tit stringbean bitch like her?*

He could move his harem here! Shit, those girls made the Playboy Mansion look like a dog pound. And there were some new ones now too, like Beverly: California tan, waxed pubes, 40 double-D's and nipples sticking out like a pair of golf cleats. *Her tits should hang in The National Gallery!* he reveled as he dug. And Melissa? *A cosmetic-surgery paragon;* she had a body on her that would put a stiffer on the Pope! Then there was Alicyn, whose vaginal barrel was more dextrous than an olympic gymnast. *Oooo-eeee!* he thought. Not to mention Shelly and Kelly, two brick-shit house redhead twins whose favorite bedroom game was "Sandwich." Rudy never hesitated to play the part of the cheese.

There were so many, an endless Whitman's Sampler of sex!

Shit yeah! I'll move them all here! The entire bimbo brigade! I'll build a fucking luxury apartment complex in the back yard! He could picture it. A different chick every day, a mass orgy every night! He'd eat Beluga caviar out of nut-tan bellybuttons, abdomens. Slurp Perrier-Jouet from Tit Valleys. *Blondes on the half-shell, baby! Redheads Au Gratin, and Brunettes Au Jus! I will live like a Renaissance prince!* Yeah. And Gormok? And Beth? Rudy's grin darkened in the moonlight. He rested a moment. Then he began to dig the second grave.

¤   ¤   ¤   ¤   ¤

"You come out here with me," he insisted. "I need you to hold the flashlight." "All right," Beth agreed. "And bring the gun."

Even bereft of arms and legs, Gormok was not easy lugging up the stairs. *The fucker weighs more than a piano!* Rudy thought between grunts. Then, as he lowered the torso into the wheelbarrow, Rudy winced as if slapped. Gormok, apparently unable to control his renal system, urinated quite liberally into Rudy's face.

Beth laughed.

"Dear Rudy, ho!" Gormok exclaimed. "My deepest apologies! Such incontinence, I assure you, is quite a contretemps!"

"Don't worry about it," Rudy forced himself to reply, dripping warmly. "I guess a man's gotta go when he's gotta go."

"And, goodly friend, hast lovely Beth enlightened thee? The wondrous news that the harvest of my loins hast given her a belly large with child?"

"Uh, yeah," Rudy replied. His back strained as he trundled the wheelbarrow along the pool deck. "That's, uh, that's why we're going out back, you know, to have a party, just the three of us."

"Great Ea! My joy comes unbridled!" Gormok exclaimed, close to tears. His stumps roved in glee. "A celebration!"

There's gonna be a celebration, all right, Rudy avowed as he grunted onward. *I'm gonna bury both of you whacks, and celebrate by pissing on your graves.*

The great back yard of the estate shimmered in quiet moonlight. It was warm out tonight, and pretty—a great night for burying people. Rudy pushed the laden wheelbarrow to the back of the property. He hefted Gormok's trunk and set it beside the first hole. The mound of freshly turned soil blocked the second hole from Beth's sight.

"But such a strange place for a celebration," Gormok's head remarked, craning atop the torso.

Rudy took the gun from Beth, who stood aside with a smirk. He checked the cylinder, saw that it was loaded, then snapped it shut with a flip of the wrist.

"Do it now," Beth ordered.

Rudy smiled. "What I'm gonna do, you torso-fucking little slut, you Babylonian-cum-swallowing whore, is kill the both of you." Then he aimed the revolver at Beth's stone-cold face.

"Go ahead," she told him. "You think I don't know what you've been planning? Use you brain, Rudy. *Think!* Gormok's an alomancer–he can *foresee* the future. If you think all we've been doing down there is fucking, then you're even dumber than I thought."

"I... You...," Rudy said in perplexion. *What the—*

"I had the guy at the gun shop take the powder out of the bullets," Beth next informed him. "It won't fire."

Rudy snapped the trigger a dozen times, each drop of the hammer resounding in a quick metallic *click!*

"But this one will."

Rudy peed his pants when Beth pointed another revolver in his face. "Now...kill Gormok," she said.

"With what?"

"I don't care. Just kill him."

The gun barrel steadied on the point between Rudy's eyes. A moment later, he had his foot behind the shovel, the blade at Gormok's throat.

"Have no fear, dear Rudy," the torso strangely commented. The silly face smiled in moonlight. "Fate beckons us all, the joy-filled summons of providence."

Beth kept the gun on him as Rudy bore down. He stomped the back of the shovel until the blade separated Gormok's head from the armless shoulders. Blood pumped from the stump, soaking Kentucky Blue sod. Rudy kicked the head into the grave.

"And now you kill me," he said, turning.

"Oh, no," Beth replied. And before Rudy could turn completely, she brought the gun-butt down hard on his skull.

EPILOGUE

Rudy would've been wise to read some of the books he'd had Beth get out of the library. Gormok had verified all she'd discovered. The spirit of a condemned salt-diviner could never be killed, only the body it happened to occupy at the time. The spirit merely moved on to possess the body in closest proximity.

Later, Beth calmly buried Gormok's head and torso. She also buried Rudy's arms and legs. Then she went downstairs, and to the basement's new tenant, she whispered, "Goodnight."

"On the morrow, my sweet beauty!" Rudy's head replied but in the familiar high, nasal warble. "I bid thee the most heavenly dreams!"

Now she could have all the babies she wanted. It wasn't like Rudy was going anywhere. And if she ever ran short of money…

There was always the ashtray, and the salt.

THE SALT-DIVINER
AFTERWORD

This is, I believe, the last story I wrote in my "Torso Period," though I wrote several stories about alomancy, and several versions of this. One version, "Private Pleasures," sold to Zebra's p/b anthology Dark Seductions, *and a few others await some future attention. The idea was given to me by a good friend in Maryland, John, with whom I worked as a night watchman. We were not very good night watchmen, by the way. Every Sunday night, we'd drink innumerable Heinekens while on duty, watch videos with titles like* Lawnmower Woman *and* One Million Years D.D., *throw up in garbage cans, leave the site and go to bars in the company vehicle, and essentially not discharge ANY of the duties we were being paid to discharge.*

Every Sunday night for ten years.

Certainly, we should've been fired....but, hey, we never got caught.

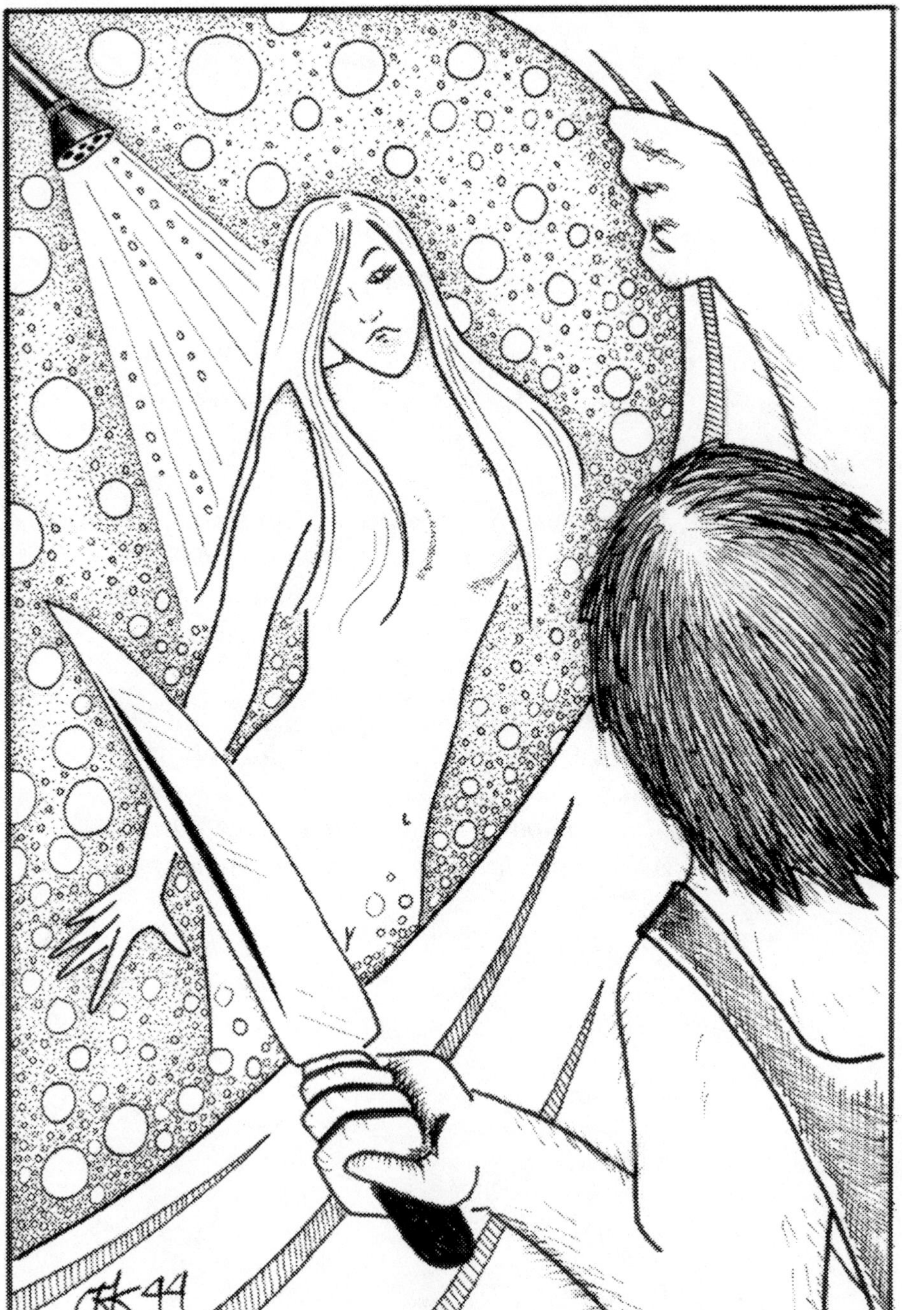

The Man Who Loved Clichés

A FEW MINUTES later, she died.

"Some night, uh-huh," he muttered. He washed his hands in the sink, and watched her blood swirl down the drain. What a wonderful cliché, this gentle, corkscrew vision of scarlet. The girl lay naked on the dusty floor, pallid in the bald light. *Bad, bad boy!* Harley thought, in his mother's voice. Of course—it was the cliché. Typical sociopath, victim of an overbearing mother. He'd picked this one up hitchhiking—it was so clichéd; didn't these girls know hitchhiking was dangerous?—footing it along the Route in her cutoffs, flipflops, and vivid orange halter. She was kind of chunky and cute, with stringy darkblond hair and a little vine tattooed around her wrist. She'd said she liked horror movies, and named all the ones with the best clichés. *I'll show you a cliché,* he reflected. Her pudgy flesh parted serenely as new-churned butter between the knife.

Harley liked clichés, he felt driven by them. Clichés were a proven creativity he couldn't deny. Simply killing them seemed boring, second-rate. It seemed to elude the meaning of what society defined as a sex-killer—a cliché itself. He looked at the pink loops of her unfurled innards and nodded.

The bare lightbulb hung off a long cord from the ceiling. He killed a lot of them in the basement, a great cliché. He tapped the bulb and watched it swing back and forth. Suddenly the damp cinderblock room seemed to throb in its dimensions. The pitching light made the shadows of her feet rove to and fro. *Neat,* he thought.

Harley laughed. He didn't quite feel up to another go-round—she was dead, eviscerated; the cliché was over—so he wrapped her up in the

Edward Lee

dropcloth and buried her in the yard. He buried lots of them in the yard; no one could see him way up here, in the old house that was a cliché: brooding, dark, full of antiques and threadbare carpets. Even the night was a cliché. Muggy, hot. Yellow sickle moon. Peepers and crickets trilled in a lovely, chaotic cacophony.

Harley buried her, whistling "Eighteen wheels and a dozen roses."

The lines in his face were a cliché. He frequently wore overalls and hats with patches advertizing chewing tobacco. He wore his age in a rustic, lackadaisical grace—the friendly old country bumpkin, Harley Fitzwater, the nice old badger down the road. He looked, acted, and talked like a cliché.

Once he'd seen two teenagers skinny dipping down at Duckworth's Pond one night. The girl had skimmed off her clothes and dashed into the water, laughing. Harley's clichéd piano wire made silent work of the boy, who was undressing behind some trees.

"Jorrie! Come and get me!" the girl taunted from the foggy water.

Well, Jorrie had bled out without so much as a whimper. Harley eased into the water, making only enough noise to get her going.

"Jorrie? Is that you?"

Harley swam beneath her by complete surprise, pulling at her thrashing feet. The unseen jabs from his icepick drew her death out long and slow like pizza cheese.

Once he'd chased a girl through the woods with a chainsaw. Another time some high school kids had broken into the house; Harley had donned a white sheet with two eyeholes, and killed them all with a fireax. The local lovers lane—here, the kids called it Trojan Grove—had provided a lot of good times. He'd always crawl under the car while the kids made out, and disconnect the starter. Then he'd get to messing with them awhile, rocking the car on its springs, cackling, tossing dead possums through the windows, before finishing them off with the double-barrel. What a great cliché!

You name it, Harley Fitzwater did it. Severed heads in the refrigerator, radios dropped into the bathtub, body parts delivered through the mail. Once he'd even buried himself. Old Eleanor Smoots left flowers on her husband's grave every year at midnight, on their anniversary. Harley couldn't resist. He'd done a pretty good job rolling back the sod, digging himself in, and covering up, leaving only a tiny airway and seam to look through. Round about midnight, old Eleanor knelt weeping before the grave with her flowers, and out shot Harley's groping arms. He'd slowly strangled her in the soil, muttering, "Eleanor, my love, I've come back to you."

The Man Who Loved Clichés

Then there was Wanda Tilly, the waitress who always teased him at the diner. Thirtyish, big bosom, nice backside. She'd always lean extra low over the table, giving Harley a good peek. Harley loved it—the social cliché. Youth taking a flirting swipe at age. He left her boyfriend's heart on her porch last Valentine's Day.

But there were only so many clichés. What would he do next? He liked to drive at night, to think. The long winding back roads and piny air opened his mind. Hitchhikers were getting old. How many times had he played "Riders on the Storm" after picking up some poor young pretty thing thumbing it down the Route? How many times had he offered sweets and then retorted "Didn't your mama ever tell you not to take candy from strangers?" as his victims went cyanotic and bug-eyed before him?

Harley's vehicle, naturally, was a beat-up old pickup truck–a cliché on wheels. He drove the night away, on this given night—a *dark* and *stormy* night, which seemed quite compliant with his special proclivities. Thunder rumbled, lightning slashed across the sky, and rain fell in sweeping sheets. *What a fine old night for murder,* he mused. The wipers thumped back and forth across the windshield. *Ooooo-doggie!* he thought, peering ahead. Did they gravitate to him? Was there something about the psyche of Harley Fitzwater that summoned these urchins of the evening?

Harley was convinced of this; it was his predestination.

He couldn't help but pull over when he spotted the head-bowed drenched young girl walking down the shoulder through the rain.

"Need a lift there, miss?" he inquired.

"Hey, thanks, mister," she gushed through the rolled down window. She climbed in quickly, as if fleeing killers, and closed the door. "Thanks a lot."

"Don't mention it," Harley replied. "Wouldn't be too neighborly of me to let a gal walk home in this. What happened? Your car break down?"

"No, I don't have a car," she said, in a whiny kind of smartyalecky voice. She pushed wet dark-brown locks back off her face. "I was taking the bus home and got off in the wrong town. Next bus doesn't come till morning so I figured I'd walk. Weathermen didn't say anything about a thunderstorm."

Harley laughed and pulled off. "Yeah, well, that's weathermen for ya, ain't it? Fellas must flip coins to decide the forecast." This was wonderful. *I'll be killin' this gal shortly, and right now we're talkin' about the weather!* What a magnificent cliché! "But, hey," he went on. "Where abouts do ya live?"

"Waynesville."

"Waynesville!" Harley close to exclaimed. "That's damn near twenty miles. Take ya all night to walk to Waynesville, and in this mess? You'd catch yer death of cold." This seemed quite a clichéd remark, and Harley felt proud. Besides, he planned for this young nasally voiced dish to be catching her death of something else altogether. Yes sir!

"Tell ya what," he proposed. "I live just up the road, got a spare room you're more than welcome to use. And I can drive ya to Waynesville in the morning when the rain lets up."

"Well…" Her face sort of crimped up, like this was a paramount deliberation, and that high, snotty tone of hers stretched the words out. "I don't really know you…"

Another pursing, snotty pause, "…but, yeah, I guess that's okay. I can tell you're a nice old guy."

A nice old guy. Harley smiled. This attitude of hers, one he'd seen so many times before, gave the event an extra trimming. *Like she's doin' me a favor*, like old ragtag Harley Fitz is just *cryin'* to have this cute dish stay at his place. It was difficult not to laugh outright. *Yeah, you're doin' me a favor, all right, honey. When I'm cuttin' you open like a fish, I'll ask ya what ya think about the Nice Old Guy now.*

"Okay, then, missy," he said. "We'll be there in a few." He settled back to drive. A few side glances gave his libido a perk. *Yessiree, a real looker, this one,* he concluded. Even in the dashlight, he could make her out just fine: all curvy and trim, with really dark eyes and that haughty defiant pretty face. She seemed even sexier all wet like that, the tight jeans tighter on that class-A backside of hers, and the sheer beige blouse stuck to her hooters like wet tissue paper. The rain made no secret of the fact that she didn't care for bras, and Harley liked that too. He could see her nipples through the clinging material, dark, pert, and big as Kennedy dollars.

"Home, sweet home," he said. He veered up the old gravel road to the house. The wood porch creaked as he led her up. The hinges of the front door keened like a witch's laugh.

"Nice place you've got here," came her clichéd remark in the old dusty foyer. "Thanks," Harley acknowledged. He considered offering her some candy but declined. That cliché was old; this saucy gal deserved better than that, much better.

But what? he wondered.

"Can I get'cha anything? Sandwich, a soda?"

"Naw, I'm not too hungry," she said. "But could I use your phone? I need to call my parents, let them know I'm all right."

Harley struggled not to titter. It enlivened him that he was able to respond with so grand a cliché: "Ain't got no phone, missy. Sorry."

The Man Who Loved Clichés

"No phone!" she objected.

"'Fraid not. Never had no use for one."

Now he really had her thinking. Picked up in the rain by a stranger. Twenty miles from home. Creepy old house and creepy old man.

And no phone.

She paused once more, trying not to let her slowly rising fear show through. Harley smiled. He could take her down right here if she tried to bolt. The little twig'd be putty in his hands. She opened her mouth to say something, then closed it, suddenly taking note of the assorted gimcracks along the mantle. Harley had collected some nice things over the years, things that a saucy gal like this might want to steal. *She must think I'm done et up with a case of the dumbass,* he figured.

"I'll stay," she said. "But can we leave early?"

"Sure. Crack of dawn if ya like."

"Okay. Great."

The stairs creaked with equal clichéd creepiness as she followed him up. All the while, though, Harley was thinking rather desperately: *What? What? What am I gonna do with this one?* A snotty, shifty little gal like this was perfect for the perfect cliché.

But that inspired a deeper question...

Just what *was* the perfect cliché?

"Here's your room," Harley informed her, opening the door. These hinges, too, squeaked beautifully. "Fresh towels and all in the closet. My room's right next door. Just give a holler if ya need anything."

"Sure, mister. Thanks. See ya in the morning."

Harley had to force himself not to dash to his own room. He couldn't help it, this was going to be a doozy. He kept the lights off and proceeded to his bedroom wall, where—to no surprise, beneath an old framed painting—he'd dug out the sheetrock and drilled a hole, to which he immediately put his eye.

She was sitting on the old four-poster bed. She leaned back and kicked off her shoes. A button popped. She squiggled out of the wet, tight jeans, then the panties, then the damp blouse.

Harley wanted to whistle.

His sociopathic appreciation of such visual treats was in no way hampered by his age. Time had well-proved that he could sew the wild oats with the best of the fellas, and he could tell in a heartbeat that he'd be sewing a lot of said oats tonight. Yes sir. This gal here was one of the best lookers he'd had up in some spell, a body on her like some of them city chicks he'd seen in the centerfolds. All creamy white skin, hourglass curves, and a pair of rib melons that wouldn't quit...

Old Harley just knew it, he thought next, his eye still opened wide over the peephole. *Why the little thief.* She'd taken off one of the pillow cases and was one by one filling it up with the little knickknacks lined up along the dresser: a gold music box, a crystal ashtray, a pair of silver candle sticks. Hell, she even took the brass knobs off the dresser! Harley wasn't fooled. She figured she'd wait till the old coot fell asleep, then she'd clean out the rest of the house, and be off on her merry way. But, if so, why had she taken off her clothes?

It was a good question, and the answer delighted Harley.

Maybe she wants to take a shower first...

She grabbed a towel and disappeared to the bathroom.

Harley had to think fast. In the basement he had a tank of snakes. He could plant a few of those bad boys under her blankets and see if that put some spark up her smart ass. And spiders, too—wasn't it a classic cliché that all women were terrified of spiders? Harley had a whole nest of them downstairs, in a shoebox poked with holes. Once he'd tied a gal down to the bed stark naked, and propped open her mouth with wooden pegs. Then he shook out that box of spiders right smack-dab onto her belly. She'd convulsed in terror as the little critters ranged every inch of her body, eventually finding their way into her mouth.

These were good ideas, but— *Just not good enough,* Harley quickly concluded. He knew he needed something special for this one, something...*ultimate.*

Then:

Of course!

He could've smacked himself upside the head for such incognizance. Why hadn't he thought of it before? She'd just gone in to take a shower, for God's sake! This situation was perfect. It was truly and undeniably *ultimate.*

He chose his favorite Sheffield butcher knife—a big silverflashing wedge of death. He heard the sharp metallic squeak of the faucet, then the glorious hiss of water.

Utterly silent footfalls took him out of his bedroom and into hers. His feet carried him like a dream across the carpet, toward the crisp, white glare of the bathroom light. The shower hissed on and on. Harley smiled as if to split his face when he peeked in at that gorgeous silhouette moving behind the translucent shower curtain. He stood there a moment, watching. The knife handle grew slick in his palm. The girl's shape played beyond the curtain, slowly and luxuriously caressing lather up and down her body, turning beneath the spray...

Too bad I ain't got a wig and one of mama's old ratty ankle dresses, Harley thought with a grin. He took one more step, then another, eyes

The Man Who Loved Clichés

peeled open in the ultimate wonder of this ultimate cliché.

His right hand reached forward as his left cocked back the gleaming knife. His fingers touched the plastic edge.

Then he jerked back the shower curtain—

¤   ¤   ¤   ¤   ¤

You sure took your sweet time about it, pops, she thought. It almost seemed like a cliché: crusty old geezer with funny eyes and those backwoods clothes. *Shit, I'll bet the old crank's even got a hole drilled in the wall.* She loved the way he thrashed, and the neat way his arms and legs tremored on the floor as she slowly and tenderly gnawed out his throat. She sucked him dry right there on the moldy tiles, and she really made a mess of herself in the process of her feast. Blood shellacked her throat and breasts, and shined around her mouth. He tasted salty and kind of bitter. When she was done, his face looked like a queer, dried fruit.

After which she calmly finished her shower and watched his blood swirl down the drain. Yes, quite like a cliché.

THE MAN WHO LOVED CLICHÉS
AFTERWORD

Yeah, I know, this one's pretty rough, but I've included it here because it served essentially as my first "redneck" horror story, something I'd become quite known for later down the road, with "Mr. Torso," The Bighead, Creekers, "Header," Micah Hays, etc. Something about rednecks has always fascinated me, I guess because I've always been terrified of them since reading James Dickey's Deliverance *and then seeing the John Boorman masterpiece adaptation. See, something about those two guys in that "I'll bet'cha kin squeal like a pig" scene reminded me too closely of some of the outer elements of where I grew up. Upon rereading it, there were many things I felt inclined to change, but as it turned out, I figured it best to leave the rest alone.*

"The Man Who Loved Cliches," granted, isn't a very good story, but I hope it's at least amusing, and for my interested fans, it's the first brick in a wall that I suspect I'll always be building.

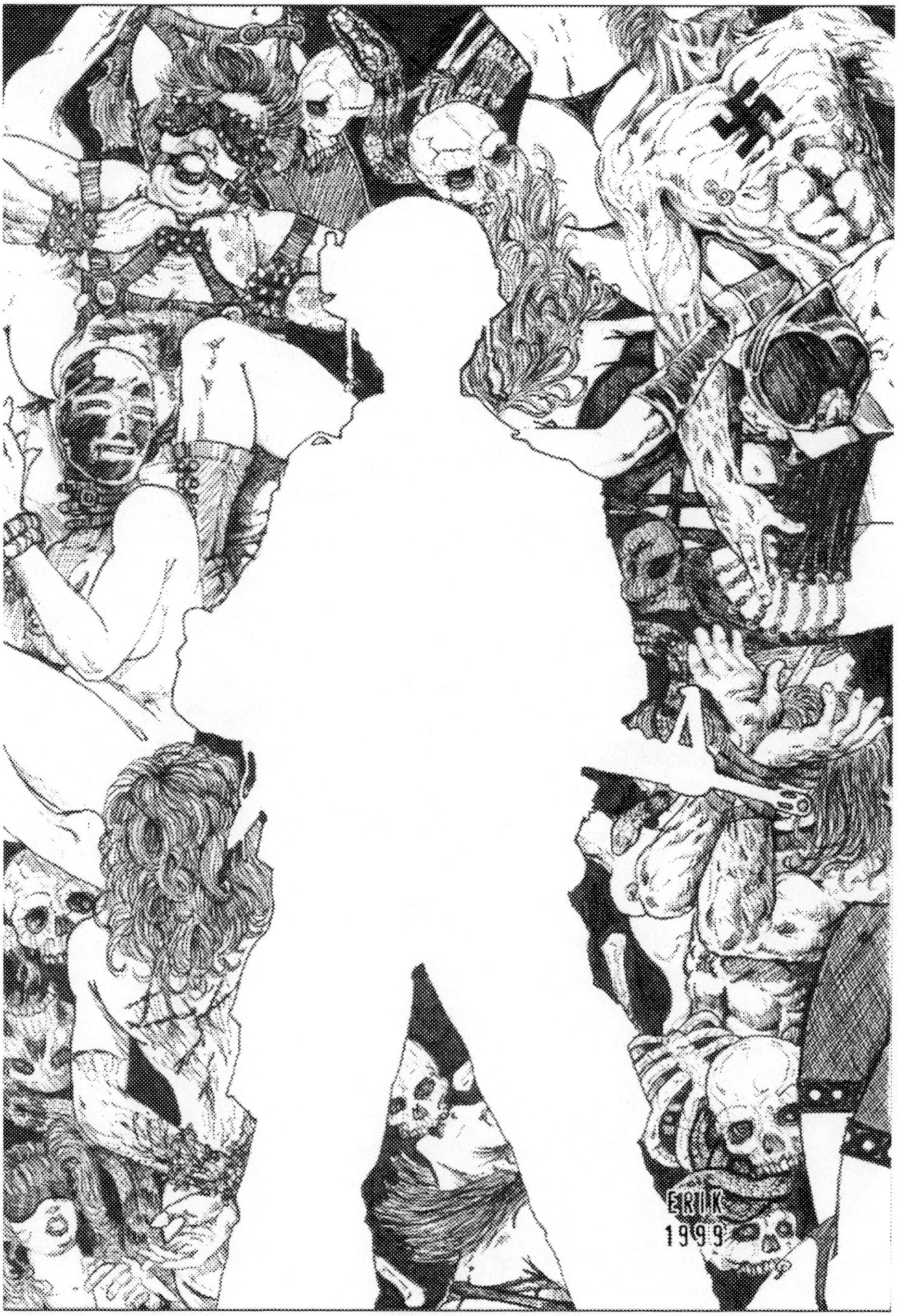
ERIK
1999

Shit-House

[-THE FINAL EDIT-]

"The world," the protagonist whispers to himself. It's a very intent whisper, and a focused one. He is gazing out the window. It's so black outside. Surreally black, like anthracite in bright light. A luminous abyss—
Yes, I think. *The world.*
In your head, you hear Howard Devoto's greatest words:
"This is forever, the final edit…"

[-delicate cutters-]

It's a song by Throwing Muses. Perhaps, one day, he'll start his own band and call them Throwing Up Muses, because that's how he feels most of the time, whenever he dares to look out his window. Music is a muse. Oh, Sisters of the Heavenly Spring, assist my verse and arm my prose, so to let the word be the mirror of the thing. Dante molested.
The protagonist has dreams based on music, like the stuff Shelley sent back in the old days, or all those Fields of the Nephilim and Skinny Puppy tapes that Hodge recorded for him. Delicate nightmares which proffer a vision that—oh, yeah!—he can really relate to. It's a cumulative process, you know. Music that taps the sewerpipe of his mind.
It's his sewerpipe, yes, but it's not his shit that flows there.
It's the world's.
Flesh melded to gray, stoic metal. Machine oil blood, ball-bearing joints, and metal-alloy bone. Time-drip iv bags droop to morphine/epinephrin needles genetically adhered to wormlike blue veins as the beat goes on…

Edward Lee

The clanging industrial metal beat of the delicate cutters in his head, boring down deep into the brainpulp.
To get to the really good shit.

[-news around the world-]

A woman a former nurse in Rio de Janeiro knocked her ex-boyfriend out with sodium amibarbitol when he awoke he was handcuffed to her bed she snipped his penis off with a pair of shingle shears injected him with Desoxyn so he wouldn't lose consciousness and then she cut the penis up into little pieces with a knife and fork and made him eat it piece by piece.
An interesting query at the very least...
What does raw cock taste like?
A heyday of cuisine!
Cock Fondue. Sweet and Sour Penis. Spicy Cajun Pecker Gumbo. Cold Poached Dick Tenders in Mustard-Sorrel Sauce.

A man in Seattle pretended to be elated when his wife announced she was pregnant when she was late in her third trimester two men pulled her out of her car at a mall drove her to a an empty office building that was scheduled to be knocked down they took her to the fourth floor and threw her down an elevator shaft then dropped cinderblocks on her belly until she miscarriaged and died.
The husband paid them $250 each for the job.

The Anne Arundel County Police will tell you that Davidsonville, Maryland, is "the best body dump" in the state.

A guy got a 25-year prison sentence for raping a 15-year-old girl and cutting her arms off at the elbows. The girl didn't die, so they couldn't charge him with murder.
He was released after 8 years for good behavior.

The Serbians have killed close to 250,000 Bosnians now and have raped, via military field order, over 60,000 women and children. Serbian guard squads that succeed in impregnating detained Bosnian women receive commendations in writing and extra weekend passes.

Who says foreign countries don't buy U.S. goods? The Chilean Secret Police use, specifically, Black and Decker power tools with which to torture "political" offenders.

Shit-House

It's a name you can trust. Black and Decker.

10,000 American children disappear every year and are never seen again.

[-pedophilia party. rockin'!-]

It's okay for a congressman to have sex with 16-year-old boys but—goddamn!—if a congressman has sex with 16-year-old girls, there will be hell to pay!

In Nurnburg, Germany, you saw a porn flick where two German guys were having sex with 6-year-olds. They greased their foot-long penises up with Vaseline, then went to work.
Very gently, of course.
After all, child pornography was legal then.

According to an F.B.I. magazine that an ex-girlfriend gave you, there is an entity in America known as "The Circuit" which entails coded "mail-drops" and anonymous "points" through which child pornography videos are distributed to eager patrons. "Kp" and "kiddy" is what the feds call it. They're not sure but it may be as great as a half-billion-dollar-per-year industry, and nobody knows about it. They snatch kids and "turn" them, put them in "the show" until they get too old—like about 12—then make them work the street till they're about 18 and considered "beat." Then they sell the kids to Mexico and Japan.

Rocco "The Eye" Monstroni ran regional "point" for a Sicilian-based "crime-pyramid." Someone dropped dime on the fuck and he pleaded for Federal Witness Protection and Identity Reassignment in exchange for turning federal evidence. He spun like a top. He sang like my fuckin' green parakeet, and the feds buried half a dozen wise guys in the stone motel for life plus ninety-nine years.
After the trial, the federal prosecutor asked Monstroni: "How could you do it? How could you perpetrate child pornography?"
Monstroni glared and answered: "I didn't perpetrate nothin'. The sick slimebags who buy the shit—they're the ones who perpetrate it. If people want somethin', and they're willing to pay, then there's always gonna be someone who'll get it for 'em. Frankly, the shit made me sick."
Interesting point, though.
Good job, Americans. Real good job!

Edward Lee

[-be all that you can be, in the army-]

"It tastes kind of like pork, when you cook it right. You grind it up and fry it, but always grind up some fat with it," Sergeant E-5 Sand told the wide-eyed, awestruck, young recruit.

"When you're in the bush, and you're starving... You'll eat."

APERS (anti-personnel) also known as "Beehive," compliments of the U.S. Army Munitions Command. A 105 or 120mm tank projectile with selectable proximity fuse. The round contains 1500 "fleshettes" or barbs which are deliberately rusted, to incite latent blood poisoning. It's a shotgun shell fired out of a tank.

"Beehive, Seymour," Sergeant Sand recommends. "If you ever go into combat, load plenty of beehive in your ready rack. One cap will clear a crowded football field, no lie. We nailed gook kids to the trees a dime a dozen with beehihve."

Bravo 1/83, 3rd Brigade, 1st Armored Division, Erlangen, West Germany. I was in our battalion maintenance shed, hand-polishing lug wrenches because we had IG inspection coming up. IG inspections are a bitch, let me tell you. So out on the pad an HE operator on an M88 crane was lifting a five-ton, 750 horse-power diesel engine out of a dead-lined M60A1-series tank. The engine is suspended about seven feet in the air, and then some black batt mechanic walks under the engine to open the trans plug. A blue static premonitory chill runs up my spine as I'm standing in the shed, watching–*He's dead,* I think—and sure enough, the operator's hand slips, and that five-ton engine free falls right smackdab on the black mechanic's head. In visual shock, I call the post medical unit, and while I'm on the phone, my platoon leader, some Johnny Brown-Bar West Point pussy motherfucker named H——, who's the commander of a armor platoon, mind you, but doesn't know the difference between a tank track and a race track, he barges into the company maintenance shed, and orders: "Goddam it, Seymour! What are you doing on the phone! Get your ass out there and hose that blood off the pad ASAP! We've got an IG in less than an hour! I'm not gonna blow an IG because you wanna waste time calling an ambulance for a dead nigger!"

Shit-House

[-the album of sergeant sand-]

You know it's all true, all the things he did...

Sand's victor, an M60-straight strangely with no bore-evacuator, backed up into a defensive position in the Vietnam jungle, a wooden stake jutting from the bustle rack. A severed human head on the end of the stake.

Sand's German girlfriend on her hands and knees, distending her anus to a round, empty hole the size of the top of a beer can, and Sand about to admit his fist.

Sand smiling in the jungle, holding up a prize. A human arm.

Sand smiling, sitting back on some crusty couch in a Saigon whorehouse. Other G.I.'s throwing U.S. dollar bills and MPC's like confetti while a South Vietnamese prostitute eats shit off the floor.

Sand's palms opened, displaying two human ears and what is probably a severed human penis.

Sand standing in the jungle with his arms crossed, looking down, and clearly waiting his turn, as an SSG copulates with the lower portion of a dead Vietnamese woman who had been cut in half at the waist when she tripped an M-18 Claymore anti-personnel mine.

Oh, yes. You know it's all true...

Because you saw the polaroids in Sergeant Sand's photo album.

[-oblique girl on the phone-]

"You don't believe everything you read, do you?" she asked on the phone that day when the light was silver and the tick of the clock was strangely loud, and she asked this with more venom in her voice than a coral snake's got in its poison ducts.
 The relationship was ending.
 "No," I answered in a voice like crumbling rocks. "But I sure as shit believe everything I see..."

[-seer-]

Such a fine line between that which serves as a blessing and that which serves as a curse.
I am a seer, you think, looking at the window.
And I...see...this...

[-the sound and the fury and the peep shows-]

The protagonist has always felt that he is a very visual person. Seeing fascinates him. He's a seer; he needs to see.
And the world has never been stingy with its sights.
The world, the protagonist thinks.
Such a visual world—

Doggone Days, Makin' Bacon, Horsin' Around: Women in sunglasses fucking dogs, blowing pigs, jerking off horses in barns. He saw them all, not surprisingly, in Baltimore. The pig bites one of the girls, and the other girls laugh. A German Shepherd frenetically humps a brunette who looks suspiciously like Martha Davis in The Motels. A dirty blonde frowns, beneath the potbellied horse, her hands jerking the lengthy pink rod until the copious release, like heavy rain, gushes into her face.
New York, 8th Avenue & 42nd Street: Fat, mustacheod bald guy busts his sausage-sized piss-hard-on into the blonde more beautiful than any woman the protagonist has ever seen in his life, all perfect, honest curves, noon-blue eyes, and white- blond hair shiny as silk. She is indefectible, paragonic. The guy sodomizes her so frenetically that at least an inch of her rectal vault prolapses with each stroke. Eventually, her rectum begins to bleed. Some time later, the man withdraws, ejaculates into her face, then wipes his bloody penis off in her lovely, silken blond hair.
Ron J. Extravaganza: Here he is, a kaleidoscope of sex with the same fat face, Ron J. slamming holes every which way, bending the gorgeous women in half, pushing their knees back to their ears, dog style, from behind, upside-down, one grueling flick after another. In one, Ron even blows himself—what a guy! And when the master is done he always obliges to charmingly release the seed of his loins into their faces or onto their backs, like someone taking a hock.
Ron Fuckin' J., yes sir. He sure knows how to treat a woman right—give yourself a slap on the back, Ron; it's a dirty job, but someone's

Shit-House

gotta do it, so it might as well be you instead of someone with a life. This hair-matted, bulbous-bellied, indecorous slob's got it all, don't he? He gets to have constant sex with beautiful women, and...he gets paid for it. I read in the Adult Video Directory that Ron J. has been in over 1000 x-rated films. Now that's what I call a real contribution to society.

If I ever see that disgusting, busted borsch-filled fat fuck on the street, I will cut him open in place, drop his guts on the pavement, and bury him like he never was born.

Poppin' Mamma: Two chuckling black guys with penises that look like things that should hang in a smokehouse take turns fornicating with a white woman who looks like about nine-and-a-half months pregnant. Eventually she breaks her water and passes out but the two guys masturbate into her hair anyway.

Champagne de Toilette: "I—I just can't help it!" she announces, stepping into the foyer. At once she lifts her skirt and urinates liberally on the floor. Washed out from a hundred dupes but still somehow glaringly sharp the blonde proves her diversity without a moment's hesitation, urinating into a big brandy snifter and gulping it right on down. "I just can't help it!" she reaffirms in a hot whine. Bright blue walls, like a Man From Uncle set, Aerosmith and Oingo Boingo playing from a boombox in the background. She couldn't possibly appear more appropriate: white high heels, black stockings, light pink blouse, dark-pink mini-skirt, black roots, smudged makeup—a real prize. She urinates steady streams into the air, douches with 7-Up, arranges herself on hands and knees and then expulses wine from her anus like a water cannon. Every so often the cameraman steps into the picture, pulls five-minute beer-pisses into her face and mouth, then ejaculates onto the side of her face. Then she's coming through the door, drops her purse on the floor, squats and urinates in the purse, then drinks from it. Next, she's in the bathroom, and what is she doing? She's inserting an entire banana into her vaginal barrel. When it's all the way in, she stands spread-legged over the open toilet and, by means of some very dextrous pelvic muscles, is ejecting the banana piece by piece into the toilet. Plunk, plunk, plunk, goes each piece. Then she gets down on her knees, licks the toilet rim, and begins to eat the banana pieces. Eventually the cameraman returns (hey, when a man's gotta go, a man's gotta go), holds her head down into the toilet, and pulls another five-minute beer-piss onto her head as she enthusiastically laps up toilet water.

Not exactly the kind of gal you'd want to bring home to meet mom and dad.

Boo-Boo's: The illustrious New York City again. In an hour of traversing this sick-fuck bung-hole of a city, I thought I'd seen everything, but, boy, was I wrong. I walked into a peep-show booth, and here's one called "Boo-Boo's." *What can this be?* I wonder as I drop in my tokens. Ah, people having sex but with a twist: all the participants possess some variation of at least one sexually transmitted disease. A pretty girl smiles, showing off the reddened bulbs of the oral herpes on her lips, while her erect suitor squeezes gonococcal pus out of his penis before he puts it in her mouth. When she's finished, another erection rages into the camera's view, the glans of which sports two marble-sized syphilitic knots. A fingernail breaks the crust off the pustules, and then the fellatio continues. Here's another girl opening her labia with her fingers for the camera, to display the thin white coat of chlamydiosis before yet another girl who lowers her tongue to probe the cheesy mess. And the final shot: a man is vigorously copulating with a sleek blond girl on what appears to be a kitchen table. He withdraws to ejaculate on her belly, then the camera zooms in for the revelatory close-up. The penis is so inflamed with herpetic boils it looks like a glistening, blood-red Pay Day. The girl leans forward to take it in her mouth, and I throw up before I can even get out of the stall.

Long Jean Silver: The woman's name is Jean, and she's about as cute as they come. The-Girl-Next-Door type of looks, honey-blonde, slim and trim, and a peaches-and-cream complexion. She was probably a cheerleader in high school. She's wearing a nice floral-patterned dress, fern-green, pretty. She quickly kneels before the other woman whose legs are thrust apart on the couch. Jean performs deft and thorough cunnilingus, and then—

Slicks her elegant, well-manicured hands up with some nameless lubricant until they shine like wet lacquer, and then—

Puts her oiled palms together and inserts both hands at once—that's right, both hands—into the other woman's vagina at the same time, until they're buried an inch past the wrists.

But is that all?

No, no, that's not all…

Jean stands up, sheds her pretty dress, and sits on the couch, chatting silently. Nude now, her beauty is even more apparent. Her flawless skin glows, her perfect blond hair seems to shimmer along with her smile. Her breasts, too, are perfect, not too small, not too large, high, firm 34B's. But—

There's something…

What the hell?

…wrong.

In time, the incongruenty becomes noticeable. Jean's left leg is arti-

Shit-House

ficial. From the knee down, the fleshtone plastic shines garishly. And then Jean calmly lifts her leg out of the prosthetic column.

What she withdraws is a long skin-covered bone. There is no foot on the end of it, just a tiny nub. Trace hair darkens the atrophied limb, which is also pocked by diminutive red sores.

She raises her thigh, wielding the emaciated lower leg dextrously, like an insect appendage. Then she begins to slick it from knee to nub with the oil after which she unhesitantly inserts it into the other woman's vaginal cavity, to a depth of more than a foot.

¤ ¤ ¤ ¤ ¤

Seen enough, seer?
Hmmm? Have you, seer?

¤ ¤ ¤ ¤ ¤

But seeing is what he must always do. It is a curse. He is helpless.
He has to see.
He has to see what the world is.

[-west street whores-}

It never fails. Whenever the protagonist leaves the Ram's Head Tavern, the light at the hotel turns red, and out they come, like pus being effused from cankers in the night. A black pimp stops short, jumps out of his beat-to-shit Camaro, and hauls a white redneck girl by the hair into the car. His fist behind the windshield rises and falls for what seems minutes, and then the girl is thrown out of the car. She staggers away in a daze, her face beaten to pulp.

tap-tap-tap, a finger on the glass. The protagonist rolls down his passenger window one inch and a skinny white hooker grins in with broken teeth. "Fifteen bucks for head," she promises. "And no rubber. How about it? I'll suck your peter so hard your asshole'll inhale."

"Uh, no thanks," the protagonist replies, thinking, *Jesus Christ, is this light ever going to change!*

"All right, ten. Or maybe you wanna fuck me. Twenty to fuck me, and you ain't gotta use a rubber, either."

"Uh, no thanks."

"Come on, let's party. How about an ass-fuck? Forty bucks. You wanna ass-fuck me?"

"No. No, thank you."

"All right, I can tell. You want the special, huh?"

"Nnnnn," the protagonist begins, but then he stops. There he goes again, with his cursed curiosity. Suddenly, he has no choice. He has to ask.

"What's, uh, what's the special?"

"Usually I charge fifty, but for you...thirty-five, 'cos I can tell you're a nice guy. What I'll let you do, see, is you can fuck me up the ass, but before you come, you pull out, and then I'll suck you off. We call it the Shit Stick Special."

The protagonist's mind reels. He floors it through the red traffic light, and gets pulled over by a city cop at the next block.

[-I street and 14th-]

A bum pisses himself in the Kojac's Sub Shop, gurgles phlegm, then dies as you're holding your half-eaten steak, egg, and cheese. A black woman taps at a vein in her corded elbow, then injects heroin whilst seated on a park bench as you and your pals stroll casually by. Mental invalids and epileptics jabber at you, rail convoluted obscenities from foaming mouths. In an alley behind the Roy Roger's, three teenagers chuckle as they urinate on a swaddled homeless woman trying to hide beneath cardboard. The city percolates, an asphalt abscess. In the stygian dark of Dave & Lee's Parking lot, a man is defecating on a car. On the corner by the liquor store there is a bloodstain shaped like West Virginia. A sound gets closer—WAP-WAP-WAP!—as you turn the corner. One man is hitting another man in the head with a two-by-four. WAP-WAP-WAP! Rats the size of puppies eat voraciously at a puddle of vomit by a dumpster. From the dumpster, a man emerges, rubbing his eyes. A short burst of machine-gun fire rings out, then a car speeds off. "Ice, Frog, Cokesmoke?" a black guy asks at the corner by Capital Books. "Tits, clits, and ice-cold Schlitz!" promises the barker in front of Benny's Rebel Room. "Seventeen tits, nine cunts, and nine assholes!" Another barker in front of a porn shack proudly announces, "Brand new films just in today, guys. Check 'em out. Fisting, shit-eating, animals. We gotta great one where this really hot chick sticks sewing needles in her tits and squeezes out blood. Come on in and get your rocks off good."

And when you're finally leaving this abyss, this canyon of human refuse, the guy is still hitting the other guy in the head with the two-by-four.

WAP-WAP-WAP!

[-summation to a philosophical query-]

Everytime I look out the fuckin' window I could just bend over and

Shit-House

throw up, more from my heart than from my belly. Yeah, I'm a seer—what a joke! If I see one more thing—

If just one more crackhead tries to mug me, if one more bum tries to shake me down for cash, one more scrawny junkie hooker tries to hit me up for a trick, if one more sociopathic white-trash Maryland redneck motherfucker in a pickup truck tailgates me for driving the goddamn fucking speed limit…

Oh, I'm sorry, pardon me for being politically incorrect. Pardon me for being insensitive to others. Pardon me for ignoring the fact that I'm to blame for every whore and rummie and drug-addict and criminal and overall amotivate that all of history has produced. Pardon me for failing to realize that it's my fault every one's so fucked up.

Porn flicks, piss flicks, animal flicks, Long Jean Fuckin' Silver and her hairy skin-covered bone, herpes, AIDS, hepatitis-B, junkies, pimps, dealers on every corner, pederasts teaching junior high gym, daycare centers where they sodomize four-year-olds, skinheads with swastikas tattooed on their chests, evangelists busting virgins, United Way execs taking the Concord to have lunch in London, murderers sprung from the pen after doing three years, burglars bust into your house and when you shoot them, they sue you—and win. Liars, thieves, con men, everybody out for themselves and fuck everyone else, North American Man-Boy Love Associations, satanic churches where membership requires one ounce of your first-born's blood and KKK and L.A. riots and it's okay to rape and kill and loot because four asshole cops beat the shit out of some asshole with a mile-long rap sheet who was driving drunk a hundred miles per hour down a residential street and serial killers cooking biceps and crack addicts getting pregnant on purpose to get more welfare and gang bangs and nail parties and nerve gas and 5kt nuclear warheads the size of a can of Coke and people pissing and shitting in the fucking street and jacking out ninety-year-old ladies for their social security and then raping them to boot and S&M support groups and rehab for killers and Sex Addicts Anonymous and "fag-bashing," and gay Maryland congressmen who pick up sixteen year-old boys at night and vote against gay rights during the day and senators taking dope and writing call girls off on their taxes and judges taking graft and still more congressmen fucking kids and staying in office because it was only an "error in judgment" and lobbyists selling the country down the river and state legislation banning the dispensation of free condoms in high schools and the CIA buying heroin and log-rolling and deficits and cops on the take and nine-year-olds with MAC-10's and three-hundred-pound women in Safeway using foodstamps to buy better steaks than I've ever eaten in my life and still still still more congressmen missing votes in the house because they're out raking in honoraria at speaking engagements since they can't possibly live on $180,000 per year and newborn babies left in dumpsters and do-it-yourself abortion kits and how-to-make-two-step-exposive-devices-with-common-kitchen products manuals and psychopathic war vets and baby-stealing clubs and guys fucking pregnant girls till they break their water and killers for hire in the backs of magazines and hot shots and street gangs raping nuns and priests sodomizing boys in the confessional and death camps and rape camps and Shit Stick Specials...

So allow me now to unfold before you the summation of this inquirous philosophical manifest:

The world is a fucking shithouse.

[-the final edit-]

Yes, the Devoto song again. The protagonist is driving through the dank, rank, ever-familiar night. It has just rained; hence the black streets glitter like a strange, otherworldly frost. The State House dome glows blue in twilight, an azure skull. A redneck in a pickup truck tailgates him for driving the speed limit, and at the light a black kid spits on his car, and says, glaring, "White muv-fuck," like it's the protagonist's fault that the guy's ancestors were slaves, and then a hooker breathes "Fuck you" into his face with corpsepile breath when he informs her that he is not interested in her proposed exchange of currency for sexual services.

But now the protagonist shrugs and smiles. He's cool, he's together...

He looks out the windshield and thinks, *The world...*

In his trunk, conveniently purchased before the Omnibus Crime Bill, is a brand-new anodized Colt AR15A2 semi-automatic assault rifle with three forty-round clips and several hundred rounds of Winchester 5.56mm full-metal-jacket ammunition, not to mention a Zeiss low-light 3.5x scope.

Yes, the world is a shithouse, he acknowledges. *Am I'm going to start cleaning it up right now.*

Then the light turns green, and the protagonist drives on. It shouldn't take him too long to find a nice, dark alley where he can lock and load.

SHIT-HOUSE
AFTERWORD

I can't recall exactly when I wrote this, but I do remember that it was one of those "fugue state" sorts of things. I just sat down one day and started writing. It felt like a wound draining. No, I do not possess the sentiments of our obscure "protagonist." But in reality, don't we all get pissed off when people abuse us or take us for granted or, worse, take us for suckers, etc.? When elected officials lie to us, when charity organizations pump up their six-figure salaries with our donations, and when police make tracks for the donut drive-in, pretending not to see that guy bleeding in the street? Or when you give money to a street person and he frowns at you as if to say "Is that all you got?" I think there's some dark shape in all of us that might on occasion harbor some negative emotions about the people around us.

Hasn't there been at least one occasion when some asshole has tailgated you, then passed and given you the finger? And what did you think then?

At any rate, when I wrote this story, it exploded into a work over 10,000 words, so I cut it into two pieces. One piece is "Shit-House," and the other piece is "The Ushers."

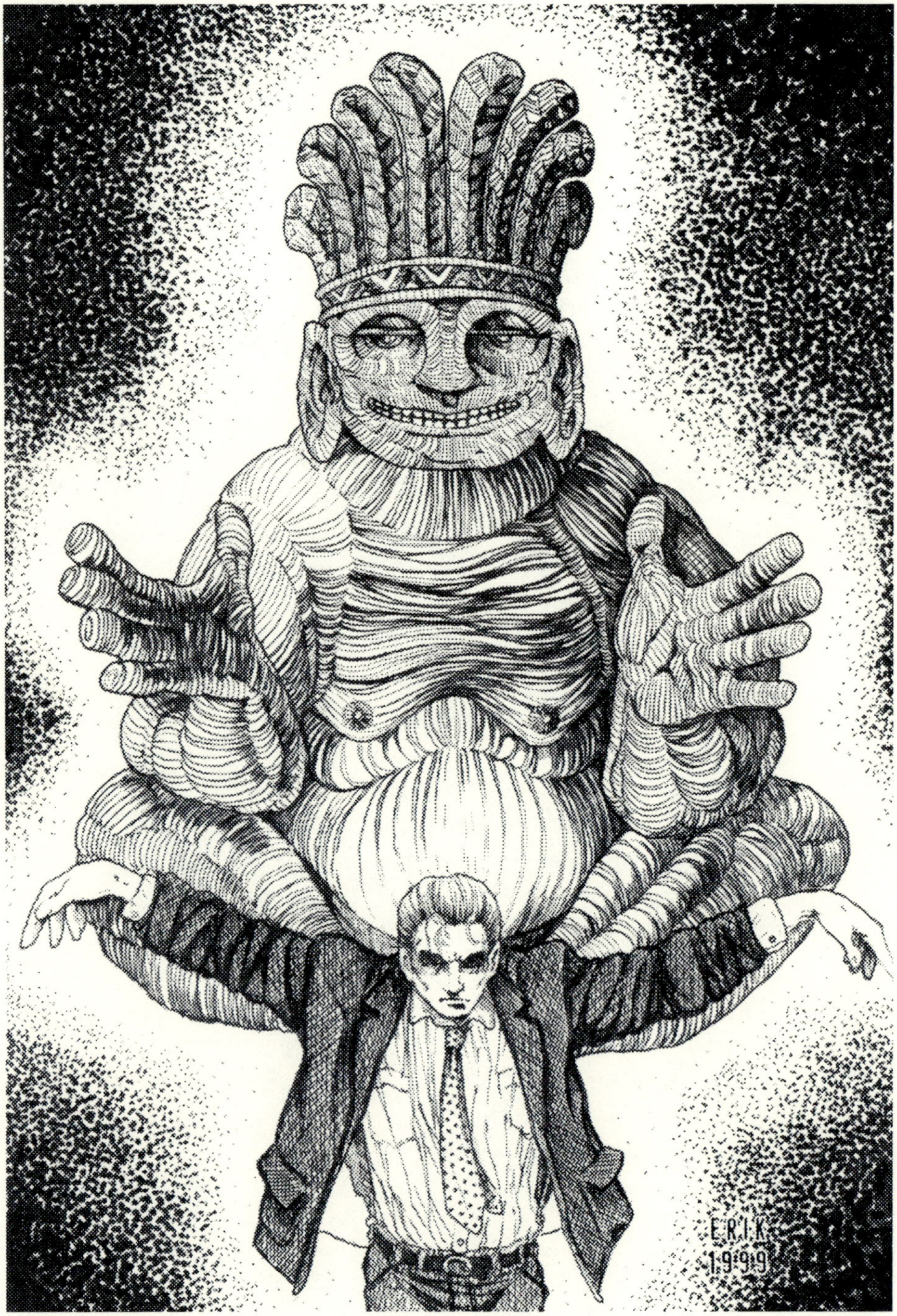
ERIK
1999

XIPE

THE SMILE—VAST, empty—oozed across the back of his mind. Pudgy hands reached out for him through a rain of blood.

Smith's eyes snapped open. The ceiling was rushing past; he was flat on his back. Dark faces, like blobs, hovered over him. He heard casters squeal and bottles clink.

A voice, a man's, exclaimed: "Desé prisa!"

Smith had a pretty good idea he was going to die.

The smile again, huge, empty—what was it? He closed his eyes and saw a muzzle flash, smelled cordite. He saw twin figures falling through dark. Then he heard a scream—his own.

A sign loomed: STAFF ONLY/PERSONAL UNICAMENTE. Doors parted clumsily. The gurney wheeled into a padded elevator, and at once the breathless, jagged motion ceased.

Images dripped back into his head: memories. Smith's heart shimmied. *I was set up,* he thought, astonished. *That swine Ramirez, he must've turned.* The guy must've gotten himself fingered and was trying to deal his way out. There'd been a fed in the room, hadn't there?

More pieces fell into place: a clawing weight on his hack, a window bursting, the unmistakable kick of a .38 full of hot loads. But Smith carried a Glock. *Did I shoot a Justice agent tonight?* With his own piece? And good luck to that scum Ramirez if he thought he could spin on Vinchetti's network. Smith couldn't remember a whole lot, but he was sure of one thing: Ramirez was dead.

The elevator hummed. Smith felt dreamy. "What hospital is this?"

"San Cristobal de la Gras, Meester Smeeth," said the blurred doctor. "We are taking you to where you will be safe."

Edward Lee

Great, Smith mused. *More Mexicans.* But what could be expect down hare? At first he thought they must be taking him to the jail wing, but then a nurse said in a warm whisper, "The government men do not know you're here." She squeezed his hand. "We will protect you."

Smith felt exorcized. Vinchetti must've arranged this, must've paid off the right people to have Ramirez protected. Otherwise, Justice would be all over the place.

Thank God, he thought.

Then, in a jolt, he remembered the rest. The face behind the empty smile, and the name.

Xipe.

¤   ¤   ¤   ¤   ¤

"It's Xipe," said the barkeep.

Smith was staring at the tiny stone figure which sat atop the register. It was black. It looked like a Buddah with a feathered headdress. Squatting, it held its arms out and smiled.

"What?" Smith said.

The keep, rail-thin, enthused in a thick Mexican accent. "Xipe protects the faithful. He is the Giver of the Harvest, the Seer of Beauty and Growth. He is the Great God of Good Will. Like your severed rabbit foot, Xipe brings luck."

You look like you've had plenty, buddy, Smith concluded. La Fiesta Del Sol, like all the bars down hare, was an erect dump. Sticky floors and walls, seamy light, jabbering Mexican music. A young G.I. fussed with two whores at a corner booth, but that was it. Ramirez always picked shithouses like this. Perhaps they reminded him of home.

Smith was Vinchetti's coverman; he handled the southern region of what the feds called "The Circuit," the mob-operated underground porn network. Vinchetti said the southern region grossed a couple of million per year, a far cry from what they'd been taking before the advent of VCR's and x-rated videos; but then they weren't losing anything anymore, either. Nobody worked in loops and stills now; it was all video. A single _ -inch master could be duplicated a thousand times and sold to pointmen for a thousand dollars apiece. From there they stepped on them any way they wanted, depending on the orders. In other words, the days of running truckloads of the stuff out of South Texas were long gone. Just a handful of masters kept The Circuit going for mouths. It was almost too easy, and risk free. Vinchetti's plants in Justice, working with set-ups from Smith, gave the feds plenty of old stuff and overstock to seize, and a couple of wetbacks to bust. Justice thought they were effectively fighting underground pornography, while Vinchetti lost nothing and made millions per year. The net was even safer from the distribution end; everything was mail drops these days, coded mailing lists and untraceable names. Even Vinchetti didn't know who most of his point clients were, and on rare occasions when Postal agents busted a point at a drop, Vinchetti skated because the points didn't know who he was, either.

The stuff, of course, was all made on the Mex side; the states were too hot, unless you were pure-ass stupid like those Dixie Mafia lightweights or the Lavender Hill people. The Circuit dealt only in what the feds called "Underground"; real S&M, torture, snuff, and lots of kiddie. The fucking perverts stateside paid big money for "kp," as much as three bills for a 20 minute double dupe, as long as the kids were white. Smith made the buys and had the masters muled to San Angelo; Vinchetti's dupe labs took it from there. Smith saw no shame in what he did. Supply and demand—hey, it was a free country, wasn't it? The only real real worry was getting the masters across the border, and that was Ramirez' problem. Smith didn't know how the guy did it-he was either a very good mule, or a very lucky one.

Where the hell is he? Smith thought. Lapeto was a ghost-town, like any of the notorious Texas border stops, a grim meld of rapid babble, dark faces, and sneers. The pop was 99% Mex, half or more wet. All that kept these little pisshole towns alive were the EM's from Lackland and Fort Sam. The kids would come here, rent rooms, then cross over to catch the donkey shows in Acuña and Fuenté. For all Smith cared, the entire border could burn.

"I've never been robbed," the keep said. He was drying glasses, grinning.

"Huh?"

"Never been robbed like other bars, never been shaken. Never problems."

"Big deal." Smith sputtered.

"Is Xipe. He is good luck."

Idiot. Smith stared at the figure again. It smiled much like the keep, emptily. Smith didn't believe in gods, stone or otherwise. Gods wre bad for business. "Another." he said, and hopped off his stool.

In the John, he scanned incomprehensible graffiti. Most of it seemed to lack Spanish extraction altogether. Xoclan, ti coatl. Ut zetl! Huetar, Coatlicue, ay! Me socorro! Someone had drawn a humming bird eating the heads off stick figures. Smith grimaced and zipped his fly. A shadow swung behind him. He spun, shucked his Glock, and drew down…

But it was only a trinket swinging from the light. A black plastic figure with pudgy hands and a big, empty smile.

Xipe.

This place gives me the creeps. He couldn't wait to get back to San Angelo and the real world. A little coke, a little pussy—enough of this wasteland. A slim figure in a smudged azure-blue suit sat stooped beside Smith's bar stool. The head turned as if psychic, big white smile with a gold tooth, greasy hair, greasy face.

"Amigo," Ramirez greeted. "How is my favoreet yankee?" He offered a pale hand, which Smith declined to shake.

"I've been waiting a fucking hour."

"Hey, we Mexicans, we're always late, isn't that right?"

"Come on, we've got business."

Ramirez nodded, grinning, and paid the tab. The gold-flecked grin seemed permanently fixed. He led Smith out, slinking like a junkie after a mainline.

The street stood empty. It stank of dust. A lone whore yammered at a couple of G.I.'s getting out of a cab. She gazed at Smith once, then quickly looked away. The main drag wasn't even paved; it was dirt, strewn with litter. Smith checked the alleys for tails, but only emptiness returned his glances.

"I have much good stuff for you tonight, Meester Smeeth." Ramirez held the door for him at the motel. PARADISA, the neon sign glowed. *Jesus,* Smith thought. Dark lamps lit the lobby. Ridiculous felt prints of matadors and Spanish women adorned the stained walls. A greasily rouged fat woman tended the counter, hair in a black bun. From a shelf of curios, the tiny figure of Xipe smiled. Smith frowned.

They mounted stairs which smelled of beer-piss and smoke. Ramirez' room smelled worse. *La Biblia* rested on a nightstand, beside a stained bed. Used condoms stuck to the side of the wastebasket. Ramirez was zipping open a battered suitcase, but Smith's gaze turned to the room's only wall painting. The quetzl-feathered head on a plump, squatting body. Its arms outstretched as if to invite embrace. The smile huge yet empty.

"Xipe," Smith muttered at it.

Ramirez looked up, grinning gold. "The Giver of the Harvest, who protects the faithful. The Great God of—"

"Good Will, I know," Smith interrupted. Xipe's eyes were empty as it's smile, its fat hands empty. Perhaps it was the *mode* of the trinket's emptiness that distressed Smith so. It seemed to him a kind of vitality— a *knowledge*— hidden deep beneath the black facade. An emptiness that somehow yearned to be filled.

"He brings luck, Meester Smeeth. He guards us from our enemies."

Smith blinked. A shiver of vertigo, like standing up too quickly after a neat shot of Uzzo, seemed to transpose Xipe's smile to a momentary hollow grimace.

Smith turned away. He didn't feel good—bad beer or something. In dismay, he glanced down. "Jesus Christ, you bring the stuff in a suitcase?"

"My people, like yours, we pay."

"You can't buy every Customs officer on the line."

"Of course not." Ramirez grinned at Xipe. "The rest is *buena snerte*."

"What?"

"Luck."

Smith felt a chill. The painting distracted him. "How many masters?"

"Ten. New faces, all new stuff. And chiquitas—the best."

Smith carried forty large. He was authorized to pay three grand per master, but only if the production was good. The way it worked, if the larger-formatted master wasn't excellent, the second dupes would look piss-poor. Ramirez plugged the first tape into the VCR he'd set up on the dresser. Now came the grueling part, having to watch a sample of each. Smith steeled himself, crossed his arms, and addressed the screen.

His eyes bulged when the image formed.

He expected the usual phantom scenes: stark-lighted rooms, hollow-eyed children and sneering spic studs, women gagged and tied and jerking as fingers sunk needles into banded breasts. Instead he saw a grainy black and white of a man getting out of a car in front of a San Angelo warehouse.

The man was Smith.

Next: himself walking down the concourse at the Dallas/Ft. Worth air terminal. And next: himself giving Vinchetti's Justice plant some pad and a list of phony bust points in a vacant Del Rio parking lot.

Ramirez' gold grin glowed. "Good stuff, eh, Meester Smeeth?"

"You greaseball pepper-belly motherfucker!" but before Smith could even think about yanking his heat, a hammer cocked behind his head. Smith's face felt huge as he turned. He was now looking down the barrel of a 3-inch S&W Model 13.

"Good evening. Mr. Smith. My name is Peterson. I work for the Department of Justice. I'm arresting you for multiple violations of Section 18 of the United States Code." It was just a young punk, the "G.I." in the bar. He gave Smith an empty smile. "Mr. Ramirez has given us enough documentation to send you up for thirty years. I want you to know that you have the right to remain…"

The words melted. Behind him, Ramirez was giggling. All Smith could think was *I'm not going down,* over and over. Federal time on a kiddie porn rap was as good as a death sentence. He'd be "boy-cherry." They'd turn him into a cellblock bitch in five minutes.

From the wall, Xipe smiled, seemed to lean over Peterson's shoulder. Smith made his move. The half-second disarm he'd learned in the Army worked well enough; his hands snapped up, grabbed the revolver and Peterson's wrist, and pushed. A round went off and burned a line across Smith's scalp. Peterson's wrist broke, and suddenly Smith had the piece. He squeezed off two Q-loads into Peterson's chest. The kid crumpled beneath Xipe like a tossed offering.

Ramirez jumped on his back. Smith tried an elbow jab but missed. The Mexican was clawing at him, was biting into his ear. The revolver hit the floor. Smith staggered back, screaming as his right ear was separated from his bead between Ramirez' teeth. The front wall diminished, yet the framed, grinning Xipe seemed not to; the empty smile followed him. Smith meant to slam Ramirez into the back wall.

Instead, he collided with the window, and the window gave.

It was nothing so trite as slow motion. Smith and his piggyback rider fell very quickly, but the hot night seemed to rise more than they seemed to fall. The street greeted them like a brick slammed down onto copulating frogs.

Something crunched, then collapsed. Smith rolled off Ramirez, who'd broken his fall. Was something looking down at them? Stupefied, Smith managed to stand, shuddering as he removed a long glass shard from his armpit and another from his belly. He was cut bad, but perhaps Xipe had brought him luck after all—Smith had risen from the two-story drop intact, while Ramirez lay crushed, organs punctured by cracked bones.

Smith caught an overhead movement, or he thought he did. He stared up. Was someone leaning out of the window, looking down at him? Maybe Peterson had had a backup man. Smith shucked his Glock, but when he lined up the three-dot sights, the window was empty.

Giggling bubbled at his feet. Ramirez spat out Smith's chewed ear. Despite ruptured organs and a broken spine, the Mexican grinned, somehow, in glory.

"Looks like today is not your lucky day, Meester Smeeth."

"Luckier than yours, bean-eater." Smith pumped eight rounds of 9mm hardball into Ramirez' head. The skull divided, as if trying to expel its contents. The gold-toothed smile froze emptily up at the night.

Smith limped away. Heads popped out of La Fiesta de la Sol. Curtains fluttered in lit windows; faces queried down. Several seemed to wear smiles like empty gouges, like cut-out masks.

Numbness throbbed where his ear had been. His breath rattled, and blood ran freely down his leg. He'd probably cut arteries, punctured a lung. Like a dimmer, his vision began to fade.

Xipe

I'm losing it, he thought. *I'm...*

But, more good luck. The cab idled in the alley, as if expecting him. He fell into the back seat, slammed the door, consciousness draining in pulses.

"I'm bleeding like a fucking tap. Get me to a hospital."

The cabbie turned, a blurred, vacant grin. "No hablo Ingles, señor."

Smith peeled off a grand in ball notes from his roll. "Hospitala!" he attempted, throwing cash. "Pronto!"

"Anytheen you say, Meester."

The cab pulled off into dust. Before Smith passed out, he sensed plump outstretched hands, a smile vast as a mountain rift. A plastic toy, like a kewpie doll, swung fitfully from the rearview.

Xipe.

¤   ¤   ¤   ¤   ¤

Smith blinked from the gurney. They'd rushed him to an ICU. Around him stood a coven of hospital staff. Starched white uniforms and intent faces. A beautiful dark-eyed nurse patted his brow with a damp cloth, while another timed his pulse.

Am I dying? Smith thought.

"You are safe now" said the doctor. "We have stopped the bleeding."

But like a mirage, a man had risen from the corner. He wore a black suit, a white collar.

Smith gulped. A priest.

Indeed he was. He took Smith's hand and asked, "Are you sorry for your sins?"

Smith felt plunged into darkness. "No, no," he muttered. "Don't let me die. Please.."

The holy man's crucifix glittered in the light. He looked solemn and kind. He was holding a book.

"Are you sorry for your sins?" the heavy accent repeated.

But Smith didn't hear the words. His eyes were busy, having at last noticed the incongruity of the priest's silver crucifix. No Jesus could be found at the end of the chain—it was another figure, who wore a crown of quetzl feathers instead of thorns. Pudgy, dark hands bore no nails. The bottomless smile beseeched him.

"Xipe," Smith whispered.

In Nahuati, the native language of the Toltecs, the priest began to speak. The knife he raised was not of steel but of flint. And from the book he commenced the recital, not the Catholic Sacrament For The Dying, but the Aztec Psalter of the Sacrifice, and the Great Rites of the Giver of the Harvest.

Smith's heart beat like thunder in his chest.

Xipe
Afterword

I wrote this one a long time ago, so long, I can't really remember when. All I can remember is this: it was originally published by a magazine called "The Barrel-House," and the publisher paid decent money at a time when I needed it.. But even before that, I'd composed the piece because a friend of mine's relative worked for the tv show Tales From the Darkside. *I thought this story might work very well there, and my friend sent it in via his contact. Silly me.*

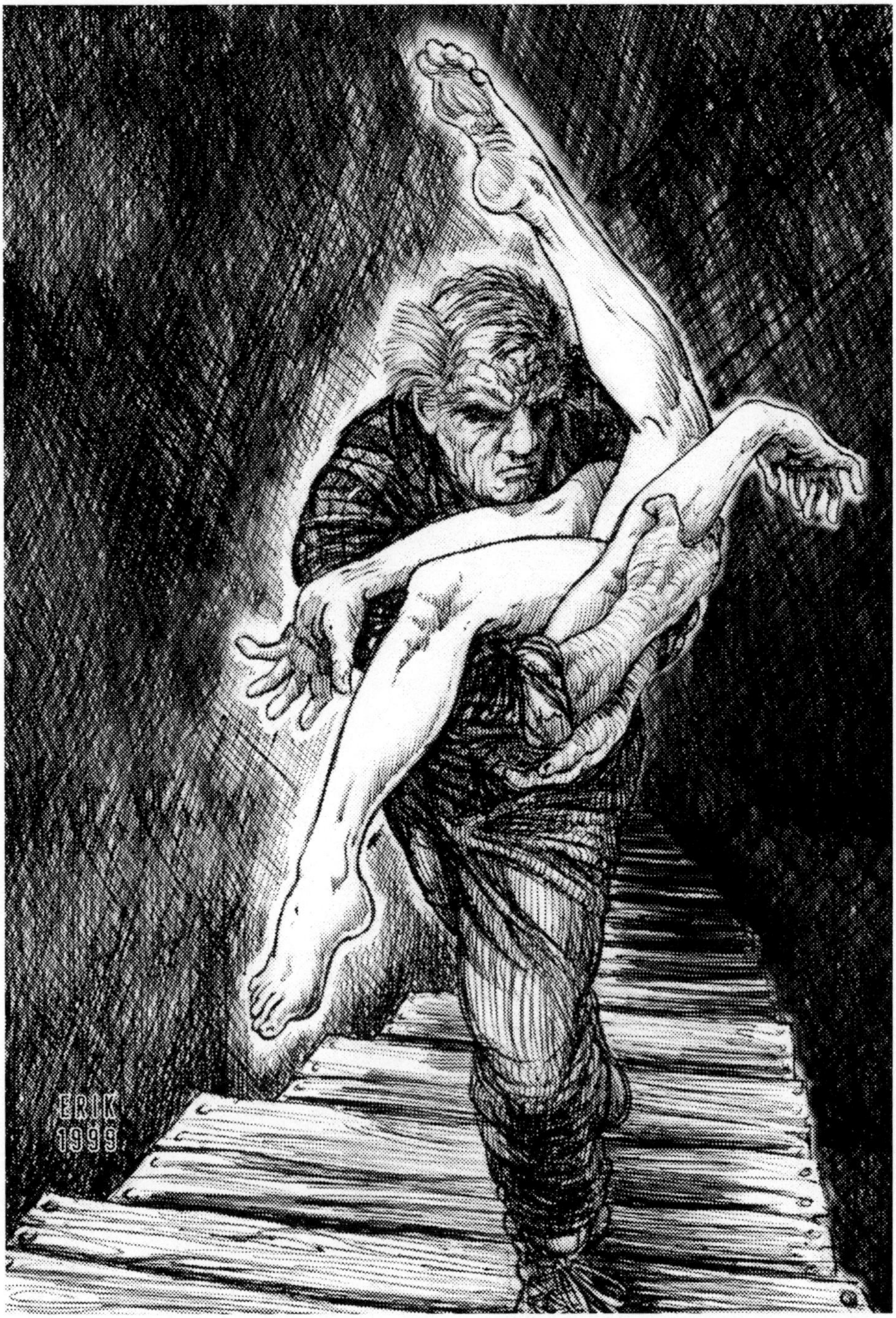
ERIK
1999

Mr. Torso

OL' LUD KNEW he was givin' 'em purpose by what he was doin'. This was God's work according ta the books he'd read, and Lud believed it might fierce he did. *Yessiree,* he thought. *That's gettin' it.* He gandered cockeyed down at Miss August outa *Hustler.* As purdy a blondie as he'd ever seen. *Ooh, yeah.* Awright, so sometimes it took awhiles. Sometimes he had trouble gettin' the ol' crane ta rise, but jimmy Christmas, at sixty-one, what fella wouldn't, ya know?

What'd these gals be doin' otherwise? *Gettin' diseases an' all, smokin' the drugs, gettin' cornholed by fellas.* 'Stead Lud was helpin' 'em ta be what The Man Upstairs intended 'em ta be, an' givin' ta those without what they'se wanted fierce. And acorse paid fer. Ya know?

Lud's mitt needed ta jack hisself up a tad longer 'fore he'd be able to get it, so's he stared on at Miss August, one mighty purdy splittail with that velvety lookin' snatch on her an' that dandy pair of ribmelons. Yessir!

But it wasn't that he was no preevert or nothin' by's doin' this everday. He was puttin' some real meanin' in these gal's lives, just like the books said. He was givin' 'em purpose.

Once he was able ta pull hisself a stiffer an' get to it, he wondered what the gal in the August centerfold'd look like without any arms n' legs on her. *Problee not too good*, he reckoned.

But acorse sometimes God's work weren't purdy.

¤ ¤ ¤ ¤ ¤

Tipps was contemplating the tenets of didactic Solipsism and its converse ideologies when he disembarked from his county car. *Positive teleology?* Tipps didn't buy it. It had to be subjectively existential. *It has to be*, he thought. *Any alternative is folly.*

County Technical Services looked like scarlet phantoms roving the darkness. Sirchie portable UV lamps glowed eerily purple. The techs wore red polyester utilities so that any accidental fiberfall wouldn't be confused as crime-scene residue by the Hair & Fibers crew back at Evidence Section. But Tipps, in his heather-gray Brooks Brothers suit, already harbored a clear notion that TSD was wasting their time.

The moon shone like a pallid face above the cornfield. Tipps walked toward the ravine, where red and blue lights throbbed. Maybe, by now, these south county boys were getting used to it. A young sergeant rested on one knee with his face in his hands.

"Get up," Tipps ordered. "You're not a creamcake, you're a county police officer. Start acting like it."

The kid stood up and blinked hard.

"Another 64?" Tipps asked.

"Yes sir. It's another torso thing."

Mr. Torso, Tipps thought. That's what he'd come to think of the perp as. Fifteen sets of limbs dumped on county roads like this the past three years. And three torsos, all, white cauc feems. The perp yanked their teeth and did an acid job on their faces, hands, and feet. Tipps ordered up the new g/p runs on all the parts but thus far to no avail. Ky jelly and sperm in the three torsos; the sperm typed A-pos. *Big deal*, Tipps thought.

"Down there, sir." The cop pointed into the lit ravine. "I'm sorry, I just can't hack it."

This is getting to be a hard county, Tipps told himself and descended toward TSD's lights. Techs crawled on hands and knees with flash-hats. Field spots had been erected; they were looking for tire indentations to cast. "Mr. Torso strikes again," Tipps muttered when he glanced further. At the culvert, two more techs were pulling severed arms and legs out of the pipe. Then a figure seemed to drift out of the eerie light. Beck, the TSD field chief.

"So we got another torso job," Tipps said more than asked.

Beck, a woman, had thick glasses and frizzy black hair like witch's. "Uh—huh," she replied. "Two arms, two legs. And another torso that doesn't match with the limbs. What's that total now? Four torsos?"

"Yeah," Tipps said. The torso lay off to the side, white slack breasts descending into its armpits. The stumps, like the others, looked healed over. The face was an acid scab.

"I'll know more once I get her in the shop, but I'm sure it's just like the others."

The others, Tipps reflected. The previous torsos had been crudely lobotomized, according to the deputy M.E. A hard pointed instrument thrust up through the left anterior eye socket. Eardrums punctured. Eyes

Mr. Torso

glued shut. Mr. Torso was shutting down their senses. *Why?* Tipps wondered. "Do another g/p run," he said.

Beck half-smiled. "That's been a waste so far, Lieutenant. We're never gonna get a records match on a genetic profile."

"Just do it," Tipps said.

Beck's sarcasm dissolved when she looked again to the ravine. "It's just so macabre. This is the sixteenth set of limbs he's dumped but only the fourth body. What the fuck is he doing with bodies?"

Tipps saw her point. *And what in God's name*, he thought, *is the purpose behind all this?* Tipps felt strangely assured of that. His philosophies itched. He knew there was a purpose.

¤   ¤   ¤   ¤   ¤

Ol' Lud's purpose, acorse, was ta get the gals knocked up. Then he'd wait till they dropped their rugrat an' he'd sell it ta folks who couldn't have critters of their own. An' he wasn't profiteerin' neither—he'd use the green ta pay the bills and give the leftover ta charity. Nothin' wrong with that.

Acorse he had ta do the job on the gals first. Seemed only proper an' humane like, to relieve 'em of the mental turmoil. An' he'd cut off their arms an' gams so's they could get by on less viddles and so's he wouldn't hafta worry 'bout 'em gettin' away. Ol' Lud poked their ears 'cos it didn't seem right fer their jiggled brains ta be hearin' things an' gettin' all confused, and same fer gluin' up their eyes. These gals didn't need ta be seein' stuff.

And 'cos he felt for 'em, he jiggled up their brains a tad just like the way his daddy'd do years ago when some of the cows an' hogs got too feisty. See, all ya do is stick the carvin' awl up under a gal's eye socket till ya hear the bone break, then ya give the awl a quick jiggle. Wouldn't kill 'em, just messed up their brains so they couldn't think. "'Botomized 'em," daddy called it. Lud didn't need fer the gals ta be thinkin' things an' all. That'd be cruel seein' that they couldn't see or hear no how, an' couldn't walk no more or pick stuff up. Acorse, he had ta be careful doin' the jiggle. See, a coupla gals kicked on him after awhiles, so's that's why Lud always disinfected the scratch awl now, so's no bad germs'd get up in their noggins. Yessir, Lud felt mighty bad about the four that died, but what could he do, ya know?

So he dumped 'em. Yanked out their pearly whites with a track wrench, an' burned up their kissers so's the cops couldn't recanize 'em and maybe figure out how he was nabbin' 'em.

Lud had 'em all rowed up in the basement, twelve of 'em. He'd lay each of 'em in a pig trough with one end cut out so's their lower parts'd kinda hang out over the edge. That ways all Lud had ta do was drop his drawers standin' right there when he gave 'em some peter and they could whiz an' poop without makin' a mess of thereselfs 'cuz Lud kept a milk bucket under each trough. He fed the gals three squares daily, good potatomash an' milk an' heathly stews 'cos he wanted nice *strong* critters ta sell. An' the gals could swaller 'n chew just fine 'cos Lud didn't pull their choppers unless they up an' croaked on him on account he seed on CNN one night 'bout how the coppers could 'denify dead folks by comparin' their teeth with dental records and some such.

Lud's routine was monthly. That's why he had twelve gals, ya know, one fer each month. Fer instance, right now it was August, so that's why he this very second had his peter in the August gal. He'd give it to her 'least three times a day, ever day fer the whole month. That way it'd stand ta reason she'd be good an' preggered by the time September rolled around. Then acorse he'd start givin it to the gal in the September trough. An' when he wasn't dickin em, or gettin' 'em viddles or washin' 'em up, he'd go upstairs and check out the city paper classified fer folks lookin' fer a critter to 'dopt. Lot of them folks was rich and they'd pay good scratch with no questions asked rather'n wait a coupla years ta get a critter legal like through the 'doption agencies. An' in his spare time, Lud'd kick back an' read his favorite books 'bout the meanin' of life an' all. He liked those books just fine, he did.

Only problem was the task of gettin' it on with the gal's. See, sometimes it took awhiles ta get his peter hard enough ta give 'em a good pokin' on account it was no easy thing fer *any* fella keep a stiffer when the gal was, like, ya know, didn't have no arms or gams. An' worse was the noises they made sometimes while Lud was tryin' ta get his nut, kinda mewlin' noises an' another noise like "gaaaaaa—gaaaaaaaa" on account of 'cos Lud had jiggled their brains. Yessiree, downright unappealin' they was ta look at an' listen to which is why ol' Lud'd put one of the girlie center-folds on their bellies so's he had somethin' inspirin' ta look at whiles he was givin' 'em the wood.

Lotta times too he'd go limp right in 'em an' pop out, like right now with this red hairt gal in the August trough. "Dag dabbit!" he cursed 'cos Lud, see, he never took the Lord's name in vain. Couldn't get a nut out noways like that! So pore Lud stepped back from the trough with his pants around his ankles so's he could jack hisself back up but meantimes the ky in the gal's babyhole'd get gummy. See, 'fore Lud got ta dickin' a gal he'd have ta give them a squirt of the ky on account the gals couldn't get wet no more thereself 'cos of the brain-'jiggle he gave 'em. But like just was mentioned, see, that ky up there'd go gummy sometimes just like right now with this red-hairt gal, so's Lud'd have ta kneel down an' hock a lunger right smackdab on her snatch ta wet her

Mr. Torso

up again, all the whiles he's jackin' his peter. It got a right frustratin' sometimes. "Ain't got all blammed day ta be beatin' my peter 'front of a torso!" he hollered aloud. "Jiminy Christmas! Can't keep a good stiffer, can't hardly come no more!" Acorse when such things happened ta cause Lud ta pitch a fit, he'd let hisself calm down and get ta thinkin'. Shore, it weren't easy sometimes, but this was God's work. He oughta be grateful—lotta fellas his age couldn't get a stiffer at all no more and they'se shore as heck couldn't have out with a nut. The books made it clear ta him. It was The Man Upstairs Hisself who'd called on him ta do this deed an' by golly there weren't no way he was gonna fail The Man Upstairs! His work weren't always easy, weren't supposed ta be.

So Lud gandered down real hard at that girlie centerfold of Miss August, pretendin' it was her in that there trough 'stead of this red-hairt gal with no arms or gams goin' "gaaaaa—gaaaaaa!" an' he was jackin' hisself real hard an' fast eyein' them purdy centerfold hooters and that nice paper cooze an— "Yeah, lordy!" he celebrated 'cos there his peter went finally gettin' hard again. "Yeah, oh yeah! Here she comes, August!" he promised an' just as ol' Lud'd have his nut he stuck his peter back inta that stump sided red-hairt snatch an' got a good load of his dicksnot right up theres in her baby-makin' parts.

"Gaaaaa! Gaaaaaaaa!" went the gal's droolin' mouth.

"Yer quite welcome, missy," Lud replied.

¤ ¤ ¤ ¤ ¤

Next morning Tipps' Guccis took him up to the city-district squad room where some newbies from south county vice swapped jokes.

"Hey, how's a torso play basketball?"

"How?"

"With difficulty!"

"Hey, guys, you know where a torso sleeps?"

"Where?"

"In a *trunk!*"

The explosion of laughter ceased when Tipps' shadow crossed the squad room floor. "Next guy I hear telling torso jokes gets transferred to district impound," was all he remarked, then moved to his office.

The sun in the window blinded him. Tipps didn't want the answers most cops wanted—he didn't give a shit. He didn't even care about justice. *Justice is only what the actualized self makes it*, he reflected. Tipps was obsessed with philosophy. He was forty-one, never married, had no friends. Nobody liked him, and he didn't like anybody, and that was the only aspect of his exterior life that he liked. He hated cops as much as he hated bad guys. He hated niggers, spics, slant-eyes. He hated pedophile rings and church coteries. He hated God and Satan and atheists, faith and disbelief, yuppies and bikers, homos, lezzies, the erotopathic and the celibate. He hated kikes, wops, and wasps. Especially wasps because he himself was born a wasp. He hated everybody and everything, because, somehow the nihilistic acknowledgment was all that kept him from feeling totally false. He hated falsehood.

He loved truth, and the philosophical calculations thereof. Truth, he believed, could only be derived via the self-assessment of the individual. For instance, there was no global *truth*. There was no political or societal *verity*. Only the truth of the separate individual against the terrascape of the universe. That's why Tipps had become a cop, because, further, it seemed that real truth could only be decrypted through the revelations of *purpose*, and such purpose was more thoroughly bared in the *spiritual* proximity to stress. Being a cop got him closer to the face that was the answer.

Fuck, he mused at his desk. He wanted to know the *purpose* of things, for it was the only way he'd ever discover *his* purpose. That's why the Mr. Torso case fascinated him. *If truth can only defined on an individual stratum via one's conception of universal purpose, then what purpose is this? Tell me, Mr. Torso.*

It had to be unique. It had to be—

Brilliant, he considered. Mr. Torso was making effective efforts to avoid detection, which meant he was not pathological nor bipolar. The m.o. was identical, painstakingly so. Nor was Mr. Torso retrograde, schizoaffective, ritualized, or hallucinotic; if he were, the psych unit would've discerned that by now, and so would the Technical Services Division. *Mr. Torso,* Tipps thought. What purpose could there be behind the acts of such a man?

Tell me, Mr. Torso.

Tipps had to know.

¤   ¤   ¤   ¤   ¤

Lud always 'ranged ta meet 'em out in the boonies, with phony plates on his pickup. Old lots, convenience stores an' the like.

"Oh thank God I can't believe it's true," yammered the blueblood lady when ol' Lud passed her the fresh, new critter. The critter made cute goo-goo sounds, its pudgy little brand-spankin' new fingers playin' with his new mommy's pearl necklace. She was crying she was so et up with happy. "Richard, give him the money."

Lud scratched his crotch sittin' back there in the back seat of this fancified big lux seedan, one of them 'spensive kraut cars was what he thought. But the gray hairt guy in the suit gave Lud a bad look. Then, kinda hezzatatin' an' twitchy, this fella asked, "Could you, uh, tell us a little bit about the mother?"

Mr. Torso

She's a torso, ya dipstick, Lud thought. *An' it was my spunk preggered her up. But what'choo care anyways? I got'cha what ya wanted, ain't I? Jiminy Christmas, these rich folks!*

"I mean," the suit said, "you're certain that this arrangement is consentual? I mean, the child wasn't...abducted or kidnaped or anything like that, right?"

"No way this critter here's kitnapped, mister, so's you's got nothin' to worry about." Then Lud felt the fella could use a reminder. "Acorse, no questions asked is what we agreet, weren't it? Like ya said in yer ad, conferdential. Now if yawl gots second thoughts, that's fine too. I'lls just take the little critter back and yawl can sign back up at the 'doption agency, 'acorse if ya don't mind waitin' like five er six years.."

"*Give him the money, Richard,*" the lady had out in a tone'a voice like the devil on a bad day. Women shore did have them some wrath now an' again. "Give him the money so we can take our baby home! And I mean right now, Richard, *right now!*"

"Er, yes," mouthed the new papa in the suit. "Yes, of course." And then he passed ol' Lud an envelope full 'o hunnert' dollar bills stuffed like ta the tune of twenty grand. Lud shot the folks a smile. "I just knows in my heart that yawl'll raise yer new critter fines an' proper. Don't ferget ta teach 'im ta say his prayer ever night, an' make shore he's raised in the ways of The Man upstairs now, ya hear?"

"We will," said the suit. "Thank you."

"Thank you thank you!" gushed the new mommy all silly-face happy and teary eyed. "You've made us very happy."

"Don't'chall thanks me 's much as The Man Upstairs," Lud said an' scooted outa the big lux kraut seedan parked at the QWIK-STOP. *Cause it's Him that called me ta do this*. After the rich folks left, Lud hisself drove off in his beat-ta-holy-hail pickup, thinkin'. He had work ta do tonight. What with that skinny-ass brownyhead dyin' on him yesterday (Lud figured she musta got some bad germs up in her noggin when he jigged her brain, and that's why she didn't live long). He had to swipe hisself a new gal an' get her torsoed up 'cos the June trough was empty now. Acorse, 'fore he did that he figured he best git home ta that red-hair August gal ta lay some afternoon peter on her, get some *good* spunk up her hole. After all, Lud had future orders now, and it didn't seem fit ta hafta keep God's work waitin'. An' he also knew, from his fav-urt books, that The Man Upstairs kept his mitts off the world itself, ever since Eve put her choppers ta that apple, so's there was physerology in play too, which was why ol' Lud knew he hadda get his dicksnot up the girl's hole many times a day as he could manage so's she'd be shore ta get preggered up just fine.

And bring new life unto the world.

◘　◘　◘　◘　◘

Tipps wore the morgue's ghastly fluorescent light like a pallor; he could've passed for a well-dressed corpse himself, here in such company. Jan Beck, the TSD field chief, set a bottle of Snapple Raspberry Iced Tea on a Vision Series II blood-gas analyzer. "Be with you in a minute, sir," she offered, matching source-spectrums to the field indexes. Tipps wondered how she applied her own notions of truth to her overall assessment of human purpose. Did she *have* such an assessment? She histologized brains for a living, autopsied children, and had probably seen more guts than fishmarket dumpster. *What is your truth?* he wondered.

"Your man wears size-11 shoes."

"That's great!" Tipps celebrated.

"Ground was wet last night." Beck chewed the end of a fat camel's-hair brush. "Left good impressions for the field boys." Rather despondently then, she closed a big red book entitled: *Pre-1980 US. Automotive Paint Index.* "I checked every source index we got, and it's not here."

"What's not here?" Tipps queried.

"Oh, I forgot to tell you. When he backed up to the ravine last night, his right-rear fender scraped the culvert rim. I ran the paint-residuum through the mass-photospectrometer. It's not stock-auto paint so I can't give you a make and model. All I can tell you is he drives a red vehicle."

Tipps felt delighted. Finally they had a real lead…

Beck continued, sipping her Snapple. "And that g/p-run you asked for? Well, you hit pay-dirt this time, Lieutenant. We got a positive match with the state CID records index. Torso Number Four has a name. Susan B. Bilkens."

"Why the hell's she got a genetic-profile record?"

"She's a whore, er, was. Six busts, five city, one county. Pressed charges against her first pimp last year so the city asked for a g/p-material sample. The pimp cut her up a little, they hoped the g/p-sample would match blood on the pimp's clothes." Beck let out a humorless chuckle. "Too bad it didn't wash in court, fuckin' judges must be out of their minds. But at least it gave the girl's name for a rundown."

"Susan H. Bilkens," Tipps repeated. He appraised the naked torso on the stainless-steel morgue platform which came complete with removable drain-trap and motorized height-adjustment. The torso's acid-burned face more resembled a mound of excrement, and her y-section had been stitched back up like a macabre zipper. "You said she's a hooker?"

"*Was* a hooker, that's right." Another chuckle. "She's just a dead torso now. Worked the West Street Block, the dope bars, till she shit-

Mr. Torso

named herself with the pimp thing. For the last year she was turning her tricks at a truck stop up on the Route."

"This is...*wonderful,*" Tipps intoned.

"The postmortum gave us more of the same. Teeth manually extracted shortly after death. Eardrums ruptured, eyed glued shut with cyanoacrilate aka Wonder Glue. Minor insult across the lateral sulcus in the frontal lobe. He lobotomized her just like the others. Oh, and I was able to match her body with the arms and legs we found in Davidsonville four months ago. You ready for the bombshell?"

Tipps looked at her.

"Tally this up, Lieutenant. Like I said, we found her arms and legs *four months* ago."

"I heard you."

Beck sipped her Snapple. "When she died she was *two months* pregnant."

¤   ¤   ¤   ¤   ¤

Two month's pregnant, he recited, motoring down Route 154 in his unmarked. It seemed spectacularly...hideous. With each revelation, Tipps felt beckoned to unveil Mr. Torso's conception human truth, and, hence, his empirical purpose.

Mr. Torso, Tipps thought. *I'm going to get you, buddy, and I'm going to find out.* Not only was Tipps a conclusionary-didactic nihilist, he was also a proficient investigator. A records check dropped the prostitute's life into his lap. Twenty-five years old, Caucasian, brown hair, brown eyes, 5'5", 121 pounds. Tipps wondered how much she weighed *without* her arms and legs. Since she had been run off the red-light block in town, she worked a truck stop near the county line called The Bonfire. Truck stops were the first places banished prostitutes fled to, and there was only one in all of south county ...

He parked between two Peterbilt semi's at the end of the lot. The little dive of a restaurant glowed beyond, peppered with minute movement in its plate-glass windows.. Tipps sung a tune in his mind, with a slight lyrical modification— "Eighteen Wheels And A Dozen Torsos "— scanning the Bonfire with a small pair of Bushnell 7x50's. In the binocular's infinity-shaped field, he could see them in there: Unkept, nutritionally depleted, desperate. Most, he knew, were clinical drug addicts, their only human purpose in the universe being to cater to the axiomatic and primordial male sex-drive in exchange for crack money. They fluttered about the restaurant interior, fussing with corpulent truck drivers whose stout arms provided tattoo-tapestries. Some of the girls dawdled outside, hidden amongst the gulf of shadows.

Tipps wondered about them, these sex-spectors. Did they even realize their place in the ethereal universe? Did they ever ponder such considerations as existential verity, psycho-societal atomism, tripardite eudaemonistic thesis? *Do they ever wonder what their purpose is?* Tipps wondered to himself. *Do they even* have *a purpose?*

At once, Tipps sat up. The Bushnell's fine German optics easily revealed the dilapidated red pickup truck that pulled into the lot, as well as the long fresh scratch along the rear-right fender.

¤   ¤   ¤   ¤   ¤

Lud loped outa the Bonfire, wearin' the usual overalls an' size-11 steel toes, totin' a bag of mags. See, the Bonfire up 'fore the register had thereselfs a rack of the girlie mags and a lotta the September issues'd just come out. Lud never quite reckoned why, for instance, the September mags always come out third week of August, not that he much cared. Next week'd be time ta start gettin' his peter up inta that lil' blondie with the hairlip sittin' cozy an' limbless in the September trough. She had a nice set a' milk wagons on her but a joyhole big enough ta take a ham hock. What'd fellas been stickin up this gal ta get her so stretched out—their blamed heads? Or was she just born that way? Acorse bein' real big likes that'd make it easier fer her ta drop critters-Jiminy, big as she was she could problee drop a whole kindergarten at once! An' the lips 'round her snatch looked like a bunch of hangin' lunchmeat er somethin'. 'Least she didn't make a ruckus like the gal in the August trough who Lud was gettin' a might sick of by now. See, that's why Lud buyed hisself new mags each month, ta open the centerfolds onta their bellies so's he could get his peter up proper an' come. An' on account of the June gal up an' dyin' on him an' his havin' ta dump her last night, Lud needed hisself a new gal ta take her place. These hookers always hanged out at the Bonfire 'cos the truckers was ferever tryin' ta get their peters off in some splittail 'tween their long hauls, and ways it was set up, that big tookus-lot with all them semirigs parked alls over, Lud could propersition a gal right quick and have her outa there without no one bein' the wiser.

Walkin' down, though, he sawed all them rubbers layin' on the cement, like a whole lot of 'em, an' this made Lud right sad. *Don't fellas know nothin' these days?* Didn't fellas ever use their brains fer more'n skull-filler? The dicksnot, see, was fer more an just feelin' good whiles it was comm' out'cher peter. It s a 'lixer of life, it was. It was a special gift The Man Upstairs gave ta fellas so's they'se could have their peters in gals proper the way He intended an' get ta makin' critters once that good spunk got up there inna gal's baby-makin' parts. Givin' life an' all, that's what the dicksnot were all's about, see? Droppin' new rugrats onto the earth ta carry on with things the way God wanted. And it was

Mr. Torso

a blammed shame seein' all's this good spunk wasted just fer the sake o' havin' a nut... Weren't supposed ta be shot inta some infernal conderm! These little things layin' all over lot, they was like a slap ta the face of The Man Upstairs in a way of reckonin', a way mankind'd figured on cheatin' the ways things was supposed t' be. Lud had a mind ta collect up all these rubbers each night an' empty 'em like maybe inta a soup bowl er somethin', them git hisself a turkey baster so's he could give each of his gals good squirt without havin' ta do it hisself. Acorse, that might not be such a hot idea considerin' all the devil-made diseases goin' 'round these days. Just seemed a cryin' shame fellas'd see fit to wastin' their juice like that, kinda in a way of like puttin' a little bit of God in a bag an' flushin' Him down the crapper or throwin' Him down on some dirty trucker parkin' lot—

"Hey, pops, for twenty bucks I'll suck your cock so hard your balls'll slide out of your peehole."

Lud gandered this little stringbean who'd came outa the shadows. They'se was all mostly rack-skinny like this one an' all had there-selves lank straight hair on 'em an' mostly little-type hooters 'cept 'acorse fer his September gal with that big ol' pair of the chest melons. "Well, say there, missy, that sounds like a right deal ta me," Lud enthused "Just foller me yonder to my truck'n we'll have ourselves a *dandy* ol' time"

They gots in the pickup an' Lud had his peter out even 'fore she could pussy-pocket that double-sawbuck he gave her. Then she opened her yap an' got ta work lickety-split. Lud figured he'd let her suck awhiles, not that he was plannin' ta waste a perfectly good load of his critteragoo on her yap but just ta let her get on it awhiles so's he'd be good'n boned up fer later when he were givin' his August gal her beddy-bye pop. Lud in fact 'preciated it. It made things easier later ta have his stiffer all hot'n bothered by a gal who still had her arms an' gams connected to her, yessir, right nice change ta be with somethin' other'n a, brain-jiggered blabberin' torso with a girlhole full of the ky. An' this little stringbean here was just a'smokin' his pole like a regler trooper she was, an' kindly givin' his ballbag a good feelup while she was goin'. *Lordy, can this gal suck a peter!* Lud exclaimed in thought. *A regler machine she is, like ta suck the peterskin right off my bone!* Then she stopped sucking a speck an' kinda snotty said, "Hey pops, I been doing this a while. You getting close?"

"Wells, try ta be patient, missy. Ol' fella the likes of me sometimes takes awhiles ta get his nut out."

She sucked awhiles more, harder an' faster with that little hand of hers just a pumpin' away on his sac like it were a full-up milkbag on a cow, an' she was a'slurpin' an' lickin' an really goin' t'town down there on his meat an' makin' more noise than a couple 1000-pound Hampshire hogs havin' a row in the mudhole, but then she stops again an' bellyaches, "Come on, pops. Hurry up and come, will ya? I ain't got all night."

"What'choo *got*, missy," Lud kindly corrected, "is yer whole life ta turn from the errah of yer ways an' starts ta doin' what gals was meant ta do in the eyes of The Man Upstairs, like havin' critters and per-petcheratin' the species. What I'se talkin' 'bout, missy, is the purpose of the whole ball of wax we calls life," an' just right then lickety-split, Lud gave her a thunk fierce on the bean with a empty Carling bottle an' put her little lights right out. He stuffed her down inta the footwell an' droved outa the lot with his peter still out'n stickin' up all high an' mighty from that humdinger of a suck she were givin' him, an' it kinda seemed a shame, ya know, what he'd hafta be doin' ta her shortly.

¤ ¤ ¤ ¤ ¤

Way he'd do it, see, is he'd take 'em downstairs an' make 'em swaller a bowl of potatomash full of horse trank, so they'd be out deep fer a good spell. Then he'd glue up their eyes an' poke their ears an' 'botermize 'em with the scratch awl so's they wouldn't sense no more an' not be confused an' all. Then he'd lop off their arms and gams with his field adze, which were like a axe only the blade went crossways, and acorse before he'd do that he'd tie off each arm an' leg right close with heavy sisal rope so's the gals wouldn't bleed ta death once he had off with their limbs.

And that's just what Lud did when he gots back ta the house with that little suckjob gal he picked hisself up at the Bonfire. Each time looked a little neater, 'fact bys now Ol' Lud could have off with a gal's arms an' gams just as neat'n clean as you'd ever want, provided acorse that you'd ever in the first place *want* a livin' torso in yer basement. The stumps'd heal over just fine in about a coupla weeks, then he'd be all set ta get ta pokin' her. This is one here, now that she were buck nekit, had some right nice little hooters on her an' a nice big clump a'hair down there' s on her babyhole, an' she even had a real fine little line'a hair goin' from her snatch ta her bellybutton which Lud always thought was just as cute as could be. One thing he didn't much care fer, though, was the tattoos—lotta these gals had tattoos on 'em—-like this here brownyhead who sported one just overs her right tittie, a silly little heart with a knife in it it looked like. Seemed a blammed shame ta Lud that gals'd have so little respect fer their bods ta scar 'em up like that 'cos the ways Lud saw it , 'least accordin' ta the books he'd read, was the body was a temple of the Man Upstairs and ta scar it up with silly tat-

Mr. Torso

toos were just the same as like throwin' garbage in a church or spray-paintin' the swear words on the altar an' bustin' up the stainglass winders with stones an' such. Didn't matter now, though, not fer this stringbean little brownyhead 'cos now she were well on her way ta some real godlylike meanin' in the scheme of life. Lud'd wait a spell 'for gettin' her settled down inta the June trough though, an' meantime, he bandaged up her stumps so's she weren't get no 'nfections. Then he picked up her arms an' gams'n carried 'em upstairs ta put 'em in the truck fer dumpin' a little later after he burned up the hands 'n feet with mercuric acid, an' he's walkin up them stairs his size 11s goin' *clump clump clump* but, see, he stopped in his tracks on the top landin' 'cos first thing he sawwed was some fancified fella in a suit waitin' for him an' this fella had in his mitt a big tookus-gun that he was a'pointin' right smackdab at Lud's face…

¤   ¤   ¤   ¤   ¤

"The blammed tarnations!" exclaimed the old man in overalls. He'd stopped cold on the landing, his arms heavy-laden with—

Limbs, Tipps realized. *He's carrying severed limbs.* "Don't move." Tipps stared at the wizened man, astonished. He kept a headshot bead in the adjustable sights of his Glock 17, whose clip was full of 9mm Remington hardball. His brain seemed to tick with arcane calculations. "Now," Tipps said. "Drop the…limbs."

The old man frowned, than released his burden. Two arms and two legs thunked to the hardwood floor.

"Sit down in that chair next to the highboy. Keep your hands your lap. Fuck with me and I blow your goddamn head off."

Wincing, the old man seated himself in an antique cane chair that creaked with his weight. "Ain't no call fer swear words, son, and no call ta be takin' the Lord's name in vain."

Tipps kept the gun on him. "You're the guy… Mr. Torso."

"That what they'se callin' me?" Mr. Torso sputtered. "Blammed silliest-ass name I ever did hear."

But Tipps' thoughts revolved in a kaleidoscope of wonder, triumph, and conceit. *I got him*, he thought. *I got Mr. Torso.*

"You're a blammed copper, ain't'cha?" Lud asked. "How'd ya find me, son? Tells me that."

"I followed you from the truck stop"'

Lud could'a smacked hisself right in the head. *I am just done ET UP with a case of the DUMBASS!* Led this poker-kisser copper in the fancified Ward an' Roebuck suit straight to him! *Jiminy Christmas I must'a passed my brain out my butthole last time I went ta the crapper!*

But, acorse…

Lud believed in proverdence. He believed what he eyeballed in them there books, an' he believed The Man Upstairs shore worked in some strange ways. An' it was proverdence he reckoned that this copper'd made him sit in the chair right next ta dead mama's old highboy. And Lud knowed full well that in the top drawer was daddy's big ol' Webley revolver...

¤   ¤   ¤   ¤   ¤

Tipps' gaze flicked about. It was an untold fantasy: *I'm in Mr. Torso's house!* "I want to know what you've been doing."

"What'cha mean, son?"

"What do I mean?" Tipps could've laughed. "I want to know why you've dismembered sixteen women over the last three years, that's what I want to know. You're keeping them alive, aren't you?"

Mr. Torso's white hair stuck up in dishevelment, his chin studded with white whiskers. "Keepin' what alive?"

"The girls! The...torsos!" Tipps yelled. "My forensic tech told me the torso you dumped last night died within forty-eight hours, you crazy old asshole! We matched her body to a set of limbs you dumped four months ago, and she was *two months pregnant!* You're impregnating them, aren't you? Tell me why, goddamn it!"

Mr. Torso shut his eyes. "Aw, son, would ya *please* stop takin' tha Lord's name in vain? Come on, now."

Tipps took a step forward, training the Glock on the old man's 5x zone. But at that precise moment his flicking gaze snagged on a row of books atop the veneered highboy. *What the... hell?* Many of the titles he recognized, many he owned himself. The chief works of history's most preeminent philosophical minds. Sartre, Kant, Sophocles, and Hegel. Plato, Heidegger, and Jaspers. Aquinas, Kierkegaard...

"You...," Tipps faltered, "read... *this?*"

"Acorse," Mr. Torso affirmed. "What, just 'cos I wears overalls 'an live in the sticks, ya think I'se just some dumb-tookus rube with no hankerin' of the meanin' of life? Lemme tell ya somethin', son. I ain't no sexshool preevert like ya problee think. An' I'se ain't no psykerpath."

"What are you then?" Tipps' question grated like gravel.

Calmly, Mr. Torso went on, "I'se a perveyer of sorts, ya know? A perveyer of objectified human dynamics. Volunteeristic idealism's what they'se call it, son. See, the abserlute will is a irrational force 'less ya apply it ta the mechanistics of causal posertivity as a kinda counterforce ta the evil concreteness of neeherlistic doctrine. What I mean, son, is as inderviduals of the self-same unerverse, we'se all subject ta the metterphysical duality scape, an we must realize what we'se are as transcendental units of bein an' then engage ourselves with objectertive

Mr. Torso

acts, son, ta turn the do-dads of our units of bein' into a functional deliverance of subjecterive posertivity in the ways of The Man Upstairs, see? No, I ain't no psykerpath. I'se a vassal, er a perpetcherater of Kierkegaardian fundermentals of human purpose."

Tipps stared as though he'd downed a fifth of Johnny Black in one chug. *Holy fucking shit!* he thought. *Mr. Torso...is a teleologic Christian phenomenolist!*

"It's takin' things inta our own mitts, see? Like with the gals, livin' in a neeherlistic void of spiritual vacuity. I do what I do ta give 'em the transertive *purpose* thats they'd never reckon on their own. I'se savin' 'em from the clutches of human aberlutism, son, ya know, savin' 'em from wastin' their potential as posertive units of bein'. All they'd be doin' otherwise is gettin' the AIDS, the herpes, gettin' abortions, smokin' the drugs, an' gettin' thereselfs problee beat up an' kilt. But alls forces in the universe is cyclic—like, ya know, one unit of bein' feeding the other to's a aberlute whole. Shore, I'se sells the critters but only ta folks who can't have none thereselfs no ways. An' the scratch I don't need ta keep good care of the gals, I gives to charity."

Tipps felt stupefied, locked in rigor. His astonishment caused the Glock's front sights to drift...

"It's all purpose, son. Human aberlute *purpose.*"

Purpose, Tipps paused to wonder—

—and in that pause, a size 11 steel-toed boot socked up and caught Tipps square in the groin. He went down—the pain was incalculable. Through blurred and spider-cracked vision, he saw Mr. Torso standing now, rooting through the highboy's drawers.

"Daggit! Where's that big-tookus Webley!"

Tipps' gunhand trembled as he extended his arm. He managed to squeeze off a double-tap—*pap! pap!*—and somehow both 9mm bullets hit Mr. Torso between the legs, from behind—

"Holy Jesus Moses ta Pete!" the old man wailed, collapsing and clutching the bloodflow at his groin. "Ya blammed neeherlistic copper bastard! Ya done shot me in the *dickbag!*"

Tipps, still shuddering in his own pain, crawled forward to finish the job. He could scarcely breathe. But when he raised gun—

What the—

—his foe's crabbed hand slapped up and pushed it away, and at the same time a terrifying arc-movement fluttered overhead.

Then came a hideous *kaCRACK!*

Tipps' world blanked out like a power failure.

¤   ¤   ¤   ¤   ¤

"Bet'cha got yerself a headache like a Old Crow hangover, huh?" A chuckle. Movement. "Yeah, I cracked ya a good one right smackdab on the bean with the butt of my daddy's big-tookus Webley .455. Took ya right out, it did."

When Tipps woke, he felt elevated somehow, drifting...

"Was all fired up ta kill ya but then I gots ta thinkin'."

To the right and left, Tipps saw a long row of what appeared to be open-ended metal troughs on stilts. Twelve troughs in all, each labeled by masking tape with a different consecutive month. Tipps throat swelled shut...

Each trough contained a torso.

"Say hello ta my gals, copper."

Each lay naked in their trough, their skin lean, white, and sweating in the basement's heat and incandescent glare. Healed-over stumped hips were visible at each trough-end. As the line of torsos progressed, Tipps couldn't help but note an increasing state of pregnancy: the later torsos sported bellies so distended they seemed on the verge of rupture, white skin stretched pin-prick tight against the burgeoning inner human freight. Fleshy navelbuds turned inside-out. Breasts heavy with mother's milk.

Immediately before him lay a wan torso with matted red hair. The slack face with sealed eyes twitched, the head lolled. "Gaaaa!" she said. "Gaaaaa!"

"This here's my August gal," Mr. Torso introduced. He stood at Tipps side. "Been spunkin' her up daily since the first of month so's ta git her good'n preggered."

"Gaaa! Gaaaaa!" she repeated.

"A regler chatterbox, ain't she? Blabbers like that on account I'se 'botermized her, ya know, jigged up her brain a tad so's she won't worry an' be confused an' such. Don't seem fair fer the gals ta keep their senses, bein' in such a state. S'why I glued up their eyes too, an' poked their ears. But don't 'cha worry none, 'cos all their baby-makin' parts works just fine."

Now Tipps deciphered the drifting sensation. His vision cleared further, and four shuddering glances showed him that he'd been divorced of all four limbs. His torso was suspended in a harness that hung from a hook over the trough. Eleven more such hooks we sunk into the ceiling rafter before each torso.

"Oh, I'se ain't gonna fiddle with *yer* eyes an' ears," Mr. Torso promised. "Nor's I gonna 'botermize ya either. See, a fella's sexshool responses are all up in his noggin, so's I can't be jiggin' yer brain like I'se done ta the gals. Can't very well git yerself a stiffer with yer brain all jigged up, now can ya?"

Mr. Torso

Tipps groaned from deep in his chest. He swayed ever-so-slightly.

"It's proverdence, son. Okay, shore, ya shot me right smack in the balls, but see, old as I am I was havin' a rough time keepin' the crane up anyways, and sometimes I'se just couldn't get a nut outa me ta save my life."

"What," came Tipps' desolate, parched whisper, "did you say about providence?"

"This, son. Me, you, the gals here—everthing. This is *God's* work, ya know, an' I figure that's why he sent ya to me, so's you can continue with His work. Keep up the human telerlogic cycle that proverdence ordained fer us. Ya know?"

Tipps' brain reeled. The hanging harness which satcheled him continued to sway ever-so-slightly. He saw that his butchered hips were exactly aligned with the red-head's stump-flanked vagina.

"Ain't much point at all ta life if we don't never comes ta realizin' our unerversal purpose…"

Tipps groaned again, swaying. The word, once ever-important to him, was now his haunting, his curse. And somehow, in spite of what had been done to him, and equally in spite of how he would spend the rest of his life, he managed to think: *You asked for it, Tipps, and now you got it. Purpose* .

"An' don't'cha worry none. That's why I'se here, son, ta help ya," said Mr. Torso as he opened the brand-new centerfold and carefully lay it on the red-head's belly.

Mr. Torso
Afterword

I like dichotomies; I like the idea of opposites colliding. I'm also intrigued by...rednecks. A while back, I went through a zone which my friend Lucy Taylor jokingly referred to as my "Torso Period." I wrote four stories in a row involving torsos (three of them are included in this collection). The fourth was a rough draft which was then deftly rewritten by Jack Ketchum, entitled "I Would Give Anything For You.") At any rate, I can't really explain the impetus for this salvo of torso stories. I guess I just had torsos on the brain.

But getting back to dichotomies.... I liked the notion of transitions switching back and forth between fervent existential philosophy and a bumpkin redneck chopping off arms and legs. When I sold "Mr. Torso" to HOT BLOOD 4, the editors enthused about the piece but simultaneously warned me that the editors at Pocket might bump it for its extreme edge. I prepared myself for the worst.

But it never happened. The piece made Pocket's cut and probably is my most widely read mass-market short story.

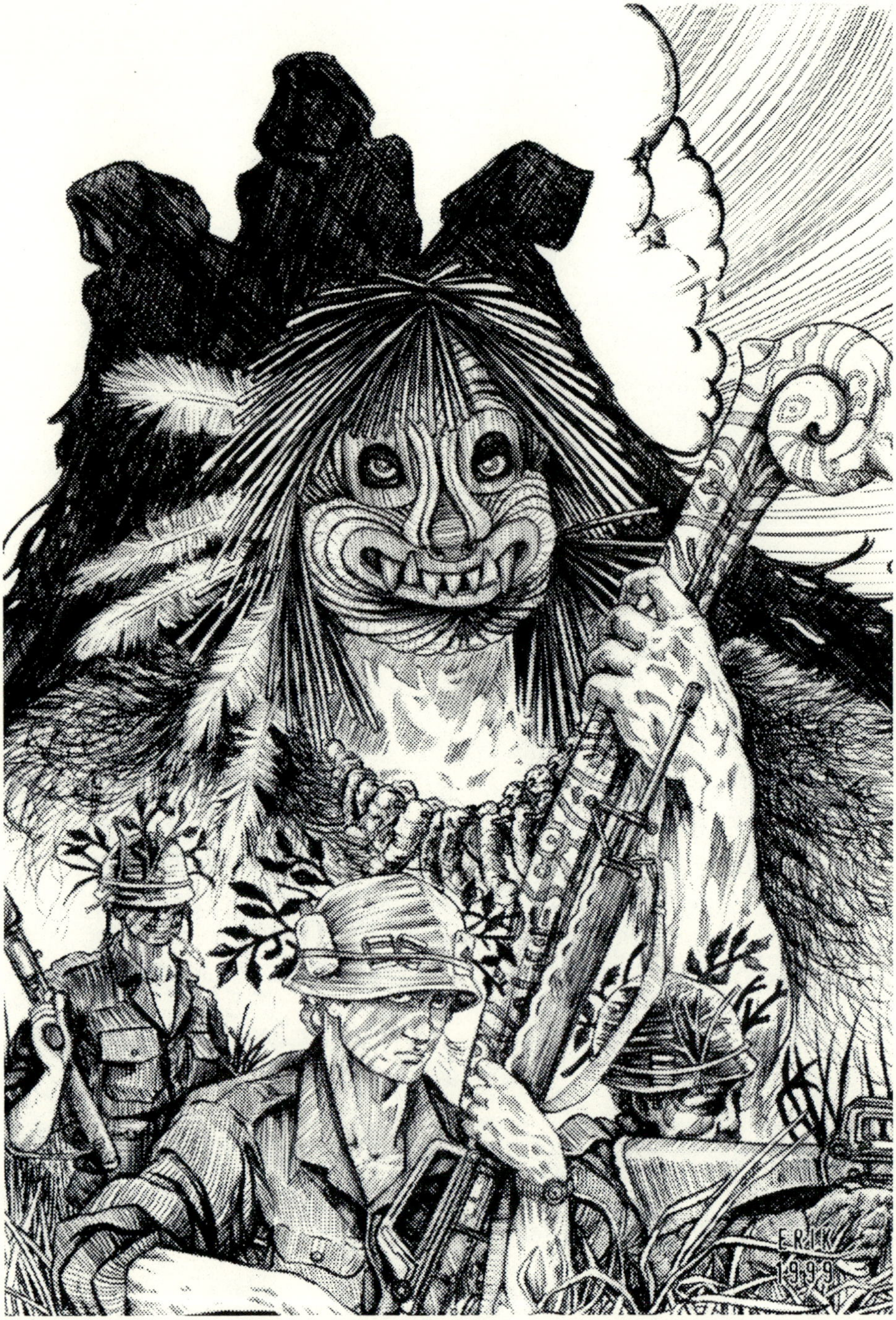
ERIK
1999

The Ushers

WHAT...IS *THAT?*
A figure in the dark?
Footsteps?

(—paramental entity—)

They are the protagonist's worst fear, his phobia incarnate.
The ushers.
His ultimate fear of going to hell.
Sometimes he thinks he can see them. In snatches, in glimpses. In hallucinotic blinks and visual shivers. The pretty British girl in the Goth record store turns momentarily monstrous. The figure in the dark, nondescript yet, somehow, disturbingly familiar. Or he'll glance into the next car at the traffic light, and the occupant will point at him with a fat, taloned hand.
Sometimes he sees them in his window at night...

What you fear most of all are the ushers. An abstraction, really—an aesthetic one.
After all, you're a horror novelist.
The ushers are spirits, they're ghosts. At least in this world they are. For there's another world where they are solid flesh and bone, all hot skin, teeth, and ageless
blood...
The ushers, you think.

Edward Lee

An outland of your perceptivity, but rooted, of course, in your wasp faith, and your prevarication thereof. You put pennies in the Jerry Lewis jar and think that means you're a good person. You'll be on your way to the D.C. strip joints with your buddies and sometimes you'll give a bum a couple of quarters or a couple of bucks.

You think that means you're going to heaven.

(—ghosts—)

He wanted to kill his father.
He came home from work one morning, trudging up the steps. He looks into his parents' bedroom and sees his father adjusting his tie in the mirror. "Hi, Lee," his father says.
His father has been dead since 1986.

You remember going to the hospital every day, watching your father's muscles turn to pudding, watching his brain turn to puree. Each day, you swear you're gonna bring your .38 to the fucking hospital and shoot the slack-armed thing in the railed bed, pop him quick in the head because you'd rather die yourself than bear any more witness to what nature is doing to him. Load up a Glaser Safety Slug, put the pillow over his face, and fire. Take your chances in court. If the shit-head Maryland judge sends you up to the joint, fine, then you'll pop yourself too. No big deal really. Life ain't *that* great. You'd rather be dead than be a cellblock bitch...

"That's not my father!" he wants to scream at the nurse. "That *thing* is not my father!"

The night after he died—Christmas Night—he saw his father standing in the living room, draped in white sheets like something Dickensian.
Pointing with a bone-white finger.

(—nutty girl you picked up one night in a bar—)

"One time I had an out-of-body experience. I went to this horrid black place, and when I woke up, I was covered with tiny flecks of wet hair. But the hair disappeared in a few minutes."
"Hmm. Flecks of hair. I think I've read about that."

The Ushers

"Do you believe in genetic memory?"

"I, uh—well..."

"I believe in psychical residuum. I believe in ghosts, I've seen them. Ghosts aren't always spirits of the dead, you know. Any kind of anguish, torture, or torment can leave a psychical stain."

"Psychical. Hmm."

"I mean, the person doesn't necessarily have to die. Why should they? The anguish is enough to leave a ghost."

"Interesting, uh— Interesting point."

"Do you believe that you have lived before?"

"Gee, you know, I really don't think—"

"Do you believe that you can be haunted in *this* life by someone you murdered in a *past* life?"

(—midnight shift—)

Asleep in the Lodge, always the dutiful security guard. After a 6-Heineken buzz, and several videos–*The Bird With The Crystal Plumage, Three On A Meat-Hook,* oh, and, *Backside To The Future*—you fall asleep and dream.

the eye of your dreaming mind is like a movie camera. you are the eye roving through untainted Maryland woodlands in the early 1700's of what is now St. Mary's County and Kent Island.

you are the killer. you are the destroyer.

you are the Conoye warlock...

women and children first, they're much more fun to rape and kill. the thunder of hoofs so dense it reminds you of the surf. you and your tribe unleash slaughter with impressive dexterity. great waves of dust unfurl in the wake of your hundred horses. screams unfurl too, bright beautiful screams, bright as sunlight. into blissful pandemonium you pour into the horde, encircling them as they try to flee. like threshers and scythes, the warhammers serenely rise and fall, felling arms, dividing skulls. one man is running away with a tradeax in his head, brains shining pink in the newly formed cleft. another man runs off in the opposite direction, waving gushing stumps.

you've trapped them now, and cut them down like weeds. back and forth your squads of war-painted horsemen gallop over the dying and the dead, sewing blood and offal into the soil. then the dust abates, replaced by the wood-smoke of the pyres. the heavy aroma is intoxicating on the evening breeze...

a job well done, all in a day's work.

it's sacrifice, you know.

you are *sacrificing* the pale white intruder to the holy windingo of the forest.

here is our sacrifice!

hear our prayer, we beseech thee!

the few men left alive are systematically beheaded and dismembered. you stoop to dig out beating hearts with your flimsy trade-trowels, and squeeze the still-hot blood out of the meaty chambers, to drink. penises and scrotums are shorn out of groins. you use the scrotums for tobacco pouches, and after each raid you add a penis to the catgut war-necklace around your throat. your necklace, in fact, hosts more penises than any other member of the tribe. nearly one hundred.

the pregnant women are saved for last. you slice the milk-swollen breasts off a screaming pale thing whose belly is stretched pin-prick tight with child.

you sacrifice the gleaming child.

And wake up.

To see the two pallid-gray figures leaning over you. Faceless. Eyeless. One tall, one short.

They are both pointing at you.

A psychic ex-girlfriend who doesn't love him anymore told him in bed one night that she dreamed a strange man was in the room, leaning over. The man was showing her snapshots of a dead person.

"But it wasn't really a person," she queerly stated.

"What do you mean?"

"It was *half* a person. A woman, I think—everything from the waist up, like she'd been cut in half."

"Hmm. Strange."

"She was walking on her hands. She was walking on her hands…through a jungle."

And then there was always Aunt Annabelle. I woke up one night to a slow creaking. A rocking chair.

But there was no rocking chair in my room, there never had been. But here was Aunt Annabelle nonetheless, rocking away–*creak-creak-creak*—dead less than two days, and still shiny from mortician's makeup and formalin-based embalming fluid.

I could smell it.

"Aunt Annabelle?" I asked, leaning up in bed.

"Yes, it's me," she said.

"But you're—"

The Ushers

"I know."

With an eerie quickness, she stood up, and, yes, pointed at me...

"Do you remember Brad?" she asked, and was gone.

(—brad—)

Dougie and the fat kid were loping home from Summerset Elementary, down Shetland Lane. The fat kid was pissed because the day before, that asshole Donnie What'shisname had beaten him up, and he ran home crying. Thank God, he'd been alone then. No one had seen him cry.

A ways ahead of them, they could recognize the exclusive, wavering gait of Brad, toting his clumsy bookbag. Dougie and the fat kid were mad at Brad because he squealed on them to Miss Wendell, for throwing paper airplanes, so Dougie and the fat kid had to take notes home to their parents. Not good.

"Let's mess with Brad," Dougie enthused.

Anger burns in the fat kid's face. Not so much that Brad had gotten him in trouble but because that asshole Donnie What'shisname had made him cry yesterday.

"Okay," the fat kid agreed.

Brad walked funny, like a wooden marionette strung to the fingers of a drunk puppeteer.

Brad was crippled.

Dougie ran up from behind, like a Stuka descending, and snatched Brad's bookbag from his palsied hand. They jogged circles around Brad, right there on the corner of the fat kid's house. Brad wailed, almost fell...

Dougie and the fat kid were really laughing it up, tossing the bookbag back and forth over Brad's head. Brad's face puffed, the brink of tears, as he reached feebly at each toss.

"How do you like that, Brad?" Dougie laughed. "We're not giving it back. We're gonna throw it in the creek!"

"No!" Brad wailed.

"Come on!" the fat kid implored. "Let's really do it! Let's chuck it in the creek!" Then the fat kid paused a moment.

"Let's get him crying!"

Brad moved back and forth with all the finesse of a crab out of water, and he started crying forthwith. Dougie and the fat kid loved it!

A car came down the street, so they flung the bookbag over Brad's head and let it skitter across the asphalt. Brad, walking as though he had cinderblocks tied to his feet, picked it up and teetered home. Crying.

"See ya tomorrow, Baby Brad!" Dougie shouted.
"Yeah!" gusted the fat kid. "*Cry*baby!"

"Yeah, Aunt Annabelle," I whispered to the empty room, in tears. "I remember Brad."

(—sergeant sand—)

"It tastes kind of like pork, when you cook it right. You grind it up and fry it, but always grind up some fat with it. Shit, when you're in the bush, and you're starving...
"You'll eat."

When I was in the Army, I was stationed in Ansbach, West Germany. This was back in the days when there was still an East and West. I was a tank gunner. Man, I could pick fucking cherries at 4000 meters. *Ba-BOOM!* The Army did a great job of turning high-school punks into homicidal machines—man, I *still* see HEAT and SABOT reticles in my head sometimes when I close my eyes, drawing a 105mm bead on a T-72. "Aim for the turret ring," my platoon leader always harped. "Then hit them with a HEP and spall the commie motherfuckers." HEP means High Explosive Plastic. What this round does is it impacts the side of the enemy turret, covers the turret with plastic explosive, then drives a delayed primer into the shit. Makes everything on the turret wall break off and cut the crew to ribbons at a velocity of about 1,200 feet per second. Popping caps, we called it, and these were big caps. I was such an asshole. I thought I wanted to kill Russians for my fucked-up, irredeemable country.
Truth is, they would've killed me first.
Anyway, there was a guy in my barrack named Sergeant Sand. That's right, Sand, like the shit at the beach. He was in The Nam. 11-Echo, tanker. Hell on fuckin' wheels, man. You put 'em up, we churn 'em up. We eat napalm for breakfast and piss transmission fluid. Grease our fuckin' treads with your 16-year-old girlfriends, man, and your mamas too, and your daddies. Hey, Ivan, where you wanna be buried after I pop your victor with enough HEAT to fill a fucking bathtub, huh? Roast Toasties, that's what we'll make ya. We'll rock your fuckin' commie world, man, oh man!
Anyway, this guy Sand, I thought he was cool. I worshiped the guy. At 18, I thought that if I could be like anyone in the world, it would be Sergeant Sand. A one-man brass-ball battalion.
He's dead now, or at least that's what I heard. He got TDY'd back to

The Ushers

Fort Knox to train on the new M1A1's that came out in '82, 1500hp turbine engines, full main-gun stabe. Turned out to be a piece of shit till they upgraded them to A-deuces. Anyway, I heard Sand got in bar fight one night in one of the "wet" counties of Kentucky, and got himself shot in the belly by some 'neck who thought Sand was putting the make on his wife. Knowing Sand, it was probably true. But that's beside the point.

Or maybe not.

Anyway, this guy Sand, he'd put cigarettes out on his tongue, then smile, then swallow. Killed Charlie Comm, lots of them, and had Polaroids to prove it. Said he'd get antsy if a week went by and he didn't kill anyone. In The Nam the 11-Echoes'd drive M60 straight series, and they'd roll through the jungle with severed heads on stakes sticking out of their bustle racks. Said he'd throw the Vietnamese kids moisture-activated fire pellets 'cos they'd pop 'em in their mouths thinking the shit was candy. Said he did a stint as a prison guard at Manheim, killed a guy who bit him on their way to transport, whapped the guy in the head so many times with his billy the guy's brains started coming out his ears. Sand had a German girlfriend who said her father was a gate guard for the SD at Belsen. "She can stand on her head and then lean over and go down on herself," Sand bragged, and it was true; I saw the Polaroids. "She's turned on by me 'cos I've killed guys," Sand claimed. "She used to be a whore at The Wall in Nurnberg, she'd do gang-bangs for forty marks per G.I." Sand said she could swallow twelve-inch knockwursts whole. Didn't believe it till he showed me the Polaroids.

Back to the story. This guy Sand, I used to party with him. We'd drink these big bottles of Hofbrau, room temperature. For some reason when you're in Germany, the beer doesn't have to be cold. And, anyway, Sand's got this foot locker under his rack, and I ask him what's in it.

"You don't wanna know," he says. "You ain't got the belly for it."

"Come on, Sarge," I drunkenly plead. "What'cha got in that box?"

Sand gets up then. Looks at me with a face like it was carved out of rock. And he slides that locker out from under his rack and opens 'er up.

First thing he showed me was a bone. I dunno, two feet long or thereabouts. I looked at it real hard, but I was drunk, see? Took me a while to realize it was a human femur. Said he'd party in Saigon with the 176th MP's and these Navy SOG guys and Aussie Special Forces, they'd get a bunch of hookers together and pay them to eat shit. Didn't believe him till he showed me the Polaroids.

Pulled a jar out of the locker, had a baby's hand in it.

Pulled a leather bag out of the locker, full of human teeth.

Pulled out a crinkly wallet, made of skin.

Pulled out another bag full of scalps.

"Tell me a story, Sarge," I asked.

"Me and this guy named Winslow, we were on the same crew, he was TC, I was gunner. We didn't have SABOT in those days, we carried lots of HEAT and HEP, and BEEHIVE in the ready rack, and we also kept a few Willy Peter's around in case we had a gook bunker to paste. So we're on a road march one day real close to the safe end of Highway 13 and we blow our neutral safety switch, which, as you know, the fuckin' PAC won't run without. So we dial up maintenance on the AN and ask for help, figure those chuckheads'll dispatch a recovery vehicle. Those chuckheads would probably deadline the victor and we'd get to go back to the firebase and knock the bottom out of some whores' asses. Anyway, engineering batt says they've got an M88 on the way but it won't be there till morning, so we got a lot of time to kill and we're sittin' right smack-dab in the middle of some hot bush. So tell me what we did, kid."

"Set up a defensive perimeter?" I guess.

"Right. Draw the range card, line up the landmarks, haul on the cammie net, all that happy horseshit. And we're sitting there all day with our M-3's out, waiting to deal some serious lead poisoning to any dink who thinks he's gotta pair big enough to fuck with us, but nothing happens. So it gets dark, and we know we're shit for brains if we don't set up a hot line, so me and Winslow set up the Claymores around the site. You know how to lay Claymores, right?"

"Sure, Sarge. You kidding? Can do it with my eyes closed."

"So anyway, we lay a hot line out. Most guys, they wouldn't bother, too much trouble, you know, but those guys are the chuckheads who always catch the MAC flight back to the World in a body bag. So me and Winslow, we sit in that hot bush all night hoping to get into the shit, and let me tell ya, you go out on a field problem in The Nam jungle for 20 days or so, and your OD's will *rot* right on your body, you pull your cock out to piss in the weeds and it stinks worse than a couple of dead Charlie Comm cooking in the bush for a few days, and bugs? Man, they had bugs over there that'd carry your mom away. Slugs with teeth, and fuckin' red fire ants big as your thumb. Lotta these ARVN guys were double agents; they'd walk off grid coordinates and wire 'em back to the VC arty crews. So we'd stake the fuckers naked to the ground, pour some sugar water on 'em, and, brother, those ants'd be eating their skin off in less time than it takes you to wipe your ass. They'd spin like tops, tell us anything we wanted to know, then we'd leave 'em there. And I swear they had spiders as big as fucking golf balls, and when those fuckers bit ya you were in the infirmary for a week."

But I'd heard all this shit before, from lots of guys. I wanted to hear about the hot line. "Come on, Sarge. Don't pull my dick."

Sand smiled, he knew. "Anyway, it was me and Winslow sitting up on watch. We had these two other guys on our victor, two niggers, Solkie and Buck—and I *swear*, the guy's name was Buck! But those two 'gers were cooping in the turret."

"Yeah, yeah," I said eagerly, "so it's you and Winslow on fire watch, waiting for the shit."

"Right. And we're sitting there with cocked M-3's, Winslow on the back deck, me on the front slope, dreaming about the World, about all the pussy we're gonna bust wide open, and how we're gonna drink enough beer to fill a fuckin' fuel gore, and then one of the Claymores gets tripped, like about 11 o'clock on the range card, and me and Winslow just about shit our OD's, 'cos you know what a Claymore sounds like going off. And we go check it out and find what it was that tripped the wire, some gook girl, probably 12 or so—dunno, maybe she was a sapper, or maybe just some kid prowling around, and what the Claymore did to her, she was like right on top of it when she tripped the fucker. Anyway, that Claymore cut this gook chick right in half..."

I was repulsed, yet simultaneously fascinated. Imagery, man. I've always been intrigued by imagery. And this was some image.

A girl cut in half.

"The two niggers pop hatch, they're shit-scared," Sand went on. "They think it's Giap and the entire North Vietnamese Army coming down on their asses or something, or like maybe the fly boys off loaded a daisy-cutter by mistake, but we told 'em it was nothing, just a boar tripped the wire, so they go back down in the turret to coop. And me and Winslow are standing there with our M-3's, looking down at this mess. When I say this chick was cut in half, I mean like everything from the sternum up was lying face down in a puddle about ten yards away, arms out like a ref signaling a touchdown, and everything from the sternum down was laying right there at our feet."

Sergeant Sand paused then, cracked open another Hofbrau, lit a butt. Was this the end of the story?

"Well...yeah?" I asked, flummoxed. "What happened then?"

"We took turns fucking the lower half of the corpse," Sand said, and swigged his beer.

I stared at him, mortified.

No, no, I thought.

I didn't believe him.

Until he showed me the Polaroids.

Yeah. Back then I thought Sergeant Sand was cool. I wanted to *be* Sergeant Sand.

God forgive me.

Edward Lee

¤   ¤   ¤   ¤   ¤

(—the ushers—)

It is a fear-driven thing, these demented visions, these demonian ghosts born of the abyss in his own mind.

He often considers that he may be insane, or worse: premonitory.

Sometimes a week will go by and he'll dream of baseball scores and they're always right the next day. Sometimes he dreams of a beautiful Asian woman whispering numbers into his ear. One day she whispers "five three three four," and the next day he gets a freelance check for $5334. One day she whispers "one-five-one" and later his agent calls to report a three-book sale, and the time on the clock reads 1:51 p.m. One day she whispers "three-one-four," and then that night at work he responds to a gunshot call which turns out to be a suicide, but the address on the house is 314.

He's prone to absolutely ludicrous dreams, often involving cruise ships and conventions in preposterous places and grocery stores full of sex fantasies and bakeries full of french crullers and apple twists. He dreams of tidal waves and sinking ships and seafood markets, of lost loves and loves never to be asserted, all in the most unseemly locations.

In late-November, 1998, he fell asleep on the Rte. 6 bus back from Chinatown–another bus crashed on the same route at the same time, killing several passengers—and dreamed about a girl he really likes a lot but never had the balls to tell her. Then the Asian woman's face appeared in the dream and whispered "She will hate you on Monday, she will hate you on Monday," and a week later–on a Monday–the girl he likes hates him.

Sometimes he knows when his friends will sell a story or a book.

Sometimes he sees auras.

That nutty girl he'd picked up in the bar that night. She'd said something else, hadn't she?

"If you create something in your mind, and if you think about it hard enough, you can make it real."

He thinks now of golems crafted of clay with his own hands. The maker destroyed by what he makes.

He gives them a scene in all of his books. The ushers.

It seems appropriate. After all, he's a horror novelist.

Pug faces on stout, corded necks. Flesh the feel and hue of riverbed clay, pit-nostrils and chisel slits for eyes. They are bulldog-like in a sense,

The Ushers

with limbs of bloated, bundled muscles, squab hands, and sausage-fat fingers with talons on the end.

They are malefactors, adjuncts, myrmidons.

There's a black moon in a red sky, a vale, horrid and vast, refulgent with luminous fog, and a lake of steaming excrement.

From fissures in the black rock, the pitiable naked horde is expulsed. A great black grackle flies overhead, its black-marble eyes gazing down in reverent delight. The horde is a mass of screaming bodies, terror incarnate, living chaos.

And from the steaming lake, the ushers arise to bull into the horde amid suboctave chuckles, their fat hands at once twisting arms and legs quickly out of sockets, wrenching heads off flexing necks, yanking whole spinal columns out of stretched open mouths. Fire gushes in the distance, greasy black smoke pours from cracks and rabbets in the vale's stone face. The smell in the air is so sweet: boiling excrement, human fat cooking over crackling flames. The ushers travail, complacent in their servitude—honored in the call of their duties. Stout, stiffened pinkies calmly squash eyeballs in howling faces. Skin is flensed from bare backs as easily as wall paper being peeled, ears, noses, lips, and fingers are bitten off and nibbled as tidbits. Talons swipe to lay open bellies, misshapen fists are thrust into rectums through which innards are extricated like tissue paper from a gift box. The ushers grunt and chuckle, plodding on, popping heads with malformed feet, inhaling blood, holding faces steadfastly down to drown in the tarn of bubbling shit from whence they came.

Yes, it is a grand day in hell. An *eternal* day.

Monstrous penises rise in heady arousal, any available orifice plundered for carnal pleasure. Their luciferic seed spurts in endless, globular gouts, vesicles drained only to be immediately refilled for still more lusty revel. No registrant of this horde of the damned can be left out, and here there is no discrimination as to gender. Rectums are fastidiously plumbed, vaginas routed to the point of prolapsation, mouths jam-packed with veined members as long and stout as rolling pins. Uteri are set aside upon hot rocks, to cook. Tender, pink brains are swallowed whole. Raw testicles are eaten like M&M's.

And when it's over, the ushers stand proud over the gorgeous carnage. Smiling ever faintly. Their bellies filled. Their groins slaked.

Yes, when it's over, only to begin again and again and again forever and ever, recompense without end…

And one of the ushers steps forward then through the hot smoke of the jubal, its black-slit eyes leveled, its forked tongue licking feces off its lips.

Its inhuman hand slowly rises, and its finger points…

(—talk show—)

An old woman with clown-orange hair claims that she's psychic. She predicts that Ross Perot will run for president and take 20% of the vote. Then she predicts that in 1993 a wave of genocide will explode in East Europe, that death camps and rape camps will reemerge. Some of the audience actually laughs at the absurdity.
She talks about crystals, about Kirlian Photography and remote viewing and OBE's and trance-channeling.
And ghosts.
"Our sins are ghosts, too. They always come back, and if you look closely enough, you can see them…"

(—the neighbor has a dream—)

The bane of any writer is when non-writers ask the infernal question: "Hey, how's the writing coming along?" Jesus.
I was raking leaves last fall in the front yard, a real pain in the ass. I had three book deadlines on my head, but I gotta blow off a day of writing to rake up and bag all these ridiculous leaves. Anyway, the guy across the street's got nothing better to do than jack his jaw, so he meanders over with a beer, and I roll my eyes even before he says: "Hey, how's the writing coming along?"
"Uh, all right, I guess."
"Oh, man, you'll love this," he said next, "seein' that you write all that horror stuff. Last night I had a dream that'd make your hair stand up. A real doozy."
"Oh, yeah?" I asked without much of a choice.
"Yeah, man. I dreamed I woke up in my own bed, and I hear footsteps outside. So I get up real quiet 'cos I don't wanna wake the wife. And, anyway, I look out my bedroom window, out into my front yard, and I see this army guy down on one knee, all dressed up for combat. He's got the paint on his face and branches sticking out of his helmet like he's in Vietnam or something and he's holding a rifle. And, get this—the guy's guts are half-hanging out 'cos someone had shot him in the belly."
I kind of raised a brow. "That's it? That's your dream?"
"Oh, no, man," my chatty neighbor laughed. "Not by a long shot. This army guy's kind of looking around, like he's scared, like he hears something. And then…*I* hear something too."

The Ushers

I wanted to groan. "What did you hear?"

"Well, more footsteps. Only they weren't as loud as his. Then all of a sudden he raises his rifle and starts shooting at someone coming around the side of my house,

but—you know how dreams are—"

Dreams, I thought.

"—sometimes things don't make no sense, and I guess that's why his rifle didn't make any noise when he was firing. I could see the muzzleflash, but—"

"No sound," I said.

"Right. And then this army guy with the belly full of bullets drops his rifle on the lawn and runs away down the street, screaming."

"Screaming?" I asked. "But I thought you couldn't hear anything."

"No, no, I meant I couldn't hear the guy's gun going off, but I could hear everything else, and this guy was screaming bloody murder."

I nodded. "Hmm. Pretty weird dream."

"Oh, but that's not all. After this army guy runs away—"

"Runs away screaming, with a belly full of bullets," I reminded him.

"Right, after he runs away screaming with a belly full of bullets, I finally see what he was shooting at."

"The footsteps you heard."

"Right, the footsteps coming around the side of my house."

It is then, presumably for effect, that my motormouth neighbor momentarily paused his story, looking at me with a wise grin.

I tied up the last pain in the ass bag of leaves and decided to accommodate him. "All right, who was it?"

"It was legs, man."

"*Legs?*" I ask.

"That's right. Legs. They looked like a girl's legs, kinda slim and pretty. But anyway, that's what I saw in the dream. Two legs walking across my front yard. And you know what they did then, these legs?"

By then I was feeling a bit sick. "The legs followed the army guy, right?"

"Well, no. That's what you'd *think* they were going to do. I mean, that would've made sense, but… You know how dreams are."

"Sure." I looked at him then, a light sweat breaking out on my forehead. "So what did they do then, these legs?"

"Here's the part you'll love!" my neighbor guffawed. "They didn't follow the army guy at all. Instead, the legs started walking across the street, to *your* house!" My neighbor, then, slapped me on the back. "Pretty weird dream, huh?"

"Yeah, man," I concurred. "Pretty weird dream…"

Edward Lee

❏   ❏   ❏   ❏   ❏

(—butcher—)

The conventioneer rushes to ready himself; he's got a panel in forty-five minutes, and he wants to grab a beer first, with Dallas, in the hotel bar. Well, maybe two beers—panels make him a little nervous. He gets out of the shower, dries himself, hurries to the bedroom in the muffled hotel quiet.

A pregnant woman is lying on the clean Scotch-Guard carpet. Her clothes have been torn off in shreds, what appears to be an off-white bustle dress like the kind of stuff women wore hundreds of years ago, only now it's streaked bright-red with blood, and she has been butchered right there on the floor via a manner of demented expertise too diabolical to describe.

The conventioneer stands slack-jawed. The image is *teeming*, stark and clear and sharp as a bezel in its clarity. Then the conventioneer blinks and, of course, the image is gone.

But he remembers the last thing he saw:

The woman's face split by a Conoye warhammer.

(—homecoming—)

Ocean City, Maryland, 1991. Yeah, that's where you and your pals went for a week in late-July. You drank a bottle of Sapporo while driving your brand-new car across the Chesapeake Bay Bridge. A straight shot down Route 50, and you're there.

Party hearty, man! Partyin' on the beach! Bikini City every day, it's enough to drive you nuts! And drinking in the Green Turtle every night—what a commendable way to live!

You stayed at a high-rise called the Atlantis. It looked like something out of a Fritz Leiber story: tall and thin with gunslit windows, a spire of drab-beige cement. One day you're sitting on the can—what a deserving place for creative enlightenment—and you get an idea for a novel that you're sure will make you a million. Little did you know then that the book would never sell.

On Thursday night you wake up at exactly 3:15 a.m. You can't sleep. You have this funny feeling you're being watched, so clichéd but so true. You go out onto the balcony in your underwear, sit down, light a cigarette. Forty-four floors up, you're sitting there totally alone. The sky is drab, the color of disconsolation. A storm is coming. At times you swear you can feel the building actually move, and from somewhere you hear a washed-out voice yell:

The Ushers

"Hey!"

To your left the waves crash but you can barely hear them because it's so windy. And to your right...

Another high-rise. Dark. Not one of its hundreds of windows are lit. But by now your eyes have acclimated to the gloom. You're staring at the other building...

And you see someone.

The tiniest figure. It seems to be standing on the opposing balcony. Just... standing there.

It's so weird. You stand up, grab the binoculars someone had brought to scope the girls on the beach in their bikinis. You're leaning out over the steel rail, focusing on the figure.

It's a boy, a seven or eight years old. But not dressed in beach garb. He's wearing long pants, a long-sleeve shirt buttoned at the collar, big clunky shoes.

He's holding a bookbag, staring right back at you with a face bereft of eyes...

Then he hobbles away and disappears.

¤ ¤ ¤ ¤ ¤

A figure in the dark?

Footsteps?

Is it me?

Or is it getting hot in here?

¤ ¤ ¤ ¤ ¤

The novelist shuts his computer down. He just got it and he hates it. He hates having to own one because writing seemed much more real on a manual typewriter. There's something obscene about all that technology existing between his fingers and the paper.

Progress.

He lights a cigarette and polishes off a Heineken, then looks out the window.

It's a beautiful night.

He gets ready, listening to This Mortal Coil and The Teargarden, puts on heather-gray slacks, a Lord & Taylor shirt, decent shoes, then he leaves. He's walking down desolate M Street with his pals, gearing up for the D.C. beer-snob bars and strip joints.

"Hey, man?" comes a destitute voice. "Can you spare some change?"

A hooded bum is standing there, with an overcoat of rotten rags.

"Just a bit of change to help me out?"

"Sure," the novelist says. Why not? He's sold thirteen novels, short stories out the ass, comic scripts; he even sold film options on two books! *Yeah, why not?* the novelist decides, and then, ever the generous Christian, he digs into his pocket to help this poor bum cop a bottle of hooch.

"Thank ya, man. God bless ya."

The bum reaches out. But he doesn't open his hand to take the money.

Instead he points.

The fat taloned finger points right into the novelist's face, and within the hood, the usher smiles, and in a voice like crumbling rock, it says:

"Your ass belongs to us…"

The Ushers
Afterword

If I've ever written a story about me and my experiences and my fears—this is it. My nightmares, my trepidations, my worldly sins–this is it. I guess the best way to say it is thus: damn near everything in this story is true.

EDWARD LEE PUBLISHING HISTORY

NOVELS:

NIGHT BAIT, (as Philip Straker), Zebra Books, May, 1982.
NIGHTLUST, (as Philip Straker), Zebra Books, October, 1982.
GHOULS, Pinnacle, July, 1988.
COVEN, Diamond/Berkley, February, 1991.
INCUBI, Diamond/Berkley, August, 1991.
SUCCUBI, Diamond/Berkley, March, 1992.
THE CHOSEN, Zebra Books, November, 1993.
CREEKERS, Zebra Books, May, 1994.
SACRIFICE, (as Richard Kinion), Zebra Books, August, 1995.
THE BIGHEAD, Necro Publications, April, 1997.
SHIFTERS, (w/John Pelan), Obsidian Books, March,1998.
PORTRAIT OF THE PSYCHOPATH AS A YOUNG WOMAN,
    (w/Elizabeth Steffen), Necro Publications, June, 1998.
THE BIGHEAD, (author's preferred version; illustrated),
    Overlook Connection, Summer, 1999.
DAHMER'S NOT DEAD (w/Elizabeth Steffen) CD Publications,
    Summer, 1999.
THE STICKMEN, CD Publications, Fall, 1999.

COLLECTIONS:

SPLATTERSPUNK: THE MICAH HAYS STORIES, (w/John
    Pelan), Sideshow Books, March, 1998.
THE USHERS, Obsidian Books, May, 1999.

NOVELLAS:

"Header," Necro Publications, August., 1995.
"Goon," (w/John Pelan), Necro Publications, August, 1996.

"The Pig," INSIDE THE WORKS, Necro Publications, Nov., 1997.
"Family Traditions," (w/John Pelan), forthcoming from Bereshith Publishing.
"The Horn-Cranker," TRIPTYCH, Sideshow Books, Summer, 1999.
"Operator 'B'," CD Publications, Summer-1999.

COMIC SCRIPT SALES:

"Mr. Torso," Verotika, Issue #6;
"Grub Girl," Verotika, Issue #8;
"Headers," Verotika, Issue #14;
"Grub Girl Returns," Verotika, Issue #15.
GRUB GIRL, Book #1, Verotik, Inc., August, 1997.

GENRE-RELATED SHORT STORIES/ARTICLES/COMMENTARIES:

"The Horror of Chambers," Eerie Country, May, 1982.
"Guts for Fun and Profit," Mystery Scene, June, 1991.
"Prophesy," Mystery Scene, September, 1991.
Appreciation Piece: Pocket Author Douglas Clegg, Tekeli-li: Journal of Terror, Summer Issue, 1991.
"Almost Never," Cemetery Dance, Fall Issue, 1991.
"Psychological Motivations in Horror Fiction," Afraid: The Newsletter for the Horror Professional, June, 1992.
"The Man Who Loved Cliches," Bizarre Bazaar 92, June 1992.
"The Inn," Bizarre Sex & Other Crimes of Passion, September, 1992.
"Preceptor," Gothic Light, Fall Issue, 1992.
"Sex and Death in Horror Fiction," Tekeli-li: Journal of Terror, Summer Issue, 1992.
  "Xipe," The Barrelhouse: Excursions into the Unknown, Winter Issue, 1993.
"The Seeker, Pay Me, The Goddess of the New Dark Age," SEX, TRUTH & REALITY, a limited-edition chapbook pub-

lished by Tal Publications, November, 1992.
"Death, She Said," Bizarre Bazaar 93, March, 1993.
"Interview," Cyber-Psychos, A.O.D. (a lengthy interview with the author, plus horror-related poetry and reviews), March, 1993.
"The Wrong Guy," Cyber-Psychos, A.O.D., June, 1993.
"Equal Opportunity," Cemetery Dance, Winter Issue, 1993.
"World Horror Con 93," Deathrealm, June 1993.
"HWA 93/Doug Clegg Interview," Deathrealm, Fall Issue, 1993
"The Providence of the Ghosts," Obelisk Books, Summer, 1994.
"Succubi," (the original prologue from the Berkley novel, Bloodsongs (Australia), May, 1994. Also published by Eulogy, with an interview of the author, Summer, 1994.
"I Would Give Anything For You," (with Jack Ketchum), Bizarre Sex & Other Crimes of Passion, Masquerade Books, June, 1994.
"Portrait of the Psychopath as a Young Woman," (collaborative novel excerpt), Merrimack Books, Fall, 1993.
Interview, Horror, interview with the author by t. Winter-Damon, Winter Issue, 1993.
"The Wrong Guy," Into The Darkness #4, May, 1995.
"Almost Never," Bloodsongs (Australia), Sept., 1994.
"Equal Opportunity" (long version), Bizarre Bazaar 94, March, 1994.
"Shit-House," Palace Corbie Six, 1995
"Shit-House," THE BEST OF PALACE CORBIE, Merrimack Books, slated for late-1999 release.
"Portrait of a Sociopath," Heliocentricnet Annual, 1996.
"The Police Officer's Cock-Ring," (w/John Pelan), Palace Corbie Seven, 1996.
"The Police Officer's Cock-Ring," (w/John Pelan), chapbook edition, Dark Raptor Press, 1998. .
"Please Let Me Out," VOICES IN THE NIGHT, Maclay Associates, May, 1994.
"Horror Ain't Dead," Horror #7, 1996.
"Private Pleasures," DARK SEDUCTIONS, Zebra Books, October, 1993.

"Mr. Torso," HOT BLOOD 4, Pocket Books, Nov., 1994. (Nominated for HWA's 1994 Stoker Award).
"Grub Girl," HOT BLOOD 5, Pocket, April, 1995.
"Dead Girls In Love," (w/Gary Bowen) HOT BLOOD 6, Pocket, Oct., 1995. (Pocket also did a hardcover edition of this volume.)
"Love Letters From The Rain Forest," (with Jack Ketchum), HOT BLOOD 7, Pocket, June, 1996.
"Night of the Vegetables," WHITE HOUSE HORRORS, DAW Books, Sept., 1996.
"Grub Girl in the Prison of Dead Women," Wetbones #2, Fall, 1997.
"Transcendence" (w/John Pelan), The Brutarian, Summer, 1997.
"Stillborn," (w/John Pelan), IMAGINATION: FULLY DILATED, CD Publications, May, 1998.
"The Scarlet Succubus" (w/ John Pelan), ZOTHIQUE: THE LOST CONTINENT, Bereshith Books, April, 1999.
"Almost Never," THE BEST OF CEMETERY DANCE, CD Publications, Summer, 1998.
"Stick Woman," DARKSIDE, edited by John Pelan, Darkside Press, May 1996, mass-market paperback by ROC, January, 1998.
"Transcendence," (w/John Pelan), Bloodsongs, Nov., 1998.
"Secret Service," THE UFO FILES, DAW Books, Jan., 1998.
"Charlie's Web," (w/John Pelan), OF SPIDERS AND PIGS, Bereshith Books, Spring, 1999.
"Driving," Squane's Journal, Spring, 1999.
"The Piece of Paper," OUT OF THE CAGE, Obsidian/Sideshow, late-1999.
"Equal Opportunity," FORCES OBSCURES, edited by Marc Bailly for Editions Naturellement in France, Spring, 1999.
"Scripture Girl," ALIENS, Pocket Books, Jan., 1999.
"ICU," 999, Avon Books, November, 1999.

OTHER:

The author has also had non-genre articles, interviews, reviews, short fiction, and poetry in the following literary and small-press magazines and newspapers: Calvert (Literary Journal for the University of Maryland); Mynd; Amanita Brandy; The Annapolis Critique; Hanson's: The Magazine of Literary and Social Interest; OTHER VOICES IN POETRY (a trade paperback anthology); All About Beer; Guns; Thin Ice; The Capital (newspaper); The Phoenix (newspaper); The Annapolis Voice (newspaper).

FUTURE PROJECTS:

"Strangle Me," an incomplete hardcore novella.
C.I., (working title for a speculative novel in progress).
WHITE HOUSE COUNSEL, (mainstream novel in progress).
BAG OF BOY, (abstract novel in progress, the first 100 pages of which won a grant from the Maryland State Arts Council).
THE EAST TENNESSEE AND GEORGIA RAILROAD COMPANY (an incomplete hardcore horror novel).
UNTITLED NOVELLA COLLECTION, contracted by Necro Publications and will contain "Header," "The Pig," and a new short novel. Undetermined publication date.
COVEN, INCUBI, SUCCUBI, GHOULS: limited h/c editions of these novels will be published in their uncut forms over the next four years.